S.L. CHOI

Bad Girls DRINK BLOOD

BLOOD FAE DRUID | BOOK ONE

BAD GIRLS DRINK BLOOD

S.L. CHOI

This book is a work of fiction. Names, characters, places, and incidents either are products of the author's imagination or are used fictitiously. Any resemblance to actual events or locales or persons, living or dead, is entirely coincidental and not intended by the author.

BAD GIRLS DRINK BLOOD
Blood Fae Druid, Book 1

CITY OWL PRESS
www.cityowlpress.com

Cover Design by MiblArt. All stock photos licensed appropriately.

Edited by Heather McCorkle.

For information on subsidiary rights, please contact the publisher at info@cityowlpress.com.

Print Edition ISBN: 978-1-64898-147-0

Digital Edition ISBN: 978-1-64898-148-7

Printed in the United States of America

PRAISE FOR S.L. CHOI

"With tantalizing hints of a wolfy blood tryst, a heavy dose of sisterly love, and plot twists to make the ride a surprise, S.L. Choi's, *Bad Girls Drink Blood* is too much fun. This brand-new world and mythos are a pleasure to explore. Solid world building, easy to grasp politics, hints of future romance and plenty of snark are the perfect scaffold to a story about finding that your scars are only the signposts of your hidden abilities, and that the part of you that brings you the most pain, can also be the wellspring of your deepest satisfaction. If you like the Hollows, you will love this." — *Kim Harrison, #1 New York Times bestselling author of the Hollows series*

"Welcome to a sexy, *new* spin on the fae. Deliciously gritty and full of snark, you'll find your new hero in Lane Callaghan." – *International and award-winning author of the Weird Girls UF romance series, Cecy Robson*

"Bad Girls Drink Blood is an action-packed good time that delivers wit, grit, and an unforgettable heroine." – *Kat Turner, author the Coven Daughters series*

"*Bad Girls Drink Blood* has everything I love: a heroine that can put bad guys in the dirt, side-splitting humor, and characters you're invested in from page one. In a debut that is both heart-wrenching and wildly hilarious from start to finish, Choi carves out her place in a crowded genre with what I hope to be a long series." — *Gabrielle Ash, author of The Family Cross and For the Murder*

"Magic, modernity, and multiple dimensions collide in the richly imagined world of S.L. Choi's page-turning debut *Bad Girls Drink Blood*, where a snarky, badass heroine with a monster complex and a sexy spark of friends-to-lovers romance will delight fans of urban fantasy and fae intrigue." – *Erin Fulmer, author of Cambion's Law*

"This urban fantasy debut will have readers on the edge of their seats as they follow Lane's action-packed adventure! Choi's voice and style pulled me in right away and I instantly loved Lane, who is a total badass. I also adored her sisters and Teddy and loved the found family theme--it's one of my favorites! I hated to put this book down and I found myself wondering what would happen next for Lane and company. I am thrilled to read the next installment in this series and can't wait for more adventures with one of my favorite characters to date. Fans of urban fantasy will want to sink their teeth into this brilliant debut!" –*Ashley R. King, author of Forever After, Painting Lines, The Wilde Card*

"Want a fast-paced urban fantasy with a badass fae heroine, a hunky love interest, and a snarky cast of mythical beings? How about found family, sisterly love, and multi-layered world building? Then sink your teeth into *Bad Girls Drink Blood*. Craving satisfied." –*Sarina Dahlan, author of Reset*

"I was thrilled for the chance to read an advanced copy of Bad Girls Drink Blood by S.L. Choi and let me tell you, it did not disappoint. This story hits the ground running and sprints full-tilt to the end until I was turning pages faster than my kindle could keep up! The writing is crisp, the characters delightful, and the worldbuilding is absolutely phenomenal. Faes, shifters, druids, and a hot bartender who's not what he seems. Yes please! I loved Lane and her sisters so much, and I can't wait for more stories about them and their detective agency. Bad Girls Drink Blood is a sparkling urban fantasy gem with a gooey romance center. Highly recommend." –*Jess K Hardy, author of Love in the Time of Wormholes and I, Bionic*

To my cat, Cronos, whose insistence on laps kept my butt in the seat writing.

1

I'M A BAD GIRL

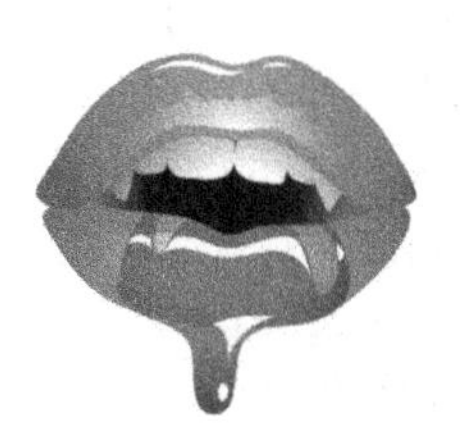

I'D BEEN NURSING MY DRINK FOR THE PAST HOUR, ALONG WITH MY PRIDE. I didn't want to face my sisters. I didn't want to tell them I'd screwed up.

The morning sun broke through stained-glass windows high on the far wall of the shotgun-style front room. It illuminated the rich mahogany bar top and the pale red layer of melted ice atop the disgusting virgin Bloody Mary I'd made the mistake of ordering.

"I don't smell nos blood." A hand large enough to crack a watermelon like an egg slid in front of me and tapped a chipped fingernail on my glass.

"Too early for that stuff." He didn't need to know I was allergic. That type of info would ruin my rep. "Tomato juice and plenty of vodka."

"Yous should go straight vodka. Don't mess with that vegetable stuff."

"Fruit."

"What?"

"Never mind." I swung around on the well-worn saddle of my stool and faced the ogre. Rip, a regular fixture at the bar, had a remarkably expressive face for something that resembled an unfinished block of gray sculpting clay. Broad as a refrigerator and somewhere close to seven feet tall, he dwarfed my already short stature. Both of his ever-roaming—and more than a little creepy—chameleon-like eyes landed on me.

"Lane Callaghan." He pinched the lapels of my jacket to straighten it. The shifting sides revealed a shoulder sheath holding a push dagger under each arm, and he tweaked one with a thick finger. "What's a bad girl like yous doing in a nice bar like this?"

Despite playing into the corny cliché, I snatched his finger and bent it back, stopping before it reached the point of pain. "Never touch a girl's hardware unless you're prepared to lose a finger." I tempered the action with a wink. Though, I meant it. Don't touch my blades.

"No touch. Gots it." He threw his hands in the air. Such a drama queen.

From the front of the bar voices rose, furniture clattered on the hardwood floors, and a bottle shattered. The only one to react was Teddy, the bartender, bar owner, and resident eye candy, who appeared from behind the bar and easily vaulted over the counter before the fighters could cause any damage to his establishment.

A nice bar, indeed. Nice was relative in Interlands, but the ogre did run a bookie business from the booth he rented here, so he was biased. To be fair, Teddy kept the place in surprisingly good shape, considering the locals and some of their shady side businesses. Myself included.

Cleanliness was not a typical werewolf trait, not that I'd ever seen Teddy go furry. Not in the seven years I'd known him, but it was obvious in the way he moved, the way he easily cowed other wolves—and just about anyone else, really.

I hitched my elbows on the bar behind me and leaned against it. "What's up, Rip?"

He rolled his thick shoulders and did a quick side-to-side look, as if there might actually be someone in here who didn't know why he'd approached me.

"Yous lookin' for work?"

My nostrils flared with a slow, deep breath. The crisp grapefruit scent of whatever cleaner Teddy used to keep a bar full of humans, fae, and other degenerates suspiciously clean invaded my senses. If I said yes, my sisters would be pissed. I was already on a job, but I'd screwed it up, and we were less than a month away from having our electricity cut off, so why not?

"You know, being propositioned for work in a bar would offend most women." I tugged my ponytail forward and began twisting the deep auburn strands into a fat braid. A red so deep it was nearly black, but not the black-on-black of a true blood fae.

The ogre's full belly laugh sounded like stones rattling inside a bass drum.

His gut was about the size of one, too. "Most don't get paid to beats up folks and take their money."

"True." My business card might say private investigator, but as my failed attempt to tail someone solo proved this morning, I should stick with being the muscle of my sibling trio, even if my sisters insisted otherwise. "All right. Who is it, and what's the timetable?"

"Lotta whos. Grounders. A pack of them."

I barked a laugh. "You want me to shake down a bunch of overgrown hamsters?"

The trenches carved into the big guy's forehead deepened. "Yous don't know much about them, do you?"

"Enough. Doesn't matter. I'll swipe the Easter Bunny's carrots, so long as you're paying. Here." I pulled the palm-sized pad emblazoned with the business name, YML Investigations, from my jacket pocket and handed it to Rip. "Details. Names, descriptions, their usual haunts. You know the drill."

The pad disappeared into Rip's massive mitt. He paused. His thick lips pressed into a tight line. "Yous don't underestimate these guys. Theys not so easy."

"Hey, I'm the big bad blood fae, remember?" Blood fae enough. "That's why you hire me. Let me worry about me."

Rip reached across the counter, grabbed a pen, and began scribbling the info. "Yous still on that other job?"

My turn to frown. Although, I shouldn't be surprised. Information kept him in the bookie game. "How'd you know about that?"

"Word gets 'round. I gots money on you bringing her in by end of tomorrow." He paused his scribbling to look me in the eye, which took getting used to. His protruding, conical-shaped eye sockets swiveled in all directions. "Yous gonna deliver?"

"Geez. Is there anything you don't run bets on?"

"Nope." His broad grin revealed two cracked teeth and a whole lot of pride. "Yous company is popular. YML makes me good money. Stupid tourists bet against yous. House wins."

"Why didn't I know about this? As the L in YML, I should have. I could've been double dipping, doing the jobs and betting all along." And paying bills on time.

Rip returned my pad. "Didn't seem ethical."

"Riiight. Because you're all about ethics. Put me down for a grand. I'll have your money by three."

One conical eye remained on me while the other rotated to the clock above the bar. His hairless brow shot skyward. "Almost noon. Yous telling me yous wrap this up in three hours?"

"Yup. I got this. Odds?"

His puffy lips pulled wide in a slow grin. "No bet. Yous bring my money in three hours or less, yous keep half."

"Let me guess, if I'm late I don't get paid?"

Rip tapped his bulbous nose, smiled, and pushed his way through the crowd toward his booth in the far corner. A brass plaque embossed with his name hung on the wall above the back bench.

Hot damn, half of what the grounders owed. They better owe a lot. It'd been a slow year for YML Investigations. Good for me and the more physical jobs—money collection, intimidation, even a little bit of protection. Those jobs were fun, for me, but didn't pay nearly enough to cover our bills. Unfortunately, it wasn't easy to drum up investigative business in a town of degenerates and criminals that didn't want to be investigated. The job I'd bombed this morning was meant to be our big payday.

I returned the pad to my pocket, but it caught on a bar napkin I'd shoved in there. Not from this bar, but to the bar in the fae-friendly casino I'd trailed my mark to this morning. Notes were never good. The one scrawled on the napkin was no exception. I tugged it free and fit the pad into place. Instead of replacing the napkin, I smoothed it on the bar top and stared down at the spindly black script.

Better luck next time, hybrid.

Fury roared through me. My ears burned and scalp tingled.

"What the hell is that?"

I spun with a snarl. My fangs elongated instantly, painfully.

Teddy's tall, lean frame bent over my shoulder as he read the napkin. My body thrummed with the surge of unspent adrenaline and possibly the intimate proximity. I flexed my fingers, curled them, flexed again.

"It's nothing." I snatched the napkin and jammed it into my jacket pocket. I'd deal with how exactly that woman knew I was a hybrid later. That was a secret for me and my sisters, and I aimed to keep it that way.

There was only one hybrid, and I was the unlucky genetic winner. It wasn't for lack of fae mixing, that was something they did often and copiously, but offspring were always of one race. It kept their magic powerful, and if fae worshiped anything, it was power. My existence wasn't an exalted position.

"But—"

"It's nothing," I stressed, my gaze steady on his. I meant business.

"Okay, okay." He tipped his forehead toward my face. "You should holster those things before you hurt someone besides yourself."

Crap, not again. All at once my lip became a persistent throb, reminding me of the pain from my fangs punching out. I dragged a finger along the edge of my mouth. It came away sticky, warm, and wet. When startled, I had zero control of the things. It was embarrassing.

Teddy tucked a clean napkin into my palm and pulled me close to whisper, "You shouldn't be wasting blood when you refuse to drink it."

His hot breath warmed my neck and tickled my ear. The heady mixture of woods, earth, and vanilla—Teddy's distinct scent—filled my nostrils, made me dizzy. Something melted and puddled in my core. My gaze fastened on the way my dark red hair danced with his bourbon-brown strands. The way they both brushed against the hard line of muscle leading from his neck to his shoulder.

Damn it.

That delicious scent shouldn't be so strong. My olfactory sense was the same as any other fae, unless I'd smelled their blood. Then again, with the amount of brawls Teddy broke up in this joint, he was bound to have bled at some point.

I stepped away and scowled in a desperate attempt to hide my reaction. "And you should mind your own business." What was wrong with me lately? I'd known the guy for years, but recently Teddy seemed more flirt than friend. I felt disgustingly girly when he got near.

"Whatever you say, sweet fangs." He chucked a knuckle under my chin, letting it linger long enough to turn the gesture from playful to intimate.

I rubbed my chin on my shoulder. This was Teddy. He couldn't possibly be flirting. He'd known me since I roared into Interlands at fifteen with way more balls and bravado than sense. More importantly, I wasn't his type—empty headed and easy.

He swaggered toward the end of the bar, and some mysterious magnetic force pulled my appreciative gaze to the way he filled out his denim. My view disappeared as he stepped behind the counter. When I looked up, Teddy watched me with a knowing grin. I bared my fangs. He laughed.

I growled under my breath and turned to leave as he circled the bar and headed for the spot across the counter from me.

"Why take these jobs, Lane? They're bad. You're so much more than this."

Teddy's earnest words stopped me, and I looked back. His bottomless black gaze gripped mine.

My chest tightened. Teddy didn't know how misplaced his faith in me was. I grabbed a freshly filled tumbler full of amber liquid from the bar.

"Hey!" The owner of the drink turned, opened his mouth to say more, and laid eyes on me. I raised my brows in a dare. The guy wisely spun to face the bar and tapped the counter, ordering a new drink for himself.

"Because I'm really, really good at it. Besides, haven't you heard?" I slammed my confiscated drink. The taste of gasoline chasing cinnamon scorched a path down my throat. My nostrils burned and eyes watered. I shoved down the sensation and flashed a smile filled with a whole lot of fang. "I'm a bad girl."

With that mic drop moment, I turned away from the bar prepared to swagger my sweet ass out the door and instead came nose to leather-clad chest. I stumbled back and focused on the crest pinned to the left pectoral area of the moon fae who wore it. A silver moon, intersecting a gold sun, with a tree rising in front of both—the Royal Fae Guard insignia. Or since that was more breath wasted on fae who didn't deserve it, the RFG.

"Duskmere," I said and straightened.

"Malaney Callaghan, there is no bad. There is no good. There simply is."

What was with the self-help, infomercial crap? "Don't waste your philosophy lessons here. I don't give a damn what anyone thinks of me."

His silver eyes tightened. Duskmere was all hard angles and sharp lines, just like his personality. Narrow face, slashing cheekbones, the elongated points to his ears, even the way his lips compressed into a razor's edge. His spiky, close-cropped silver hair didn't dare have a strand out of place. He nodded to an occupied booth near the door and headed that way, not waiting to see if I followed.

I blew an angry breath from my nose and stomped after the moon fae.

Duskmere stared down the patrons in the booth. Judging by the two empty pitchers on the table, the trio were deep in their cups but not so far gone to miss the lethal energy emanating from the moon fae. They quickly scooted from the benches. I grabbed a half empty mug from one of the former booth occupants as he passed. He glanced at me and kept moving.

With a sigh, I slid onto the still-warm seat and waited for Duskmere to settle across from me.

He set his elbows on the tabletop, leaned forward, and wasted no time getting down to business. "Once you have captured the banshee, Etta'wy, you will bring her to us."

I barked a laugh. "I'll do no such thing."

"You will."

"Uh, no, I won't." I held out a fist and flipped up the index finger. "First, you're RFG, so by use of the royal 'us,' you mean the sun fae. There is no scenario where I help them."

He opened his mouth to respond, but I continued and popped a second finger.

"Second, Etta'wy is a job. Someone hired my sisters and me. That someone is paying us to bring her in, so they're the one we'll be delivering her to." I held up another finger. "Third, since you didn't seem to hear me the first time, I will never help the sun fae."

"I am aware you were hired by the banshee's husband. He has agreed to allow for delivery to us in his stead. We will pay your fee."

"Nope." I slapped my palms down on the tabletop and pushed to my feet. "I'd say sorry you wasted your time, but I'm not. See ya around."

Duskmere surged from the booth and grabbed my elbow. He leaned close, voice going low. "The sun stones have been stolen."

"So? Get some more."

"You misheard," Duskmere said. "The sun stones have been stolen. The stones. The source. There will be no more shards."

A slush of ice coursed through my veins, and my nostrils flared on a sharp inhale. I met his pounded steel gaze.

"The banshee was involved. It is imperative we question her. The stones must be found."

I didn't know Duskmere well, but he'd always been a stoic, by-the-books prick who never showed emotion. The desperation, the intensity of his plea punched me in the gut.

"That, I am sorry for, but I'm not the one you should be asking for help." I swallowed and turned to focus on the door. Escape. "Good luck."

"There are many things said about you, but petty was not among them." I sneered at his insult, and Duskmere's grip tightened. "You issue a death sentence with your refusal."

"Doubtful. This is a sun fae problem we're talking about. They're resilient. They don't need me."

"Sun fae problems affect all fae." He tilted his head. "You're fae."

Something bitter and vile twisted inside of me. I clenched my fists on my thighs.

"I think the word you're looking for is abomination. Monster is a popular choice. Or you could be trying for something fancy like mistake of nature. I've heard them all."

"Perhaps there is something wrong with my hearing." Duskmere's voice came at me soft and sly. "I thought you said you do not care what anyone thinks of you."

My stomach clenched. I looked up and let him see everything in my mismatched eyes—one black, one violet. Eyes which forever set me apart. All the rage, all the pain, the black hole of sadness I would never escape no matter how much I lied and told myself I didn't care.

"Trust me, even if the sun fae did need me, they wouldn't want my help. They would rather die than accept anything from the likes of me. Who's the petty ones in this situation? Good luck, Duskmere," I said again, and this time I meant it. I could at least give him that.

The moon fae's hand dropped from my elbow. Ignoring the way his gaze went dull, I turned away and headed for the exit. Time was ticking. Getting hijacked by Duskmere had eaten up twenty minutes of my deadline with Rip.

With every step I took toward the doors, away from Duskmere, fae problems slid from my conscience.

Outside, the stale afternoon air filled my lungs. I slipped on my sunglasses and smiled. This was going to be easy money.

My feet hit the cobbled sidewalk that ran along the front of the bar as the door swished open behind me and heavy footsteps followed onto the wood porch. "Hold up, sweet fangs."

I froze, a snake of anticipation coiling around my spine, pulling it taught. If I didn't shake this reaction I'd been having to Teddy, I'd have to move my place of business. He was less eye candy these days and more serious distraction.

Warm fingers gripped my elbow. They glided to my hand, engulfing it, and he tugged me around to face him. “That moon fae giving you trouble?”

He didn’t drop my hand and heat bloomed up my arm from his touch. I licked my lips. “Nothing I can’t handle.”

Teddy’s head dipped closer to mine, and the smile that curved his lips was nothing short of criminal. The mouth-watering scent of musky forest and sweet vanilla teased the knots from my back that the encounter with Duskmere created. Anticipation left my spine to settle in my chest, pressure shortening my breath. His lips brushed my ear, and goosebumps skittered across my neck, tickling my scalp.

“I know,” he said and chuckled. The soft laughter fluttered my hair, and my lips parted at the airy caress. Still gripping my hand, he straightened. “But I’m here for you if you ever need me. You know that, right?”

Damn, it was hot out here, or was that just my proximity to this male? Nothing rattled me, except a nice ass and devilish dark eyes, apparently. Seven years I’d known Teddy, and suddenly my hormones decided to have a party and issue him an invitation.

“I heard the job Rip is sending you on.” Teddy released my hand at last and leaned against a porch post. “He wasn’t wrong. There’s more to those guys than size indicates. You want back up? Zee’s here and it’s slow, I can take a break.”

“Thanks, but I’ve been doing this for a while. I think I know what I’m doing.” I ran a hand over the hairs escaped from my loose braid, tucking several behind my still-tingling ears.

“I have no doubt that you do. Just offering a helping hand. Remember, grounders are really sensitive about their fur.” He winked and strolled back into the bar.

“What the hell does that mean?” I shouted at the swinging door and rubbed at the suspicious vacancy the evaporated pressure left in my chest.

2

LET'S DO THIS

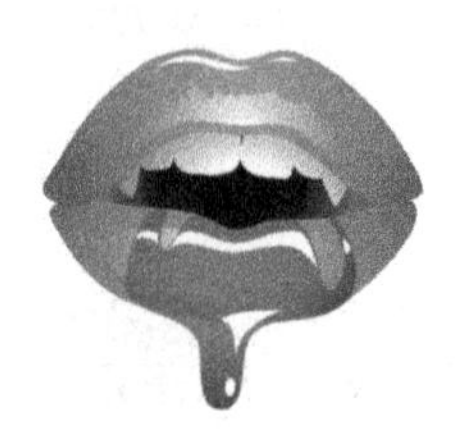

I TORQUED THE WHEEL LEFT AND MADE A SHARP TURN INTO THE MOSTLY empty gravel parking lot. Seeing as it was the middle of the day and this was a seedier part of a seedy town, there weren't many humans, fae, or otherwise out and about.

Ace in the Hole was the last dive Rip listed I might find the grounders gambling their tiny hearts out. The clock was running out, and I'd be damned if I had two failures today. They better be here.

The back end of my '94 Bronco shimmied on mud and gravel but held steady. I swung parallel into the space before the front door. "That a girl." I patted the dash and hopped out of the SUV to scope out the lot. I spied a handful of furry, scaly, and feathered mounts, some tied up, some not. Unfortunately, nothing small enough for a grounder. Three cars, too, but a big enough booster seat didn't exist for the grounders to drive. If they were here, they had walked.

"Not a parking spot," the muscle-bound mountain blocking the door said. He spotted me as I rounded the SUV's hood and straightened on the wall he leaned against. With a chin nod of recognition, he waved me by.

"Good lookin' out." I gave the bouncer's swollen bicep a pat and pushed through the doors, leaving the sun-bright morning behind.

Inside the gloom and dank, a mix of clove cigarettes, fried food, and booze-soaked carpets wrestled for dominance in my nasal cavity. I snorted and shook my head to clear away the obnoxious scents.

Another aroma rode beneath the others—death. Stale and old, but heavy. This place had seen plenty of it. Drunk humans searching for something legendary, something fae, something supernatural, frequented these dark corners of Interlands. Most returned to the bright lights of Vegas. Some didn't. The unluckiest found their way across the border to Ta'Vale.

I tried to slide my sunglasses into the inner jacket chest pocket I normally carried them in, but the wadded-up napkin didn't leave much room. Instead, I slipped them into a shallow inner pocket near my hip and cursed myself for neglecting to put in my lenses this morning. The lenses didn't just disguise the very non-blood fae, one black, one violet color of my oddball eyes, they let me see in the sunlight without suffering excruciating pain. Kind of a big deal.

My shadow-loving eyes needed no time adjusting to the dim light, and I scanned the room. Large round tables dotted the floor, each thick with gamblers, with no less than two grounders in every group. A cantaloupe-sized fixture hung above each table leaking watery yellow light.

Seated on low-backed booster stools dead center in the room, a pack of wannabe teddy bears traded tiles at an extra-large table. Only three of the twenty-two gamblers at what, I assumed, was the VIP table, were not small and furry. While I watched, the largest grounder in the room tossed what looked to be a modest-sized ruby onto a pile of coins, paper cash, and random items in the middle of the table. The pile grew as the betting intensified.

Knowing the hamster nugget I needed to shake down when I saw it, I cracked my neck and stalked in that direction.

"I'm here to collect for Rip." No acknowledgment. "Hey, furballs, I said I'm here for the money you owe your bookie."

One of the grounders rearranged its tiles and threw a gold coin from my homeland, Ta'Vale, onto the pile. Still, none of them looked up.

A growl vibrated deep in my throat. I thumbed open the dagger holster on my right thigh. Sure, I had claws, but sometimes steel made the bigger impression.

The sleek black carbon whispered from its rigid leather sheath. I twirled it in my palm, leaned forward, and slammed the blade through a hundred-dollar bill. Coins jumped and slid from the mound of bets. Something bright winked from beneath the pile. A rich amber stone, rough cut, the size of half a golf ball. Recognition tingled across my scalp, and my eyes widened. Not a stone, a sun shard.

Of course it had to be a sun shard. I reached for it.

"Hey! Ours. Fair pay for a job." The biggest of the fuzzballs protested and lunged for the shard. First it had to climb its small, slightly rotund body onto the table.

I didn't know shards this size existed. Parting with it would be like severing a limb to a sun fae.

The grounder's short legs scissor kicked until it hefted itself onto the table and made a beeline for the intended treasure.

"Right." I snorted. My reach was longer, and I got to it first. "You trying to tell me some sun fae legitimately paid with this so a pack of rodents could dig a hole? Because that's what you do, right? You dig holes."

"Not rodents, not a sun fae, and we dig good. More than a hole." It stood on the table and sneered at my obvious ignorance of holes.

"So you weren't paid by a sun fae." Morbid curiosity, not my desire to help Duskmere with his problem, made me ask, "A banshee hire you?"

"Not banshee," the big grounder replied, daring a step closer.

The shard was smooth on one side, three sides rough, chipped, as if it had been broken off an even larger piece. A theory took root in my brain. Ridiculous. Improbable, but not impossible. I guess it wouldn't hurt to follow up, so long as someone was willing to pay.

"Banshee hired us, moon fae paid."

The shard wobbled in my palm. This could be a problem. Considering the most prominent moon fae left after the Great Fae Divide was Duskmere, it might be smart to hold off on that follow up.

"Right, well, I don't care how you got it, it's mine now. Consider it payment for not shearing you. You know how much I could get for all that blue fur? Now move."

The grounder bared its teeth and hissed. I bared my fangs in return. The small beastie twitched but didn't move, so I moved it with a shove. It tumbled from the pile and over the far side of the table. With a shrug, the duffle I'd carried in with me slid from my shoulder to land on the floor with an empty whumph. I nudged it forward with my foot and leaned over the table to drag the pile of money into the waiting bag.

"That should cover what you owe Rip." And what he'd owe me when I won my wager. I zipped the bag and hoisted its now considerable weight, positioning the strap crosswise across my chest, its bulk on my back. I rolled the confiscated shard between my thumb and forefinger. "Got any more of these?"

As one they puffed and chittered. The big grounder leaped back onto the edge of the table. I kicked it. The heavy table jumped, scattering coins and returning the angry ball of fluff to the floor. Gamblers scrambled to grab whatever remaining cash they could.

"Stay. Anybody else?"

Once again, the grounders puffed and chittered at me but were not dissuaded from getting their greedy paws on whatever currency they could. "Smart. I'll ask again, any more shards?"

With a hard stare into each of their beady eyes, I pulled my dagger from the felt tabletop and slid it home. Each grounder returned my look with bare hostility. Three gamblers at the table weren't with the grounders. The first, a human, counted ceiling stains, the second, also human, busied herself adjusting her chip stacks. The third, a werewolf, stared dead on and dragged his gaze to a satchel hanging on the empty seat of the big grounder I'd kicked to the floor.

I straightened and strolled around the table to the bag in question. The closer I got, the more the fuzzballs puffed. The saddlebag was heavier than expected. I unzipped the corner, got a good look at a bag full of amber crystals, and dropped the shard I still held inside, gave the bag a jingle, and smiled at the rattle and clink. The sun shards were a massive windfall Rip didn't need to know about.

"Good doin' business with you. I'll see you next time you skip out on payin' your debts." I winked, rapped my knuckles on the table, and swaggered toward the door.

Speaking of debts, maybe now I could pay one or two of mine. Maybe a lot more if my sister didn't question where whoever paid the grounders got these shards.

Outside the sun blasted my sensitive pupils, and I threw a forearm across my eyes to shield them and fumbled in my pocket for my glasses. Damn it, they weren't there. No way was I going back inside for them now.

Of course, today had to be the first cloudless day in two weeks. Sunlight knifed into my overblown pupils. My eyes watered, screaming for a return of the deep gloom inside the gambling den. As a hybrid, my blood fae strengths were watered down, but I didn't lack for their weaknesses. Extreme light-sensitivity, for example.

Instead of stopping, I kept heading in the direction of my SUV I'd left feet from the door and the extra pair of sunglasses I kept in the glove compartment. Should be able to find it with my eyes closed, which they were.

"Son of a bitch." My foot squelched ankle-deep into a mud puddle. Sandwiched between the dry-as-bone Mojave Desert and lush lands of Ta'Vale, the small bubble dimension that was Interlands generally followed the weather patterns of its neighbor, Las Vegas. Except for the extremely brief but powerful rainy season that left behind a month-long headache of flooded roads and mud traps, and we'd just gone through the heaviest rains I'd experienced since moving here.

Despite their watery protest, I forced a squint and limped around the front of my SUV, shaking sludge from my combat boot as I went. Damn, these were my favorites.

I slid into the well-worn driver's seat, fished my sunglasses from the glove compartment, and slid them on. With the mirrored lenses came sweet relief. I sank into my seat and waited for the sun's halo to fade from my now protected vision. I'd be damned if I neglected my contact lenses again.

Something banged and cracked. The sudden noise had me upright in my seat. My neck tightened and phantom claws tickled my scalp. I twisted toward the building. The front door of the gambling den was flung wide. It hung askew against the wall. The oversized doorstop of a bouncer lay on his back. With a serious lack of grace, he regained his feet, but instead of moving toward the door, he backed away.

"Shit." Small they might be, but there were a lot of them. The big blue furball I'd bullied stood huffing and puffing in the opening, its buddies crowded in behind. Not only the ones from the table, but all of them. I stopped counting at fifteen where their fuzzy forms disappeared into shadow.

The leader bared its longer than should be physically possible pointy teeth, the smaller less-than-cuddly fluffballs behind followed suit. Not good. It flexed its paws, and claws half the length of its fingers popped. Worse.

I should have known there was more to them than blue fluff. If it couldn't eat your face, it wouldn't survive in Interlands.

A deep throated croak from the large leader silenced the manic chitters of the pack. Three more successive croaks, and the group's tiny legs flew into motion. They speed-waddled for my SUV.

"Shit," I repeated. My hand shook. It took three tries to fit the key. I cranked the engine, yanked the gear shift into drive, and stomped the gas to the floor. In the rearview, gravel and mud sprayed the pack as they converged on the spot I vacated.

I chuckled under my breath and sped from the parking lot, heading for Creek Ridge. Aptly named, it ran parallel to the creek bed, and while it might be flooded in places, it'd get me to Teddy's bar and my payday faster than the meandering route I took to get here.

The driver's seat hugged me as I relaxed into it. Unspent adrenaline jangled beneath my skin. My arms trembled, and I eased my death grip on the steering wheel. Thank the stars my sisters weren't here to see me run away from a pack of grounders. Especially Y'sindra, who at three and a half feet tall wasn't any bigger than the biggest of them and would have laughed her little snow fairy ass off.

Thunk. Thunk, thud, thunk.

The Bronco's rear fishtailed mid-turn on a thick layer of deep-orange creek mud. I wrestled the SUV straight on the narrow dirt road and stomped the brakes. The vehicle was still skidding to a stop as I spun in my seat and stared out the rear window. Maybe my eyes suffered from sunlight overload, but what I saw made no sense.

The road moved, boiled, a blue tide rising and coming for my rear bumper. How had those Smurf farts caught up to me?

Thud! Thunk, thunk, crack! One by one they pelted the SUV. A furry body slammed into the back window. A crack formed beneath and spiderwebbed across the glass.

How the hell was I going to pay for that? Anger swelled through me, and I grabbed the door handle. "That's coming out of your furry blue hides!" The door opened a sliver and a paw shot inside. Finger-length claws punctured the door panel, eliciting a loud click when claws met the metal frame.

"On second thought, maybe not." I flung the door wide and knocked over a cluster of grounders, but my tenacious hitchhiker hung on and reached toward me with its free arm. "Oh, no you don't." I pulled the door closed with all the strength I could muster. Which was considerable.

It screamed. I smiled.

Once again, I threw the gear shift into drive and stomped the gas. The

SUV's tires spun for purchase and sent a geyser of the mud toward the pack. The blue beasties turned orange. I cackled into my rearview. The wheels caught and the Bronco surged into motion.

Each bounce over the extremely uneven road elicited a thump from the trapped grounder's body against the door, probably ruining its trespassing arm for life. It shrieked, and with its free arm, pounded against the window with renewed vigor.

"Let this be a lesson to keep your fucking paws to yourself," I shouted, and without slowing down, cracked the door, letting the grounder fall away.

In the rearview, its body bounced, rolled, and was lost beneath the undulating tide of mud-caked furballs rolling toward me.

"What...?" The oncoming swell of grounders was an ever-moving herd of blue and orange. They'd tucked themselves into balls, more teeth and claws than fur, and rolled after me in rabid pursuit. Rip hadn't said a damn thing about this metamorphosis.

My knuckles went white on the steering wheel, and I stomped the already floored gas. The SUV dove through a crater of a pothole, mud flew, splattering the windows. I hit the windshield wipers and jammed the window down button. The driver's window stuttered. I pressed the button until my fingertip bleached white. The window whined open. It scraped the caked-on mud from the glass onto the sill and oozed down the door. Fat, sticky rivulets obscured my side view mirror.

Thank the stars for all the fast food I eat and resulting wad of napkins stashed in the center console. I used the napkins to scrape mud from the mirror and eased up on the gas pedal. I couldn't afford to lose a wheel driving into one of the even bigger potholes. Plenty of them hidden beneath the mud.

Surprise performed somersaults in my belly as something latched onto my elbow and pulled it down, banging it on the outside of my door. I dropped the napkin and lifted my arm. "What the...? Get off me!"

The angry yellow eyes of a mud-caked furball met mine above my arm where it had attached itself, fangs first. Its dagger-tipped feet scrabbled against my door.

"Cut it out, you little shit." I shook my arm, glaring between it and the road. A small tear opened on my jacket. The grounder's chitters of protest were muffled behind the mouthful of my leather it refused to spit out. I extended my arm out the window and whipped it up and down. Fabric tore.

A breeze kissed my bare skin. The grounder's shriek was swallowed by the wind as it performed a broken cartwheel along the side of my SUV.

"Sure, no problem! Three hours. I got this. Yeah, I so *don't* got this," I shouted and slapped my steering wheel.

Rip warned me, but in my professional opinion, *theys not so easy* didn't cover it. He could have told me that the two-foot-tall tooth-achingly cute blue teddy bears would turn into demonic fucking fuzzballs.

I gunned it through the next turn, veering wide to avoid the epic pothole beneath the mud and turned onto Creek Ridge. I risked a quick glance into the rearview. More grounders than I could count rolled toward me, faster and faster, all fangs, claws, and fur flying. The wheels hydroplaned. I slowed to avoid a spinout, and the grounders gained.

A hill rose ahead of me. This was my chance to put some distance between us. I slammed the gas pedal to the floor as I crested the slope, and my SUV took flight. The Bronco cannonballed into sludge. Mud sprayed over my vehicle, and then rained down, painting my side through the still open window. I stomped the gas again, but the Bronco didn't move. The tires spun in the mire but refused to budge. My vehicle handled the Interlands terrain like a champ, but off-roading through a lake of mud? Not so much.

"Shit! Shit, shit, shit!" My hearts punched my ribs. I jerked my gaze to the rearview but couldn't see the road. I twisted to look behind me. A solid sheet of wet clay coated the cracked window. I didn't want to get out.

New napkin in hand, I scrubbed at the mirror again. When I could see a reflection through the streaks, my side view told me objects in the mirror were closer than they appeared, and they appeared to be right on my ass.

My knee jerk reaction said gun it. Logic said that was the last thing I should do. That's what got me into this mess, but I was freaking out. Logic wasn't a factor, fight or flight was, and I wasn't ashamed to flee.

A grounder latched onto my braid. My head yanked to the left, half out of the open driver's window. The hamster spawned in the fiery pits of Hell scrabbled for purchase. My ear bounced against the window frame. "Get..." I grunted and whipped my head to the right. "Off me, asshole!" A fire screamed to life in my scalp and tears rippled across my vision. I'd shaken it loose, but the thing took a handful of my hair with it. Warm blood welled beneath the cold coating of mud on my head.

"That's it." I shoved open the door. The Bronco wasn't going anywhere. Sitting inside and letting these things take me apart one tiny chunk at a time wasn't an option. I hopped down, orange muck swallowing my boots. Push daggers appeared in each hand as I ripped them from the underarm sheath and faced my attackers.

What did Teddy say about their fur? They were sensitive about it? Time to test that statement. Teeth bared, I stared at the grounders who had all stopped in a ragged line a safe distance from the vehicle. They seemed shocked to see me standing there. I'd be shocked too if I wasn't so pissed off.

"All right, let's do this, bitches!" Lip curled back from my lengthening fangs, I rushed them.

3

FATE'S A FUNNY BITCH

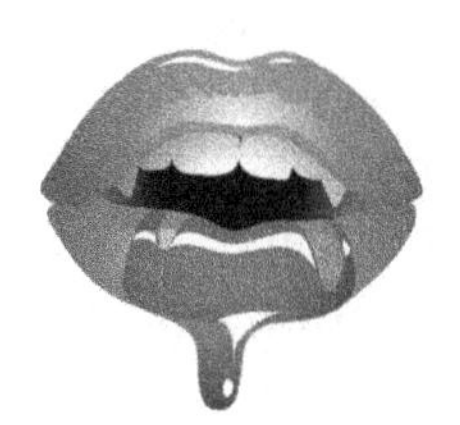

I DROPPED THE BAG OF MONEY ON THE TABLE IN FRONT OF RIP. DROPLETS of mud splattered his lap, and without a word, I held my hand out for payment.

One of the ogre's eyes swiveled to the bag while the other stayed on me. He stood. When my nose was somewhere between his pecs and his belly button he started laughing. "I's told you, don't go alone, girl."

"Yeah, yeah. Lesson learned. Size doesn't matter, got it. I'm under three hours, pay up." I wiggled my fingers impatiently and caught sight of my sisters at the bar. Mae's gold-hewn complexion paled, her aristocratic features locked in a shocked mask. No surprise, in contrast, the pint-sized Y'sindra snickered and pointed. Her opalescent wings hummed, spraying snow over her neighbors at the bar. Thank goodness of the fae, only fairies had wings, because those things were obnoxious.

"Here yous go." Rip pulled my attention back to him, tucking a roll of bills in my palm bigger than what he owed. "Call it a bonus. I's coulda maybe told yous about their bad attitude." Both eye cones rotated to the ceiling, and he huffed.

Oh stars, he'd been drinking kiwu. Nasty stuff. Made from fermented mushrooms, black garlic, and molasses, ogres favored it. My stomach clenched and flipped in rebellion. I wrinkled my nose but resisted stepping away as not to offend.

"I's don't think I's loan to them anymore."

"Oh, no, I expect they'll pay on time in the future." I dropped a second bag on the table, larger than the first, but with a fraction of the weight.

Rip's hairless brow shot up. He studied both me and the bag at the same time. With extra caution he pulled the strings cinching the burlap sack, and it sagged open. He pegged the contents with one eye, and then the second eye rotated down to join the first. He boomed with laughter, and his breath blasted me once again. My liquid breakfast rode a wave of nausea to my throat. Offense be damned, I took the step. Three slow breaths through my mouth, not my nose, and the threat passed.

"I's can?" Rip gestured to the bag.

"Sure, there's plenty, and I wouldn't have it without you sending me after them." Rip dipped his fingers into the bag, oddly delicate as he sorted and plucked just enough fluff to fill his palm.

I looked at the mound of fuzzy blue fur inside the bag and smirked, pretty damn pleased with myself.

I'd held every single one of the fuzzballs I could catch down and gave them an impromptu shave with my blades. My jacket was shredded, and I could feel the dried blood beneath the sleeves where their claws had cut me through the stiff leather, but it had been worth every scratch and bite. I'd gotten ahold of eight. Well, eight and a half. The last one squirmed out of my mud-slick grip and beat a path after his friends, down the road, away from me. I'd walked to the bar with a bag of priceless shards, a duffel full of money, and a sack full of pelts, whistling the entire way.

"Bring that banshee to the husband by tomorrow, and I give yous half my winnings." Rip finished tucking the fur carefully into a satchel on the bench behind him. He stepped close, returning the bag and leaned in to speak low. I cringed and held my breath. "Is a lot. Yous should finish that job."

I studied Rip for a moment, nodded and headed for my place of business at the bar where my sisters waited. A scowl tugged my lips as I passed Teddy. He leaned on the bar top, his arms folded on the glossy slab of wood. The sleeves of his flannel were rolled up to reveal a mouth-watering amount of forearm.

When did I start finding forearms sexy?

Teddy's dark, bottomless gaze caught mine and followed me from over the shoulder of a customer. He winked. I sucked in a breath and turned my glare to the floor.

He'd been wrong this morning, not about the grounders and their fur, but about me, and thank goodness. I'm not better than these types of jobs. Considering this new arrangement with Rip, these types of jobs weren't just going to pay the bills, they were going to make me rich. Respected, too. Maybe not the kind of respect my sisters and I had been chasing as we tried to build our business and be taken seriously, but I'd take any kind I could shove up the snooty noses of every sun fae who forced me to leave Ta'Vale.

I slid onto the stool my sisters kept empty for me. The seat was chilly. They'd been waiting awhile.

"What was that about?" Mae asked. As with most sun fae, my sister was tall, nearly six foot, and she looked down her slightly sloped nose at me. Her ripe, blueberry eyes scoured my dirt and blood-crusted self. Ever the neat freak, she frowned at the flakes of dried mud collecting below my seat. I half expected her to ask Teddy where the broom closet was.

"Had a complication this morning. I got the pictures of Etta'wy meeting with her guy." I felt under one arm and patted the zipped side pocket along my ribs where I'd stowed the camera. "She gave me the slip before I could bring her in."

The delicate wing of Mae's white-blonde brow arched in surprise. I was a good tracker. Nose like a bloodhound if I'd scented the blood, and the banshee's husband had provided an old sample. It had been faint, but still ranked among the most unpleasant I'd ever smelled, like the putrid water she came from that hid rotting things beneath its placid surface.

"Yeah, I know. She disappeared but left this behind." I pulled the wadded-up napkin from my jacket pocket and handed it to Mae. "Swamp bitch thought she was funny."

Mae's wide eyes jumped from the note, to me, and back. "How?"

I shrugged. "No one around here knows." At least I didn't think anyone knew.

Unable to resist her orderly tendencies, she placed the napkin on the bar, smoothed out the creases, and folded it into a neat square. I had no idea how she could tolerate living with me. My laundry hamper was the floor. All of it.

"Anyhow, I assume you heard about the other job I took. Those furry little bastards were more trouble than I gave them credit for. Here, this should keep the lights on a couple months." I put the wad of money and bag of fur on the bar top and slid them to her, accidentally knocking the neatly folded note behind the bar. Damn.

Mae pulled her obscenely large purse into her lap and dropped the money inside.

"Thanks," I said. "Don't think I have a pocket that isn't full of mud."

She poked the burlap sack. Tufts of blue fur poked out. "What do you want me to do with this?"

"I don't know. You're into fashion, have it made into a coat. A throw rug would be nice."

"Mmm," she hummed and slid her gaze to the bag still slung over my shoulder. The one I'd taken from the grounders. The one I hadn't given to Rip.

"Later," I said with a meaningful glance around. I didn't want anyone else to know what I carried.

Teddy rounded the bar and wedged himself between Mae and me. He swiveled me toward him and tucked the note I'd dropped behind the bar into my hip pocket. Even the brief touch sank tendrils of heat through my denim, made my skin feel too tight. That could also be the pants. Y'sindra and I had gone on a junk food binge and trashy reality show marathon every night this week.

"Thanks." I drew in a deep breath, my shoulders loosening with relief. No one needed to read what was on the napkin. Teddy might have seen the scrawled taunt, but so far, no judgement, no questions. He was good about keeping his nose out of his clients' business, unless they were about to spill blood in his bar.

Teddy searched my eyes. "You shouldn't hide your eyes. They are who you are, and you are phenomenal. His hand, still on my hip, tightened and then fell away. The lingering touch branded me through my denim, and my flesh beneath tingled.

A sudden feeling of claustrophobia from his nearness, his perception, his interest, squeezed my ribs.

My gaze broke from his and slid to a spot on the counter, but Teddy hooked a finger under my chin and angled my face to his. A crooked smile curled his almost too-perfect lips, and he proceeded to take his time appraising my filthy, bloody appearance. "New look?"

"Don't," I warned, and the onslaught of suffocating emotions instantly evaporated.

Teddy's chest, still so close to me, rumbled his amusement.

My lips twitched, humor at the situation slow coming. "Hey, think you can get me a tow? My Bronco is bogged down in mud on Creek Ridge, just past 'Little Dipper.'" The legendary pothole had a name.

"Sure thing. I'll get it after my shift and drop it by your place."

"Thanks. I owe ya." For this and a million other small things he'd done for me over the years.

"Yeah, you do. I've got a few things in mind." He slung the dish towel over his shoulder and retreated behind the bar. The thin white T-shirt beneath the cleaning rag grew damp, clung to his skin, accentuating the muscles of his back.

My mouth went dry.

I tore my gaze away and pressed cool hands to my flushed cheeks.

A snowflake landed on the bar. I frowned and slid a look to my right. Y'sindra had her pert snow fairy bottom perched exactly where it shouldn't be—on the bar top. Her pearlescent wings shivered as the heels of her dainty ballet slippers thumped the front of the counter. Each exaggerated swing of her legs set the cloud of white curls bouncing. She gave me a slow wink and grinned.

"Shut it," I snapped. On my left, Mae flashed her pearly whites. "Not you too."

"You've had your eye on that one for a long time, and Teddy's scrumptious, so why not?" She shrugged and flipped a strand of her honey-and-ice blonde hair off her shoulder. The afternoon sun set her gold-tinted complexion ablaze.

A sun fae, Mae was essentially the antithesis of me and my nearly translucent self. Even if the blood fae DNA I got from Mom was clouded with my father's sun fae, I didn't look a lick like my adopted sister. Didn't look much like a true blood fae, either. Fortunately, blood fae were a young race and rare enough that no one in Interlands realized the difference.

We were the result of magic, dark and horrible magic. A forced evolution. A last-ditch attempt by the moon fae during the Great Fae Divide to create immortal soldiers. We weren't immortal, but we were damn hard to kill. Also, damn good at killing. I lived off the reputation and legend of my more than formidable race.

The whumph, whumph, whumph of the saloon-style front doors pulled my gaze to the mirror behind the bar. Its reflection revealed a banshee in a crisp white pantsuit rocking a snarl of hip-length, mossy green hair. My banshee. I chuckled under my breath. Sometimes, Fate's a funny bitch.

I shot a triumphant grin at Rip and rubbed my forefinger and thumb together. Hot damn, the ogre was about to owe me more money.

Banshees were bad news who rarely came to town. The knock of a drink hitting a table ricocheted through the hush that fell over the room. Someone scooted their seat, and the chair whined against the floor. My sisters swiveled to face the source of the sudden silence. In the mirror, the banshee locked eyes as murky as the swamp water she'd been born to on my back.

"Hybrid. You have something that belongs to me."

Oh, she did not just out me. My talons dug into the edge of the bar.

"Hybrid," she called again.

My fingers tensed. Wood shavings curled onto the counter. Maybe if I ignored her no one would know she meant me?

"Malaney Callaghan. Bring me the shards."

So much for that idea. I groaned and turned slow enough to count three ticks of the clock.

"Listen, crazy lady, why don't we step outside."

"The shards," she repeated.

"I have no idea what you're talking about, but I do know your husband wants you returned and hired me to make sure that happens." I pushed from the stool and flicked a pair of zip tie cuffs from a side pocket. Traditional cuffs were a bad idea. Brittle, and easy for the locals to break. With a discreet nudge of my toe, I pushed the bag of stones beneath Mae's stool and faced the banshee. "Why don't you come along easy, and I'll put in a good word for you with Palough."

"Like hell," Y'sindra muttered and stood. I elbowed her over the side of the bar before she caused a situation. Situations were her specialty. She cursed and hopped back up, but kept her trap shut.

The banshee tilted her head and cackled. "You may tell my husband he's officially back on the market."

"You know it doesn't work like that. He's a kelpie prince, and you married him. That's a lifetime gig, lady."

"The shards."

This again? My top lip peeled up in a snarl. "Come and get 'em."

"Lane," Mae warned, too late.

Etta'wy's stomach went concave while her chest swelled and shoulders pinched back.

"She's gonna blow," Y'sindra shouted. Her wings spun into a snowy flurry, and she lifted off the bar.

The banshee's wail rolled over the room. Bodies dropped and writhed. Y'sindra plummeted to the counter with a hard thud and bounced behind the bar.

Shit.

"Lane," Mae screamed. Her hands pressed hard against her ears, she doubled over.

The frequency was too high to affect me. Thanks to my blood fae genes, I basically had built in audio tuners. Most days my blood fae skills came up short, but right now, I was fucking winning.

Etta'wy spotted me—the only person left standing. I gave her a full-fanged grin and shot forward. Three steps in and a werewolf spontaneously furred up. His writhing bulk, four thrashing legs, and snapping jaw blocked my path. Damn things were worse than puppies. No control.

Without breaking stride, I sidestepped and vaulted onto a tabletop. Teddy had sturdy furniture, the kind of furniture that took more than one hit over the head to break. The table absorbed my weight without a wobble. I leaped to the next table, taking an elevated route to the door. The haphazard layout forced me to make a long jump to the next, little more than a skip after that. Why was this room so long?

"Lane, hurry." Mae's plea carried above the howls of pain. I turned to check on her.

The room was a sea of bodies. Spines bowed in agony. They twisted, rolling in their own vomit. Ruby drops swelled on earlobes, streaked down cheeks, throats, pooled on the floor. A forbidden hunger roared. It demanded I taste. Lick. Absorb its power. My nostrils flared and filled with a cacophony of smells. Above the booze, above the sick: blood. All blood smelled different—dark chocolate, cinnamon, onion, rosemary, almond. My head swam with euphoric overload.

"Please, Lane." The thready note of Mae's voice snapped me out of it. She'd fallen to her side, arms curled over her head.

Eardrums would burst soon. Some might have already. Death wouldn't be far behind. I had to hurry.

Fury burned a path from my lungs. My legs bent deep, muscles bunched, and I propelled myself two tables away. With a snarl, I met the banshee's increasingly panicked look. Her wail broke long enough to drag in another lungful of death-shriek air. She let loose, upping the volume. The vial of swamp water dangling from a chain between her breasts exploded. Behind me, next to me, everywhere beings sobbed in pain.

"You're going to regret that," I shouted and lunged to the next table, and then the next. Her precarious position must have finally sunk in because her wail wobbled. She began backing toward the door.

Three tables left between us, but they veered from the door. I spared a glance for the path and winced. Barely a square of floor showed between the squirming bodies. Nothing to be done.

I sprang and landed a good five feet from the table, balanced on my toes between two forms. One writhed manically, one suspiciously still. Too late. I was too slow. The failure was an anchor pulling my hearts to my gut.

The banshee scrabbled back. My attention caught. My bleary gaze focused, snapped to her. I could almost reach out and grab her. She turned, dropped the death wail, and surged for the doors.

"Not so fast." My hand came down hard on her bony shoulder. Something cracked and she screamed. Hot satisfaction swept through me.

She tried to roll from my grip. I dug my extended talons into her flesh, shoved her forward, and rode her to the ground. We tumbled through the front door. The banshee's face slapped the rough wood planks of the porch. Her nose burst. Blood shot out to frame her head. It stank, like the stagnant swamp she came from.

Somewhere in my race for the door I'd dropped the cuffs. I grabbed her by her snarled hair, wrenched her head back, and slammed her forehead into the hardwood—once, twice. Third time, she went limp.

Sometimes, a girl's gotta improvise.

4

HAD TO GO THERE

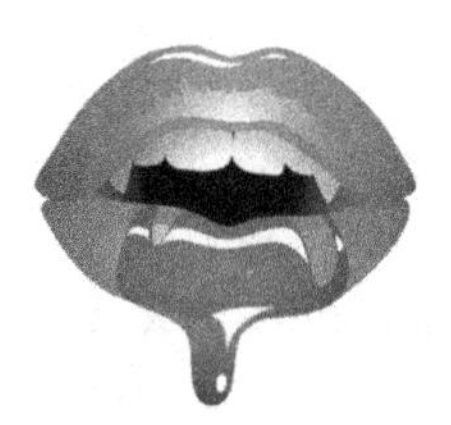

I SHAVED THE TIP OF MY DAGGER ALONG THE UNDERSIDE OF ANOTHER talon. *Phwipt Phwipt.* Bits of blue fur still lodged beneath my claws fluttered to the forest floor.

Late afternoon light played across the sparse grass and dead, dried leaves. Time flew when one was occupied trussing up an unconscious banshee. Hauling her from what passed for downtown Interlands to the home my sisters and I shared took another hour.

While my sisters had gone inside to recover, I'd dragged Etta'wy to a clearing about a hundred yards behind the house, along with a chair which I'd tied her to. She was still out, her snores chewing through trees with the cadence of a dying chainsaw. The sock I'd confiscated from one of the werewolves that went furry at the bar and shoved in her mouth forced her to breathe through the broken ridge of cartilage. A deep black and red bruise covered the swollen flesh of her ruined nose butterflied across her cheeks and swept up to paint her eye sockets.

Bitch deserved it. Deserved worse. I scraped beneath the next nail. Hopefully her nose wasn't so damaged she couldn't smell *eau de* wet dog on that sock when she woke up.

Too bad Palough hadn't asked us to take her out. When beings could live for thousands of years, they rarely made their togetherness official. A whole lot of heavy magic was required to create that magnitude of binding, and it took drastic measures break. Death would do it, and right about now I'd be happy to deliver just that.

Landscape here was a mishmash of Mojave and Ta'Vale. An ecosystem all its own. Our property, far from Interland's dusty downtown, was a full-on forest. The trees surrounding our land rose to a hundred feet or more. The thick canopy of branches spread to one another like seeking arms. Long swaths of pink and yellow, blue and green appeared from behind the dead strips of bark curling away on trunks so thick several people in a ring couldn't fully embrace them.

Mom gifted me the house when I left home. She'd given me so much more than she'd ever know. This house, this forest, they'd become a lifeline back to myself. The property had been vacant for generations, and the forest had overtaken by the time I got here, but it was love at first sight. The trees had become my savior, helping me to overcome a crippling fear of heights as I'd practiced climbing higher, always pushing further, until I reached the top.

I drew in a deep, calming breath ripe with rich forest scents. It lingered in my lungs and eased out over my lips.

Across the clearing, light from the falling sun played across the unconscious banshee. I'd lost yet another pair of sunglasses in my barroom brawl, but Mae, bless her fastidious soul, had come across my forgotten contact lenses and brought them with her. I peered up, into the light, trying to gauge how long Etta'wy had been out. Two hours, maybe three. Idiot put too much magic in her wail. Then again, it could be my fault. I hit her pretty hard. But again, she deserved it.

Irritation rubbed under my skin. Y'sindra and I should be stuffing our faces full of cheesy poofs and Ho Hos while we vegged to a DVR full of reality TV. If I'd had my way, we'd have dumped Etta'wy on her husband's mudbank. Unfortunately, Marrowghan Swamp was another half-day's ride, and after the attack, my sisters were in no shape for that trip.

Phwipt. I scraped beneath the next nail. A twig snapped, and I brought my head up. Mae entered the clearing, pausing to assess our captive. I raked a look over my sister, making sure she was all right. Three beings had died under the banshee's wail.

"That sock from the werewolf that went furry in the bar?" Maerwen, freshly showered and smelling of rosemary soap, strolled into the clearing and nodded in the direction of the banshee.

"Hmm," I hummed my affirmation.

"Nice." Arms folded across her chest, she cocked her hip against a tree next to me. No more than ten seconds passed when she asked, "Is that Hello Kitty on the sock?"

A laugh burst out of me. Leave it to Mae to spot that strange fashion detail. "Yep, guess the big bad wolf is a big bad kitty lover." I glanced at her and grinned. "He had boxers to match."

Mae's eyebrows tried to merge with her hairline.

"I didn't undress him, geez. His tail made a giant hole in his jeans. I could see the boxers through it."

Deciding not to acknowledge the werewolf boxers—unexpected, considering the number of wolves she'd slept with—Mae got down to business. She cleared her throat and not-so-casually consulted her manicure. "I checked the bag."

"Worth a lot." If she didn't insist we do something noble like return them. "I'm sure you could use a few more, too."

"You know Duskmere came here for you?"

My dagger stopped mid-scrape, and I glanced at the banshee to make sure she wasn't awake. Another labored snore vibrated from her blood-clogged nostrils.

"He didn't say what for, but after seeing what's in that bag, I have a pretty good guess." Mae gripped the sun shard pendant she wore. A smooth flat oval half the size of her thumb, the shard was bigger than most, but still far smaller than any in the bag. Our father gifted it to her when she followed me from Ta'Vale. "No one should have that many shards, Lane. Not that size. Did Duskmere ask for help?"

"More or less. He wants her." I waved my dagger at the slumped banshee. "The sun stones were stolen."

"There are more missing than what's in the bag?" Mae's thumb worried over the smooth surface of her shard. It responded to her touch. A warm, gold light heated its center.

Having recently been through this with Duskmere, I understood her confusion. The sun stones were sacred, worshipped. I didn't know a soul who had ever seen them up close, but the stones were alive. They grew and shed chips of themselves. Those were the shards, and someone had to collect them.

"Mae," I said. "Listen to what I'm saying. The stones are missing."

"The stones?" Her restless thumb froze.

I nodded.

"The stones?" The pitch of her voice drove a flock of birds from the treetops. "Who in the stars would do that? *How* could they do that? I thought maybe the palace of Eodrom had been raided, royals robbed of their shards. The stones are inaccessible, no one can get into the sun garden."

"Apparently, someone did, and Duskmere thinks Etta'wy had something to do with it," I told her. "I don't know if the grounders were involved, but they were paid for a job with that bag of sun shards I gave you. They confirmed a banshee hired them. Right after that, Etta'wy came for the shards. So I think we can safely assume she was the banshee."

I studied Etta'wy with pursed lips. "You know what bothers me about all this? That hag knew we were tailing her this whole time. How else would she have known I took the shards from the grounders, not to mention how she gave me the slip this morning?"

"That's what bothers you?" Mae shook her head.

"Mostly." I had no idea what else should be bothering me, maybe the hybrid thing, but my sister's judgy tone implied otherwise. "On the bright side, Etta'wy's impromptu visit makes our job easier. We can load her up, drop her in her swamp, and get paid."

"Are you kidding? We've got to take her to Duskmere. He's RFG. He will make Palough understand."

I shrugged, wouldn't meet her gaze. *Phwipt*. The knife's edge scraped the next talon. "He already did. Duskmere said they'd pay what Palough owed. I explained we had a contract, and we were going to honor it. It's all about reputation, right?"

"Lane, if she knows where the stones are, we've got to hand her and the shards from the grounders over to the RFG."

And with that we were back to being broke.

Mae threw her hands in the air and paced a small circle. Mouth tight, she stared at me and paced another circle. Finally, she stopped. "Listen, I know you don't have magic."

The blade jerked beneath my talon, its edge caught the side of my finger. Blood beaded from the cut and dropped onto my boot. She must be really worried to be so careless with her words.

"You don't understand what losing the stones means," she said.

"No." I holstered my dagger and leveled a flat look on my sister. "I don't."

She went soft, wilting like a delicate flower beneath the rain. Miniscule creases of concern puckered her smooth brow. "Oh, Laney, I'm sorry. I didn't mean it like that." She wrapped me in a fierce hug.

"S'okay," I mumbled into her shoulder, squeezed, and disengaged. "I know you didn't, and you're right, I don't have magic. I have no idea what it means, and I don't give a damn. Hang the sun fae. You know how they treated me. Hell, how they treated you."

"I'm sun fae. Dad's sun fae."

I stopped breathing for a good five seconds. Low blow. Mae was adopted, but she was still sun fae. Mom might be blood fae, but my father was sun fae. My arms fell to my sides and dangled. "Had to go there."

"There will be consequences, that's all." Mae puffed a breath and threaded her arms tight across herself, gripping her elbows. "I'll stand behind you whatever you decide. My magic took a hit the second I left Ta'Vale. I don't regret it, but Dad..."

"But Dad," I repeated.

"Magic is his everything. Dad's sun fae, but more importantly, he's the chief royal wizard. Magic is less choice and more necessity. These shards," Mae flattened a palm over the scotch-hued chip resting against her chest, "they're used as a focus to funnel the magic through, to keep the magic from scorching his mind."

Despite my abominable hybrid nature that weakened my powers, my father's position was never in question. No one would dare. He was an undisputed magical powerhouse.

I worked my lip beneath a fang. Terror, relief, and a bucket-load of guilt for feeling that relief chewed into my gut. Terror for my sister and for my father. Relief for myself because I'd never have to worry about magic. Guilt for such a selfish, shitty thought.

"Dad's shards will eventually lose their juice, then that's it. With the stones gone, there's no more shards. Dad will have to stop practicing or risk frying his mind. That's how magic works." Mae gave a slow shake of her head. "Do you think he'll stop using magic?"

"Fuck me." I tilted my head back and stared unseeing at the darkening sky. Magic was as important as air to the great Finnlay Callaghan. Mae was right. I had to help the sun fae. At least I could make sure they knew who saved them. Shove it down their throats. Here's your hero: the mutt, the abomination, the monster. I'd have posters made.

Of course, I'd have to find the stones first.

"All right, but we need to figure out what to do with Etta'wy. We're not taking her to Duskmere." Mae's mouth opened to object, I pushed on. "Our banshee hired the grounders, but they were paid by a moon fae."

Her mouth clicked shut and her jaw worked, clenched, chewed, no sound coming out.

"Exactly," I said and tousled my freshly cleaned talons through my hair. The ends, still heavy with clumps of dried mud, thumped against my lower back.

Mae tugged at the edge of her lip. "It can't be Duskmere, he's a captain in the RFG. He's loyal as they come."

"You know him that well?" He stopped by periodically with news from Eodrom or from my parents, but that hardly put us on a friendly level. The little I'd interacted with him he'd been aloof at best, a pompous ass at worst.

"Not well, but you know how Mom likes to talk." Mae waved her hand in a dismissive gesture and continued. "Stars, Laney, Duskmere saved our parents."

"Sure, he saved a whole lot of fae, but that was over a hundred years ago. Things change, fae change, and there's no other explanation." Except, I didn't entirely disagree. From everything I knew, Duskmere was disgustingly loyal. In fact, he was a damn war hero. As a boy working in the moon fae kitchens during the war, he'd had the balls to sneak not only my parents, but over twenty other captives out of the moon fae dungeons and across the border to Eodrom—the jewel of the Grian Valley, the cradle of the sun fae domain.

"What's your gut tell you?"

"That I'm a crappy detective and to follow the facts."

"Tsk." Mae's eyes made an exaggerated circuit around their orbs. "Stop dismissing your instincts. They're good."

"Except when she thinks someone's tapping our communication crystal." Y'sindra flew from the trees on a wobbly trajectory to us, smelling of berries. Crap. I leaned down and sniffed. Yep, and booze. "Or when you insisted we go to the poison marshes—*hiccup*—to follow a lead and ended up coming home with nothing but a rash. Then there was—"

"We get the idea," I ground out.

She shrugged and pulled a stainless-steel travel tumbler from the folds of her baby doll dress.

I lunged for it, but she spun away, surprisingly quick for someone with such short legs. A large nozia berry she must have swiped from the bar appeared from her other pocket. She stopped swaying long enough to lock her polar-blue gaze on mine, grin, and pop the top of her tumbler. "Oops," she said and dropped the berry inside.

This didn't bode well for our night. Booze alone couldn't compete with a fairy's metabolism, but throw in a couple berries and watch out.

Y'sindra didn't bother resealing the tumbler but put it to her lips and gulped. I slapped it from her hand.

"Hey!" She flew cock-eyed after the cup as it rolled across the clearing, bumped against the banshee's toe, and stopped. Y'sindra crawled the last few feet. "Great, it's empty. Thanks a lot."

"You're welcome. We've got work to do." I nodded toward Etta'wy, who was finally awake and whose narrowed eyes plunged daggers at the snow fairy at her feet.

"Fairy farts!" Y'sindra fell on her rump and crab crawled away.

"Classy."

"Like you're much better." She waved a finger in my direction.

"Shoo," I waved my hand at her. "The adults are talking here."

"I'm older than—*hiccup*—the both of you."

So she claimed, but I wasn't so sure. I shook my head and turned to Mae. "The banshee's awake, so I say we question her ourselves. Take her to Palough after and wipe our hands of her."

"Agreed. We do need to figure out what to do about the," her eyebrows climbed her forehead, "you know."

Mae worried the banshee might catch her implication that we had the shards, but it wouldn't matter even if she did. Etta'wy was tied up and not going anywhere until we took her somewhere. I glanced across the clearing and snorted. Mae had nothing to worry about. Etta'wy was locked in a death-match glare-down with Y'sindra, who had moved closer and stood swaying less than a foot from the chair. The banshee's right shoulder hung at an awkward angle, dislocated or broken from where I'd hit her, but she was completely invested in her staring match with my sister.

"We could make a lot of money," I said. "Pay the electricity before we're sitting in the dark, maybe get ahead for once. After today I could use a new jacket, Y'sindra ate my last Ho Ho, and I bet you could use...shoes?"

"If you think we are better off keeping them than returning them, that's what we'll do."

Damn Mae for always supporting me. I couldn't do that to her or to our father.

"No, I don't think that's what we should do." I stopped spending the money in my head and kicked a seed pod the size of an apricot. It hit the back of Y'sindra's knee, which gave out. Her wings fluttered double-time, sending a pile of snow into the banshee's lap.

Y'sindra spun side to side and glared into the trees at the other dangling pods.

I smirked but turned to find Mae studying me. One arm crossed over her middle while she chewed the thumbnail of her other hand.

"Spit it out." Whatever she had to say, I wouldn't like it. Mae was as fastidious about her appearance as she was about cleanliness, which meant nerves drove her to chew that nail.

"You need to talk to Dad."

"That's it? I thought you were about to suggest I pay a visit to Eodrom or something. Yeah, sure. I'll call him after we're done."

"No, you need to go talk to him. You might be right about our communication crystal being tapped." Mae moved from her thumbnail to index. "How else would the RFG know about our job for Palough? We only told Mom and Dad about the job yesterday. I still don't think Duskmere has anything to do with the theft, but it can't be a coincidence he came here today."

My hearts beat out of sync—*skip—pound—pound—skip*. Her words drove ice into my chest. It spread, heated, crept up my neck and down my legs. "How'd I miss that?"

"You didn't." Mae let her hand fall free and shrugged. "I'm better at logic. You would have come to the same conclusion eventually."

"I wouldn't be so sure," I mumbled and wrung my hands, one over the other.

"Laney." Mae gripped my restless hands, stilling them. "You're strong, yes, but you're also brilliant. Trust your instincts."

I didn't agree, but her calm confidence fed me. I pulled myself to my full five-foot-zero inches and nodded. "Let's get some answers from the swamp bitch."

Y'sindra had passed out, thankfully, out of kicking reach of the banshee. A snowflake fluttered in the stream of my sister's breath before drifting down to settle on her cupid-bow lips, repeating the cycle with her next breath.

The banshee tracked every movement Mae and I made. Behind me the trees rustled. Etta'wy's focus shifted to the noise. She shouted behind her sock gag. Fear overrode whatever pain her injured shoulder might cause as she wrenched her hands up with such force, she stretched the loops of rope binding them to the chair's arms and banged them again and again.

A noise like the rising whistle of a tea kettle pierced the air a second before a writhing ball of black light slammed into the banshee's chest. The chair rocked from the force. Her eyes went comically round. The impact jarred the sock from her mouth, and it fell onto her leg. Saliva glistened on her lap. It soaked into the white pant leg of her suit, dirty now from being dragged through the woods.

The black mass rippled, writhed, and the bindings across her body disintegrated. Etta'wy pushed forward on the seat. She made to stand, but her chest caved in, imploded. The center of her became a red slush of torn flesh and flayed muscle. Stark white slivers of bone jutted from her shorn ribcage.

It happened in seconds and then accelerated—a lit fuse. Magic like I'd never known rushed over her body, burned it, consumed it. Etta'wy's impossibly wide jaw opened further, dislocated. Fell and bounced off her rapidly dissolving thighs.

A pile of ash lay where moments before there had been a living, breathing, pissed-off banshee. A blackened jawbone lay in the dirt.

I hadn't even had time to scream.

5

FIGHT OR FLIGHT

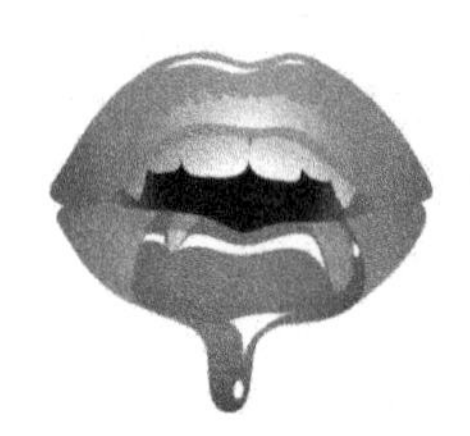

I COULDN'T GET ENOUGH AIR. I GULPED IT. MY CHEST HEAVED.

A pale gold orb rippled around Mae and me. Mae's magic. She'd instinctively surrounded us with a shield.

Across the clearing, Y'sindra was safe inside a smaller bubble and still out cold. She'd slept through the entire thing. I wiped a trembling hand across my face.

Low laughter, deep and dark and full of malice, drifted from somewhere above. Mae's head whipped side-to-side, her eyes round and wild.

Another flutter of leaves.

I followed their path and found the assassin. Perched in the path of the falling sun, the source was little more than a silhouette—a male silhouette. His shoulders faced me directly. We looked at each other for a heartbeat before he leaped away and vaulted toward the canopy.

"Got him." I propelled myself toward the tree line and didn't break stride as I jumped into the low limbs. My palms barely grazed the first branch when I swung myself to the next, going higher and higher. The assassin wove steadily away and up, a dark smudge in a sea of shadows. The air grew chilly with the height.

Still, he pushed higher, and I pursued. No choice. I had to catch this guy. Etta'wy was dead, and we needed answers. The rapidly dwindling daylight gave me the advantage. I might not have the night vision of a full blood fae, but it was still damn good.

The sharp, spicy smell of pepper, the nostril-puckering tang of vinegar, and something sour, like old meat, brought my pursuit to a standstill. A subtle hint of jasmine lay beneath all the unpleasant. Quickly, I searched the limbs, the leaves, the trunk. A bright red handprint smudged the bark, and a victorious flush of excitement ignited in my chest. Once I got a scent, I never forgot. "You can run, but you can't hide, asshole!"

Ahead, the shadowy figure paused. *That's right, I'm coming for you.* I chuckled beneath my breath and flew into motion, maneuvering faster, gaining ground. The figure leaped to another tree. Metal flashed. It dug into a tree trunk. The assassin took longer to manipulate that climbing hook than me with my talons. I didn't need the scent. He was mine.

The chilled air slashed across my cheeks as I sailed for the next tree. I landed and clung to a limb half the width of my thigh. Panting, I looked up. It was still a good twenty feet to the top. The narrowing trunk swayed with the impact. My arms and legs tingled, trembled from the strain as I held on. I eased to a crouch.

A whistling started. My hearts tripped over one another and muscles locked. I froze. The sound shrieked by my head. Loud. Close. A deafening boom shook my bones, and splinters burst into the air. I grunted and threw myself flat on the limb. The scent of burned wood tore up my nostrils, and the left side of my face throbbed with heat. Too close.

Behind me, an ear-splitting crack echoed. I looked over my shoulder at the charred indentation dug nearly through the trunk in the blackened wood. Holy. Shit.

But the tree still stood. The magic wasn't spreading. It wasn't what hit Etta'wy, but it could still kill my ass.

Panting, unable to focus on any single detail in the dust of ruined leaves and tree, I drew myself back into a crouch, searching for my attacker. Where was he? There. He huddled no more than fifteen feet away in the shadowy crook where the limb met the trunk.

"Oops, I missed." He laughed, and it reminded me of a dull knife scraping burned toast.

"Slow down and I promise I'll give you another shot." My taunt would have sounded much cooler if it didn't end on a lame wheeze.

He pushed forward from the shadows, and my stomach twisted. He wasn't just locked in shadow, with his dark hair and slate-gray complexion, he blended perfectly. A moon fae, but this one wasn't like Duskmere. Thick black—no, red, dark red—veins worked their way up his throat, across his cheeks, a meandering roadmap on his face—the corruption.

I shoved the live wire of fear inside of me into a tight ball of fury. He'd killed my banshee, tried to kill me. It was fight or flight, and I planned to fuck this guy up.

The moon fae's bloodshot gaze found mine while he flashed a barracuda grin. "Come and get me," he taunted and let go of the tree with one hand to curl his fingers toward himself in a gesture to echo his words.

"Gladly," I growled and physically shook myself, shedding the shock of seeing a corrupted moon fae.

He still hadn't moved. Cocky. Probably didn't think I could make the jump. Coiling my legs against the tree limb, I pushed off, leaping across the space between us. My hands curved into lethal weapons tipped in sharp talons ready to sink into my target.

Still, he didn't move. Idiot. I flew at him, my wide-open eyes aching from the cold. We were mere feet apart. The bastard was mine.

With a pop of air, a void opened behind him. He stepped inside an inky portal. I got the one finger salute right before he and the mini black hole vanished.

The air froze in my lungs. Terror gripped the hands of time. Everything slowed. I seemed to float on a cushion of air, and then I fell. A scream, part surprise, part fear, and a whole lot of rage tore out of me. The sound clung to the treetops.

"Huuuh!" The belly flop onto a tree limb shoved every drop of air from my lungs. There was no bounce, no pause, it snapped. The hideous crack echoed into the twilight, followed by another, and another.

I kept going, crashing from tree limb to tree limb. I flailed. Tried to dig my talons into the tree but came away with splinters and leaves. Bits of wood scratched and tore at me, ripped at my hair. Sharp bursts of pain fired everywhere on my body. I threw an arm across my eyes before I lost one.

Memories flashed behind my shielded eyelids: the impetus to my move to Interlands; the day I turned fifteen, when an anonymous note lured me to the apex of the impossibly tall sun bridge arching over Eodrom with irresistible promises of the things I craved—friendship, acceptance. What was it with me and notes?

I had been pushed and left for dead that day.

One final crack. "Oof!" A cloud of fluffy snow erupted from the mound where I'd landed. I opened my eyes to take in the patchwork of blue sky far above. My hearts beat so hard against my ribcage, the bones threatened to crack, but unlike my fall from the sun bridge when I was fifteen, I wasn't broken this time. I hadn't been abandoned.

"Thanks for the snow, Y'sindra," I croaked and took a second to regain the breath I'd lost a hundred feet ago. "I thought you were passed out. Good thing for me you're not, I guess."

"You were making more noise than a cyclops with a cataract crashing through those trees. Like I could sleep through that?" *Hiccup*. She crested the snow pile she'd made for me.

I tried to look down my body, check for injuries, but my neck seriously hurt.

Mae's head appeared over the snowbank. "Are you okay?"

"You tell me." I flopped back into the fluffy snow. My sisters would probably tell me if I was missing an arm or had a tree limb sticking out of my chest. Again.

Mae chewed her lip and shook her head.

"You're in one pieceses." Y'sindra swayed and tumbled from the snow crest.

"Can't say the same for you." I roll-wiggled myself over the edge of the snow pile and onto solid ground. I paused to look up the tree and the path of disaster I'd made on my way down.

Asshole. I'd like to take that finger of his and—

"Ahem," Mae said, pretending to clear her throat. "You find anything out before you fell?"

"I didn't fall."

"Funny, then why did I bother with snow?" Y'sindra yawned. She'd burned a lot of energy with the amount of snow she'd made for me, which was probably more the reason for her slurring and swaying than the drink.

"Fine, I fell, but it wasn't my fault. He vanished. A portal opened and he jumped in. I was about to grab him, and then he was gone." I snapped my fingers. "Just like that. Gone."

A leaf waved at me from a twig protruding from my right forearm. I tugged it loose and swore. Stars that hurt. Tonight would suck. I had enough wood in me to start a bonfire.

"Anyhow, he was a moon fae," I said and wrapped my hand over the frayed and bloody hole of my completely destroyed jacket. "But that wasn't moon magic he hit Etta'wy with, not even the corrupted kind. We would have read about something like that. At least you would have." I nodded my chin at Mae, who shook her head, indicating she hadn't. "Guess they've learned a thing or two since their exile."

"Why do you think he was one of the exiled?" Mae asked, bright blue gaze still bouncing from my head to my toes, ensuring I escaped my romp through the trees unscathed.

"Because he had the corruption." Bomb dropped.

Y'sindra snorted. "You must have knocked your head good since that's not possible."

I sneered at her. Though, if I hadn't seen it, I'd be skeptical, too. Outside of Duskmere, I'd never met another moon fae. Sure, I knew some uncorrupted moon fae escaped Lann Ridge, their homeland, during the Great Fae Divide. The sun fae might hate lil ol' hybrid me, but they embraced the uncorrupted of their sibling race and settled them in Eodrom—a place I avoided like the burning dumpster fire it was (in my mind).

No corrupted moon fae remained, since after the sun fae victory in the war, all corrupted had been exiled to another realm called Shadwe. To prevent those moon fae from ever returning, the door to the neutral realm between Ta'Vale and Shadwe was sealed, the bridge between those two realms broken. It should not have been possible to find one here, but I knew what I'd seen.

"I didn't hit my head, smart ass. I mean, I probably did, but I know what I saw."

"Right, and I'm a tooth fairy."

I ignored Y'sindra. Something about the moon fae encounter nagged at me. I scraped a fang over the edge of my lip. The thought was there, bobbing below the surface.

Focus, Lane, Focus!

Reaching for the moon fae's image, I turned it over in my mind. His complexion, his eyes, the color of old blood. And the corruption. The scrawling veins. The thick ugly throbbing from temple to cheek. I'd never seen the corruption on a living, breathing being before. It had been the beginning of the end when the ruling moon fae family decided they needed more—more power, more strength—and they delved into shadow magic.

Others were eager to follow, others were forced. The combination corrupted their blood. Shadow magic hadn't played well with their moon magic.

Realization slammed into me, and I let out a surprised gasp. "His corruption wasn't the right color. It was dark red, not black. I've only seen it in the crystal projections, but his was definitely wrong."

"Whoa," Y'sindra said.

Shock sculpted Mae's expression above the hand covering her mouth.

"Yeah, exactly." I pressed my face into my palms. Pains and protests slowly fired through my body. "Well, I guess that's that. We've got to talk to someone. We're going home."

Not the home I wanted to return to, the place I shared with my sisters. We were going to Ta'Vale. Specifically, Eodrom. The place I hadn't set foot in since I left as an angry broken thing years ago. Life as an outcast and abuse that culminated in an attempt on my life was a perfectly reasonable reason for *staying the fuck away*.

A pit churned in my gut and not just from my disgusting, liquid breakfast. Falling out of a tree had sucked. This would be so much worse.

6

SIDE-EYE

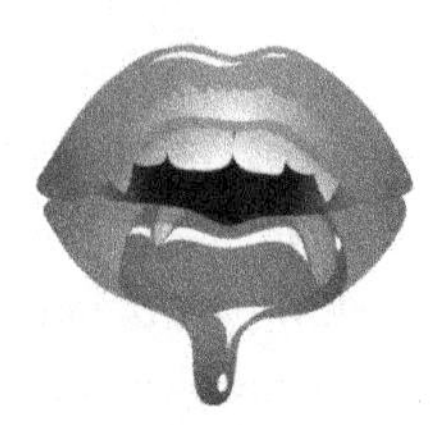

THE WALK HOME TOOK LONGER THAN MY WEARY BONES WOULD HAVE liked. I liked the sight of who stood in our driveway even less.

"What's that d-bag doing here?" Y'sindra really embraced human curses. That wasn't entirely accurate; she embraced all foul language.

"Keep it down," I hissed.

"Why? The d-bag sees us." Y'sindra's voice boomed in my ear.

I cringed and rubbed the offended ear to my shoulder. I'd agreed to let her ride home piggyback-style, since she'd burned herself out helping me, but she was fine now. I stood straight and pushed her legs from my ribs.

"Hey!" She bobbed in the air, unsteady, but caught herself and hovered in my face. "That was rude."

"So are you." I smirked at her, and she wrinkled her nose. "I'd prefer not to find out what Duskmere's doing here with a fairy on my back."

"Fair enough." She blew me a kiss and darted ahead.

Like the desert climate Interlands bordered, the darker it got, the further the temperatures fell. The dense forest surrounding our property grew cooler faster, and my newly ventilated jacket wasn't a whole lot of help. I crossed my arms and hugged them tight to my middle.

If I was honest with myself, I'd probably admit the chill came as much from my recent brush with whatever just happened as it did from the temperature. Probably more so, since Duskmere inconveniently showed up and I'd have to tell him all about it. I'd planned to lean on my father's slightly more sympathetic shoulder and let him deal with Duskmere.

I blew into my hands and glanced at Mae walking next to me. "On the bright side, now we don't have to pay a visit to Ta'Vale."

Instead of responding, she jutted her chin toward the house. "Who's that?"

"Uh, Duskmere. I thought you said you knew who he was?"

"No, not him, the other guy."

Sure enough, a sun fae male walked from the trees that hid a pond along the drive. He led two mounts with him. Aloughtas—towering deer-like carnivorous creatures the sun fae favored and the same breed of mount Mae used. Y'sindra, Mae, and I still needed mounts for the rare occasion when we traveled to Ta'Vale where automobiles didn't work. Little human technology did.

Technically, Y'sindra didn't need a mount. She could fly. She was also lazy.

Duskmere turned to his approaching companion, and an aloughta, the one with the midnight coat, walked to his side. It lowered its head and butted its nose against the moon fae's shoulder. Duskmere ran a hand through the short spiky mane sprouting from the ridge of the beast's neck and scratched between the rapier-like antlers perfect for impaling.

A scowl weighed down the corners of my mouth. Of course he had to be nice to animals. Never mind the fact that the animals were as intelligent as him or me and could eat his face. I didn't want there to be anything more beneath the asshole veneer Duskmere wore so well.

I scowled and shifted my weight from my aching left leg to my aching right leg as I waited and watched. It could just be me who had a problem with the guy. His no-nonsense, uppity attitude rubbed me the wrong way. My parents loved him, the aloughta obviously adored him, even Mae seemed enamored—which wasn't actually a ringing endorsement, since she liked just about anything with a pulse. But as far as I was concerned, he was an asshole.

The sun fae turned to watch our approach. Like all sun fae, his hair was silky-straight, but this guy leaned more toward an unusually dark, brassy tone, as opposed to Mae's honey and ice. He was taller than Duskmere, who wasn't quite six foot. The cold eyes he studied us with were disguised by the early evening shadows.

He folded his hands behind him—military style. The duster jacket he wore parted to reveal a vest beneath and the RFG insignia on the left side of his chest.

"Sun fae rarely leave Ta'Vale, and suddenly Interlands is infected with the pompous jerks." I nudged Mae with my elbow as we walked. "Present company excluded."

Y'sindra flew by the pair. She glared, but thankfully kept her opinions to herself. I loved that girl, but she could stir up trouble better than a mixologist making a martini. The trouble-making fairy flew toward the house and the open second floor window, but made a sloppy landing. Her toe wedged beneath a wooden roof tile and she stumbled, going down on her knees before she hoisted herself through the open window.

Guilt pinched my stomach. I shouldn't have forced her to fly so soon.

"She'll be fine," Mae said. But when I glanced at her to respond, she only had eyes for the sun fae in our drive.

I looked from Mae to the sun fae and back. Guilt pinched harder. I shoved my hands into my pockets. Seven years in Interlands, and I'd never stopped to consider if Mae missed the company of other sun fae.

"Would you have been happier if you'd stayed in Eodrom?" I blurted the question.

Mae stopped walking and swung toward me. "Now? You want to ask me that now?"

"No. Yes. Maybe?" I ran a hand over my face. "I never thought about it before now, but seeing you and that sun fae over there—"

"Your father...our dad," she corrected, "might have rescued Y'sindra and I, two abandoned outcasts that no one wanted. Mom and Dad might have adopted us into the family, but you, Y'sindra, and me, we're sisters. We don't need to share blood for that to be true. Where you go, I go. Where we go, Y'sindra goes. You came here, so we did too." I opened my mouth, but she waved me into silence. "I'm a big girl. If I wasn't happy, I'd do something about it. You and Y'sindra are all I need, so no more of that, okay?"

The vise constricting my chest relaxed. I dragged in a breath and nodded.

"Good, because I want a taste of that." Mae dipped her head to the side, toward the pair of fae loitering in our drive. "Let's go find out what they want."

"Which one?"

Mae shot me a wicked grin. "Both."

I snorted a laugh. There was my promiscuous-and-proud-of-it sister. To be fair, that wasn't unusual among the fae, long lived and all. Of course, with only twenty-three years under Mae's belt, she was well ahead of the curve.

In an unspoken agreement, Mae hung back and I took the lead. No point beating around the bush. "Your banshee's dead, and there's a moon fae jumping through portals in your backyard."

"He has no backyard," the sun fae said.

Seriously? Not dealing with the brightest bulb in the box here. I arched a questioning brow at Duskmere. "Who's your buddy?"

"Cirron Brightstone is my partner."

*Ha, Bright*stone. *Ironic.*

"Well, Cirron Brightstone," I drawled, "it's a figure of speech. I was referring to Interlands. You know, this blip of space between Ta'Vale and Earth. Ta'Vale's backyard."

"This is Interlands," Cirron managed in a monotone that sounded irritated at the same time.

"Ding, ding, ding, genius." I shook my head and gave Duskmere a pointed look. "You should think about a new partner."

"You killed Etta'wy?" Duskmere gripped my bicep.

I pressed my lips together and squinted at his hand, my fingers tapping on my thigh. "No, but thanks for jumping to that conclusion. Aren't you the least bit interested in the moon fae I mentioned?"

"There aren't many moon fae remaining in Ta'Vale, but we still exist. I am simply a more public figure. So, no, I am not interested." Duskmere released his grip and crossed his arms over his chest.

"Others? How? Where?" Suddenly wide awake, I pressed my palm against the surprise fluttering beneath my breastbone. I'd heard the rumors of moon fae in the Grian Valley, even living in Eodrom, but I'd never seen them. I shook my head, leave it to me to get distracted. "Never mind, it's not important. Do they have the corruption? Because this guy did, and he killed Etta'wy."

Duskmere's posture went rigid.

"The banshee is dead?" Cirron asked.

"Are you going to keep repeating everything I say?" I snapped. "Yes, she's dead. Nothing left but a pile of ash. Moon fae killed her."

Duskmere shook his head. "It is not possible. All the corrupted were banished. Sealed in Outerlands and Shadwe, for those who dare that dark realm."

My fingers tapped faster on my thigh. "Listen, it's been a long day. I don't understand half of what you said, but I also just fell out of a tree, and there's a good chance I hit my head. Somehow, I'm still alive and on my feet, so let's speed this up before I'm not."

"You are sure the banshee is dead?" Cirron asked.

"What part of 'pile of ash' did you not understand? I'll get you a dustpan and broom if you want what's left of her." I sneered at the sun fae, who, despite my tone, was distracted and not at all offended.

"Anyhow," I said to Duskmere, angling away from this Cirron character. "This afternoon Etta'wy tried to wail an entire bar to death, my sisters and I included. We caught her and brought her here. I planned to question her about her involvement in the whole sun stone thing, but she got nuked by the moon fae I chased. Rude bastard flipped me off and hopped a portal to who knows where."

"You were unable to extract information?"

"It happened fast after she woke up. We didn't get the chance."

Behind me, the sun fae exhaled loudly.

My teeth scraped together, and I slid him the side-eye over my shoulder.

The obnoxious pair of fae males huddled together and whispered.

"Well, Etta'wy's gone, and it's a long ride to Eodrom, you should hit the road." My not-so-subtle suggestion went ignored.

I shoved my hands into my hip pockets, but my fingers caught on a piece of paper folded into my right pocket. Those pockets were never used for anything but my hands.

Teddy. He'd put the note I'd dropped in that pocket. A phantom tingle spread over my hip remembering his touch. I tugged out a familiar napkin, unfolded it and read. Warmth bubbled in my chest at the words. Below the dead banshee's scrawl was Teddy's bold script. *"You are so much more than this."*

My lungs were suddenly too small for my breath. I blinked at the ache behind my eyes.

No spite, no hate, no false promises, just belief.

No one believed in me. No one but my sisters. But Teddy, with his bone-melting glances and award-winning ass, why?

"I am sorry to hear this," Duskmere said, and I jumped at his voice.

Carefully folding the napkin, I ignored the slight tremble in my hand as I tucked it back where I'd found it. This would have to remain a mystery to solve later, after a shower, a nap, and a drink—maybe a lot of drinks. I swallowed the emotion lodged in my throat and looked to Duskmere. "Why are you sorry?"

"This leaves the path we must take clear." Duskmere sounded resigned. "Malaney Callaghan, daughter of Finnlay Callaghan, Queen Iola has requested an interview with you."

Mae gasped.

Fear clawed from my scalp to my toes. The formality of the request—no, the demand—made it even worse. "Queen Iola?" I swallowed and rubbed my neck. It wasn't that she had a reputation for removing heads on a whim, quite the contrary. Being the queen of all fae and wanting to see me was odd enough. But my very existence was an embarrassment to the fae. The daily abuse I went through before getting the hell out proved it. She might have decided to get rid of that blight. "Yeah. Yes, of course. I'll ride to Eodrom tomorrow."

"There is no time. You will come now."

"No, I won't." I took a step backward, away from Duskmere. My hearts pounded a tandem song of panic against my ribs.

Duskmere ignored my retreat. He turned to his partner and handed Cirron a communication crystal, the fae equivalent of a cell phone. "Call and make them aware."

"I will see you on my return tomorrow," the sun fae responded. He placed a hand on his aloughta's arched neck and beckoned Duskmere's mount to his side. "I will see you on my return tomorrow."

My feet stumbled over one another as I turned and walked toward the house.

"Lane," Mae called.

"No," I shouted and kept going. "Every inch of me hurts, and I need a bath. I said I'll go, and I'll go. Tomorrow."

Duskmere caught up to me and blocked my path. I lowered my head, ready to go right through him, and growled.

"Malaney Callaghan, we must go now."

"And I said no. I'll be there bright and—"

With a sound like shredding paper, Duskmere ripped open a slice in space. A flat disc of darkness yawned.

"I'm sorry," Duskmere repeated and shoved me into the portal.

7

WOULD THIS BE MY FATE

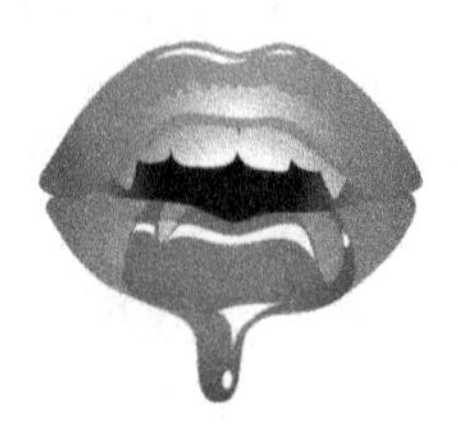

My knees burrowed into gravel, and I threw my hands out to catch myself. Tiny shards bit into my palms. Light shone from behind me, weak and watery. A black, crushed pebble floor, dark walls, and bottomless shadows surrounded me. I twisted toward the light. The tiny rocks beneath me shifted and ground further into my jeans.

The portal was still open, the image inside wavy. Duskmere's form grew larger as he approached the open wound into my yard. Mae shouted in the background while Cirron held her back.

One foot, one leg, pushed through the portal. I didn't wait for the rest of Duskmere but scrabbled away. Bloody handprints followed me. I struggled to my feet, legs wobbling, and staggered a step, two, five, and came up against a set of slick black bars.

I was trapped. Caged.

"No," I shouted. "No, no, no!"

Heedless of the dizzying pain, I gripped the cold bars and shook. They didn't move, but I did. I screamed my rage, my blinding terror.

Light from the opening behind me reflected on the bars and winked out. The portal sealed with a whip crack. I panted and strained to see anything. Not even a trace of my pale fingers on the bars showed.

Though the portal's light had revealed space between the bars, my arm couldn't push through. I felt for one bar and then inched my hand to the side until my fingertips brushed against the next bar. Whatever blocked me gave but didn't give up. It absorbed the pressure I exerted.

Why would Duskmere do this? *Why was I in a cage?* I couldn't be here, wherever here was. I had to get out.

My chest expanded and squeezed, expanded and squeezed. I pressed my forehead into the magic memory foam and focused on slowing my harsh breaths. Panic wasn't going to help me. From head to toe, the fine hairs across my body shivered in reaction to something. I inhaled. The scent of strong magic—hot metal, electricity.

"Malaney Callaghan." Duskmere's disembodied voice hung in the absolute darkness.

"Don't come near me." My shoulders tightened, my neck pinched.

He sighed. I heard him shift position. The stiff leathers he wore creaked, but no steps followed.

Along the high ceiling of the corridor, a rope of pale blue lights winked once, twice, stayed on. Marble-sized globes with tiny flames suspended in their center. A faint tinkle of music hummed—fae lights.

I traced the strand to the right and left. The hall went on and out of sight in both directions. Two cells were visible opposite me, but far enough away and spaced wide enough so that it would be impossible to pass or even throw anything between them. At this angle, I couldn't tell if they were occupied.

Duskmere hadn't pushed me into a cage, he'd put me in some sort of jail—a dungeon if the damp chill was any indication. Was this what the queen had wanted? To have me locked up—hidden from sight? Maybe Duskmere was just pissed the lead he was so desperate to get his hands on was dead, and he thought I did the deed.

"I knew you were cold, but this is low. I told you I didn't kill your banshee." My voice came back to me muffled from the invisible sheet of magic.

Duskmere didn't respond, not that I'd expected him to. I stretched my arms wide and traced along the unnaturally cool bars on either side of me. My seeking fingers paused on a deformity. The bar to my left bent to the left and pulled slightly inward. To my right the bar had an identical, but opposite, turn. Someone or something, did this. If they could do it...

I gripped the parenthetical bars and pulled, twisted. Heat ignited my cheeks, and my already dim vision grew fuzzy at the edges from exertion. The bars didn't budge.

Whatever did this, I never wanted to meet it. If I was to be a new resident here, hopefully the thing that bent these bars was long gone from this place. Frustrated, desperate, I grabbed the bars and shook again. They still didn't move, but it made me feel better.

In the distance, a flicker of light bloomed. I angled toward it and tensed. The light grew, bobbing as if being carried. "Hey! Help," I yelled. "I shouldn't be here, help me."

Duskmere's sigh was heavy, full of annoyance. Gravel whispered and hissed as he walked toward me.

I banged my palms on the bars. "I need help!"

No response came. The speed of whoever carried the light did not increase.

"Ugh." I shouted out my frustration and kicked the bar. It didn't even vibrate.

Thank the gods for steel-toed boots because damn, that hurt. Defeated, I rested my forehead on the unnaturally cool metal and waited for whatever fate was coming.

My fate arrived in the form of a blood fae wearing the RFG leathers adorned with their moon, sun, and tree insignia. My spine snapped straight with shock, and I pulled away from the bars. There were very few blood fae for a reason. Only a handful were created.

Created.

There were even less blood fae offspring, like me, like the blood fae on the other side of the bars. Except, she was the real deal. I was an imitation.

Ice coated my hearts. My arms trembled, biceps twitched. I couldn't blink, couldn't look away. I didn't understand what I was doing here, and Duskmere wasn't clarifying the matter. If this blood fae was here for me, I was fucked. I figured I could take Duskmere on a good day—which today was not—but never a blood fae. Mostly because I was half of what they were. Scratch that, I was half of a half of that, since the enhanced power of the blood fae came from drinking blood, and my inconvenient allergy prevented that.

I let go of the bars. Outmatched or not, I wouldn't go down without taking several chunks of them with me.

The blood fae growing clearer with each step had the same pale complexion as me and was, surprisingly, the same height. That is where our similarities ended. She had the black eyes and raven hair expected of a blood fae, and much larger fangs, which she bared at me and elongated slowly. Of course she would have that sort of control.

Even if she was here to kill me, I didn't take it personal. It was an instinctive reaction to the way I smelled—wrong.

"Sir." The female's velvety rich voice had the smooth, deliciously sweet feel of hot chocolate. She'd already forgotten me, her love-struck gaze on Duskmere. No accounting for taste. "I apologize for the delay. Cirron requests I inform you it took longer than expected before he could contact us."

Hot satisfaction flared in my chest. That was my sister. I hoped for at least one black eye when I saw the sun fae again. If I saw the sun fae again.

"The door," Duskmere ordered, always business.

A fresh wave of fear rolled through me. Careful to keep the blood fae in my peripheral, I shifted my glare to Duskmere. "I won't let you leave me in here."

Empty threats. I didn't have much choice, but I wouldn't make it easy.

Duskmere's gaze remained on the RFG female as he spoke. "Malaney Callaghan and I must hurry."

"Er." Wait, what? What game was this? I scowled and shifted my weight from foot to foot. "I'm not falling for that."

Duskmere rolled his eyes—actually rolled his damn eyes. Mr. Stick-Up-His-Ass showed emotion, annoyance, of all things. I gaped as he made a hurry motion to the female.

The lock clicked, and Duskmere walked past me. He kept going down the hall in the same direction the other guard had come. He didn't stop, didn't look back. He... He left me.

Shock rooted me to the floor, and I watched his retreating figure. What was happening here? Did that portal lead to the Twilight Zone?

"This way, Malaney Callaghan." Duskmere's bored voice echoed down the hall.

I snapped my gaze to the blood fae. She didn't look at me, and she didn't look at Duskmere, either, but she wanted to, I could tell. Her black eyes kept pulling toward him before she jerked them away, as if he were her gravity. *Gross*. My lip curled at the very idea, and I shuffled for the door. I kept my gaze on her in case she tried anything, and she kept hers on the far wall.

Our eyes met briefly, but that was all I needed to see her opinion of me.

Monster. Abomination. Mistake.

The taunting mantra of my childhood played on loop in my brain. My stomach cramped, and I wanted to curl into a ball. I let my head fall forward, the sweep of my waist-length hair shielding my face. I focused on the gravel pushing over my toes as I shuffled past the blood fae and began down the hall. So many years gone by, and the pain of the past, of being back here, gnawed at me, fresh as ever.

As I followed Duskmere down the hall, maintaining a healthy distance, I drove my talons into my raw palms, relishing the physical pain. I could deal with physical pain, heal from it. That sort of pain wouldn't test my sanity. An ember of anger ignited. A tendril wrapped around my hearts.

Calm down. Breathe. One day, you'll show them all how wrong they are about you. You're not a monster. You're not a monster. You're not a monster.

Some distance behind me the cell door clanged shut. I turned and watched the blood fae walk in the opposite direction.

My body relaxed, and my thoughts were no longer a hysterical mess. If we traveled through a portal and were met by another member of the RFG, it stood to reason we were in Eodrom. In a dungeon but somewhere in Eodrom. I let my eyes slide shut. The heavy thump of my slowing hearts drummed in my ears. I pulled in air until my chest ached with expansion, and let it out slowly. Inhale. Exhale.

A hiss came from my right. Adrenaline scorched the aches from my body. I danced away from a dark cell. Something shifted in the shadowed corners of the small room, and the gravel murmured with the movement. A smell—sun lily and musk—floated from the cell. Something terrible rode beneath that scent—sick, rot.

Bones lay against the far wall. No, not bones—legs. They bent askew, and a sun fae leaned into the watery light. Her lanky hair was an unidentifiable shade of blonde and had fallen out in places. The knobby bones of her once-alluring facial structure jutted unnaturally against her dull, gold-touched flesh. She pressed her lips together and swallowed. Small tears formed and bits of dry skin flaked away. An open sore on her cheek oozed. Azure eyes, rich but vacant, looked through me.

I inched closer to the glistening black bars. The movement sparked life in her. For a heartbeat she focused, and our gazes met. Her mouth opened and closed as if trying to speak, but she said nothing. Fresh fissures split open on her dry lips, and a sigh rattled from the woman. Her eyes glazed. She sank into the shadows, only her thin legs remaining in the light.

Would this be my fate?

The fae never wanted me. I was a monster, a hybrid. Half sun fae, half blood fae, with no sun magic and my blood fae abilities were parlor tricks compared to the real stuff. I was less than even the lowliest fae, reviled, and treated as such—ridiculed, broken, and made an outcast. Easy to lock me up and forget about me down here.

I pulled away from the cell and resumed my journey in the direction Duskmere had taken. After the moment of stillness, the shock of all my aches and pains nearly stole my breath. Each step felt like pushing through quicksand. My body couldn't keep up with the abuse I'd put it through today.

Maybe if I risked it. If I drank the blood of the emaciated sun fae, just a taste, enough to kick-start my healing.

My shoulders sagged on a sigh. I closed my eyes and pressed the heels of my palms into their sockets. No, I'd been down this road before. One taste led to a second, and before I knew it, I was waking up the next day with little recollection of anything in between. My nasty reputation in Interlands came in large part due to the aftermath of my allergic reaction, or blood-drunk episodes, as my sisters called them.

I rolled my tight shoulders and squinted into the dark distance half expecting to find Duskmere watching me—judging me—but he was gone. Oh well, he'd wait for me, or he wouldn't and I'd find my way home.

Gods I hoped he didn't wait.

With each step, my feet sank at least a half inch into the layer of pulverized gravel. It was an easy solution to any rock the architects of this pit ran into when they were digging it. On a normal day, this would be fine. Today was not a normal day, and right now, I was miserable. My calves cramped, and a fire blazed in my thighs. I focused on lifting one foot, another foot, again. The hall felt alive with the echo of my harsh breaths.

I passed three more cells, all empty. Time dragged, I dragged, but I kept going. As I neared the end of the hall, I spotted a form leaning against the arching doorframe. Damn. He'd waited for me.

Duskmere's back was to me, his shoulder and the side of his head leaning into the doorframe. His close-cropped hair was a spiky mess, its moonlight-silver strands a ghostly blue beneath the fae lights. I could hear his even breathing in this vacuum of stillness. Had he stopped for a power nap?

Whip fast, his head swung to the side, putting his profile to me, and he watched me over his shoulder.

Startled by the sudden movement, my fangs punched down and nicked my tongue. Fuck. I swallowed the puddle of blood that pooled in my mouth and licked my lips. "Listen, I'm tired, sore as hell, and my sisters are probably losing their minds. You need to answer some questions." I settled into a wide-legged power stance and crossed my arms over my chest. "Why am I in a dungeon? I told you, it wasn't me who killed your damn banshee."

Duskmere pushed from the wall and turned to face me. "I believe you."

"Then why did you kidnap me?" Kidnap was a strong word, but I was definitely here against my will.

"Come," he ordered rather than answer my question.

I planted my feet wide and crossed my arms over my chest. "I'm not going anywhere until you tell me why I'm here."

"You are here at the request of Queen Iola." Duskmere raked a scathing look over me. "I am not privy to the reasons for her request. I cannot begin to understand why she would need to see a bratty blood fae who ran away from home, but it's not my place to question."

"Sounds like you just did," I muttered. Who the hell was he calling a brat?

"Now you will come with me."

"Or?" I prompted.

The straight slash of Duskmere's brows lowered over his narrowed eyes. "Or I leave you in the dungeon."

That might be preferable to the disdain, the ridicule, the disgust I would likely face in this place, but I bet they didn't have cheesy poofs down here. Or food, in general.

"Well, when you put it that way." I pulled myself straight, forcing some steel into my spine, and walked past Duskmere, heading into the pit of vipers that was Eodrom.

8

I'M NOTHING

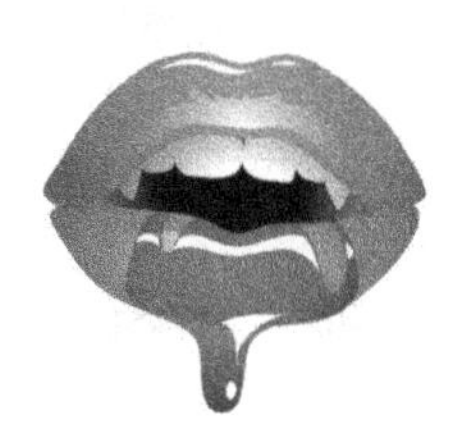

If I'd known an endless climb in a frigid stone stairwell was in store, I might have opted for the dungeon. At least I could have lain down.

We'd been climbing for at least five minutes and with each step, it was more of a fight to lift my legs. Above and to my left, another tall arch cut into the stone, identical to the one I went through in the dungeon. I'd lost count of how many we'd passed. The scent of damp, churned earth filtered from the darkness beyond the arch into the stairwell. Not very dungeon-like.

"Since we have all this time," I said. "What's up with you and that blood fae? You two a thing?"

The look he shot me was all kinds of foul. I'd annoyed him. One bright light in this blackhole.

"I mean, she obviously has it bad for you."

Duskmere grunted. "Not my type."

My already sore muscles tightened on a flash of anger. "Because she's blood fae?"

"Because I am her superior." His statement was matter of fact.

What an uptight prick. Mae could be good for this guy, loosen him up, make him bearable to be around. Not that I liked my sister finding him attractive. But damn, he needed something to break him out of his mood. He resumed climbing, and I limped behind. "How about my sister, Maerwen? She'd probably go for you."

"Not my type."

"Are you kidding? Mae is everyone's type."

He slid me an irritated look. "You aren't going to stop, are you?"

"Nope."

"I am spoken for."

"What about Cirron?" My sister wasn't picky, and she'd had her eye on both of them back in Interlands.

"Taken."

Always ready to be my sisters wing-girl. "How about both of you? She's never one to turn down an adventure."

"Both. Taken." His voice was tight, clipped.

Whoa. Didn't see that coming. I stopped walking and gaped after Duskmere's backside, which honestly wasn't half-bad in those snug leather pants. I mean, fae were fluid, totally normal, but Duskmere and Cirron? I figured Duskmere would prefer brains to pretty boy. To each their own, I guess.

Duskmere rounded the spiral above me, disappearing, though I could still hear the relentless clomp of his boots. I pushed my reluctant muscles harder to catch up, but being the inconsiderate jerk he was, he continued to stay far enough ahead to keep me struggling and unable to pester him with more questions I was dying to ask. In my haste, I clipped a toe and nearly kissed the steps. Muttering, I slowed to focus on the monotony of one step after the next.

The gaps between floors were significant and the distance between each random. I counted as few as ten steps between one floor and then sixty-seven to the next. It was doubtful each level was a dungeon, but I couldn't begin to guess what else they'd be used for this deep underground. We seemed to be climbing for the sun and the stars in this winding staircase to nowhere.

"Think you guys coulda put this dungeon any deeper?" I focused on lifting my left leg, my right. Cold sweat beaded on my brow and gathered beneath the hair on my neck. "Humans have these great things called elevators. Heard of 'em? You should invest."

Duskmere grunted.

"I know, I know, technology is a no go," I continued, in part to keep my mind from the excruciating pain each step inflicted, but mostly to annoy the crap out of my climbing partner. "You fae can go wiggle your fingers and create some magic pulley system. You open portals, and what about doors, like Ta'Vale to Earth? An elevator should be easy."

"Druids."

"What about them?"

"Druids are realm walkers," Duskmere said.

Apparently, he was forgetting about the portal he opened and shoved my ass through. "You say that like it should mean somethi—" My thousand-pound leg didn't lift far enough, and the scuffed toe of my combat boot clipped the step. I fell forward, cracking my knee against the stone. Pinpricks of white light burst across my vision. I moaned and rolled to my butt, curling over my throbbing knee. "Damn it. Ow."

Several steps above me, Duskmere stopped. To his credit, he didn't ask if I was okay or try to help me up. Sure, that'd be the polite thing to do, but I probably would have tried to remove any hand he offered.

"Only druids can part the veil between realms and create permanent doors," Duskmere said.

"Are you seriously still talking about that?" If he couldn't do it, I was beyond caring about the details. I massaged my knee and speared Duskmere with a look that promised pain. "I don't actually give a shit. How much further? At this rate, you're going to have to send a rescue party for me."

"We would get there sooner if I—"

"Don't you dare say carry me. I swear I will punch you in the face."

Duskmere's jaw ticked.

"Why can't you open a *temporary* portal to wherever we need to go and toss me through? Worked for you the first time." I pressed my fingers into the slightly swollen flesh surrounding the joint, testing the injury.

"That cell is the only place one may open a portal. It was left that way to safely transport criminals into the dungeons." He looked down his nose at me—literally and figuratively—clearly judging me for my lack of knowledge and my don't-give-a-shit attitude for my home world. "You grew up here. You should know Ta'Vale has a spell woven over it to ward against portals within the realm."

"Right." I stood and carefully eased weight onto the leg. Duskmere obviously didn't know about Finnlay Callaghan's hybrid portal experiments, all from the convenience of his backyard. "Guess it wouldn't make sense to evict an entire race who could pop open some portals and come right back without first establishing precautions."

"Yes," Duskmere said simply and resumed the climb.

"It doesn't bother you?" With my right hand on the wall for balance, I followed, hugging the inner section of the spiral.

"What does not bother me, Malaney Callaghan?"

"That you serve the beings who exiled your brethren? And stop using my full name. It's an annoying habit."

"It is a sign of respect for your station." Duskmere paused again to study me.

I wrinkled my nose and fanned my hands over my filthy jacket. "My station? Wow, if anyone told you I was important, that's one twisted practical joke. And if I was actually important, you have a hell of a way of showing it."

"Queen Iola told me this."

My stomach dropped to my toes. Still, it sounded less and less like I might be a thing she wanted dead. "I've never met her. I'm nothing. She can't possibly be bothered to know I exist."

"I told you, Malaney Call—" Duskmere swallowed my last name with the same look I gave broccoli. "Malaney, Queen Iola requested an audience with you, immediately. So we must go." He turned to leave but stopped. His voice a whisper, he added "And they were not my brethren."

The reality of his words sank in as he rounded the curve in the spiral stairwell, leaving me alone. I slumped against the wall. The fury I felt for the situation Duskmere had put me in dropped to a simmer.

"Keep up, Malaney Callaghan."

Then again... I scowled at the empty stairs above me. A fresh wave of anger fueled the rest of my climb.

9

BROKEN

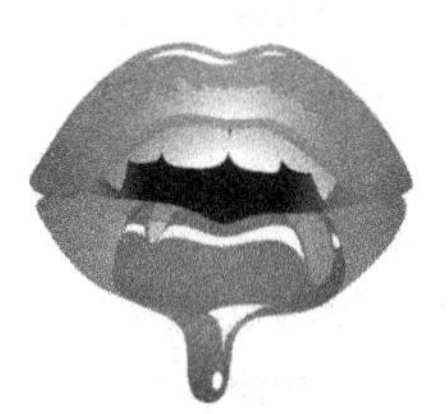

The warm scent of spiced gingerbread hit me first. That one was always the strongest, and it snapped me from my climbing coma. Close behind came the tang of overripe citrus and the cloying floral scent. A knot twisted in my stomach, and I hugged an arm across my middle.

Judging by the smells, this hallway led into the heart of Eodrom. Memories flooded me. The taunts, the beatings, the day I'd almost died.

The sun bridge stretched across the entirety of the Grian Valley, north to south and east to west. Its center was an open circle that afforded a view of the inaccessible sun garden below. A breathtaking view to most, nightmare inducing for me. All those years ago, that's where I landed, but I don't remember a thing.

Streaks of sunlight painted the curved wall of the stairs above me. Faint voices and off-key singing took the place of Duskmere's sure steps. I stopped. Voices meant that when I rounded the next spiral, chances were, I'd be inside the central palace of Eodrom—the jewel of the Grian Valley, the seat of the sun fae royals. The place I'd run long and hard to escape.

I ground the heel of my palm against the phantom pain that flared off-center of my breastbone—where my smaller heart pulsed. The larger heart had been pierced by the spiked arm of a sundial I landed on when I plummeted into the garden. It almost pierced both. I'd evaded death by seven millimeters.

When I didn't come home, my family went looking for me. They told me the search lasted for two days. It was Mae and her budding ability to follow aura trails who led to my rescue. A slow burn kindled in my bones at the memory. She later said my aura was a rainbow of color she'd always find.

Twenty-seven weeks later, when I'd healed, I still had no idea who'd lured me onto the bridge, but I wasn't about to give them a second chance. I left for Interlands. Less than a week later my sisters followed.

A sudden thought intruded on my stroll down memory lane. Mae didn't pull me from the sun garden, she never went inside, so who had?

Duskmere, having apparently backtracked, reappeared on the curving stairs above.

Too many memories. Too many emotions. I didn't want to be here. "About that offer to stay in the dungeon."

He came down three more steps toward me. "It was a threat, not an offer."

"Still..."

He put a hand on my elbow, but I shook it off. "Please come, Malaney."

It was the please that did it. Didn't hurt he'd remembered not to use my full name.

With a roll of my wrist, I gestured for Duskmere to go ahead. "I'll be right behind you. You have my word."

"I do not know you well enough to know if your word has value."

"Just go, will you?"

Duskmere arched a silver brow. I raised both of mine and stared back.

"You should not disguise your eyes. They are who you are," he said and continued up the stairs.

"I thought you didn't know me." I smacked my hand against the wall and stared at the empty stairwell. What was it with my eyes all the sudden? As a child, they'd been my stigma, my mark. Suddenly everyone thought I should let them all hang out. A frustrated growl rolled beneath my breath as I climbed after Duskmere.

The stairwell opened to the corner of a twelve-acre courtyard at the center of Eodrom. I paused and squinted at the bright, afternoon tableau. Crushed-pebble paths wound through the courtyard in an artful design. They ran along a deep watery crevasse, through gardens, and into a dark and dangerous grove. Any fae with a lick of sense would take the long way around that grove, and stay away from the water, too.

Ta'Vale was feral and breathtaking, and it was a part of my soul. I could never leave it behind entirely. I couldn't even avoid Grian Valley, since my parents were here. I could avoid the central palace of Eodrom, though, and I'd planned to until Duskmere gave me the heave-ho home.

A pair of sun fae dressed in the typical palace fashion of jewel-bedecked flowing robes and sandals caught sight of me and their noses went so high into the stratosphere, the clouds were in danger of being sucked from the sky. "Feeling's mutual," I called and smoothed a hand over my knotted hair.

"Malaney." Duskmere gestured to a small door set in a wall running along the courtyard, to my right.

Still trying to avoid venturing further into Eodrom, I ignored the gesture and hooked a thumb over my shoulder at the archway we'd just passed through. "Brilliant idea having easy access to the dungeons right off the courtyard." The acidic bite to my tone didn't faze him.

"Had you explored this stairwell when you resided here and garnered the stamina to make it to the bottom, which I doubt, you would have discovered your inability to enter the dungeon."

"Rude. You don't know me."

"Hmm." Duskmere gave me a dubious non-response and an even more dubious look. "Let us say you made the climb."

"I could." Not. Had fifteen years to do it, never did. Didn't even make it to this side of the courtyard.

"Only the bottom floors are dungeons, and to enter requires the presence of a Royal Fae Guard." Duskmere tapped the insignia on his shoulder and glanced impatiently to the door I still hadn't moved toward. "Most of the floors between here and the dungeon are comprised of spore fields, gardens for herbs, and other flora which require the absence of light to bloom. Moon fae who fled Lann Ridge during the Divide to settle within the protective walls of Eodrom reside on the top floors with the three moon stones relocated by the sun fae following the Divide." Boring recitation complete, he once again gestured for the door.

So that's where the other moon fae lived. I hadn't seen any on the climb or heard other voices. To be fair, I'd been so focused on not dropping dead, I would have missed a train coming at me.

"Fine." We stared at one another. "I'm not going first."

I sounded childish, and I also didn't care.

His exasperation finally forced another subtle eye roll. That pleased me immensely. At last he moved ahead, and I limped slowly behind. Every joint in my body an aching reminder of this shitty day.

Duskmere planted his back to the wall and held the door wide for me. How dare he have manners after pushing me through a portal between realms and dragging me up umpteen-thousand winding steps. I gave him the most brutal glare I could muster and walked past, but pulled up short inside the long hallway when music hit me. A light ethereal sound—chimes, bells, harps. Goosebumps rose along my flesh.

"I've heard this music before, but I don't remember when." I glanced to Duskmere as he let the door to the courtyard fall shut behind him and stepped inside the hallway with me. "Where are we?"

His face remained passive. He didn't reply but instead stood quietly, expectantly. I bit the inside of my cheek, feeling small, off balance.

The wall opposite the door we entered the hallway through was the faded white of old bones, filled with honeycomb holes and covered in spearmint-shaded lichen and climbing vines. Despite being indoors, bright pink trumpet-shaped flowers hung in heavy clusters from the vines clinging to the wall. Iridescent birds the size of my pinkie darted in and out of the holes, nipping nectar from the flowers and zipping away.

"You must proceed on your own. I cannot escort you into the garden."

Was he trying to be funny? Because if this was his idea of a joke, Duskmere and I had a very different view of comedy. There was nothing but solid wall reaching from us into the distance. I waved my hands wide to encompass the breadth of the wall, but he didn't crack a smile. This fucker was serious.

I ran my tongue across the tops of my tingling fangs and shoved my hands onto my hips. "Look, you seem to be waiting for something, but I don't know what. There aren't any doors besides the one we came through, so give a girl a hint."

Duskmere's forehead rippled into a frown, and he glanced from me to the wall opposite. "I thought perhaps since you hear the music, you would sense it. The Sun Garden is straight ahead."

My hands fisted the hem of my jacket. All I wanted right now was a hot bath and a trough of cheesy poofs so I could eat myself into a food coma. "Please, for the love of all the forsaken gods, tell me what I need to do, so I can go home."

"Enter the Sun Garden," Duskmere replied.

That did it. This day of bullshit ripped the top off the frustration I'd been bottling up. A shot of adrenaline burned the fatigue from my overtaxed muscles. I screeched and launched myself at Duskmere. He might be bigger, but I was stronger, and he was unprepared. I easily took him to the ground. His silver head bounced, and dark satisfaction injected life into my tired limbs.

He deserved that and more for everything he'd put me through. Before he could recover, I pulled back my taloned hand.

Sunlight streamed into the hall. I shielded my eyes and rolled from the moon fae. An impossibly beautiful sun fae female towered over me. I knew this person. *Breathe, Lane, breathe.*

The strong features of her oval face were set in amusement. Her wide mouth with lips that weren't overly full, hitched upward at the corners. A waterfall of liquid gold hair streamed over her shoulders.

When her eyes found mine, the world tilted, and my knees went weak. Her otherworldly irises looked like twin sunsets on a lake. I'd never met this woman, but there was no doubt who she was.

"Queen Iola," Duskmere said and pushed to his feet. "Apologies."

Her gliding walk brought her to Duskmere, and she placed a kiss on his charcoal brow. "Be at ease. You completed the task I asked of you."

Duskmere dipped his head and retreated down the hall.

She turned to me, the soft smile never leaving her lips. "Malaney Callaghan, daughter of Finnlay Callaghan."

I cringed at the echo of Duskmere's formal request. "Majesty?" I had no idea how to address this higher being.

"You may call me Iola." She glided to me and took my hands in hers, and it felt like dipping my hands into sun-warmed water.

Surprised by the informality, I stood a little straighter. The anxiety melted from my bones, and I returned her smile.

"Now then," she said. "I believe you may be able to help us. Please, come." She released my hands to turn and walk right through the wall.

10

YOU ARE AN EVOLUTION

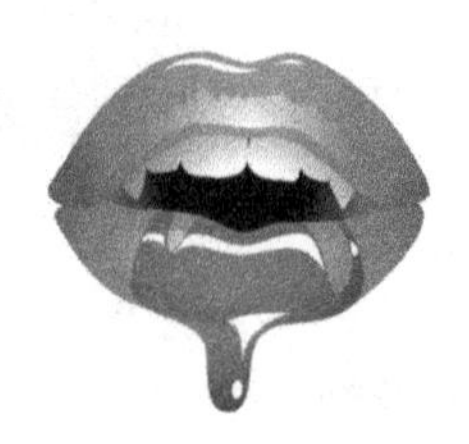

Shit.

Queen Iola walked through a wall.

A solid wall.

I mashed my hands together in front of my chest, one thumb continuously rubbing the other.

She hadn't even paused. Walked into the wall, and for the split second she passed through, sunlight had ripped into the narrow hall and a dream appeared beyond.

Only me and the birds here now.

Something green twitched at the edge of my vision. An odd pinkish-brown creature that vaguely resembled a rabbit sifted through the low hanging vines. It shoveled leaves into its mouth, packing its cheeks full. The longer I watched it, the more of them I saw. Their thick coats rippled over rolls of plant-fed fat as they chewed.

The one closest to me froze. It stopped gnawing on the vine to stare at me with its beady pink eyes. One ear twitched and it chirped. A wad of wet leaves tumbled from its mouth, showing off oversized buck teeth. Its fellow fluffballs echoed the call.

"No." I wagged my finger at the aggressively cute creatures. "I'm not doing this again."

I spun for the wall and threw my arm across my face as I barreled through...air.

Nothing but air—toasted-cinnamon scented air.

Shock slapped me into stillness, and I could do little more than gawk open-mouthed at the paradise surrounding me. I closed my eyes and breathed deep. Beneath the cinnamon came the clean scent of fresh soil, roasted citrus, and loamy lake shores. Knocked off balance from the dizzying circus of smells, my legs went weak, and I dropped to my knees in the thick carpet of grass.

A forest rose in front of me. These trees weren't tall, but they were fat and dense. The rich brown branches were adorned with leaves like wafer-thin gems. Frothy willows with long, pale violet branches swayed in the warm breeze kissing my skin. Hip-high flowers grew along a path that appeared to be made from crushed stone shards, which stretched from me into the trees.

The kaleidoscope of sensations stole my breath. I pressed both hands over my hearts. Their steady thump-thump-thump grounded me. In what felt like a dream state, a long breath ebbed and flowed over my lips while I searched the sun-dappled shadows beneath the tree canopy for any sign of Queen Iola.

I found her standing on the far side of a small red bridge arched over the slow-moving waters of a turquoise stream. She watched me with the same serene expression she'd given Duskmere. The feather-light gown flowing over her fluttered in the light breeze. I knew I was short, but she was a woman who could look Rip directly in the eye and probably also tear out his heart without losing the beatific smile curving her full lips.

The thought shook me from my awestruck paralysis, and I climbed to my feet. No, I'd never heard an evil word uttered about Queen Iola—I'd never heard much at all—but she was the sun fae queen. The queen of all the fae.

With the moon fae gone, by population and power the sun fae owned this realm. My father always warned that the sun needed the moon to hold balance in the realm. It was why, despite him being captured and tortured during the Great Fae Divide, he dedicated his life's work to the practice of melding sun and moon magic.

Hybrid magic. Probably why he'd didn't reject his hybrid daughter. I balled my hands into fists against my thighs.

The glossy wooden surface of a sundial appeared as I crested the bridge. My body flushed and then went cold. I skirted the smooth circle while my pulse tapped an anxious rhythm in my throat. The face of the ancient dial was large enough to park my Bronco on with room to spare. The top three feet of its arm had been fitted with some sort of metal. The original length of petrified wood that had been its original arm hung over my fireplace as a reminder of why I'd left Ta'Vale. My gaze inevitably drew upwards to the distant arc of the sun bridge.

"I found you that day," Queen Iola said from beside me, and I jumped.

"You? I, um..." I'd been so distracted, I hadn't heard her move. I folded my arms across my middle and looked at her but couldn't quite meet her eyes. My arms flopped to my sides, and I tugged at the hem of my jacket. "I'd assumed someone else. A guard or a gardener. Do you have gardeners for this place?"

Wow. Brilliant conversationalist there, Lane.

"Very few hear the stone's song. It has been generations, until you." She lifted my chin and smiled down at me. Her graceful fingers tucked a strand of hair behind my ear. "Your sister traced your aura to the hallway but could not find you, could not locate the garden. I broke the sundial and delivered you to your family."

I bit the edge of my lip and shrugged. "I don't understand how I'm here. I'm not a sun fae. I'm nobody."

"The stones do not discriminate, Malaney."

"I thought..." My brows pinched together. "I think I understand. The shards are the same as any other foci, like the banshee's swamp water, anybody can touch it." Not that they'd want to, ew. "But no one else can draw power from it. Or, I guess, filter power through it."

"You are correct. Only the sun fae find the stones necessary for survival." Queen Iola flexed her hand and a miniature sun rose above her palm, so bright that even with my lenses, tears obscured my vision. She extinguished the light and smiled, and it was so kind it hurt. "But fae of all races can hear their songs if the stones so choose."

My chest squeezed, and I looked at my reflection in the sundial's polished surface, at the night-black eyes that weren't mine. I removed the contact lenses, shoved them in my side pocket, and met Queen Iola's gaze with my bi-colored eyes. "But why me? I'm not sure I'm even fae."

"Come." Rather than acknowledge my gut-wrenching confession, she took my hand in her unnaturally warm grip and pulled me onto the path. "Let us get to the reason I brought you here."

Crushed stone and bits of sun shards crunched beneath our feet.

After a few moments, Queen Iola spoke.

"You are a direct descendant of the first keepers of the sun stones, and most definitely fae."

"On my father's side. The first king and queen, I know, but I'm not sun fae and I'm not even blood fae. What does that leave?" I waved a hand in front of my face to indicate my eyes. "A mistake. No magic. I'm a blood fae who's allergic to blood. Allergic!"

My breath came hard at the litany of confessions that spewed from my mouth. Why did I tell her all that? Because I'm an idiot.

"You speak of the royalty your parents are descended from."

"Am I wrong?"

"Yes and no. They were the first, but they were not royals. They were keepers of the sun stones, same as Torneh and me. These titles, king and queen, they came to be over many millennia, and before my time. It has poisoned this place." She made an elegant sweep of her hand in the general direction of the palace proper. The corners of her eyes crinkled. "This is why I ask that I am Iola to you."

"I will do that...Iola." I understood her request, but still struggled with it. Dropping an ingrained honorific was *hard*. Great, now I felt bad for snapping at Duskmere for doing the same thing to me. Wait, nope, moment passed. He was still an asshole.

"Wonderful." Her smile outshone the sun. "To answer your earlier question, your parents are each born of the original keepers, but from there, their lines diverged, many times over."

Ahead, two paths veered away from the central path. Well, if that wasn't symbolic...

Iola stopped to pick a pale-yellow globe from a tree. She peeled away the fruit's flesh to reveal shockingly deep purple segments and offered me a wedge.

"Thank you." I couldn't remember the last time I had eaten and eagerly popped it into my mouth. It tasted like a deliciously weird cross between a grapefruit and cotton candy.

"All fae are brought to the hallway of the sun garden on the celebration day of their twentieth year."

The declaration startled me. "All fae?"

"Mmm, yes. Before the Great Fae Divide, fae allegiance fell to either moon or sun fae, but no more. Now all come to us, as you and your sisters would have, had you not left. Though, we already knew you had an affinity for the garden. You don't remember, but when I found you, you were conscious briefly and told me you heard music." She handed me another segment. "It is quiet here. I had so looked forward to your company, to sharing moments such as this. Malaney, when you fell—"

"I didn't fall." The compulsion to tell the truth only my sisters knew overwhelmed me. I shifted from one foot to the other. What was one more confession? "I was pushed."

Iola inhaled sharply and dropped the fruit. It bounced and splattered purple juice across the front of her white gown. Her sticky fingers gripped mine, and I met her gaze. The sunset-orange and pink ring lining her pupils flared into brilliant star bursts and spiked across the bright blue of her irises. An otherworldly light illuminated them, and a whip-crack of fear shot through me. My breath stuttered.

"It was believed you fell," Iola said, her words slow and careful.

Only my sisters knew the truth, and I'd only told them after they joined me in Interlands. I licked my lips. "There wasn't much point in saying otherwise. I wasn't winning any popularity contests. It could have been anyone, I never saw them, and no one ever came forward to say they saw anything either. It was easier to just leave."

"There is truth in your words. I understand now why you left, but I wish you'd come to us sooner. We would have found who did this." Her grip tightened until my bones ached. "I fear it is too late, but if we ever discover the truth, justice will be swift."

My scalp tightened and tingled. Goosebumps rose on my neck.

"Oh, no. Please, no." Iola meant to see this deed done. She might reject the moniker of queen, but she had the power of one and more. "I've let that go. I don't know who pushed me, and I'm fine with that. In fact, I prefer not knowing. I'm happy with my life. I've made something of myself, and I want to prove I'm more than a mistake."

Her head tilted a fraction, and she studied me down the sharp line of her straight nose. I squirmed, swallowed my breath and held it, feeling like she could see me down to my atoms.

"Very well," she said at last, and I could breathe. "I understand. Only know you are no mistake. You are an evolution."

Iola took the lead and we continued walking. The tiny iridescent birds from the hallway zipped from tree to tree. Their lustrous feathers camouflaged them amongst the jeweled leaves. In the distance, a chestnut aloughta lifted its head from the grass to watch us. Small black pig-like creatures, the size and shape of an orange, darted across the path on bright red legs.

My steps grew heavier, and I pressed my hands to the small of my aching back. I'd traded climbing stairs for walking paths, and my body thought this was the perfect time to remind me of all the shit I'd been through today.

Focused on putting one foot in front of the other and not falling on my ass, a short note, like a broken harp string, shook me alert. My heavy steps faltered, but at least I didn't tip over. The ethereal hum of music had grown steadily louder, but there was a touch of discord, something off.

"Where is that music coming from?" I bit my lip and searched my surroundings for the source.

"The sun stones sing for you. We are close to the first now." She glanced at me and pointed upward. "The circular path in the sun bridge surrounds the stones."

Reluctantly, I tilted my face to the bridge. Sure enough, the stunning piece of fae architecture hung directly above, and it turned my stomach. "This music is coming from the sun stones? Duskmere claims they were stolen."

"Yes," she replied, putting a period on the conversation, and continued down the path, disappearing around a bend.

All this walking would be the death of me. I pushed my aggrieved muscles to catch up and found Iola standing at the end of the path with a broken stone not far beyond. A broken boulder would be more accurate.

"This is the first stone." Iola glided forward, and I got my first good look at the source of the sun shards.

Hundreds of woven reed baskets half full of shed sun shards lay in disarray around a stone that sprouted from the ground like the stump of a rotting tooth. Barely wider than I was tall, it rose to shoulder height—mine, not Iola's—with a brilliant amber base, but the surface was a mottled brown. Veins of gray, black, and brown bled into what was left of the sun stone.

Iola placed a hand on the stone.

Beneath her palm the sun stone flared, flickered. This close to it, the sharp chords and off-key notes were obvious. The light flickered, went out. My chest ached. I didn't know how I knew, but my gut told me the stone was dying.

"I cannot heal them," Iola said. "They are dying. They need your help."

My head snapped back. "My help? What can I do?"

"Finnlay has told me you and your sisters perform investigations."

"Yes, we do." This couldn't possibly be going where I thought.

"How fortuitous that we have need of someone with your skill set, and you can enter the sun garden."

Shit. It went there.

"I'm sorry, Que—Iola. I don't know what I can do to help. Even if I find the stones, what can I do?"

She placed both palms on the broken stone. Sunlight flowed in her veins. Her gold skin paled by comparison to the threads of light streaming down her arms and into the stone. A small patch of the sickly brown surface cleared. Iola gasped, wilted to the ground, and rested against the stone. Her despondent gaze rose to mine.

The ache in my chest swelled, and I pressed my hand against the base of my breastbone.

"You feel their pain." She let her head fall back against the stone. "That bit of magic was but a bandage on a mortal wound. I can heal the stones, but their severed pieces must first be returned. Whoever has taken them has rooted them elsewhere. Those stones are growing, and these stones will die."

I knelt in front of Iola. "How can those stones survive? The stolen pieces?"

"This is difficult to explain." Her tongue traced the seam of her tightly compressed lips. "Here, the stones were one. They were rooted where they sprouted from the soil, but when they were cleaved, the unrooted pieces became newborns, fresh to the world, accessible to any. Whoever stole these stones knew enough to take more than they left. No matter where they are in the universe, once they are rooted the newly made stones will draw on their mother stone's power until ours eventually die."

As she spoke, the music of the stones became unbearable. I winced at the discord.

Iola rose and laid a heavy hand on my shoulder. "I understand I ask much of you, but please find the stones." Her fingers warmed, and the gentle heat melted through me. "I will leave you now."

With weighted steps, she retreated down the path we came.

"So, tell me," I said and swiveled to face the apparently sentient stone. "How the fuck am I supposed to do that?"

11

JUST GIVE ME SOMETHING

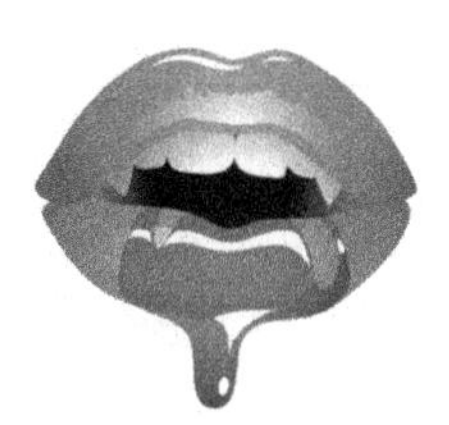

THE STONES HAD GROWN IN A FAIRLY UNIFORM POLYGON, MAKING EACH one easy to find, despite the lengthy separation between each. As I approached the third stone, which was the final broken stone, roughly a straight-line opposite from the first, the nostril-puckering scent of vinegar hit me first. I stumbled, stopped, and dragged another deep breath in through my nose.

Sharp and peppery. The sour stench of old meat. Jasmine. All faint, but still there, and I never forgot a scent.

Slowly, carefully, as if I might scare away the evidence, I paced a spiral around the stone, found nothing, did another slow spiral, moving inward toward the broken stone with each lap. Nothing again. I glanced up, turning this way and that to make sure no one was watching.

"Can we agree to never speak of this to anyone?" The stone, unsurprisingly, remained silent. I dropped to my hands and knees and crawled the same spiral, but moving outward. One palm coated in squashed mushroom juice and two grass-stained knees later, still nothing.

I growled in frustration and dumped a basket of sun shards, then another, and another, until I was almost back to the third sun stone. I shoved over another basket.

A tide of sun shards rolled out, a black pebble among them. My breath clung to my throat.

"One of you is not like the other." I stared at the oddball pebble and then swept my gaze over the spill of shards looking for anything else. Nothing. This was it. I plucked the pebble from its nest of amber shards, turning it side to side.

Unlike the uncomfortably warm shards, this thing was cold. I knelt, sitting on my heels, and rolled it between my forefinger and thumb. It was a perfect oval and as smooth as volcanic glass except for the almost imperceptible crack on one side. I couldn't see the damage, but I could feel it.

Eau de moon fae came at me stronger, closer. Unease simmered in my chest. The more friction on the pebble, the stronger the scent. Inanimate objects did not—should not—smell like blood...unless something bled on it. But this thing was smooth. No residue. The wheels were turning, but nothing caught.

I twisted in the direction of the first broken stone. I hadn't found a damn thing there, but I hadn't checked the baskets.

Excitement fed energy into my tight muscles. Riding high on my discovery, I squeezed the evidence in a tight fist and sprinted the quarter mile back to the second sun stone. The bottom of the first basket I came across was visible through the handful of shards inside, but I flipped it over and dug through the contents anyhow. No pebble. I crawled to the next basket and repeated the process.

Twenty-seven baskets later and nothing but shards. Frustration gnawed at me.

There had to be something. I smelled him. That corrupted moon fae had been here.

"You're delirious, Lane," I mumbled to myself. Falling out of a tree could do that.

My entire body sagged as I took in the mess I'd made. If I didn't find the sun stones, these could be the last of the shards. My stomach soured, and it wasn't the fruit Iola fed me. It was *feelings*. I didn't want to care, but damn it, I did.

Three stones—three extremely large stones—had been snapped in half and hauled away, but how? The half left behind was still taller than me, so it's not like they were dragged down the halls of Eodrom. They were just gone, and all I'd found was a black pebble. I hadn't seen anything else like it so far, but I'd only seen a tiny portion of the garden. It could have come from anywhere in here.

I rolled my eyes toward the sun bridge, and a quiver of remembered pain skated across my nerve endings. Leaves and small bits of debris seemed to float above the treetops. The stone falling from above was not an option. While the garden was open to the sky and to viewing from the sun bridge, an invisible barrier prevented entrance. I'd fallen through all those years ago, but apparently the stones accepted me. Didn't I feel special?

A hot rush of air exploded from my nostrils. What the hell kind of clue was a black pebble smaller than a glob of Y'sindra's spit? This job wasn't for me, not alone at least. I needed my sisters. Frustrated, I yanked out the pebble, tossed the small stone to the ground and watched it roll. I couldn't look away, felt itchy, unsettled.

"Shit." I crawled after the pebble and shoved it into the inner chest pocket of my jacket normally reserved for my sunglasses. "You better be worth it."

I tugged the hem of my jacket to straighten it and turned in the direction of the final stolen sun stone, the first stone, where Iola had left me. I walked this time. The brief burst of energy had abandoned me. When the stone finally came into view, it appeared identical to the others—broken, dying, with no hint to what happened. My upper lip twitched with annoyance. Should I even bother?

Of course. I had to check. My conscience would haunt me if I didn't—and Mae would be a fucking poltergeist if she found out.

"Argh." Banging my hands on my hips, I stomped toward the third stone. I'd tipped past the point of pain, past the exhaustion. I wanted this over with so I could go home and wallow in junk food.

I kicked over the first basket. Nothing. Sun shards pushed into the soles of my boots despite my half-hearted attempt to skirt the pieces. I probably shouldn't make such a mess.

Then again, I probably shouldn't be here in the first place, so, oh well.

An annoying thread of guilt knotted my insides. I liked Iola. She'd been nice. She'd *cared*.

I scowled and tried not to be a wrecking ball.

The tang of vinegar, while still faint, came at me heavier on the far side of the stone, but these baskets were empty.

I squeezed the bridge of my nose, fighting the frustration building behind my eyes. With no idea what to do next, I lay down and glared at the sun bridge. My fingertips dug into the soil, grass tickling my palms. The moon fae's scent was even stronger. It taunted me, like his obscene gesture.

With nothing to lose but my dignity, I flipped to my hands and knees and stuck my nose to the ground, searching for anything. I worked my way forward, stopping every few feet to sniff. *Come on, just give me something.*

Halfway around the stone the already faint smell faded. I crawled closer to the stone and began the other way. Nearly back to where I'd started, something smooth and cool pressed against my palm. Elation roared, and I jolted back. It took a moment to find it, but I parted the grass and there it was—a wink of black glinting against black soil, taunting me. I'd never wanted to be so right and so wrong at the same time.

My breath came too quickly. I counted to five on a deep inhale, held it for five, and took another five to exhale. Again. My breathing slowed. I leaned forward and sniffed. The same distasteful bouquet invaded my nostrils.

It shouldn't be possible, but the finger-flipping moon fae had definitely been here, and obviously handled the stones quite a bit for the smell of him to come at me so strong.

Triumph and anxiety went to war in my gut. I shook my hands in front of me, hopped to my feet and paced, never taking my eyes from the rogue pebble. I'd figured something out, but it shouldn't be possible. I had to be wrong.

No, I'd smelled his blood, knew that scent.

Mae's voice came alive in my head. *Trust your instincts.*

"Easy for you to say," I muttered.

I stood over the small black stone and flexed my hands. My muscles twitched. I picked up the pebble and gave it another sniff. Gods, that smell—awful.

"Definitely him." I shoved it into the pocket with the first pebble and rubbed my palms on my thighs.

There was nothing but sun garden for miles upon miles. I didn't believe for a second a moon fae could open a portal to this sacred place. But how else would he get inside? I worked my lip beneath my fang and tried to focus. Though the worst of the pains in my body had faded, I was exhausted by the erratic tides of adrenaline ebbing and flowing through me today. My thoughts were insulated in cotton.

I crossed to the dying sun stone and tapped a finger against its mottled surface. "You're stupid. It should have been Mae. Even Y'sindra would have been a better choice."

Frustrated—and a little embarrassed I'd stooped to insulting a stone—I wedged my hands into my front pockets. My fingertips brushed paper. I stilled and closed my eyes.

The stones weren't the only ones that believed in me. My family did, and Iola held some sort of inexplicable faith. I stroked the folded paper in my pocket. My hearts swelled with bitter-sweet pain in my chest. Teddy believed in me.

"Get your shit together, Lane." I rolled my shoulders, took a deep breath, and dropped to all fours.

Rustling the blades of grass, I found nothing and crawled forward.

"Malaney?"

I leaped to my feet and spun toward Iola.

"Sorry, it's nothing weird. I was—"

"You must come with me."

"Now? But I think I found something."

"Good, you may explain at a later time." She turned and headed, I assumed, toward the exit. I couldn't be sure. I was the worst at directions.

So much for desperately needing my help.

"Wait." I jogged to catch up. "I think this is important. If you wait, I'll show you."

She glanced at me, the sunset ring surrounding her pupils flared briefly. "You have a most insistent visitor."

"What? Who? No one knows I'm here." Except my sisters, but they were at least a day's ride away.

Iola walked quickly, and I struggled to keep up. By some miracle my injuries today were minor. I guess I bounced right on my way down the tree, but that didn't make me any less tired or sore. Or short. Iola had long legs.

I racked my brain as we speed-walked down the twisting path. There was no way my sisters could have made it here yet. The aches in my body said I'd been here for ages, but it couldn't have been more than half a day.

The trees thinned, and the wall came into view. I caught up to Iola as she mounted the red bridge. "Is it Mom? Did my sisters call her? Geez, I bet she's freaking out."

Without stopping, Iola glanced over her shoulder. A small frown tugged at her lips. "Why would Meghan be concerned?"

"Um, because I was kidnapped." And because she liked the court only marginally more than I did, despite her status as a respected healer.

Iola stopped. The wall was so close, I wondered if anyone on the other side could hear our conversation. I brushed at the grass stains on my knees and glanced at the honeycomb stone. Who could be here?

"You did not want to come?" Iola asked.

"No." I shook my head. "I mean yes, I planned to come, but not when I did. I'd already decided I needed to talk to someone, but I told Duskmere I'd visit tomorrow."

I glared at the wall. I hoped he could hear me.

"But you are here. I asked Duskmere to bring you. I do not understand." Iola's elegant fingers twisted in the folds of her gown.

"Fine, he didn't kidnap me, but he also didn't give me a choice." I paused and took a slow, calming breath. I wasn't doing myself any favors by losing my temper in front of Iola. "Duskmere said you wanted to see me and shoved me through a portal, which I'm pretty certain no one would appreciate. I'm not surprised my sisters panicked and called Mom."

"Your mother is not here."

"I'm sorry, but I don't know who else would care."

Iola's lips pressed together as she smoothed the wrinkles she'd twisted into the front of her gown. "He goes by the name Teddy."

With that she turned and vanished through the wall.

"What the...."

12

PUSHING STARS ACROSS THE SKY

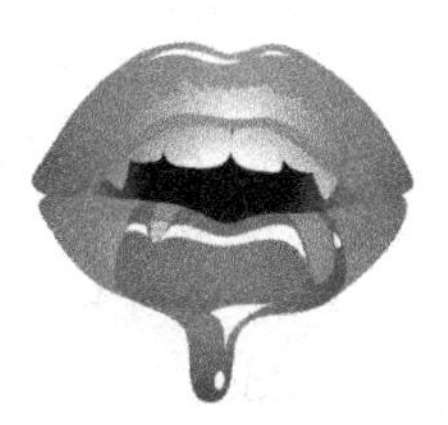

"FUCK." I SURGED FOR TEDDY, WHO HAD DUSKMERE PINNED AGAINST THE far wall by the throat. "What are you doing? Stop!"

Duskmere slapped at Teddy's arms, each hit weaker than the last. The moon fae's charcoal skin began to resemble a bruised eggplant, while the veins on Teddy's corded forearms stood out from the pressure he continued to apply.

"Where is she?" Teddy snarled in Duskmere's face.

"I'm right here." I tried to pull Teddy's forearm from Duskmere, but I might as well have tried to twist a knot in a lead pipe. Teddy shook his arm, and his elbow grazed my fang.

Salty sweet bliss exploded on my tongue. The world erupted into brilliant color. The already vibrant smells overwhelmed me. I clutched my hands to my chest and stared at the thin trail of blood welling on Teddy's arm. There was no way I got enough in my mouth for this sort of reaction, for any sort of reaction.

I growled and shook my head to clear it. Burst blood vessels crowded Duskmere's silver eyes. With one arm wrapped around Teddy's waist, I clenched my jaw hard enough to snap fangs and pulled. My shoulder joints popped. Brilliant pinpricks of white light exploded behind my eyelids. My boots—designed to grip like a mother—slid forward, but he didn't move.

"What..." I readjusted my feet for leverage. "the hell..." I grunted and strained. "...have you been eating?"

"What did you do?" Oblivious to me, Teddy shouted into the nearly unconscious moon fae's face.

What was happening? Teddy broke up fights like a pro. I'd seen him do it a hundred times. Always calm, collected, efficient—he never lost his cool. *This was not Teddy.*

My gaze skipped wildly over the empty hallway. I spun right, left, behind me. "Iola!" Where did she go? I stomped my foot. "What am I supposed to do here?"

Pushing stars across the sky seemed more attainable. How was Teddy so much stronger than me? Another blood fae could be, sure, but as far as I knew, Teddy was a werewolf. Big and scary, but not this strong.

"Screw it." I shoved my shoulder into Duskmere and slapped Teddy across the face with every ounce of strength I could muster. His head whipped to the side, but his eyes finally focused on something other than the moon fae—me. A shiver of unease gripped me, and my hearts tried to jump from my mouth. His eyes were more bottomless black than white. A thin ring of red pulsed around the outer edge. Something stared out at me, something I'd never seen before, anywhere, ever. The predator inside me said *proceed with caution.*

"What are you?" I whispered and clenched my fists against my chest.

Duskmere gurgled. I rocked on my toes and again lunged for Teddy's arm.

"You're killing him." Duskmere was going boneless. Frantic, I searched the hallway again. No one, but that didn't mean there weren't eyes on the situation. "Shit, you're going to get both of us killed. Let go."

With one final tug, Teddy's arm fell away. He stumbled from Duskmere but remained focused on me, recognition at last registering in his otherworldly gaze. His entire body trembled, and as I watched, the black of his eyes contracted, pulsed, and oozed back to normal.

"Lane. You're okay?" Teddy took me by the shoulders and stared down into my face.

"Am *I* okay?" My voice jumped to an unnatural octave. "I was fine before you showed up. Now, I'm not so sure. What was that? Literally, *what* was that? Because it damn sure wasn't you."

"I'm sorry. I thought you were in trouble. That's not how I wanted you to ever see me. It's been a long time since I lost control, but your sisters said...

then I couldn't find you..." Teddy frowned, and as if afraid of what he'd find written on my face, his gaze slipped from me to the ground.

"You know what, never mind," I said. Too familiar with that look of all-consuming shame, that feeling, my hearts convulsed. I rubbed the heels of my palms against my eyes, momentarily losing myself in the star bursts created by the pressure. "Yeah, I'm fine. I've been taking care of myself for a long time."

"Of course. I'm..." He blew out a breath and dragged his fingers through his hair. "I brought your Bronco back to your house and your sisters were hysterical. They told me what happened, what he did to you, and I promised I'd get you."

"How? It's more than a day's ride on a fast mount."

Teddy shrugged. "I'm faster."

My mouth opened, closed. I threaded my arms across my chest and gave him a long stare. What was he? More importantly, *why did he care what happened to me?* An uncomfortable, unnamable bubble of emotion swelled beneath my sternum.

Behind Teddy, Duskmere slumped on the ground, hugging his knees and coughing. At least he was alive, not that I particularly liked the guy, but Iola would be pissed if he died. I shot another anxious glance around the hallway and frowned. Why hadn't she intervened? Everything I saw of her today indicated she could have returned Teddy to stardust with a snap of her fingers.

I frowned and looked to Teddy. He'd released my shoulders and stepped away to give me space, and thank the stars for that. My body went haywire with him so near. "How'd you find me? This place is a labyrinth. Eodrom isn't exactly small."

"I followed your scent from the courtyard."

"You...what?" Discreet as I could manage—which wasn't discreet at all—I sniffed in the direction of my armpit. Sure, it'd been a bit since I showered, but that wasn't my fault.

Teddy chuckled, and it felt like home. He tucked a strand of hair behind my ear. The tips where his fingers grazed tingled.

I ignored my traitorous body's reaction to his touch and searched the hallway a final time. That female had more tricks than Houdini. "I need to tell Iola what I found before I go."

"Before *we* go," Teddy said and yanked Duskmere to his feet, though the moon fae's legs weren't entirely stable. "Tell this one instead, and we can leave."

Watching Duskmere struggle to steady himself, I felt bad. A little bad. I mean, I wouldn't lose sleep over it.

The moon fae coughed and straightened. "I will..." He flinched, his voice like sandpaper and broken glass. "I will relay the message." He spoke to me but maintained a glare on Teddy that plainly said he wanted to put an ice pick through his face.

I glanced between the two. Teddy didn't bother to acknowledge Duskmere's death stare, and instead wiped his palms on the front of his jeans. *Oh, burn.* The tension surrounding the pair was thick enough to swim in.

"Um, okay." Things were about to get physical, and not in the good way. I edged in front of Teddy to dig the black pebbles from my pocket, and handed them to Duskmere. "Here, I found these. I'm pretty sure I know where they came from, but I don't know how. I'll get in touch later to discuss my theory. I need to sleep on it, and I've got a long ride home."

Duskmere's body went rigid, and he clenched the pebbles in a fist. "This can't be possible."

"I know, right? That's what I said."

"You do not understand what these are." Duskmere's voice was low and urgent.

"Show Lane," Teddy said from behind me. "We need to return home. Show her what the stones are, and then send us back to Interlands."

I sighed at Teddy's high-handed attitude, but I was too tired to make a fuss. Later. After a nap, a trashy reality show with excessive kissing, and at least a dozen Ho Hos.

Duskmere's jaw flexed. His gaze burrowed into mine and slowly drew up to Teddy. The moon fae jerked his chin once in what I suppose was a nod and pulled a small pouch from his belt. He tugged loose the drawstring and turned the pouch over in his hand.

My eyes narrowed on the black pebble that rolled out.

"This will work similar to a homing spell. Using their blood, Moon fae bind to these stones. When someone else activates the stone, that moon fae may open a portal to the location where the stone has been used." He placed what felt and looked like a small, cold marble in my palm. "This is my stone. I am bound to it by my blood."

"Meaning, what? You bled on the stones and poof." I waved my fingers. "It's done?"

"More or less," Duskmere rasped and gingerly pressed his fingertips to his throat. "You do not need knowledge of the binding spell ritual to use the stone. The important thing to understand is that, from the dungeon area where we arrived, I can open a portal to wherever your location may be once you trigger the stone."

Bound by blood. That explained why the finger flipper's scent was so strong on the stones I found, and why this one smelled entirely different. I rolled it between my forefinger and thumb. "No crack."

"No." Duskmere drew his finger across one I'd given him. "The crack indicates it has been used."

My eyebrows shook hands with my hairline. "Uh, I thought this entire realm was warded against portals."

"As did I." The self-loathing tone in Duskmere's voice was something I was too familiar with.

"Can't moon fae just..." I waved my hands in the air. "Open a portal to wherever they want without the use of one of these?"

"It's complicated, but no. That is not how it works." Duskmere rubbed his throat and winced.

A deep red and purple bruise already circled his neck. Oh yeah, that would hurt tomorrow. I was a little bit sorry, but not really. He did force me to walk up the spiraling stairs from Hell—dungeon—same difference—after I fell out of a tree. A really big tree.

"What am I supposed to do with this?" I tucked the pebble into the same pocket I'd used for the others. Teddy shifted behind me, so close his chest brushed my shoulders. Did someone crank up the heat in this joint? Suddenly aware of how narrow this hallway was, I inched away. As much as the heat coming off him latched on and pulled me in, I couldn't get past what I'd just seen him do, what he could be capable of doing. My inner self-preservation—the one I generally ignored—screamed at me to keep my distance. For now, I'd listen.

"If you need me to open a portal, squeeze the stone and then throw it to the ground," Duskmere said. "It can be used one time, so do not use it unless necessary."

I scoffed. "As if I'd ever need your help."

Duskmere exhaled a long, aggrieved breath.

"What if I drop it? I don't need you popping in while I'm in the shower or something."

"Squeeze it and throw it," Duskmere repeated.

I huffed. This would not end well.

Teddy put a hand on my shoulder and every nerve ending in my body sang. I squashed my body's inappropriate desire to soak up his touch and stepped to the side, giving his hand the slip.

"Well, I've—" I began, but Teddy cleared his throat. I rolled my eyes to the ceiling. "*We've* got a long ride. You got mounts we can borrow? And tell my folks to let my sisters know I'm on my way before they show up, too. Trust me, you don't want a pissed off Y'sindra up in here." I might be the resident muscle of YML Investigations, but that snow fairy could wreck a day.

"Send us back," Teddy said. Someone put on their bossy pants today. Lucky for him he wasn't talking to me.

With a groan of pain, Duskmere pushed away from the wall. He gave Teddy another vicious look and then laid his focus on me. "We need to return to the dungeon. I will open a portal from there to send you home."

"Oh, you've got to be shitting me. No. I'm not climbing the Mount Doom of stairs a second time."

"Lead the way," Teddy spoke over me.

My vision pulsed red and for the second time today, I slapped him right across his too-handsome face.

13

I FOUND MY BREATH

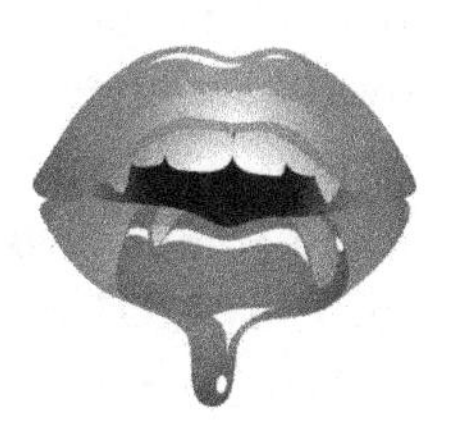

Silence accompanied us through the long descent to the dungeon, leaving me plenty of time to stew while the two males took turns attempting to flay one another with their black looks. I seethed about being dragged through portals, about being underestimated, about never suspecting Teddy was anything but a nice guy with a nicer ass.

Duskmere led us to the same cell he'd shoved me into via a portal, and his raw vocal cords cracked to life. "The portal will only remain open for moments. Move quickly."

"What—" The question died on my tongue as he quite literally unzipped space. From an oval the size of a full-length mirror, the watery light of dawn dripped over my front yard. A laugh bubbled from my chest, and I leaned closer. I'd never get used to this.

"Go," Duskmere ordered.

Teddy put his hand on the small of my back. I sprang forward at the touch and jogged through the portal, into my yard, halfway between my house and the drive. Exactly where Duskmere and I had left the night before.

A communication crystal rolled to a stop against my boot. I reached down to grab the silver crystal and turned it over on my palm, finding the small black *d* etched into its smooth surface. "Attune that to your communication crystal and contact me later," Duskmere said, and the portal snapped closed. Save for the warbling of morning birds, everything was quiet, calm.

I dropped the crystal into the pocket with the stone. The exhaustion of the past day—*days*—crushed me, and my bed called. Turning toward my house, I spotted my Bronco in the driveway parked behind Teddy's dust-covered Ford F-150. The towing chain still connected to his truck lay on the ground. I'd wager he'd only had time to unhitch the tow before my sisters descended on him.

Teddy came around from behind me and stood with hands tucked in his pockets. He angled his face toward the ground, but his dark eyes slid up to me. This was bad. I had a weakness for lost puppies. "Lane, I'm sorry. Your sisters told me what happened, and I…I was worried."

"Yeah, well, I'm sorry too. About the slap, I mean." I squeezed my arms across my chest, fighting the ridiculous urge to hug him, to tell him it was okay. It wasn't okay, and I wasn't a hugger.

"Nothing to forgive. It was necessary." He took a deep breath. My eyes inappropriately fixed on his expanding chest.

"What was that about anyhow? You're the most easy-going guy I know." Already the primal fear that tore through me at the first sight of what lurked beneath his surface had faded, almost forgotten. Thinking about how *other* Teddy had been seemed more dream than memory. "Even when that riot happened in your bar last year, you were ice about it. You got the shit handled."

One shoulder lifted and fell. "Instincts. I thought you were in trouble, and you're important to me. It's part of who I am."

Tired beyond measure, I glanced longingly toward my front porch and slid my hands into my back pockets. "You realize that doesn't make any sense? I know plenty of werewolves, and I can kick their collective asses ten ways to Sunday. Teddy, I couldn't even move your arm."

He gave another one shoulder shrug. "You should stay away from the moon fae."

"What? Wow." My head snapped back. "Way to change the subject."

"I already explained what happened."

This was some bullshit "theys not so easy" half-explanation. I gave him a long look, which he unabashedly met. The questions were all still there, but this was Teddy. The same Teddy I'd known for seven years. "Okay, fine. I'll bite. Why should I stay away from Duskmere? He's not my favorite, especially now, but he's close with my parents. Duskmere is harmless."

Except when he was shoving me from this realm to the next.

Teddy's lips pressed together. He stared into the trees and sighed. "Because I know him, too. Let's just say you'd be better off."

That got my attention. I straightened. "You know Duskmere? How?"

"Story for another time." Teddy scraped his fingers through his hair, a frustrated gesture I'd become all too familiar with over the years.

"I'm holding you to that, but I'll let it go for now." My jaw cracked on a yawn. "Because I need sleep."

Teddy rubbed a hand across his chin. "All right, but we need to talk about why I stopped by last night."

"You said to drop off my Bronco." I waved toward the driveway.

"No, I'd already towed it to the bar and was planning to check if the mud had done any damage. I would have brought it back today, but this sun fae came around asking about you and your sisters."

A bolt of anxiety knifed through me. Instantly alert, I went still. "Tall, dark, copper hair? RFG insignia? Stick up his ass?"

"No RFG, but otherwise, yes. The whole thing felt suspicious. He said he was interested in hiring you, but his questions didn't line up. How often do you travel for jobs? Where do you travel? He asked if I knew where you'd been lately and specifically about your most recent job. What it was, not if you got the job done."

I tugged the edge of my lip beneath a fang and chewed. "Was Duskmere with him?"

"No."

"Okay." Relieved, I pressed a hand to my stomach and nodded. "That's good. Not who I was thinking. It doesn't explain why someone is trying to get all up in our business, but it's better than the alternative."

"He was with a different moon fae. His hair was dark and long, so obviously not Duskmere. I couldn't see his face. He hung out down the street, stayed in the shadows."

My mouth went dry. I swallowed. Not counting Duskmere, that was two moon fae in Interlands in as many days. "How'd you know they were together if the sun fae came in alone?"

"I watched him leave." Teddy frowned into the distance as if picturing what he'd seen. "They weren't obvious about it, but they weren't discreet, either. Not a lot of sun or moon fae outside of Ta'Vale, so they probably didn't think anyone would recognize them or care."

I didn't want to believe it was Duskmere's partner Cirron, not because I liked him and gave a shit, but because this situation was already too complex. We had moon fae opening portals into impossible places, dead banshees, and jilted kelpie princes.

Jilted.

My head jerked up, and excitement fluttered in my stomach. My sisters and I need to pay a visit to Vegas, but if we were being looked into, probably followed, we needed new transportation. "I know I'm asking a lot after everything you've already done, but can I borrow one of your cars?"

Teddy had more than one car. As rowdy as Interlands could get, he made a tidy fortune renting vehicles to tourists who had theirs destroyed or vanished by the locals. Wish I'd thought of doing that first.

"Yeah, of course. Whatever you need, but you should probably get some rest." He dug into his pocket and pulled out his keys.

"No, sorry." I put my hand on his to push back his keys, and my awareness shrank to the feel of his warm hand beneath my palm. My breath hitched, and I swallowed. "Uh, no. Tomorrow, I mean tomorrow. I definitely need rest. Right now, thanks. See you tomorrow. Bye."

On a rush of words, I turned for the front door, but Teddy's strong fingers caught my hand and pulled me around to face him. He chuckled and tickled his fingers down the sides of my ribs to rest at my waist.

Arrows of fire raced through my body. My stomach floated away. Of course I'd had partners before, but this was Teddy, and things with him felt so different. It felt right, good. So good it terrified me. The feeling had been building for some time, but I'd tried to ignore it. I stepped back, but he kept a light hold on my hand and stepped with me.

"Hmm." He stepped closer, and I frowned at his chest, his very broad chest inches from my nose. Teddy wore flannel good. If I undid that top button...

Ugh, down girl. I gave my libido a mental slap.

"Didn't you say you owe me for towing your Bronco?" Teddy's breath rustled the hair at my temple. His fresh, woodsy scent wrapped around my senses.

The desert in my mouth made it impossible to swallow. "Cash only, or do you take check?"

"I think..." Teddy lifted his hands to cup my jaw before starting a slow glide down my neck, my arms. His feather-light touch felt like butterfly kisses on my skin. I shivered. "The cost is going to be steep." He traced my fingers and began the torturous climb back up my arms.

Red alert! I was in big trouble here. My fangs tingled. I licked my lips and watched helplessly as Teddy's face descended toward mine. I had the ridiculous urge to suck on his bottom lip, and not in a blood fae way. Panic overrode reason. I let my knees go soft and started sliding to the ground.

Teddy's grip shifted to my hipbones to stop me from falling. A husky laugh rumbled from his intoxicatingly close chest. It mesmerized me. Every one of my senses became immersed in this male.

"Not so fast, sweet fangs. Do you really want to go? I'll leave now if that's what you want."

My breath hitched, left me. He'd given me an out.

A million answers screamed to be heard, so many excuses to walk away.

I shook my head and all thoughts scattered when his pillow-soft lips met mine. My brain became a wide-open landscape, void of any noise for the first time in days. I found my breath in Teddy when my mouth opened to his.

"Lane!" Mae's voice broke the spell, and I stumbled from Teddy. Footsteps thundered across the front porch. Teddy's hands were slow to fall away. "Oh. You're all right. Um, sorry."

Y'sindra cackled and bobbed into my line of sight. "Told you."

With a groan, I rolled my eyes and looked at Mae.

"We'll see you inside." She began to walk away, but Y'sindra landed by my feet, grinning like a damn fool. Mae hissed, "Y'sindra."

"Fine, but we have questions." She flew after Mae but called to me. "Hurry up will ya? I'll get the DVR fired up. You want popcorn? I'll make us popcorn."

And just like that, I was alone with Teddy again. Heat scorched my cheeks. "Listen, I don't know what this is, but I'm not like Mae. I'm not like most fae. I'm not going to be one of your barfly floozies, so we should nip this in the bud now."

Teddy closed the distance he'd given me when my sisters came out and gently lifted my chin. My breath caught as my gaze met his. I wanted to live in those dark depths.

"Despite what you seem to think, I rarely get involved with anyone. I have lived a long time, and at this point if someone isn't worth the effort, I'm not interested. When I finally saw, really saw, the one female worth the effort, there hasn't been anyone else."

My fists curled on a rush of intense possessiveness. Who was she? I would... His gaze dug into mine, driving home the meaning of his words. Holy Twinkies, he meant me.

"Oh," I managed to say around the knot of confused emotion in my throat. With my tattletale complexion, he'd see the mortification written all over my flaming face. I tried to turn my head. His fingers slid from my chin to my cheek and then returned to his pocket.

He backed away, and the bubble of tension between us popped. The tightness in my lungs released, and I gasped.

"Listen, I've known for a long time, but I understand it took you awhile. This," he paused to gesture from him to me. "This is new for you."

"You knew what?" I frowned and hugged my arms across my chest. "What are you talking about?"

"You'll figure it out, Lane. I'm going to give you the space to do that. I want this to be a mutual..." Teddy took his time. "Craving."

He said it like he tasted the word, and it was delicious. Phantom fingers tripped down my spine, and I shivered.

As Teddy started walking toward his truck, like it always did, my lusty gaze dropped to enjoy the way he filled out his denim. He stopped by his bumper and turned abruptly.

I groaned. Of course he caught me taking in an eyeful. A fresh wave of heat toasted my cheeks.

"Don't worry, everything stays the same until you say otherwise. I'm not going to push you." He flashed a wolfish grin and had the audacity to wink. He opened the door and hopped into his Jeep.

I unfolded my arms and slid my hands into my front pockets as Teddy started the SUV. My hearts squeezed as my fingertips grazed the folded note.

The window rolled down, and Teddy rested his elbow on the frame. "I'll have a car ready for you tomorrow. See you then, sweet fangs."

The Jeep rolled down the dirt drive, sending dust into the sky, and he was gone. I stared at the empty drive, not sure what just happened. But something did.

Something in the foundation of the architecture of my life had shifted.

14

THEY CALL ME MONSTER

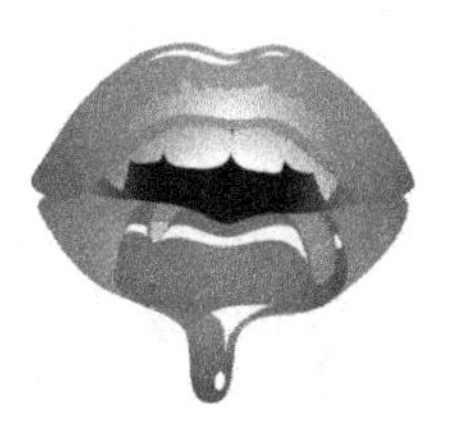

THE SALTY, BUTTERY SCENT OF POPCORN FILLED THE HOUSE. MY FAVORITE soft blankets were piled on the plaid sofa I refused to part with. On the television screen, unnaturally beautiful men and women wearing barely there beach attire and drinking champagne were frozen mid-toast on some tropical beach. My sisters' bantering voices floated in from the kitchen. Something tugged in my chest, and I blew out a shaky breath. Stars, I didn't deserve them, and I'd spend every day making sure they never regretted following me from Ta'Vale.

I padded across the wooden floors to the river rock fireplace where the broken arm of the sundial hung above the mantle. My pulse thumped in the base of my throat. Iola said she carried me to my family. I'd never considered what my family suffered seeing me unconscious, impaled on a four-foot length of petrified wood.

Reaching up, I traced the bright red streaks of my lifeblood preserved beneath a thick layer of clear shellac. After the accident, I wouldn't let them throw it away, and I wouldn't let them clean it. Instead, I'd insisted on having resin laid over the evidence of my almost-death. *Never forget.*

They call me monster, but it's monsters who haunt my nightmares, hands slamming into my back, the inexorable tilt over the side of the sun bridge, the moment of breathlessness when my feet still touched something solid as my body fought the inevitable grip of gravity. The screaming wind against my face, and the ground below rushing to greet me.

The microwave door banged. Seconds later came a curse, and I winced as a piece of our dishware shattered on the floor.

"Y'sindra! Those bowls are too big for you," Mae screeched. "That's two this week. I swear I'm replacing everything with plastic."

"No, it's not too big, the counter's slippery."

Their bickering voices overlapped one another, shoving the bitter memories to the back of my brain. I took a deep breath. It was good to be home.

The three-foot fairy teetered in with her arms wrapped around a bowl twice the size of her head. She couldn't see past it, but she managed to get it onto the coffee table and spotted me by the mantle. "What are you doing? Get over here and tell us what happened." Folding her wings tight to her back, she pulled herself onto the sofa and patted the cushion. "Buttercup will be in here soon. You know how she is."

"I heard that." Mae poked her head out of the kitchen. "Sorry, Laney, be there in a minute. Almost done cleaning *someone's* mess."

Y'sindra's eyes made an exaggerated circuit around their sockets.

My damp hair soaked the thin material of the over-sized T-shirt my sisters had laid out, along with matching fuzzy cat slippers, while I'd been in the shower. The fact Mae had ventured into my disaster zone of a room spoke to how worried they'd been.

Shivering from the chill my wet hair brought on, I pulled a second blanket to my chin.

Y'sindra propped against the opposite arm of the sofa to face me, legs running parallel to mine. Under the blankets her feet nudged my knee.

"You call Mom and Dad?" I tugged the blanket back that shifted when Y'sindra squirmed beneath. "Did you tell them I'm okay?"

"Sure did. It was Duskmere, so Dad wasn't worried." Y'sindra tore into a Snoball, her undisputed favorite food group. Coconut shavings clung to her lips as she chewed a big bite of chocolate cake and spongy marshmallow frosting.

Mae appeared in her Dalmatian-print onesie carrying a plate of sliced fruit. She bypassed the love seat to set the plate in front of the sofa. "Apparently the words portal and kidnapped didn't faze Dad."

I pulled my legs up, giving her space between Y'sindra and me. "Did you tell him about Etta'wy and the moon fae? That he had the corruption?"

"Yes." Mae reclined between us, meticulously arranging the nest of blankets as she did. "He said he trusted you would handle it."

"That makes one of us." I stretched my legs across Mae's lap.

Y'sindra pushed against my feet with her own. "Three of us. We believe in ya."

"Sending Teddy after me isn't the best affirmation of faith."

"We didn't send him. We told him what happened, and he took off." Mae studied the orange slice she'd plucked from the plate. "Although, promises to bring you home might have been made. My memory's foggy."

I sobered at the sight of the citrus wedge. It reminded me of Iola and my visit to the garden. I let out a tight laugh. "Here's a fun fact. If Duskmere ever offers you a portal to Ta'Vale, avoid it at all costs. It leads to the dungeons."

"They have a dungeon?" Y'sindra dug into the popcorn. "Tell us everything."

"Not much to tell. There are ten thousand stairs between the dungeon and the central courtyard, and oh by the way, did you know moon fae live there, too?"

"Yes," Mae said and shrugged at my incredulous look. "The dungeons aren't secret, and neither are the moon fae. I spent a lot of time inside the central palace and ran into them often. You already know most uncorrupted moon fae fled to Eodrom, seeking amnesty from the sun fae during the Great Fae Divide. Some returned to Lann Ridge after the war, when the corrupted were banished. Most stayed in the Grian Valley."

"I knew about the amnesty, but that was over a hundred years ago." Sitting up, the blanket pooled in my lap. "I assumed... I don't know what I assumed. I never thought about it. Wow, I'm a selfish ass."

Mae reached over and squeezed my hand. "No one's judging, and you aren't selfish. You avoided Eodrom for good reason, so why would you know?"

"Bunch of court bullshit." Y'sindra toasted me with her third Snoball. "May Fenrir eat them all."

"Hmm, speaking of the court and the unavoidable, I met Iola." I filled my sisters in on my conversation about royal titles, keepers, and singing stones. "Oh, and Dad isn't the only one related to the first keepers. Mom is too."

"Mom, too?" Y'sindra gave a long, low whistle. "So, you're a full-fledged royal. Do I have to bow when I enter the room now?"

I bounced a grape off her forehead. "I just told you that's not how it works."

Mae was quiet, eyes on her lap. One arm hugged her middle while she chewed on the thumbnail of the other hand.

"Hey, what's wrong?" I nudged her hand from her mouth with my toe.

"Oh, sorry, it's nothing. Chipped nail, and I didn't want to get up." She sighed and slumped in her seat. "And I'm thinking about dropping the queen in Queen Iola. That's going to be hard."

I relaxed back against my side of the sofa and chuckled. "Yeah, it's gonna be torture for you."

"Well, I understand why Queen—" Mae's lips mashed together, and she shook her head. Poor thing looked like she'd swallowed a bug. "Why Iola instructed Duskmere to bring you. Dad would have told her what we do. Easy to see why they'd turn to the one fae they know who can get inside the crime scene and have a shot at figuring out what happened."

That was Mae, perceptive as hell.

"So." Y'sindra prodded my leg with her jabby little toes. "Don't keep us in suspense. What did you find? I flew over the garden once, as close as I could get before some invisible barrier stopped me. Those things are huge. Stonehenge kind of huge. No idea how anyone could jack them."

"They're still there. Parts of them are. Whoever took them cracked the sun stones in half and mysteriously made off with the broken pieces." A vacuum of anxious silence filled the room. I took a deep breath and looked first to Y'sindra and then held Mae's gaze. "What's left in the garden are dying."

Mae's hands flew to her mouth, and she bolted upright in her seat, knocking my legs to the floor and forcing Y'sindra to sit up.

"How?" Y'sindra whispered. Her wings shivered, dusting the sofa with snowflakes.

"I don't know, but you're not going to believe this. Somehow the moon fae who killed our banshee is involved."

Mae gasped.

"Bullshit," Y'sindra exclaimed.

"It's true. He left a trail of blood during our chase, and I got his scent." The black stone Duskmere had given me sat on the coffee table. I showed it to my sisters and explained how it worked. "I found two used portal stones in the garden, but there could be more. My search was interrupted because someone let a crazy werewolf track me down."

"First, you didn't seem to mind." Y'sindra teased. "Second, if Teddy's a werewolf, call me Tinkerbell."

Y'sindra meant business. Her hate for the company who had turned the fictional fairy into a glitter-sprinkling joke was strong. "How do you know he's not a werewolf?"

She shrugged. "I don't know what he is, but it's obvious he's no pup. No wet dog smell, and he never went wolfy to control bar brawls."

All valid points, but I wasn't ready to concede. Until proven otherwise, I would maintain my theory that Teddy was a werewolf. A super strong, super alpha werewolf. "Okay, Tinkerbell, that doesn't mean a thing."

"Did he go furry?" Mae asked.

"No." I drew out the word. "He turned into something else, although *turned* isn't the right word. It was still Teddy, but something more."

Mae swiveled to face me. "What do you mean? Did he physically change?"

"Not entirely, no. When I first saw him, he had Duskmere pinned against the wall, choking him. Nearly killed the guy." I scraped my tongue across the back of my teeth. "I couldn't get through to Teddy, couldn't even budge him."

That got their attention. Both of my sisters leaned toward me. I couldn't sustain feats of strength for long, but in bursts, I could move anything. Okay, not anything, but close. I traced my fingers over the worn hem of the blanket and recounted everything to my sisters.

Mae broke into a fit of laughter. "You," she chortled. "You slapped him?"

"Told you." Y'sindra tapped her nose. "Not a werewolf. If he was, you'd be short a hand."

The glare I sent her would have turned a lesser fairy to ash.

She shrugged. "Or he'd be dead because he tried to take your hand"

"That's more like it," I agreed and glanced at Mae.

Preoccupied with wiping tears of laughter from her beneath her lashes, shook her head. "Don't look at me."

"I'm looking at you because of the three of us, you're the one who reads auras."

"Okay, fine." She studied her nails. "His aura is different. Dark as a starless night and there are ruby-red sparks swirling inside of it."

"Like his eyes." I focused on my fingers twitching over the edge the blanket and asked Mae, "Is that normal?"

"No," she admitted. "Certainly not for a werewolf. Since Earth is a magic-less realm, human auras are muted. Lycanthropy is a magic disease, though. Werewolves are human, so their auras are still dull, but they're mottled, like a bruise. I always assumed Teddy was some mega-alpha." Mae kicked her feet out to rest her heels on the mismatched burgundy ottoman.

Apparently, before this, Mae had been of the same opinion as me. I tucked this new bit of info about Teddy away to mull over later. We had bigger things to worry about.

"Teddy's not important—"

"Looked pretty important to us." Y'sindra pushed my legs with her feet.

"Lane's right," Mae said. "We've got to figure out what happened to the sun stones. I assume you're in this now?"

I sighed but nodded.

"Good. You have a plan?"

Of course, Mae would have that level of faith in me. Fortunately, I did have a plan.

"First I eat, drown my brain in reality TV, and sleep." True to my word, I grabbed the popcorn, television remote, and stretched across my sisters on the sofa. "Tomorrow we go to Vegas. The moon fae and Etta'wy are connected. We know she visited someone at the Blackthorne regularly, but we don't know a thing about him. It's time we figure out this mystery man."

15

GET TO THE JUICY STUFF

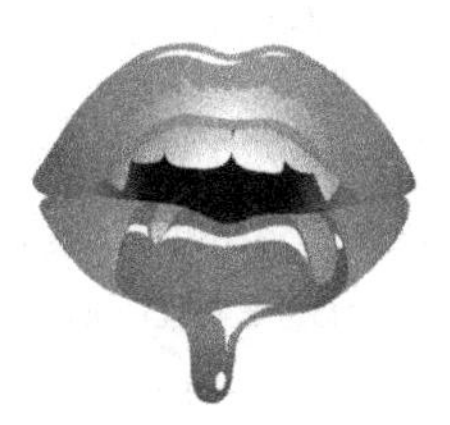

"We have two working vehicles, so tell me again why we need to borrow Teddy's car?" Mae asked as she dug a matte black tube from her purse. Today she toted a glossy white-vinyl purse shaped like a sunflower. Flipping down the sun visor, she went to work applying a new shade of sapphire blue lipstick in the moving SUV like a pro. Only Mae would doll up her appearance before a job where fists might fly, but the color totally matched her eyes.

"She wants to play kissy-face with her new boyfriend before we hit the road." Y'sindra made kissing noises on her hand.

I shook my head but didn't respond to her taunt. My sister needed no encouragement to be a grade-A pain in the ass. When I didn't rise to the bait, she went back to braiding my hair. Despite the jostling of the moving vehicle, Y'sindra was still freakishly good at styling hair. If the investigations business ever went belly-up, she had a future as a hair stylist.

"Because," I said, keeping my focus on the road. If I hit a pothole while Mae was applying lipstick, this day would be miserable. "I suspect we're being followed, and we need something that won't be recognized."

Y'sindra dropped my hair and became a whirlwind bouncing across the backseat, pressing her tip-tilted nose to every window. "I don't see anything." She resumed her position wedged between me and Mae and went back to work.

In my peripheral, Mae twisted the lipstick tube, clicked the cap into place, and returned it to her purse. Despite my argument that we didn't know what we were walking into and should dress accordingly, my fashion-obsessed sister had, no surprise, ignored me. I drummed my fingers on the steering wheel. She wore a cream tunic with a blue camisole beneath, and cream shorts decorated with lipstick-matching blue flowers. She'd topped the ensemble off with, of all things, gladiator-style sandals laced to her kneecaps. Ridiculous things.

In contrast, I'd stomped as much dried mud from my combat boots as I could manage and pulled on a black T-shirt that read *If zombies chase us, I'm tripping you*—true statement. I'd traded my denim for thick but pliable leather pants designed for fighting. Emphasizing the fighting aspect, dual thigh sheaths were sewn into the pants, each holding a push dagger. I was a strong believer in never leaving home without a blade.

"What makes you think we're being followed? There hasn't been another vehicle on the road since we left home." Mae dropped her bag into the footwell and twisted in her seat to face me. "Explain."

"We never got to the conversation I had with Teddy last night."

"Or the kissing. We didn't talk about the kissing." Y'sindra's feet drummed against the center console.

"You were so tired, I wanted to let you sleep. Someone else," Mae hooked her thumb over her shoulder, "has been so out of her mind since Duskmere took you, she drove herself to exhaustion. She passed out about the same time you did. It was cute."

"Whatever." Y'sindra flopped against the backseat. Few insults were worse than cute when it came to my snow fairy sister.

I blew her a kiss in the rearview mirror. She snorted, but her mouth kicked up at the corner.

"So, what did Teddy have to say?" Mae asked. "After he rescued you, of course."

"He didn't rescue me." I cut my sister a sharp glare. "What he did was turn into someone I don't know and create a helluva scene. I think he scared Iola away. Great first impression."

"I won't apologize for being upset when Teddy showed up. Duskmere had pushed you through a portal. You both vanished," Mae chided.

"Fair point, sorry." I cranked the wheel left, turning off the single-lane dirt road that led from our property onto Palmetto. At the edge of downtown Interlands, it was semi-maintained. The potholes were filled at least once a year. "Teddy told me the reason he came by yesterd—"

"Technically day before yesterday, and to drop off your Bronco. We know. Get to the juicy stuff." Not one to be left out, Y'sindra crawled back onto the center console and resumed braiding.

"He came by to tell us a sun fae dropped by the bar asking weird questions."

Mae gave a startled gasp but recovered quickly. "Well, it could be coincidence."

"Doubt it. I can count on two hands the number of sun fae I've seen since we moved here." Poor Mae and her eternal optimism. "Teddy said he had copper hair. How many sun fae do you know with dark copper hair?"

"Not many." Mae clacked a freshly painted fingernail against her teeth. "It doesn't make any sense though. I suppose he could have been trying to get a sense of whether he could trust us. This is a sensitive deal. I imagine the RFG, and whoever else is in the know, wouldn't want it leaked that the sun stones are missing."

"Could be." I took the turn onto Root, the main road running from Ta'Vale, through Interlands, all the way to the Las Vegas strip. Y'sindra teetered backward along with my hair.

"Watch it before you lose more hair," she grumbled and used my braid to Rapunzel herself back onto the center console.

"You don't think it's a coincidence, do you?" Mae fanned the hem of her billowy tunic over her lap.

"Nope." I flexed my neck to get a little slack into Y'sindra's tight braids. "Teddy said the sun fae asked a lot of suspicious questions. Not the type of thing a potential client would ask, like our success rate, work ethic, or even fees. More about our daily routines and our travel."

"Not a smoking gun," Mae said. "But suspicious."

"There was a moon fae waiting for him outside, and it wasn't Duskmere." I dropped that bomb.

Look-on-the-bright-side, Mae diffused it. "Lots of moon fae live in Eodrom. I'm sure there is more than one in the RFG."

There was. I'd met one, and she was a judgmental bitch.

It wasn't quite nine a.m., and I managed to snag a parallel parking spot near the bar. It helped that it was too early for the afternoon tourists on the hunt for something more dangerous than roulette, and too late for the night crowd to be heading home.

A cloud of dust swallowed my feet as I hopped down from the Bronco. I stepped onto the cobblestone sidewalk—the single concession made to gentrify Interlands for the tourists—and studied the street. There had been a total of five other vehicles on the road between home and here, but I had spotted neither a sun nor moon fae in any of them. Realistically, I didn't think they'd be driving. Seeing as vehicles didn't work in Ta'Vale, and sun fae rarely visited Interlands, they had no reason to own one. Plus, the more obvious reason—Teddy hadn't mentioned it.

"Out of the way ladies. Time to get my drink on." Y'sindra pushed her way past Mae and me and headed toward the front entrance of the bar.

"Berries only," I shouted after her. "We need you sober."

I shook my head in exasperation and pointed several blocks away at the grocer, creatively named Groceries. "That's where Teddy said the moon fae waited for Cirron."

"If it was Cirron." Mae's lips pursed, creating waves in her blue lipstick. "Let's not toss around accusations until we have proof."

I glanced at the cloudless sky. Feeling uncharacteristically bold and confident this morning, I wore clear lenses designed to protect my pupils against the painful rays of the sun but not to disguise the color of my eyes. Mom had them made for me and sent them along with my sisters after I moved. Seven years later, I'd finally worked up the courage to wear them.

"I haven't seen anything to indicate we're being followed." I nibbled the edge of my lip and frowned at Mae. "I've got this feeling, though. Maybe I'm crazy."

"You aren't. Remember the conversations with Mom and Dad you were sure someone was listening in on? Makes a lot more sense now."

My neck itched, and I cupped a hand over the spot. "Let's make this quick."

"That's what she said." Mae broke into a fit of giggles at her not-so-clever joke.

I groaned. This was going to be a long day.

"Watch Y'sindra?" I asked Mae.

She busied herself smoothing and fluffing her tissue-thin tunic until it laid just so. "Of course. So, you're going to talk to Rip after you get the keys and then we go?"

"That's the plan."

"You really think he can help?" Mae finished her ensemble by fitting the sunflower purse strap crosswise over her body.

"Definitely. That ogre has his finger in so many pies. He's sent me after people you wouldn't believe."

"But will he help?" Mae tugged her tunic free of the crease her purse strap made.

"With the right bait he will." I shrugged into a different jacket woefully lacking in pocket space, but at least it wasn't ventilated. "This should be quick. Get Y'sindra and meet me by Rip's booth. I asked Teddy to park near the rear exit."

Mae headed across the sidewalk and into the bar with me following.

The doors swished shut behind me, but I only had eyes for the bar. Teddy wasn't there. A pang of disappointment pinched inside my chest. Zee glanced up at my approach and slid across the counter from me. The rainbow-haired bartender gave me the once over, a slow smile tilting her lips. She nodded toward the stairs leading to a handful of rooms for rent—and Teddy's apartment. My mouth went dry.

"Sweetheart, I don't know what you two got up to, but he's been out since he got back from your place." She leaned her elbows on the bar and rested her chin in her hands. "Tell me everything."

The sting of a blush lit my cheeks, and with Y'sindra's fancy braid, I had no hair to hide behind.

"Nothing to tell."

"Pity. The big guy never shows interest in the ladies. I'd hoped you two..." Her words trailed off with X-rated implications.

"Sorry to disappoint." I swiped a hand over my lips. My neck and chest flamed remembering the interrupted kiss with Teddy.

Zee wagged her gold-studded brows. "You sure nothing happened?"

I gave her a blank stare and drilled my talons on the counter.

She chuckled and held her hands up, palms out. "Okay, I'll drop it." She winked. "For now. Next ladies' night, all bets are off."

"With promises like that, I feel the flu coming on." I fake-coughed.

"Sorry, sister. Not buyin' it. You never get sick. Oh, here." Zee walked to the register and pulled an envelope from the till. Hips swinging, the outrageously curvy she-wolf returned and slid the bulging packet in front of me. "Boss said this was for you. He also said you can go give him a kiss goodbye."

"What?" A wave of heat to rival the Mojave rolled down my body.

"You should see your face. Tells me everything I need to know." Zee howled with laughter and slapped the counter. "I made that last bit up, but he did say he'll see you when you get back tonight."

Lips curling up, I bared my fangs at her. Zee pinched my cheek and sauntered away to attend to her thirsty customers. Inside the envelope was a chrome key chain with a black wolf's head and a GM key attached. Interesting choice of cars. I slid the envelope into my jacket pocket.

Rip waved to me from his booth, cradling a whole pot of coffee in his other hand. And my sisters thought I had a caffeine problem.

"Yous needed to see me?" he asked as I slid into the u-shaped booth. I sat on the end, while Rip's massive form took up the entire curve.

"Yeah, appreciate you getting up early to meet me. I need a favor."

With a meaty finger, he stroked his square, hairless chin. "What I get from this favor?"

I'd thought about this. What I needed was important, but as Mae said, this was a sensitive case. I had to tread carefully. "First, you tell me if you can help me. If you can, we'll talk trade."

Rip lifted the pot of coffee and sipped through a straw. I struggled to keep a straight face, despite the horrible slurping noises. "Okay. I know yous. What yous need?"

"I need a contact at the Blackthorne. Someone who can get me into a room." I bit my lip. "Here's the tricky part, it's one of the floors that requires an elevator code."

"Yous want in a VIP resident room?" The booth back whimpered as Rip thumped against it. "That's a big ask."

I nodded. "I've got a big scoop for the books if you can help."

More than one head turned at Rip's booming laughter. He dragged his sausage fingers beneath his eyes and slurped from the coffee pot straw. "This why I like yous. Yous know the way to my heart. Okay, yeah. Lucky for yous, I got someone who owes me big. Couple more weeks and I'd send yous anyhow."

"So, we call this good? You don't need the tip?"

"Yous know better, but whatever it is, I'll cut yous in." Rip sipped his coffee—less sip, more guzzle.

Catching Mae's eye, I waved her over. Y'sindra stayed where she'd planted herself next to a tray of drink accoutrements.

"Ready?" she asked me and watched in fascination while the ogre sucked down the last drops of his pot.

"Almost." Scoping out the room to make sure all eyes had turned away, I handed Mae the envelope containing the borrowed car key. "Grab the fairy before she eats all the maraschino cherries and meet out back."

Mae peeked in the envelope. She nodded and headed for Y'sindra, who saw her coming and quickly shoved a fistful of cherries in her mouth.

Time to get down to business. I clicked a talon on the tabletop and laid out the details I'd decided were safe to share with Rip. "Here's the deal. No one knows this yet, but Etta'wy's dead."

"I knew yous a bad girl." Rip tapped his bulbous nose and pointed at me.

For crying out loud. "Wasn't me. A corrupted moon fae did the deed. No idea where he came from, how he got here, or how he tracked her to my back yard. Last I saw him he was hopping a portal to who the hell knows where. The sun fae want him, and I plan to deliver him to them."

Rip pulled out a pad and flipped it open. He grinned at me and started scribbling. "That's good stuff. In fact, I's not takin' a bet from yous. I's give you a percentage. One percent. That kind of bet, yous lookin' at an easy ten thou."

I choked. "Ten thousand dollars? You said one percent."

"Made more off the banshee take down. I's told you, I's make good money off yous. Outcome's not predictable, but the house—that's me—wins most of the time." His thick lips stretched in a smug smile.

"Who says ogres aren't smart?"

Rip chuckled and scribbled on the legal-sized note pad. He ripped off the paper and slid it to me. "The name. Good luck."

I stood, rapped my knuckles on the tabletop, and strode for the employee-only exit. Between me and daylight was a storage cellar and two walk-in coolers.

When I crossed the threshold into the hallway, I couldn't resist one final look. My gaze climbed to the second floor. There he was—Teddy with tousled hair fresh from the pillow, an unbuttoned flannel, and gray sweatpants riding wickedly low on his lean hips. He lifted a hand and mouthed, "Tonight."

My breath quickened with my pulse. A flush rolled over my skin. I wasn't afraid of much, but this thing with Teddy terrified me.

He stretched and the flannel opened to reveal a toned chest and rock-hard abs. Lots of abs. The shirt fell into place and my eyes snapped from his torso to his face. He laid a brain-melting smile on me and nodded toward the stairs. An invitation.

With no shame, I turned and fled.

16

I'D JUST EAT YOU

The atomic orange '99 Firebird Trans Am roared down the road, eating up the miles. We'd made it to the outskirts of town in under fifteen minutes.

Mae busied herself opening the glove compartment, flipping the visor, and digging into every nook and cranny she could find. My insatiably curious sister's roaming hands finally reached the thing I knew she'd been dying to get to.

"You going to push it?" Mae asked and flicked the yellow sticky note on the radio. Teddy had exchanged the vintage knob and button tuning system for something sleek, shiny, and modern.

"Hmm." I'd spotted the note as soon as I slid into the driver's seat. It read *PLAY ME* and featured a smiley face with hearts for eyes beneath. I didn't do adorable, but this was that, and I liked it.

A snore trumpeted behind me. Y'sindra was sacked out under the rear window, and it kept frosting up. I jabbed the rear defrost button again.

Mae groaned. "Well, if you won't, I will." She hit play.

Bon Jovi "You Give Love a Bad Name" blared from the speakers below Y'sindra. She shrieked and surged up, spraying snow and thwapping her forehead against the inclined window above her.

Mae and I looked at one another and broke into fits of laughter. Despite the dusting of snow on my shoulders, a kernel of warmth bloomed in my chest and spread through my body.

"That male's humor." Mae's shoulders shook with laughter. "You better hold onto him."

My fingers flexed on the steering wheel, and I smiled. Based off the kiss still tingling on my lips, I'd be holding on for longer than my sister could guess. Longer than I was yet ready to admit.

"Thor's tiny testicles," Y'sindra cursed and rubbed her head. Wings folded and tucked tight to her body, she rolled from the window ledge and into the backseat that couldn't fit anyone much larger than a fairy. She smacked my shoulder. "Thanks."

"Hey, that was all Mae, and didn't I tell you to wipe that curse from your Rolodex of foul-mouthed slurs?" I scowled at Y'sindra in the rear view. It was all fun and games until the subject of said curse showed up on the doorstep intent on proving his "hammer" didn't lack for size. Norse mythology was alive and well in the Drifta mountains, Y'sindra's homeland.

She grumbled and pulled her knees to her chest, an unseemly thing to do, considering her typical baby doll dress. I didn't need a view of her skull and crossbones knickers.

We sailed past a large green sign declaring *Las Vegas Twenty Miles* in reflective lettering. I shifted in the black leather seat, a stupid smile still lingering on my face. Even Y'sindra's deliberate kicks to the back of my seat didn't faze me. I couldn't be sure what this thing with Teddy would turn out to be. It terrified me and thrilled me in a hands-to-the-sky, top-of-a-roller coaster sort of way. I did love a good coaster.

Ahead, nearly undetectable, the road wavered like hot asphalt beneath a blistering sun. It wasn't the sun, it was the border—the tear in the veil between Interlands and Las Vegas—or more accurately, Ta'Vale and Earth. Interlands was a buffer of space between the two, the universe's way of ensuring two realms don't collide with one another.

The border offered no resistance, and we slid across smooth as creamy peanut butter. Root, the main road that ran from Earth all the way through Interlands and to Ta'Vale, would dump us out east of State Route 604—Las Vegas Boulevard. Earth side of Root was paved because humans paved everything.

Very few human developers braved the possibility of an expanding Interlands border, but over the years as the border remained where it was, more and more developments spilled closer and closer to Interlands. Aside from a hamburger joint right outside of the Interlands border, there was still miles of open desert dotted with cacti, clusters of fat-limbed elephant trees, and the flowering branches of desert ironwoods.

I dropped a lead foot on the gas until we hit traffic waiting to turn onto the Strip. The Firebird idled through the long line, slowly creeping toward the stoplight at about five minutes per precious inch. Foot traffic clogged the intersection, and Mae busied herself flirting through the passenger window with the sappy-eyed humans struck dumb by her big blue eyes and gracefully pointed ears.

Y'sindra wedged her shoulders between Mae and me. "It's getting close to lunch. I say we hit the Noodle Shop when we get to Blackthorne."

Mae pursed her lips. "It's not even ten-thirty."

"Yeah, almost lunchtime."

I drummed my fingers on the wheel. Still idling in place four cars from the turn, I angled toward Mae and gave her a sheepish smile. "I'm not, *not* hungry. I forgot to eat breakfast."

Mae's generous lips flattened into a tight line. "When we're done. Hopefully this won't take long."

"Okay, Mom." Traffic moved, and I rolled forward a whole car length. "I take that back, Mom would encourage us to eat."

Ahead, the signal arrow turned green and stayed long enough to navigate onto the boulevard. Fortunately, Root took us to within blocks of the Blackthorne Casino and Resort, on the northeast end of the Strip.

Smaller towers housing everything from a parking garage, an amphitheater, and high-end shops surrounded the main building, which was crowned by an inexplicably lush garden. In the early afternoon light, the tall building cast a spindly shadow over its neighbor, the Wynn.

The Blackthorne's mysterious and magical air fed the delight of humans, but it catered to the supernatural with everything from specialized food and beverage to the "No Humans Allowed" entertainment rooms. Considering the wide bands of deep reddish-brown wood that flanked its main entrance ran from the ground to the sky garden and never rotted, it was a safe bet at least one of the owners was also fae.

I turned right onto the long arm of a U-shaped drive leading to the covered front entrance. A large group of humans stepped from the curb, but when I didn't slow down they quickly reconsidered. The Trans Am screeched to a diagonal halt in front of the valet stand. I left the car idling and rounded the trunk as the valet, a hunky young thing, was waylaid by Mae.

She might be all business, but a pretty face was my perpetually horny sister's Achilles' heel. I hooked Mae's waist with an arm and peeled her away.

Giving Mae a shove toward the casino entrance, I slipped the valet the keys and a hundred-dollar bill, courtesy of the grounders. "Park it in the VIP section. We won't be long."

Y'sindra fluttered to my side. "A hundred?"

"Ten spaces in the VIP lot and only two open." I nodded to the small, private parking area adjacent to the loop. "I don't want to wait thirty minutes for our car when we're done. Do you?"

"Guess not," she conceded and dropped to the ground to walk.

We strode toward the casino's massive revolving doors. All three of us stepped inside the same pie-wedge partition wide enough to fit a party of ten, or a single ogre. Maybe two.

The casino was cool and comfortably lit with soft, artificial light. The enormous entry featured polished wood floors that to the left led to the typical carpet of colorful whorls meant to disguise dropped casino chips. While to the right was a deep green, slate blue, and copper shaded carpet featuring a barely there layer of memory foam. The clever design kept the long queues of guests comfortable, and more patient, while they waited to reach the bank of check-in counters manned by both fae, humans, and human supernaturals. Massive chandeliers that appeared to be upside down trees adorned with fae lights hung from the high, half-dome ceiling.

While Y'sindra and I went left, Mae veered right. She bypassed the lines and headed straight for customer service. Heads turned, but no one objected. When Mae approached the desk, I nodded Y'sindra toward the closest bank of slots where I could keep an eye on Mae and wait.

Y'sindra plopped down at the machine next to me. A frizzy-haired lady in a hot pink velour track suit with a voucher in one hand and a platinum membership card in the other was a fraction of a second too late confiscating the same spot.

"What?" My comically evil sister laid a wicked mean-girl stare on the woman. "Move along. This seat is mine, honey. Be glad I'm only taking the seat and not your coins, too."

"I never..." The lady reeled back.

"Well now you have." Y'sindra continued to stare her down.

The woman huffed and stupidly opened her mouth, but I needed to cut this off before it escalated.

"Word to the wise, lady. You're in a fae establishment. Don't fuck with the fae. This fairy could turn you into an ice sculpture. Oh, and me?" I flashed her a fang-heavy grin. "I'd just eat you."

The woman turned a shade paler with each declaration. Her eyes wobbled between us. She spun abruptly and bolted.

"Tourists," I said and turned to find Y'sindra holding out her hand.

"Got twenty bucks?"

The fun-sized troublemaker liked gambling almost as much as berry-booze.

"Mae won't be long." I leaned to the side for a view of the front desk and sure enough, she was already crossing the lobby with a man in a light gray suit at war with his considerable muscles. Mae was one smooth talker.

"Fine." Y'sindra slumped in the high-backed chair and drummed her heels against the seat.

Mae bumped a hip against my chair and spun it toward her. "Lane, this is Vaughn."

"Is there a problem here?" The man's voice was as deep as he was tall—a good four or five inches taller than Mae. He wore his dark blond hair in a long ponytail tied off at his nape and kept his posture stiff.

"No problem. Just a misunderstanding." My eyes climbed to his face and were met by dark gray irises set in astonishingly white orbs crisscrossed with a road map of blood vessels. Correction, not a man. A vampire. Awesome. Bunch of angsty assholes. The guy's pink complexion screamed well fed, but vampires flocked to Vegas for that reason—lots of willing throats. Unlike blood fae, vamps needed the red nectar to survive.

I stifled my groan and pasted on a plastic smile. "Hi, I'm Lane. You met Mae, and this is Y'sindra."

Y'sindra mumbled a lackluster greeting and continued to glare in the direction of the long-gone woman.

"Your delightful sister tells me you are here on behalf of Rip."

Mae patted the vampire's impressive forearm. She beamed up at Vaughn, and his lips twitched into a smile before settling back into their rigid, no-nonsense line. My sister could charm the pelt from a werewolf and apparently, the fangs from a vampire.

"We are." I didn't stand. Threats issued from a seated position was a total power play. "Rip promises to forgive your debts if you help us out."

Vaughn's nostrils pinched. His chin tilted back, and he stared down his Roman nose at me. "I'm listening."

The anticipation billowing off him was palpable. Oh, he wanted this bad. Mr. Vampire must be in deep with Rip.

I unzipped my jacket pocket and pulled out my phone. My finger swiped across the screen until I came to the single shot of the man Etta'wy came here to meet. I turned the screen to face Vaughn. "Can you get us access to this man's apartment?"

Shaking his head, the vampire took a jittery step back. "No. I can't do that."

Weird reaction.

"Listen," I said, stood, and followed him as he retreated another step. "I'm here as the nice guy asking for a favor today. If I go home without what I want, I'm going to be back next week to collect what you owe Rip. In full. And I promise, there won't be anything nice about that visit."

Vaughn's big-boy bluster vanished. Droplets of blood sweat peeked on his brow. "I can't."

I leaned in more and whispered. "If I have to come back, I'm going to remember you could have helped me."

Y'sindra whistled. "Bad news, buddy."

Mae pressed against the vampire's side. "You definitely don't want that."

The vampire's dark pupils expanded and contracted while his flickering gaze tripped from each of my sisters to me. He might be tough, but of the two of us, I was the bigger predator and clearly, he knew it.

"If he finds out..." Vaughn's big frame caved in on itself.

An electric current tingled through me. "He won't."

The vampire blew out an unnecessary breath and nodded. "I'll get the key. He's out and shouldn't return until this evening. Leave no trace and be gone by sunset."

"Done," I said and tucked my phone into my pocket. "Who is he anyhow?"

Vaughn frowned and pointed to my pocketed phone. "That's Mr. Black. The owner."

17

CALM DOWN AND FOCUS

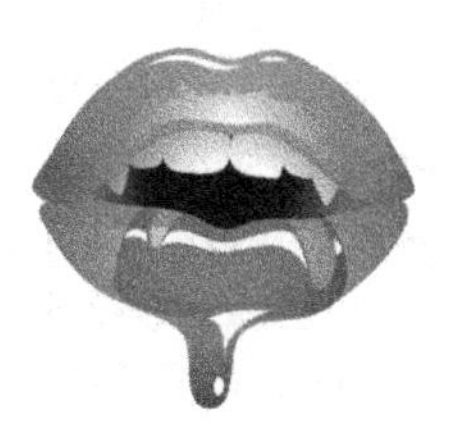

THE TRIP TO THE FORTY-NINTH FLOOR REQUIRED BOTH A KEY AND A KEY code.

I inserted the physical key, gave it a turn, and the buttons for the top four floors lit up.

"Vamp-man said there are only four apartments on forty-six and two on forty-seven and forty-eight." Y'sindra's fingers twitched as she stared at the lit numbers.

"Hmm, makes you wonder how big forty-nine is." That key would get us to the top four floors, but the penthouse required an access code once we got there.

"No time like the present to find out." Y'sindra fluttered up and punched the button with a P instead of a number. She buzzed a circle around the cylindrical glass elevator and finally settled on the far side.

The copper doors shut, and the elevator slid upward. Mae gasped as the open view of the casino transitioned to the stone face of a waterfall, complete with an actual waterfall. I gripped the wooden railing that circled the lift and watched the wall covered in climbing vines, wide-leafed plants, and enormous flowers rush by.

"Stunning," Mae breathed, and I didn't disagree.

"I could fly down here and mess with...." Y'sindra's words trailed off as a water fairy dipped in and out of the falling streams outside the elevator. "Tourists."

"Guess you aren't the first fae with that idea." I waved at two more fairies zipping past.

Y'sindra scoffed. "They're hired help."

"Snob," I said but didn't miss the way her wide eyes followed the fairies. Discarded by her clan at only twelve years old, Y'sindra had spent more time alive away from fairies than with them.

Despite the rapid ascent, the elevator slid to an effortless stop. Mae crossed to the keypad while I positioned myself in front of the door with Y'sindra on my heels. I could take more damage than either of my sisters, but Y'sindra was the sucker punch no one saw coming. The vampire said Mr. Black was out, but he could have canceled his trip or returned early without Vaughn's knowledge. Better to be prepared than not.

Mae's fingers poised over the keypad curled into her palm. "Crud. I brought the communication crystal Duskmere gave you but forgot the portal stone."

"Don't worry, I got it." I patted my left jacket pocket, the phone being in the right. "Doubt we'll need it. We never have before."

She released a long breath and quickly punched in the code.

My knees were loose but body tense. The familiar buzz of anticipation fizzled in my veins. I slowed my breathing. The doors hissed open, and while I stayed perfectly still, my gaze dug into every nook and cranny where a potential threat could hide.

Nothing. So far so good. "Stay here."

Mae gave a quick nod, finger pressed so hard to the "Door Open" button, the tip turned white.

I eased from the elevator into the foyer. Two steps down the hall leading away from the foyer and still nothing but silence. Eight steps and the wall to my right opened on a square kitchen featuring deep green granite, dark wood cabinets, and an island with a six burner cook top. Continuing down the hall, I stopped before passing beneath an impressive wooden arch that resembled a twisted knot of tree limbs and opened to a large living space. From here, I could only see a small slice of the room. If anyone waited to ambush, it would be here.

With slow, controlled steps, I moved toward the room. A sheet of glass replaced the far wall. With the desert sun bearing down on the windows, a reflection of the room was visible. The closer I got, the clearer the image. A massive sectional sofa, wooden stools tucked beneath the pass-through from the kitchen. Instead of an aquarium, Mr. Black had a living wall—a wall of plants. Two-story bookcases with rolling ladders were built into that wall and surrounded by those plants. In stark contrast, a large-screen TV was mounted on the opposite wall.

No fae, people, or pets.

"Clear," I called and walked beneath the arch. The ceilings soared, and a second-floor balcony ran along two walls above the living space. Two were separate hallways and three doors led off the balcony, but the lights were out, and nothing moved there.

Mae and Y'sindra strode past me into the room. Despite the sofa and big-screen TV, the space had a grounded feel to it. The wood floors were buffed smooth but not polished, as if whoever lived here wanted to feel the knots and whorls beneath their soles. All the earth tones, wood, and potted plants screamed that despite residing in a desert high-rise, Mr. Black loved the outdoors.

Tucked into the wall on my left, a door stood ajar. Like the rest of the penthouse, the lights were off, but enough natural light from the living room filtered in for me to see it was an office. I glanced at my sisters. Mae was busy studying the spines of books, pulling one out every few feet to check the space behind, while Y'sindra buzzed the top shelves searching for anything Mr. Black wanted to keep hidden.

I took a step toward the study and stopped. No, I needed to stick with this living room. Better to clear one room at a time and be thorough.

A round dining room table stood between the kitchen pass-through and the open living space. I reached for the first stack of papers scattered across its surface but pulled my hand back and curled it against my chest. A fissure of unease cracked open inside of me. The table was made of the same ashy shade of petrified wood as the sundial in the garden.

My tongue flicked nervously over my lips, and I sought my sisters. They didn't notice. They'd started on the second bookshelf.

"Coincidence, Lane," I whispered to myself.

I picked up the first slip of paper and released a shaky laugh—a grocery list. Next was a list of random design and renovation thoughts for the casino and some beach-front motel. The tension eased from my shoulders as I flipped through the mundane papers. I quickly scanned a slip with the names of some construction companies and was setting it down when my hand began to shake. Beneath names like Solid Rock Builders, Key Construction, Five Star Building Group, someone had scribbled a single word—grounders.

"Hey guys, you need to see this." I tapped a nervous finger on the note. No one answered me. I glanced up to find the glass wall was in fact sliding glass doors and they were open. My sisters roamed the balcony beyond. I took out my phone and snapped a picture of the incriminating paper.

More innocuous lists were piled on the table. I shuffled through them quickly until I came across another list of names. Running my finger down the list, I tapped the single name I recognized—Etta'wy. While the other names weren't familiar to me, Duskmere might know them. We needed to get out of here as soon as possible, so I took more pictures and moved on.

Finished at the table, I headed for the office, but when I looked out to the balcony to let my sisters know, they were gone. I frowned but shrugged. We were over seven hundred feet up, It was not like they jumped. At least Mae didn't.

The office door swung open on squeaky hinges. My hearts thumped, and I held my breath. Though I was certain Vaughn was right and the place was empty, I had an itch between my shoulders that wouldn't let me relax.

"Lane!" Y'sindra's voice trumpeted across the room.

My stomach clenched.

"Don't *do* that," I hissed. "And keep it down."

"What? Can't hear you," she continued to shout. "Hey get out here, you gotta see this."

I rubbed a hand across my face and scanned the dark room. Like the dining room table, piles of papers spilled over the large desk. There could be no doubt Mr. Black was involved with the missing stones, and he obviously wasn't worried about leaving incriminating evidence lying about. I should definitely check the office.

"Laney, you really need to see this," Mae called.

Giving in, I headed for the sliding glass doors. I'd recruit Mae to go through the papers with me afterward. Her methodical sensibilities should make it through that pile in no time. I'd send Y'sindra to check out the upstairs while we did that.

A stunning view of the Las Vegas Strip greeted me from the balcony, but my sisters didn't.

"Up here. You're not going to believe this." Above me, Mae leaned against a chest-high partition wall made of glass. She gestured to a spiral staircase I hadn't noticed in the corner of the balcony. "Over there."

The climb was further than I'd realized, probably because of the ten-foot-tall sheet of metal that began at the roof and ended at the base of the glass half-wall. My mouth dropped as I crested the stairs and found a literal forest in the Las Vegas sky. *Whoa.*

"I know, but this isn't why we called you out here." Mae beckoned me to follow.

"It's not?" I swiped a hand over my numb face. Trees, no more than ten feet tall, but healthy, sprang from a thick carpet of grass. I crouched and danced my fingers across the blades. Real. "How is this even possible?"

Ahead, Mae shrugged. "I'm guessing that thick platform allows space for roots and a watering system."

"Well, the garden is visible from the ground. I shouldn't be surprised."

"Yeah, but it's not public. The balcony is the only access point. Y'sindra and I checked." Mae stopped walking. "This is what you need to see."

"Wow, a pomegranate tree." I headed for the ruby red fruit. "Mr. Black's got his own fruit farm in the sky. Dude must be some kind of magician."

"He's some kind of something," Y'sindra said. "Over here, dummy."

I rolled my eyes toward the smart-mouthed fairy and caught sight of the real reason they'd dragged me to the roof. A wave of dizziness washed over me, and I clutched my hands to my sternum. "Holy..."

"Shit. Holy shit, right? That's what you were going for because what in the name of Odin's beard is this doing up here?" Y'sindra buzzed wildly around a wide circle of tall stones. She bobbed in front of each, cataloging the intricate runes carved into them.

The sun inched past its zenith, casting long-fingered shadows from the stones and across the grass. I took a wary step toward the circle. This was something I'd read about.

"Mr. Black might not be a magician." I licked my lips and laid hands on the cool stone. "But he's a druid, and this is a damn portal circle."

"No way!" Y'sindra did a Daytona 500 speed lap around the stone circle.

I dragged a finger along the runic engravings and shook my head in wonder. "Druids disappeared after the Great Fae Divide. I don't know how this is possible."

"Druids disappeared from Ta'Vale." Mae strolled into the center of the circle and slowly spun to take in the sight. There were twelve stones. Most were hip high or smaller, but four were as tall, if not taller than Mae.

"Hmm, well there is the bogeyman story. The druid who drained the power from all the druids who followed him and left behind their lifeless husks." I stood and studied the next stone. "Could be Mr. Black."

Y'sindra landed next to Mae, tugging nervously at the hem of her buttery yellow baby doll dress. "You don't think?"

"Nah, I'm teasing. It's a story the older generation gets their jollies scaring us with. Be good or the big bad druid will come drain you." I hoped it was just a story.

"Well, I don't like it. None of this." Y'sindra spun in a circle, waving her hands. "This shouldn't be possible."

She wasn't wrong.

Crouched by one of the smaller stones, my legs began to cramp. They weren't entirely over the marathon of stairs.

The moment I crossed the perimeter of the stones an electric bolt streaked through my body. I froze and looked between my sisters. "You feel that?"

Mae frowned. "Feel what?"

"Nothing, I guess." It was definitely something, and it wasn't the stairs.

I took another step. Electricity burned across my shoulders, up my neck, down my arms. I breathed in and out through my mouth. By the time I reached my sisters, my blood felt fizzier than the cans of soda Y'sindra liked to shake up.

"I can't believe you don't feel this. It's like I'm walking on a live wire." I rubbed my hands on my thighs and studied the area. This was a place of magic linked to another circle somewhere.

"Everything okay?" Mae's forehead wrinkled with concern.

Hugging my arms tight to my body, I nodded. "I'm good."

"Wonder where this goes?" Y'sindra said.

I squeezed my arms tighter to my chest, trying to ignore the energy zinging through my body. "Or how we go—"

The world went dark.

18

THE EDGE OF THE WORLD

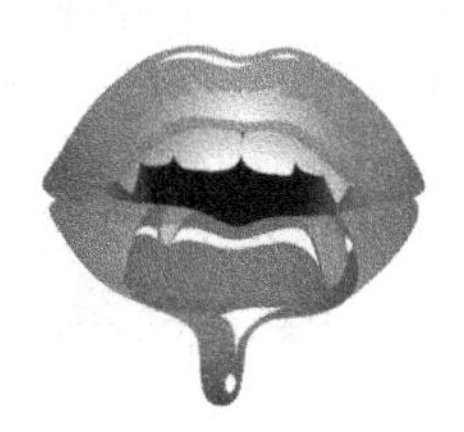

I STUMBLED MY WAY TO THE CLOSEST STONE JUTTING FROM THE POWDERY sand, doubled over and dry heaved, waiting for yesterday's buffet of junk food to make a second appearance. Y'sindra performed loops like a punch-drunk fairy while Mae lay face down, groaning.

Mae's perfect lipstick application kissing the ground? Unthinkable.

"Oh man, what was that?" I asked between retches.

Mae lifted her head and spit out sand. "You said go, and we went."

"That can't be right." I tried to stand but ended up on my butt. Last thing I wanted was a repeat of whatever just happened, so I crawled outside the circle. "Only druids can navigate these things."

"We don't know if that's true." Mae sat up and brushed clumps of hair from her face. "The circles in Ta'Vale have been dormant for longer than we've been alive, and there aren't many documents on druids in the libraries."

As if I bothered with history or libraries. Maybe I should have paid attention to Duskmere's unwelcome lesson on druids.

Y'sindra crash landed a few feet beyond me. She jumped up, spraying sand in all directions. "Don't do that again, Lane!"

My glare was ruined by another dry heave. "I didn't do anything. All I said—"

"Shut up!" both my sisters shouted in unison.

Probably for the best. No reason to wave the red cape at Fate.

I rolled onto my back. Above, the sky had gone from a bright blue afternoon to the bruised purple of twilight. I ran my fingers through the sand. It had the same stinging heat as Las Vegas sand, but with a soft, powdery texture.

Beneath my sister's mutterings a roar rose, followed by a long, hissing whoosh. The scent of salt and fish filled my nostrils. Unlike the bone-bleaching dry desert, the briny air here clung to my skin like a wet rag.

We'd left Vegas, but where did we end up, and how were we getting home? I didn't believe for a second we'd made it here—wherever here was—because of me and the magical word "go." I might not know how portals worked, but I knew for damn sure I couldn't work them. Our fancy coffee machine was the extent of my wizardry. This had to be a fluke. The druid could have activated the portal, but that begged the question: Where was this mysterious druid?

Unease festered in my belly, and the question brought my tired muscles to life. I lifted my head to look down the length of my body, past the stone circle, past my toes. A small hotel that resembled one of those 1970's off-strip Vegas casinos crouched on the beach's crest, but it was painted powder blue instead of the typical desert beige. No lights on and no other buildings nearby.

I rolled to all fours, pushed to my feet, and looked in the opposite direction.

My lungs turned to lead.

A glittering, undulating sheet of dark water rolled to the edge of the world. Twilight-blue waves crashed on the shore, leaving behind a foamy line on the white beach.

"Wow." My legs went shaky, and I plopped down in the sand. Ta'Vale was a single landmass world, and though surrounded by water, neither my sisters nor I had ever seen an ocean. A brilliant layer of orange and pink and purple bands drenched the horizon. The flag of colors waved across the water's surface. Goosebumps rose over my sweat-slick skin. "Wow," I repeated, dazed.

Mae crouched next to me. "I've never seen anything like this."

"Hey, you two." Y'sindra flew between us, her usually silent wings—the only stealthy thing about her—buzzed with speed and agitation, spraying snow over sand. "Guys, we gotta move."

I waved her away.

"Seriously," she said. "While you two were over here taking in the view, I scoped out the area, and we're gonna have company soon."

Twisting to look behind me, I leaped to my feet. The lights were now on inside the hotel lobby as were the floodlights on a deck attached to it.

"Don't beat yourself up, it was dark when we got here." Y'sindra flew backwards and motioned for us to follow. "Come on, there's two guys in the lobby, one's a moon fae. I'd bet a year's supply of Snoballs they're headed to the circle."

That probably made the other guy the druid, and I had no intention of meeting Mr. Black. Not today, not ever. Grabbing Mae's hand, I hustled after Y'sindra. She flew low, leading us to the left of the portal stones and away from the wood plank path leading from the circle to the deck.

Deep but faint voices carried above the ocean's music to my sensitive ears.

"Hurry," I whispered. "Voices."

Mae nodded and increased her pace. She vanilla-cursed as sand flooded her sandals. Still, her long legs forced me to ignore the burn in my thighs and push to keep up. My feet dug deeper into the loose sand with each step.

Y'sindra zipped upward. "It's the two I saw. They're standing outside the doors talking, but we gotta hurry."

With each step, the sand sucked at our feet. We sprinted in slow motion, following Y'sindra to the ridge of dunes.

"Lots of footprints," I panted. "Hopefully ours will blend in."

"They're hiding the druid circle in plain sight. Tourist feature," Mae said, not sounding the least bit winded. "Same as the Vegas rooftop feature."

Clever planning. Long game planning. Smart and scary.

We reached the first dune and dove behind. I rose to a crouch and peeked past the tufts of long grass. A tall brown stalk topped by something resembling wheat waved in my face. "We got out of there just in time. They're headed this way."

"Now what? We're hidden from the hotel, but they'll see us from the circle," Mae asked as she shook her sandals free of sand, only to have the fine grains flood beneath her soles each time she put her foot down. She met my gaze and scowled. "I already know what you're going to say and don't."

I shrugged but didn't bother to hide my smug smirk.

"Be right back." Y'sindra stayed low and winged silently toward the hotel.

I held my breath watching her small form blend with the shadows creeping from the rolling mounds of sand. My pulse thumped against my eardrums. I rose from my crouch enough to see over the dune. Far enough away and silhouetted against the patio floodlights, details of the pair were hidden from even my sharp eyes. Still deep in conversation, they continued to stop and talk. It bought us time.

Y'sindra landed in a spray of sand. Her wings drooped and she gasped for breath. "It's gonna be tricky, but here's what we do." She dug her hands into her sides and looked to me. "Where are they?"

The two figures hadn't made it very far. "Not even halfway. They keep stopping. One of them has a cane, probably slowing them down."

"Good." She licked her lips. "We go up the side of the dunes, the same direction I flew. We'll only be exposed if we're passing at the same time and get caught in the open."

"Okay," Mae said and unlaced her sandals, tied the ends together, and slung them over her shoulder. At last, a practical decision. "We need to time it. You'll tell us when."

"Let's move." I knelt for Y'sindra. "Climb on, we don't know what we're in for. Can't burn you out before we even make it inside."

For all her snarky faults, she knew when it was time to be serious. Y'sindra dusted off her hands and climbed onto my back.

Fire licked my thighs as I rose to a half-crouch and waded through the loose sand toward the hotel. I bit the inside of my cheek and breathed through my nose, trying to ignore the shake in my legs.

"I promise I'll take a shot of blood when we get home," I swore to the universe. Not too much that I got blood-drunk, but enough to speed the healing I desperately needed.

"Just like Ma taught you." Y'sindra patted my head.

Mae snorted. "Or you could start exercising with me. Do some squats."

"Sure, that'll happen, never." I shrugged my shoulders for Y'sindra's attention. "Keep an eye out."

With her palms pressed to my shoulders, knees digging into my ribs, she stood on my back. "They're on the move. We'll pass them soon."

I eyed the wide gap from one dune to the next. "This is going to be tight."

One dune, two. We kept moving forward, and my sister continued to rise and keep watch, her wings tucked tight against her back to prevent drag.

"Wait," Y'sindra whispered. The urgency in her voice instantly brought Mae and me to a halt. "Once they pass, make a break for the hotel."

I tensed, waiting for her signal.

"They're passing now." Her words were little more than a breath. "Hold. Hold..."

My muscles coiled. Anticipation crawled over my scalp. I focused on my goal—the deck.

"Go!"

Keeping low to the ground, Mae and I shot forward. Y'sindra tucked close and stayed quiet through the sprint.

Fifty feet. Forty.

Y'sindra rose to check behind us. Her fist knotted in my collar, knobby knees digging into my ribs.

Thirty.

My hearts threatened to explode from my chest. Twenty-five.

"Shit. The moon fae is coming back. Abort, abort!" Y'sindra pushed from my back to tuck and roll while I dove for a small sand ridge.

Cheek pressed to the sand, I panted. My head felt so light, I wasn't certain it was still attached to my body. Next to me, Mae lay on her back, both hands pressed to her belly. Even she gasped for air.

"The moon fae's downhill. He'll see us if we move." Y'sindra crouched in the sand, her arms wrapped tight around her knees. She was right, this close to the deck, the dunes were little more than ripples.

"He'll see us from the deck if we don't move," Mae said.

"Way to shit on an already shitty situation." I wrinkled my nose at my sister.

Y'sindra's hands fisted in the skirt of her dress. "What now?"

"Whatever it is, we don't have much time." I knelt in the sand. Things couldn't be worse. No one knew where we were. *We* didn't know where we were, and a moon fae in league with a druid who helped to steal the sun stones was about to trip over us.

I tilted my neck back. A single star winked above the roof line of the hotel. A shadow moved in front of the star—a bird, lots of birds, more than I could count. I laughed under my breath. We might have a chance.

Mae's smooth brow scrunched in concern. "You okay?"

"I knew it'd happen. She finally cracked." Y'sindra shook her head.

"One day, but not yet." I pointed to the hotel roof.

Y'sindra scowled but followed my finger. It took her a second, but she finally saw them and grinned. "On it. Hold tight."

"What's going on?" Mae asked.

I scanned the patio for a good hiding spot. Not the cabanas—the curtains were sheer and tied open. The stacks of lawn chairs were iffy. My gaze skipped to a tall, square bar, about twelve feet wide and long, and lined on all four sides with stools. To get behind the counters we'd need to reach the opening located on the side furthest from us. We'd be exposed longer getting there than anywhere else, but it was our best shot.

"There." I indicated our goal to Mae. "Be ready. When we get the signal, run for the bar and get behind the counter."

"What signal?"

Watching the roof line, time seemed to hold its breath. My body tensed. *Please work, please work.*

A dark smudge streaked in from the far side and dove through the birds. The hair on my arms stood on end as my anxiety twisted into overdrive. The humid air felt alive, breathing, and waiting. Suddenly a cloud of gray and white birds burst into the sky in a cacophony of hoots and squawks.

"Go!" I shoved Mae into motion and raced behind her, hoping the distraction would be enough. The ground firmed as we neared the deck. We moved faster. Mae leaped for the deck, but the sand collapsed beneath her foot. She landed off-balance and tilted backwards into my arms as I jumped up behind her. I spun her toward me and threw her over my shoulder.

My vision became hyper-focused, muscles pulled to their snapping point, waiting for the shout to come from behind us, waiting to be caught.

The three of us could take the moon fae, but he might have a way to call his druid buddy back. Druids were the big bad unknown.

A spike of white-hot fear propelled me past the stools lining the counter. I dodged one pulled out too far and angled toward the narrow opening cut into the corner of the bar.

We'd been in the open for too long. This was such a reckless idea. Stupid.

I reached the corner and grabbed the counter, flinging myself around the end, knees going weak with relief. My pulse hammered in my eardrums as I collapsed behind the safety of the tall bar. Mae tumbled from my shoulder and rolled away, all elbows and bare knees scraping on the cement. She cried out but quickly mashed her lips together, cutting the sound short. Her chest rose and fell as she breathed through the pain.

Y'sindra flew low between the gap, her wings brushing the patio deck to land beside us.

There were no bottles or kegs behind the bar. This place had to be new—not even open. I found a roll of paper towels wedged deep on the back of a shelf, tore loose a handful, and pressed them to Mae's bleeding knee. She nodded her thanks.

We wedged ourselves against the counter where we'd be hidden from sight. Mae's blood smudged the center of the open square space. If we were lucky—and we often weren't—the guy would walk straight past the bar.

"Good news and bad news." Y'sindra kept her voice low.

"Bad news." Always get the bad news first.

"The guy with the big stick left through the portal, so it's pretty obvious he's Mr. Black. We need to find another way home."

"Not great, but if we can figure out where we are, we can figure out a way home." Some days it really sucked to be right. Worry wound a knot between my shoulders, but I kept my voice even. Panic spread faster than wildfire, and this situation called for level heads. "What's the good news?"

"The birds were a smart distraction, the moon fae was too busy avoiding bird bombs to notice you two."

My pinched shoulders went loose, and my body relaxed on an easy breath.

"Problem is, now he's headed this way. Once he's inside..." Y'sindra gestured behind me.

I turned, and my stomach dropped to my toes. Well, there was the bad news she should have led with. One way into the bar, and the lobby had a clear view.

We were trapped.

19

WE WERE SCREWED

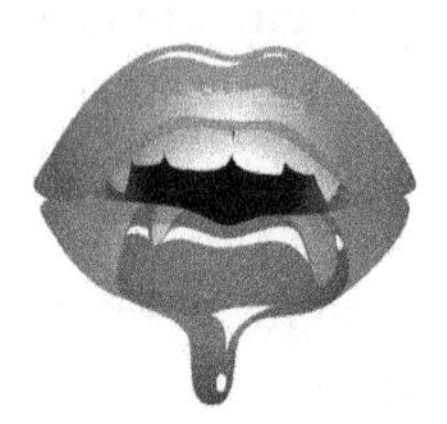

FOOTSTEPS SCRAPED ACROSS CEMENT. A HOARSE MALE VOICE MUTTERED something about arrogance and entitlement. There was talk of kicking that tree hugger's ass. I locked gazes with Mae and arched a brow. She shrugged.

I always considered dryads the tree huggers of the fae world, but sure, why not druids, too?

"...need a drink," the moon fae said.

You and me both, buddy.

Somewhere on the other side of the counter he yanked opened a door, and a burst of artificially chilled air hit my nostrils. The door sighed on his fading footsteps and closed with a decisive whoomph.

With my back against a liquor well and legs pulled to my chest, I pressed my forehead against my knee. How had I made such a horrible mistake? One way in meant one way out. So stupid. I pulled my head back and hammered my forehead against my kneecap.

"Stop, Lane." Mae put a hand on my shoulder. "We were exposed, and you got us to safety. We'll figure this out."

I grunted and rolled my cheek to my knee. It'd been a hellish three days, and it all started with the tiny blue terrors. No, that wasn't true. It started with Etta'wy giving me the slip. At least now I knew I hadn't entirely screwed up. There was a perfectly reasonable explanation as to why I'd lost her scent—swamp bitch hopped a portal out of that hotel. Even my super sniffer couldn't track through time and space.

"That's weird. I think he's closing up shop," Y'sindra said.

A sigh eased past my lips, and I rolled my head again to rest my chin on my knee. Y'sindra crouched by the bar opening and peeked around the corner. I could mention her snow-white head stuck out like a hitchhiker's frostbit thumb, but I was too deep into my sulk to care.

Mae pushed my shoulder. "Stop feeling sorry for yourself and get us out of here."

"What do you expect me to do?" Mae must've knocked her pretty blonde head on the ground when I dropped her. I rolled onto my knees, planted my hands on my thighs, and glared. "Sprout wings and carry us all home? We don't even know where we are."

"Step one, we figure that out." Mae waved her step one finger. "We're still Earth-side. Druid circles don't cross realms. They can open the veil and create a door between realms, but that's something different. That's how Interlands hap—"

"Ugh. Spare me the lesson." Mae flinched at my sharp tone, and a needle of guilt stabbed me. Life might have kicked me when I was down, but my sisters picked me up. *Don't be an asshole to them.* The only rule I lived by. I forced a half-smile. "Of course you'd know that. How do you accomplish so many dates with the amount of reading you do?"

"It's a gift," she said and unknotted the sandal straps that somehow stayed on her shoulder during our run.

"If only that gift could divine where we were."

She shrugged and began the arduous task of lacing her absurd sandals. "You're better at spontaneous, shifting details than Y'sindra or me. I have faith in you."

Without a doubt, we were screwed.

"He's turning off the lights," Y'sindra called. "Get over here."

I crawled toward Y'sindra, my fighting leathers holding up against the rough cement much better than jeans ever could, but my knees still hurt. I reached the cutout in the bar and peered into the lobby.

A figure moved inside, hitting light switches as he went. His features were indistinct, the details of his appearance washed out by the exterior floodlights. He walked into a back room and it went dark. The moon fae came out and crossed the lobby to approach a light panel near the window. I held my breath, willing him not to see us. Though he would have to look out and down, all it would take was a slight turn to the left and our disembodied heads would be visible.

"What's going on?" Mae asked, and I waved a hand behind me to shush her.

The moon fae flipped a switch and the lighting inside the doors blinked off. He hit the next switch and out went the floodlights. I blinked away the lingering halo and the lobby came into crisp focus—as did the moon fae. He turned from the window and headed toward the front desk, but I'd seen his face.

"Son of a bitch!" I surged for the bar opening, but Mae grabbed my ankles and pulled me back. Knocked off balance, I fell forward and bounced my chin on the concrete. Skin split and my teeth clacked together on impact. My shirt caught on the cement and rode up as she dragged me back. Red hot needles of pain ripped into my stomach and palms where flesh pulled in the struggle to wrench myself forward. "Get off me. That's the guy who killed Etta'wy."

"Oof." Y'sindra landed hard on my back, pushing the air from my lungs.

"Got her," she crowed in a stage whisper. Everything was a game to her.

I growled and flipped over, sending her tumbling into an empty liquor shelf.

Mae let go of my legs long enough to wag her finger at me. "Lane, no."

"Do I look like a damn dog? Get off me." I vibrated with need to get at that moon fae.

"Not until you settle down. Stars, Lane, you're not thinking." Mae shook her head. "Yeah, you could storm in there and take him out, but then what?"

"Yes. Exactly that." My legs ached with want for movement.

Y'sindra wandered over, glaring and brushing dirt from her dress.

"Tsk," Mae popped her tongue on the roof of her mouth. "Don't be daft, you're smarter than this. We have no idea if there's anyone else in there, and you want to run in and take out the target who can tell us what's going on. This situation calls for finesse."

I snorted and shook my leg. "Let go, I won't go inside. Yet."

Mae's grip on my calves tightened.

"Look, it's cute you think he's an easy mark. You remember what happened to Etta'wy?" I yanked my legs from her grip, the force throwing Mae off balance. She caught herself quickly and remained crouched over me like a gorgeous blonde vulture protecting its carrion. "Let's not forget he can hop through a portal of his own anytime he wants."

She pinned me with her bright gaze. "All true, and all the more reason not to charge in there unprepared. We don't know for sure if he's alone. There could be ten more inside just like him."

The fight left me. When Mae released my legs, I rolled over and sat up. Every last vibrating molecule inside of me wanted to get in there and eviscerate the guy, but Mae was right, and it sucked.

"Fine." I threw my hands in the air. "Let's get eyes on him—see what he does."

"On it." Y'sindra hustled to the bar pass-through and hunkered down.

"Here." Mae shoved the roll of paper towels at me. "You look like hell."

"Your fault." I ripped off a sheet and pressed it to my chin. Keeping my back bent below the bar top, I followed Y'sindra and poked my head out above hers. Mae put her hands to my shoulders and edged her head out above mine, capping our deranged totem pole imitation.

"Don't bleed on my head," Y'sindra whispered, as if she finally worried he might hear us, after all the noise we already made. "He's behind the check-in desk."

Beyond the exterior walls of blue concrete and floor-to-ceiling windows, ambient light emitted a soft glow inside the lobby. From the muggy twilight we had a clear view of the details with the exterior floodlights turned off.

The front desk was a wide horseshoe halfway between the dark front entrance and an elevator tucked against the left wall. I did a double take. An elevator? The logistics made no sense. The wall behind appeared too narrow to support a functioning elevator. Stranger still, the doors were elaborately carved wood reliefs. I frowned and scanned across the lobby. Another elevator faced the exterior windows, this one with the typical shining silver doors.

My gaze skipped over the rest of the lobby details. Aside from the odd elevator that appeared more decorative than functional, nothing screamed evil moon fae lair. A set of double doors to the right of the bar led inside to a small box-like hall and another set of glass double doors. Clever design to keep the cooled air in and the swelter out. A sitting area, and behind that a bar and small dining area made up the front and right side of the structure. The space was simple but attractively decorated with small indoor palm trees, peace lilies, beachy paintings, framed maps, and mirrors scattered across the lobby.

The moon fae pulled a bottle from behind the desk and unscrewed the cap. He took a long gulp and dragged his arm across his mouth. Half-empty liquor bottle in hand, his prowling strides carried him to the wood-door elevator—the one I'd dismissed as decoration. The moon fae punched his knuckle against a glowing orange button and leaned a shoulder against the wall, back to us.

His relaxed posture offended me on every level. In life, Etta'wy had been an awful individual. Being dead didn't change that, but she didn't deserve that manner of death. No one did. I bit down on my lip as an image of the banshee's silent scream invaded my brain. The way the writhing black ball of magic ate through her chest and consumed her body.

Y'sindra smacked a palm against the concrete. "What's taking so long?"

My stomach cramped, and I tasted bile in the back of my throat. I blinked rapidly, shedding the memories of Etta'wy's last moments.

Mae moved to crouch behind a beer tap. From my peripheral she edged forward, leaning over the countertop. "The elevator light went out. Something's happening."

Inside the lobby, the elevator door slid open and the moon fae stepped inside. I gasped. Shock and anger lanced through my chest.

"No, no, no!" I leaped to my feet and ran not for the door, but in the opposite direction, toward the side of the building, both my sisters on my heels. "This wall isn't wide enough for an elevator. If that wasn't an exit, he's gone."

There was nothing but beach behind the ornate doors the moon fae entered, and I'd been right—the wall was not thick enough to house a real elevator. I don't know how he did it, but that moon fae was gone. I slapped a hand on the rough stucco building face.

"We don't know that," Mae said. She reached for me but stopped herself.

How could I let him get away? Frustration beating a war drum in my chest, I glared through the windows, half-hoping I'd find the moon fae staring back. How could I let him get away? "You say trust my gut and my gut says this place is empty." I pointed behind her, toward the door leading into the lobby from the deck. "I'm going in. Maybe I'll find something that makes losing our only lead worth it."

Y'sindra hovered next to Mae, her mouth turned down and brow pinched in an angry scowl. "You sure it's about the case and not your pride?"

Heat singed my cheeks. "Not fair."

"It's okay, we'll find him." Mae rested a hand on my arm.

"How do you know?" I shook off her hand and stalked around her, toward the door. I couldn't believe he got away—again.

Mae's leather-soled feet slapped the ground behind me. "We will."

"Ending up here when we did, seeing who we saw? Absolute fucking chance." I stabbed at the empty lobby. "There went our chance."

"Pull your panties out of your crack and be reasonable." Y'sindra's angry face dove in front of mine. "The guy didn't make a portal. He pressed a button and stepped into an elevator—an elevator none of us could see inside. For all we know it's only for employees and the size of a broom closet."

My steps slowed until I stopped, just steps from the back door. A tingling heat crawled over my cheeks, and I blew a sharp burst of air from my nostrils. Y'sindra had called me on my pride, and there was a chance she wasn't wrong. "You could be right. Sorry."

Mae's arm threaded through mine and she pulled me to the door. "Don't worry, Laney. You've been through a lot this week. We'll get that guy, and we'll get the stones. This'll be over soon."

I rested my head on her shoulder. "It's been a real shit show so far. How are you so sure?"

"Because we're that good." Mae yanked open the back door to a pop of released suction and stale air. My sister tossed me a saucy wink and swaggered inside.

Idiot moon fae hadn't locked the door. Either they had nothing of value to take, or more likely, they didn't understand the ways of humans.

A smile tugged at my lips. Mae was right, we were that good.

I caught the closing door and followed my sisters into the hotel.

20

DISCOVER THE RICHES

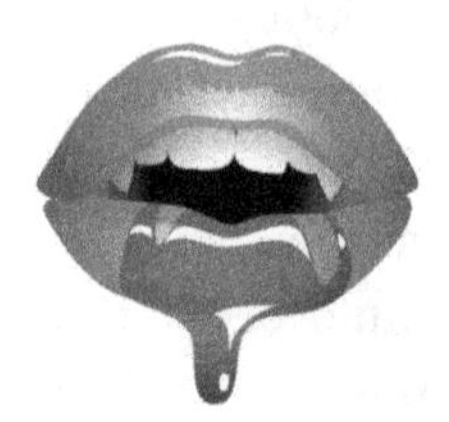

The lobby smelled of new construction and artificial coconut. Somewhere an HVAC hummed, but the sudden absence of surf and wind overwhelmed me.

The main elevator was the typical wide, polished silver doors and illuminated panel indicating floors—there were ten. Y'sindra bypassed the potential noise in favor of the stairwell to check floors and confirm the hotel's vacancy.

I glanced to my left at the weird elevator and its carved, wooden doors the finger flipping fae had disappeared through. It didn't seem possible to fit an elevator shaft behind that wall.

"This is eerie." Mae's whisper rattled to the high ceilings. She caught the direction of my gaze and put a hand on my arm. "I know you want to figure out where he went, and we will, but let's check for clues about what's going on here first, okay?"

I grunted my acquiescence. My jaw flexed and molars attempted to merge together. This case would drive me to the dentist, and dentists hated fangs, but as usual, Mae was right. My instincts were action, and to hell with the consequences. Sometimes it worked for me. Sometimes it got me mauled by fuzzy blue rodents.

She squeezed my arm and walked to the right, her steps a whisper as she moved through the sitting area on her soft-soled sandals. I guess they weren't completely useless. Mae glided through the lobby, dragging her fingers over textured throw pillows propped on sofas and chairs, and disappeared into the bar area on the far side of the silver-doored elevator.

Dragging a fang across my bottom lip, I studied the space. Beach paintings, a number of decorative maps mounted in driftwood frames, wide bowls of shells, plastic greenery. Aside from the rare splash of greens, blues, and yellows, the space was a neutral color palette, too bland to be either appreciated or offensive.

A wire rack with brochures stood against the entry wall opposite the check-in counter. Vegas hotels always had those, pamphlets advertising everything on the Strip and off. Hoping to find a hint of where we might be, I crossed to the entry and began pulling trifolds from the rack. Unlike Mae, my heavy boots clomped on the tile floor, and I rolled to my toes to muffle my steps.

The first brochure was about a sandcastle contest, and no way were the sculptures in those photos made from sand. Might be worth a return trip. Second brochure advertised something called parasailing. I pulled the next trifold and *jackpot*! Thick bold text across the image of a blue-green ocean and sandy white beach declared "Discover the riches of Treasure Island, Florida!"

At least I had an answer as to where we'd traveled, conceptually. I'd seen maps and knew Florida was a state, and knew how far we were from Las Vegas—we weren't walking home. I remember learning somewhere in Mae's boring lessons that druids had a one stone circle limit. Technically two, since there was one on each end, which begged the question, why Florida?

"What's that?" Y'sindra's voice hit my ear at full volume.

I jumped, banging my knee against the wire rack which rocked against the wall. The noise echoed through the lobby. Good thing we were trying to be quiet. "Don't sneak up on me like that."

"This place is stone-cold empty. Creepier than Odin's eye." She bobbed to the ground and snatched the pamphlet from my hand. "I wasn't trying to be quiet. If you didn't hear me, that's on you, baby fangs."

"Rub it in, why don't you?"

"Don't worry, I hear size doesn't matter, it's how you use them." She tapped the brochure. "Oh! Do you think there's treasure here?" Y'sindra skipped to the seating area and hopped into a chair to peruse the brochure.

What a brat. I ran a thumb down a fang and glared after my sister.

My chin itched. Damn thing was starting to stitch together. I fisted my hands at my sides and fought the urge to scratch as I wandered to the horseshoe-shaped front desk. The skin on my palms and belly pulled, also healing from the drag across the concrete. Minor wounds. They'd be healed before we got home.

My phone vibrated against my ribs, and I jumped, snapping my fangs together and almost piercing my tongue. *Who the hell?* Hands shaking from the rush of adrenaline, I pulled my phone from my pocket and thumbed open the screen. It was a new text from Teddy. This was no time to check my messages, but the longer I deliberated, the more convinced I became something dire happened after we left.

"Fuck it." Standing at the locked front doors, I swept a glance over the lobby behind me ensuring we were still alone, tapped the message, and almost dropped the phone. Fumbling to secure the device in my suddenly sweaty hands, I read the words again.

Drop your sisters at home and come to the bar for dinner. I'm cooking. Clothes optional. He'd added a wink-face emoji.

I rocked forward and rested my forehead on the glass. Did he just ask—no, order—me to join him on a date? At the bar. Where his apartment was. Where his bed was. A low heat coiled in my belly, shortened my breath. I curled and then flexed my fingers, the skin pulling across my palm. Hopefully, my torn flesh would be smooth, and I'd get the feeling back in my hand for this date, because there were definitely things I wanted to feel.

Shaking out my hands, I blew out a breath. While this diversion was a pleasant avenue to stroll down, it was also dangerous. I straightened, smoothing my hands over my jacket, and checked behind me once again. Still clear, thank the gods. What had I been thinking? Anyone could have strolled up and shanked me. Disappointed in myself, I pressed my lips into a tight, unforgiving line and shoved the phone back into my pocket.

Back to the task. I swallowed and gazed past the glass front doors. Outside, three pairs of headlights and a set of taillights lit the two-lane road the hotel was situated on. A driveway swept in, beneath an extended carport and past the front door before looping back to the road. The driveway had access to an empty parking lot on my right. On my left, the hotel signpost was visible, but the high carport roof blocked the marquee. I crouched for a view beyond the roof's overhang.

A bucket of ice-cold shock hit me. My breath shook as I stared unblinking at the sign—Shadwe Inn. How the hell had the moon fae escaped their prison realm and set up shop on Earth? And where were they?

I gripped the back of my neck and took in the sterile emptiness of the lobby. This made no sense. The only moon fae we'd seen was Etta'wy's killer, and he'd left.

He'd left.

My gaze strayed to the wooden doors by the front desk. Nervous energy crawled over my skin.

"We need to see what's on the other side of that elevator," I yelled, not caring about the volume. No one was here. Below the large sign brandishing the hotel name, a smaller sign read No Vacancy in red neon.

Y'sindra landed next to me. With her height, she immediately saw the sign.

"Well, damn. Guess this place is a shady front for their beach to desert travel." Her lips twitched side-to-side in the reflection.

"I'm not so sure. If corrupted moon fae started flooding the Blackthorne —an establishment crawling with fae—we'd have heard about it. Even if one started strolling through the casino, they'd be noticed."

"You're right. We're there all the time. We would've seen."

"You're there all the time."

"Truth." Y'sindra bounced on her toes. "Can we push the elevator to nowhere button now?"

"In a sec. Wait 'til we're all together. We don't know what's going to happen." I jutted my chin toward the front desk. "Why don't you see if there's anything over there?"

Y'sindra wasted no time buzzing across the lobby.

Mae appeared from the around the corner. "What are you shouting about? We've hardly checked anything out here."

"We don't need to. Come over here, you'll see why."

Mae trotted to a stop. Her brow puckered into a frown as she looked between Y'sindra and me, clearly torn. She knew our sister and her penchant for button pushing.

"Trust me," I said. "You have to see this."

"Nothin' but a phone and computer, neither plugged in, and a half-empty pack of cinnamon gum over here." Y'sindra finished her search and flew for the oddball elevator.

Mae watched Y'sindra and then joined me. "What's so important?"

I pointed in the direction of the outdoor sign. "Over there. You'll need to squat."

"Is this necessary?"

"Very." I rolled my hand for her to get on with it.

She bent at the waist in order to see past the carport. "Holy shit."

"Yup." Mae rarely cursed, not because she had an aversion, she just never did it, so the sign's impact was obvious. "Not one to say I told you so—"

"Yes, you are." She stood and covered her mouth with both her hands, her huge blue orbs locked on me.

"The elevator?" I prodded.

She nodded and together we jogged across the lobby. Y'sindra saw us coming and jabbed the button three times in rapid succession.

The silence between us stretched, tense, ready to snap. I swallowed, and it was as loud as the ocean waves against my eardrums.

"What's taking so long?" Mae's voice was a strangled whisper.

I shook my head. I didn't know.

For once, Y'sindra remained quiet. Focused. Game face.

A soft thump on the other side of the etched wood panels set fire to my nerves. My arms tensed, fingers tingled. I put a hand to either side of me, and my sisters stepped back—far enough to avoid whatever might come through those doors, but close enough to be ready to fight.

Ding.

I eased a slow breath from my lungs and allowed a calm to roll over me, steadied myself.

My shoulders bunched and legs tensed, readying to leap into action.

An inner safety lock on the elevator thumped its release, and the doors slid open on a quiet hiss.

No movement. Just a plain white box, the size of the average elevator with no moon fae inside.

"You've got to be kidding me." Y'sindra flew past me, her unspent adrenaline expending itself in a spray of snow as she went. "That's what I call anticlimactic."

I bounced on my toes and shook the jitters from my hands. Pulling Mae inside, I jammed my fist against the single button. "Let's find out where this thing goes."

The doors slid shut and the elevator thumped. Time held its breath, and then we warped into motion.

21

PARALLEL UNIVERSE SITUATION

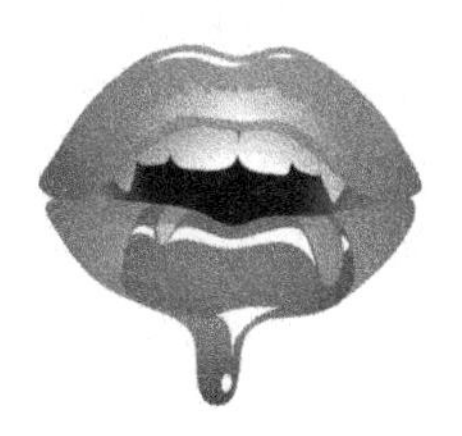

THE ELEVATOR TRAVELED NEITHER UP NOR DOWN. IT SHOT INTO LATERAL motion.

A small bubble of hysterical laughter popped from my lungs. I smacked a hand over my mouth.

"You okay?" Mae braced her legs wide and eyed me warily.

"No." The hysterics evaporated as quickly as they came on. I ground my fingertips against my temples. We'd reached critical mass of absurdity, and I was done with it. "Of course we'd go sideways, because why would this be any less ridiculous than a corrupted moon fae in our backyard? Let's not forget about the druid circle in the middle of Las Vegas that against all odds, we managed to stumble through. What's next? A trip to Candy Land?"

"Oh! Can we?" Y'sindra clapped.

"Lane—"

"I'm fine." I waved Mae off. Nothing about this was fine, but for my sisters' sake, I needed to keep a level head. "Let's be ready for whatever's at the other end of this trip."

The white panels of the elevator—if that's what we were still calling it—fell away, disappeared as if they'd never existed. My hearts stuttered, and I skipped away from the missing walls.

Y'sindra, who had her shoulders propped against the side wall, sprang toward the center of the box.

Pure color, pure light, and pure dark swam beyond the open sides. Nebulas. Stars and bits of stardust. Absolute pitch black. It all rushed by too fast to focus on any one thing.

The air pressure didn't change when the walls went clear. Y'sindra, who had been leaning against the side, didn't go tumbling into space. There must be something there.

I hoped.

My pulse thrummed like hummingbird wings inside my throat. I swallowed and extended a hand toward the missing wall.

"Lane, don't." Mae's nervous voice wobbled.

An inch from the side I curled my fingers into my palm. My tongue traced the seam of my lips. Ignoring Mae's warning, I held my breath and shoved my hand forward.

A barrier I couldn't see gave but didn't let my hand pass through. "Son of a bitch." I leaned forward and sniffed—electricity and metal, faint. The magic from the dungeon.

"What is it?" Y'sindra stepped next to me and pushed a toe against the there-not-there barrier.

"I saw this magic in—" A thump vibrated the floor, and I braced my legs.

The interstellar box's jarring speed slowed to a crawl. Mae and I held our balance while Y'sindra grabbed onto my jacket. Normal white walls replaced the view beyond. Our trip stopped with a smooth glide. Another thump and click, and the doors slid open.

Y'sindra flew for the door. I snatched the hem of her baby doll dress and shook my head, putting a finger to my lips before she set my ears bleeding with her curses.

"We don't know what's out there," I whispered. "Let's be careful."

Mae wedged herself against the wall behind me and gripped the door frame with both hands to prevent them from closing.

"I'm good, let go." Y'sindra's voice was quiet but tight. I released her and she lowered herself to the ground.

"Let me look." I pressed against the interior front wall and met Mae's gaze. She nodded, and maintaining her grip on the door, slid her hands above my head. My eyelids drooped, and I took slow breaths, held, released. As calm infused me, I rolled along the panel to my right until my shoulder edged beyond the opening, and leaned out.

Night sky hung over me, while a deserted grass road ran in front of the elevator. Well-used, matted by foot traffic—no wheel tracks in sight. The elevator itself was a small stand-alone building, easily mistaken for a shed. Dark windows of a rough wood building faced us from across the street.

To the left, the road disappeared into a forest of squat, fat-trunked trees. The grass grew thicker in that direction, the road barely discernible.

My gaze swung right, and I jerked with surprise. If the roads were dirt instead of grass, this could be Interlands, the same main street, with the same saloon-style wood buildings. What sort of parallel universe situation had we stumbled into? Was that even a real thing?

I leaned out for a better view. Cool air bit into my cheeks. I wouldn't call it cold, but the air was damp. It stung. Never thought I'd miss the dry, hot, dust-choked climate I'd come to call home.

This road dead-ended at another grass street, forming a T intersection. The turf near the intersection was also worn low by foot traffic. On the far side of what I assumed was the main street, five buildings were visible before they disappeared too far right or left down the main road. Like the building across from the elevator, they were all dark but one. Fire or candlelight flickered behind those windows. Someone was home in this ghost town.

No one moved outside. Nocturnal insects chittered, and the occasional screech of a bird broke the quiet.

I backed into the elevator and faced my sisters. "I don't see the moon fae—don't see anyone. It's a long shot, but if we're in Shadwe, we need to try to locate the stones."

Y'sindra snorted. "You're crazy. These guys can't be dumb enough to hide them so close."

"It's not that crazy," Mae said. "This is an obscure location, accessed by an even more obscure method of travel."

"Let's get this over with." I peeked out of the elevator to confirm the road was still empty. "Mae, follow me. We go across and to the right. Y'sindra, you go high and do a sweep from above. See if there is any movement out there, anything unusual, get some pictures." I dug into my pocket and handed her my phone.

She tucked the phone into a fanny pack strapped crosswise over her body and gave two thumbs up as she lifted into the air, flying out and up, disappearing into shadows that seemed to follow her.

"Hold the door a sec," Mae said and disappeared around the corner of the elevator. She returned less than a minute later carrying a large rock and wedged it on the door track, against the corner of the frame.

"Good thinking." I put my foot to the rock and gave it a nudge. Solid enough to hold the door open in case we needed a quick getaway. "Ready?"

"Yes. Let's go."

Rolling onto the balls of my feet, I moved quickly across the grass road, Mae right on my heels. With our backs pressed to the dark building, I signaled to move toward the main street. She nodded and we slunk toward the front edge of the building. A wide porch provided cover from the street.

Mae nudged me. "Nothing to the right, get a look left."

Having the better eyesight, especially at night, it was up to me to get the full scope of our situation. Inside the shadows cast from the porch, I crawled toward its front edge and looked left down the road.

Shit. Surprise galloped across my nerves.

There were others on the road. I crushed the burgeoning panic swelling in my chest with a swallow. Arm extended to my side, I made a fist, signaling for Mae to wait. Holding up two fingers for her to see, and then five, I motioned across the street.

Mae squeezed my ankle. She understood.

A sun fae female and moon fae male walked down the center of the road with a small cluster of what appeared to be guards around them. The moon fae appeared tall, his posture rigid. He angled his chin in a way that implied self-entitled ownership of everything and everyone. My lip curled on instinct. As good as my eyes were, I couldn't see the details of his face. I didn't know if he had the corruption, but I'd take those odds.

The female walked a pace ahead of the moon fae, moving with slinky grace. Her fair hair, long and loose, swung with the sway of her hips. She laughed over her shoulder at something the male said. It spoke to the ease between them and a lack of concern for their surroundings.

I focused in on the five positioned around the pair. They were definitely guards with the way they casually, but continuously, scanned the area. I hunkered deeper into the shadows. The cluster of guards included two moon fae and three...I had no idea what. They could pass for human, but then so could some fae. I didn't know what the native Shadwe inhabitants —*Shadwenians*?—looked like, either. While the silver glint of bladed weapons hung from sheath loops on the moon fae's belts, the mystery guards appeared unarmed. I'd seen enough kung fu movies to know those were the ones to watch out for.

As the group grew nearer, they angled toward the other side of the street, and my shoulders relaxed a fraction. Mae squeezed my ankle again in question, and I shook my head. *Don't move yet.*

A sliver of the female's profile was visible from this angle, and most of that hid behind her hair. The male, on the other hand, had to turn in my direction while speaking to the female. As predicted, he had the same reddish-black corruption as Etta'wy's assassin. The two moon fae bringing up the rear did also.

The group went into the building across the street. Tension spilled from my body. I relaxed and crawled back from the porch's edge.

"They went in that building." I rose and dusted bits of grass from my hands off on my pants. "Should we wait for Y'sindra or go in for a closer look?"

Quick, quick footsteps sounded, but Mae didn't appear at my side.

"La—" My sister's cry cut off.

The honeysuckle scent of Mae's blood punched my nostrils.

Adrenaline surged into my veins. I became hyper-focused and time went sluggish.

I dropped low and spun, my joints fluid, oiled. Muscle memory had me pulling the twin push daggers from their sheaths before I completed the turn. My arm swung wide, the knife's edge leading my turn.

The blade froze centimeters—millimeters—from Mae's golden skin.

My breath coiled in my throat. My arm shook, nicking her calf.

I looked up the length of my sister to find Etta'wy's murderer holding her at knifepoint. Two knives. One blade at her kidney, the other on her carotid. Blood seeped down the slope of her neck.

Furious, frustrated, my lip twitched in a snarl. Threats pushed against my teeth, but I swallowed them.

I'd made a huge mistake. I'd let myself get lost to the action on the street and hadn't heard him coming. I should have. A heavy ache sank into my chest. I had to open my mouth to breathe.

The moon fae's bloodshot eyes met mine. He sliced a malicious grin at me over Mae's shoulder. "Oh, I think we'll go in for that closer look."

22

I'D MAKE HIS DEATH SLOW

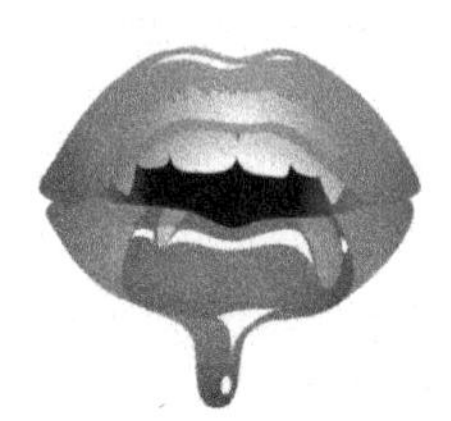

THE MOON FAE HELD ME HOSTAGE BY WAY OF MY SISTER'S LIFE. I FOCUSED on putting one foot in front of the other as my stiff legs carried me across the street.

"Come on, hybrid, move. Let's not forget I've seen you in action. You're faster than this."

How could I let this happen? Mae was one knife twist from death, and I didn't know where Y'sindra was. They might have her, too.

"How'd you know?" If I kept him occupied, kept him talking, I'd think of some way out of this. "How'd you know I'm a hybrid?"

"It's obvious."

"Bullshit." I stopped and swung around to distract him, throw him off balance. I took a wide stance and planted my fists on my hips. "There aren't any other hybrids—never have been—so you wouldn't know what was obvious if it punched you in the nose."

Which I wanted to do. I edged closer to him.

"Uh, uh, uh." The moon fae kept a dagger at Mae's kidney while he waved the other at me. I eased off the balls of my feet. A knife to the kidney wouldn't kill my sister any less than the throat. "I know what you're doing, and it won't work. Keep moving."

Palms up, I backed away.

"Good girl." His lips split wide in a sadistic grin. The red-black veins scrolling across his skin seeming to crawl with his movements. There wasn't a thing I could do, and he knew it.

I would rip out this guy's throat at the first opportunity.

The moon fae flicked his wrist up, returning the dagger to my sister's slender neck. The blade bit into her skin, but Mae being the bad bitch she was, mashed her lips into a flat, bloodless line and held in any reaction.

She and I locked gazes.

We're getting out of this and then we're going to kill this mother fucker.

The corner of her mouth hooked in a smirk. I wasn't telepathic, but my sister knew me. She read my murderous intent.

Apparently, so could the moon fae.

"Move." He bared his teeth and dug the tip deeper into her blood-slicked skin.

Mae couldn't hold back a stuttered gasp.

Arms quivering with barely controlled rage, I held my fists against my thighs and did as instructed. Gravity pulled at my feet. One step. Two.

"Etta'wy knew you were a hybrid."

"Not possible." I spit the words, but somehow it was. She'd taunted me with her knowledge. "The first time she and I met face to face was the same day you murdered her."

He snorted. "She had contacts inside Eodrom. When she found out Palough hired you to come after her, she did her research, got in touch with her contacts, and told us all about you and your sisters."

Surprise kicked me in the gut, and I jerked around. He waved me forward.

My mind spun. All that time thinking I'd blown the case, that I'd given us away, and Etta'wy had already known we were tailing her. I didn't have a thing to do with it, I hadn't fucked up. Although fleeting, considering the circumstances, I felt lighter, stood taller.

"Didn't see that coming, did you?" The moon fae chuckled. "Why do you think those guards came after Etta'wy? They caught one of her contacts, have them in custody. That's why Etta'wy had to die. Couldn't risk her getting caught and spilling what she knew is going on here and others involved."

I stared across the street at the building I was desperately trying to avoid as questions bombarded my brain. I'd bet my last bag of cheesy poofs "others involved" meant traitors in the sun fae midst. Why the hell hadn't Duskmere told me Etta'wy had a contact in Eodrom? That they had someone in custody? Guess my distrust of the RFG wasn't entirely misplaced.

"After everything I heard about you, I didn't expect you'd come after me in the trees. Pushed from the sun bridge, right?" He whistled. "Long way down. That'd make me think twice about heights, but not you."

I'd make his death slow, excruciatingly slow.

The bite of my talons against my palms kept me focused. He was trying to provoke me. Trying to get me to do something stupid. Not happening. Not with my sister a millimeter from death.

"We did have fun in the trees, didn't we? Maybe they'll let me keep you alive, and we can do it again."

I slid a glare dark look over my shoulder.

He waved the knife at Mae's neck, motioning me forward again. "Let's go ask them."

"You better hope I don't get a second chance."

All too soon we reached the porch. I rolled my shoulders and took the two steps up. There was no avoiding it, we had to go inside.

Narrow white wood planks ran the length of the porch. No furniture sat outside. Similar to every other building on the street, two windows flanked a double wide front door. Unlike every other building, lights flickered behind the smoked glass panes.

The doors stood ajar, voices mingling beyond. I paused.

"Go." This time, the moon fae's command was accompanied by a knife point against the base of my neck.

A slipknot of tension pulled tight between my shoulder blades. My talons dug deeper into my palms. I wanted to rip the blade from his hand and use it to open him from navel to neck. If I didn't have Mae's life to consider, he'd already be bleeding out on the porch.

I forced a slow breath into my lungs. The lush, calming scent of wood-fire smoke coated my senses. Chin lifted, shoulders back, I shoved through the door.

No one looked up. The three non-fae guards sat around something that resembled a chess table, but all three were playing, and the pieces were geometrical. Though the three looked human, I assumed they were native to Shadwe. The two moon fae guards sat in ornately carved, red brocade chairs facing the fireplace. Either these guards were shitty at their jobs, or there really were no threats in this town.

A male with a bleached wheat complexion, who was not fae and not with the group outside, noticed us first. He leaned forward, drawing shadows from the dancing firelight into the pockets cut beneath his sharp-boned features. Though he sat, his excessive height was obvious by the rise of his shoulders above his chair. A swath of light brown hair fell across his brow and dimples of amusement bracketed his mouth.

The female sun fae from the street stopped speaking to the brunette male and followed his gaze, angling in her seat to face us. Holy stars—she had the corruption. A sun fae with corruption. A paler, thinner map of reddish-black veins sketched across her elegant features.

I narrowed my eyes a fraction. Something about the female felt familiar, but I couldn't place her. She scoured me with bloodshot eyes but quickly dismissed me in favor of the moon fae at my back with Mae. The corrupted sun fae's posture went rigid.

"This is no way to treat guests, Nyle." The moon fae male who accompanied the female into the building reclined in his seat, an elbow slung lazily over the arm rest. Across the room, the guards came to life, but a wave —a mere flick of fingers—from this male had them sinking into their chairs. He looked past me to the finger flipper. "Let's put the weapons away."

"But—"

"Now." The male's command crushed any objection.

Nyle spat curses beneath his breath, too low for anyone but me to hear. Guess I knew who the big dog here was, and it wasn't the finger flipper.

With the slick tang of knives sliding against leather, Nyle sheathed his blades, followed by my sister's sandals slapping against the wooden floors. She appeared at my side and gave my hand a quick squeeze.

The female wiggled her fingers at Nyle. "Go make sure they weren't followed."

My nemesis's irritated mumblings faded with his footsteps. Cool air from the door he left open brushed my neck.

With azure orbs that would be stunning if not for the blood vessels worming through them, the sun fae tracked from me to my sister. My protective instincts kicked into overdrive, and I stepped toward the female before the guards once again sprang from their seats. I froze.

The reclining moon fae cut a sharp look at the group, and while they didn't sit, all five guards held their positions. Arrogant jackass. Did we pose so little threat in his estimation?

"Prince." The moniker uttered by the female moon fae guard and repeated by the rest of them sent a riptide of bile churning through my gut.

Well, shit. There was only one moon fae prince left alive by the end of the Great Divide, and he was the most ruthless bastard of the ruthless bunch. We were so dead if I didn't get us out of here fast.

My lungs were too tight for the air I needed. Without turning my head, my gaze tripped wildly over the room. It was a larger space than it appeared from outside. They were all far enough away that I might be able to grab Mae and get out the door.

Then what?

I still didn't know where Y'sindra went, and we weren't leaving without her. At least she wasn't here.

The sun fae took a step toward us.

My muscles went taut, joints loose. I'd take her down, give Mae time to run. I could survive long enough for her to find Y'sindra and get out of here.

I edged in front of Mae and let my hands drift toward my thigh sheaths. "I'm not sure how I ended up in Shadwe, but I'm going to make sure all of you stay here."

The non-fae male barked a laugh. "The small one thinks this is Shadwe. Adorable."

Small one? He died first.

A winter chill bit into my neck.

About damn time.

"Suck on it!" Y'sindra shouted, and a fat snowball sped by me to hit the female dead center of her face.

The sun fae's screech shook the rafters as she twisted and turned, shaking the sludge of snow from her eyes.

"Out!" Y'sindra dove in front of me, snow spraying from her wings. "Now!"

Chaos erupted. The guards took a step toward us, but the devious fairy sent a wave of hoarfrost across the floor. Heavy bodies hit the ground one after another, the guard's weapons shaken from their grips and spinning across the ice.

The mystery male who insulted me relaxed into his seat, watching everything with an amused smirk. Our gazes met and he winked. A shiver of unease snaked down my spine. His calm shook me more than the other's fury.

I backed toward Mae.

The prince rose, his expression violent. Glittering black magic sparked over his hands. Fear tap danced across my nerves.

"Do it, Y'sindra. Do it now," I yelled and spun, pushing Mae ahead of me toward the door.

We sprinted across the porch as the whoosh of a winter storm and cracking of ice silenced the mayhem inside the building.

"That'll buy uth time." Y'sindra's words slurred with fatigue. She dropped heavily to the street, leaning side to side like a teeter-totter.

I scooped her up and checked the door, did a double take. "What did you do?" Sometimes I forgot the power inside my smart-mouthed sister.

A deep boom shook the ground beneath us. Behind the solid sheet of ice covering the building, magic flared and faded. The coating of ice so thick, all I could make out behind it were the wavy shadows of figures.

Another boom and flare of magic. I flinched, but the ice remained.

"Uh, you've been practicing."

"I'd say so." Mae bobbed her head.

The fairy gave us a sloppy grin and two thumbs up. She swayed forward in my arms, but I readjusted my grip before she tumbled from my hold.

"Let's not waste the advantage," Mae said. "We need to get out of here and find somewhere to hide."

"Agreed." I sprinted for the elevator, holding Y'sindra's floppy, magic-drunk form to me.

The elevator building, barely bigger than an oversized outhouse, loomed closer. *Closed doors, not good.* I licked my lips. "Didn't we leave something on the track?"

"Door might have shoved it off." Mae paced in front of the doors. "No button."

"You've got to be kidding." Only I could stumble through two portals and get locked out of Earth.

Brilliant yellow orbs blinked at us from the grass. "It's the lever on the side over here."

"Fucking shit!" I screamed and skipped forward, pulling my leg back to dropkick whatever it was.

Y'sindra rolled from my arms and wobbled in front of the shadow. "No," she slurred. "Is good people. Coming wif us."

A guy, about the same size as my three-foot-tall sister, blinked huge, luminous eyes at me. I didn't see him move, but the shadows melted away. Loose fitting, dark gray clothes draped over most of his body, but the rest was covered in a fine layer of fur. Of course he'd be furry.

"What? No. We don't save strangers unless they're paying us."

"Found it," Mae called from around the side of the building. The elevator clunked and a whirring motion sounded behind the doors.

I groaned at the hopeful look the little guy gave me. Y'sindra swayed and glared.

"Look at him, he's harmless. Plus, Y'sindra likes him." Mae dusted off her hands and beamed at our sister's new companion. "She doesn't like anyone. You must be special."

His chest puffed. "Thank you. It has been so long since I was useful. It makes me very happy to help."

"Help?" I narrowed my eyes in suspicion.

"Oh, yes." He dug into a pocket and held my phone out to me. "Your sister asked me to give you this."

"Got pictures." Y'sindra wagged a limp-wristed arm at the phone.

"She allowed me to keep lookout." His wide smile was made of sunshine, and he bounced on his toes.

Well, I'd lost this argument. I sighed and tucked the phone into a zippered pocket.

"Okay, fine." I scraped my hands over my face and doublechecked Y'sindra's work. The ice still held, but she'd drained herself. "He can come with us, but then he's on his own. Got it?"

"What's taking so long?" Mae jogged back around the side of the elevator. The lever clunked twice, and she returned to stare at the doors.

"Excuse me...?"

"Lane," I said and pulled my attention from the excruciating wait for the elevator-portal to Y'sindra's new friend.

"Oh, thank you. I'm honored to know you, Lane. I'm Lonwie—Lo to my friends."

I resisted an eye roll. Lonwie had to be putting on an act. No one was this...naive, guileless. *Nice.*

Y'sindra swayed to the side, and I moved to scoop my sister up, but the little guy had her—and she let him. That fairy must have magicked herself delirious, because otherwise she'd flash-freeze his ass.

The doors hissed open, and I gawked after the pair as he trotted into the box, Y'sindra's head resting with ease on his shoulder.

Mae stood to the side holding the door, expression set with the same shock I felt.

Once inside, Lonwie turned to face Mae and me, regarding us with those round, unblinking eyes.

Ignoring his thousand-watt smile, I followed and turned to face the door. Mae stepped inside, released the door, and hit the single button embedded in the plain white wall.

"Oh, silly me, I almost forgot," Lonwie said. "Your sister asked I inform you that the moon fae returned to the hotel."

"What?" Panic ricocheted down my spine, and I twisted to look down at Lonwie and my snoozing sister.

The elevator clunked, and we shot into space.

23

PRIDE BE DAMNED

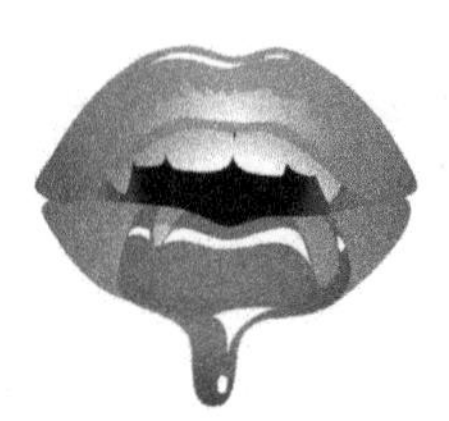

If this half-baked plan didn't work, we were screwed.

I rubbed my thumb over the ridges of Duskmere's communication crystal. Precious seconds passed with no response and then his image projected above my fingers. He scowled and leaned in toward the crystal. His face grew grotesquely large in the holograph-like image. "Where have you been?"

"Explain later. Be ready to open a portal." I closed my fist over the crystal, cutting off the connection and shoved it into my pocket.

Time was up. The elevator would hit the hotel any minute. It gutted me to sacrifice our one sure way home, but with us hurtling toward the death-magic-wielding moon fae and Y'sindra still down for the count, we were out of options.

"You promise you'll stay hidden until I give the all clear?" I asked Mae.

"I said I would." Her face screwed up like she was in pain—and she probably was, agreeing to let me face Nyle alone.

"If things go wrong, get Y'sindra and get out of here. Go back to Shadwe and hide."

"That's not Shadwe, Miss Lane." Lonwie stood by my hip, staring up at me with those enormous orbs of adorableness.

I pressed a hand to my thundering hearts. I'd forgotten the guy was there. Stealthy bugger.

"What do you mean... You know what? Never mind, explain after we get out of here." My brow dipped as I considered him. "Actually, I have a job for you. A critical job. Are you up for it?"

"Oh, yes. Anything to help." His small, clawed hands—I did a double take, yep, tiny retractable claws—steepled at his chest, and he practically vibrated.

Why the hell was he so eager to help strangers? I wanted to be dubious, but my gut didn't stir. He seemed genuine, and Y'sindra, whose tendency was to like no one, took an immediate shine to Lonwie.

"Okay, you have the most important job." The elevator gave a hollow thump and we slowed. My mouth went dry at the reminder of our imminent arrival. "It's clear you've been in that not-Shadwe place for some time. You're familiar. If something goes wrong, it's your job to keep my sisters safe. Find a place to hide until help comes."

If someone came. I had to believe they would.

"I can do that." He stood an inch taller, the fine fur covering his small form puffing and settling.

I drilled Mae with a look that brooked no argument. "You will take Y'sindra and go with Lonwie if anything happens. Stay hidden behind the wall panel but hold the door. If I say go, you go."

How they would escape from the other place, I had no idea. I could only think one step at a time, and that step would save their asses. Mae could take it from there.

"I don't like this."

"But you'll do it?" She had to.

Her jaw worked. "Yes."

A small burst of relief flared. If Mae tried to take on the moon fae, if I lost my sisters... No. I'd never let that happen.

The walls went white, and the elevator gave a second clunk. I rolled my shoulders and shoved those distracting thoughts off their track.

Mae grabbed me in desperate hug, her hot breath ruffling the loose hairs across my forehead. I squeezed and stepped from her hold.

Slow, deliberate breaths through my mouth kept my hearts from accelerating. My fingers curled into loose fists, and I lowered my center of gravity. A pulse beat in the base of my throat. With each thump, time seemed to stretch. It wasn't magic, it was training.

From the back of the elevator, Y'sindra hiccupped a snore. I kept my hyper-focused attention straight ahead, ready.

Our forward momentum eased to a stop.

I bounced on my toes. Once. Twice.

A hiss of released pressure sounded. I stilled, tensed. The doors slid open.

Lonwie kept himself tucked behind the wall while he reached to put a hand over the door frame. Leaning over him, Mae did the same.

"Oy." A distant voice echoed through the lobby. "I already swept the beach. Nobody here."

I drank in my sisters, burned the image into my brain. We'd been in some tight situations before, but not like this. One on one, I might be able to take him, but with the magic he'd proven he had access to, there was no guarantee. It was far from a sure thing that Mae would escape unscathed. Y'sindra didn't have a chance in her condition.

This plan had to work.

My hearts shook my rib cage.

I'd make it work.

Throwing back my shoulders, I stalked from the elevator.

Nyle stood by the back door. He faced the beach.

Putting distance between me and everyone hiding inside the elevator, I strode forward.

"You sure about that?" I asked.

His head whipped around, and his gaze tracked to me. "How? No, you couldn't have escaped."

"I'm disappointed. I thought you knew more about me than that." I stalked in a wide arc around Nyle, keeping him in front of me and positioning to put the dining area at my back.

I needed room to run that didn't lead past my sisters.

The moon fae's eyes narrowed, and he turned to face me fully, a smile pulling at his lips. "I wasn't sure what you could do. Etta'wy swore you were easy to handle, but I figured that swamp dweller had you all wrong."

I bristled at the casual mention of the banshee he'd murdered. No one kills my bounties but me. "Guess you're smarter than your ugly mug gives you credit for."

His smug smile dipped but quickly returned.

Never thought I'd miss Y'sindra's gold-level insults. I wanted to provoke him, get him to light up his magic and give me a probable reason to run, make him chase me. But he wasn't taking the bait.

Time to switch gears.

My dim reflection in the glass wall showed I was almost lined up with the room I'd been inching toward.

"All right." His smile grew to a full-tooth grin. "Time to play?"

"I don't play," I growled and charged.

Talons digging into the overstuffed chair between us, I swung my legs over and used the momentum to launch myself into Nyle.

He raised his hands to defend himself. I ducked low and rammed my shoulder into his gut. Something inside him cracked. The force lifted him up, and I kept pushing forward.

"Oof." His breath exploded from his lungs. Vinegar-scented blood flew into the air.

My arms circled his waist and talons dug into the small of his back. His fists clubbed my spine. I gritted my teeth against the assault.

We collided with the floor-to-ceiling window. It rattled against its frame.

I shouted out my fear. My fury. My desperation

The safety glass cobwebbed behind Nyle.

He growled and managed to wedge his hands beneath my armpits. My arms were an unbreakable band around his waist. He couldn't get the grip on my arms he was after.

I panted and kept the pressure on his abdomen.

This was the moment. I had him. It would be easy to go for his throat. I wanted that with a blinding red rage. But Nyle had answers we needed.

Every fiber in me screamed to forget the sun stones. Fuck the sun fae. They never did a thing for me except bury me beneath insults, leave me on the periphery of their lives. They broke every ounce of me. My best course of action had been to leave, and so I did. I was such a fucking coward.

To the sun fae, to all fae, really, I was nothing but a monster. A disease to be eradicated.

But my father.

Mae.

They needed the stones.

If I wanted those answers I had to follow through with the plan.

I had to let Nyle win.

"Damn it." The sour taste of defeat boiled into my mouth. I relaxed my arms, giving Nyle the room he needed to maneuver his grip. As soon as I allowed the opening, he seized it.

The moon fae knew what he was doing. I'd had a split-second moment of surprise when I attacked him. I wouldn't get it again.

His hands circled my upper biceps, and he tore me away.

"Argh!" I twisted feebly but didn't truly try to escape.

This had to work. He had to believe it.

I swiped at his face but pulled short on the reach to avoid incapacitating him. Still, the tips of my retracted talons raked his cheek. Blood swelled in the open flesh. Feral satisfaction beat in my chest.

"You hybrid bitch."

"Sure am." Time to make my escape. I pulled my knees to my chest to kick him, but he spun and used the momentum to throw me.

Bastard was wiry but strong.

I flew across the sitting area ragdoll style and plowed into the chair. It tilted backward and hit the plush area rug with a muted thump. My ribs compressed on impact, pushing the breath from my body. The backward momentum carried my legs over my head and flipped me onto all fours on the floor.

The chair lay on its back, inches from my face. A high-pitched whine dug into my eardrums, and I dropped flat to my belly. The center of the chair blew out and heat washed over my head. Fear pulled at my scalp. Too damn close.

I rose to my elbows and stared through the hole, past the tufts of melted synthetic stuffing to Nyle's madman grin. The veins scrawling across his face pulsed.

My gaze dropped to the dull moon stone hanging at his chest. He couldn't focus his magic through that stone, not completely. Without an insulator from the level of magic he was casting, he should have a brain bleed. Few races could use magic without some sort of focus, moon fae were not among the short list. Even if the corrupted had miraculously developed the ability, Nyle should be out cold from dumping so much magic.

Across the sitting area, he ducked enough to wink at me through the hole he'd made. That cocky bastard. I bared my fangs.

"There you are. Guess I missed." He laughed. A horizontal vein across his brow throbbed. In the backyard chase, the vein I'd noticed ran vertical, from forehead to cheek. I squinted. Yep, the vertical line was still there but faded.

A nerve jumped in my neck, and I stuttered a gasp. *That's it. Pulsing veins. Blood.* That was what was happening. The magic siphoned through the moonstone *and* his blood. Moon fae weren't built for that.

Blood magic.

Blood fae were the embodiment of this magic, and there was only one way to purify the blood—drink more.

"Hell no." I shot to my feet. "You won't be drinking my blood."

Nyle slapped a hand against his thigh and laughed. "Figured it out, did you?"

Pride be damned, I turned and sprinted around the corner of the dining area. I skidded to a stop. A heavy, wood-backed chair stopped my slide. It cracked against the table and wedged against my hipbone.

Footsteps thundered through the lobby. I dug into the pocket I'd stowed the portal stone, ripped it out, and squeezed it in my fist. The stone warmed against my palm. It worked. I hoped.

His footsteps grew louder. Almost here.

I dredged up every ounce of strength in my body and funneled it into the arm arcing forward. The stone hit the ground. Tile cracked. The stone wedged and didn't roll.

My body pulled taut, wide eyes twitching between the stone and the opening to the lobby. I waited. No portal appeared.

Nyle rounded the corner. His shoes squeaked on the tile as he dug in and came to a quick stop, eyes on the stone. "Tricky, tricky, tricky."

We both watched the stone, waiting. I swallowed. Still nothing. Damn it, I told Duskmere to be ready, so of course he'd make me wait.

"Too bad. You had a good plan." Nyle strolled to the inert stone. "The thing about these is that whoever is on the other end has to be paying attention. It's a subtle tug on our magic—easy to miss, easy to ignore."

His body relaxed, magic lit across his fingers, and he stalked forward. When would this dude run out of juice?

A slice in space ripped open between us. My legs shook with relief. Duskmere appeared leaning against the far wall of a familiar dungeon cell. As if standing between us, his head swiveled from Nyle to me.

I couldn't get Nyle in the portal from here, and it wouldn't stay open long enough for me to get around and push him through. My sisters and I were stuck. No one knew where we were.

Thinking fast, I yanked my phone from my pocket, snapped several quick frames of the surroundings including another decorative map mounted on the wall that I could only hope was of the area and threw the device through the portal. It hit the ground, sending gravel flying. "Code's 3975. Find us."

Through the image of the dungeon, Nyle appeared like a faded vignette. He raised his magic heavy hand and took aim at Duskmere.

"Get down," I shouted.

An avenging angel emerged behind Nyle—Mae.

She let out a roar and bulldozed into his back, sending him headfirst through the portal.

The ball of magic slithered from his fingers and hit the table at my hip. It sheered away a wooden leg, and I jumped out of the way as it crashed to the floor.

The portal snapped shut with a loud crack that echoed through the room.

We did it. My knees turned liquid, and I reached for the closest chair.

Nyle was gone. I didn't die. My sisters were safe.

Light-headed, my jittery gaze flew to Mae and then Y'sindra leaning against the doorframe, Lonwie holding her steady.

Shaking hands pressed to her chest, Mae stumbled into the wall.

The combination of blood-moon magic filled the small room with the cloying scent of dead roses.

Y'sindra toddled away from the door. "Did you..." She swallowed. "Did you use the portal stone?"

"Yes. The moon fae who killed Etta'wy is now in RFG custody, so we know the ones Y'sindra iced can't follow."

"Great, but did you also throw away our only way of calling home?"

I tugged the corner of my lip between my teeth. "Seemed like a good idea at the time."

Mae gathered herself to leave the room, shooing Y'sindra in front of her. "We'll figure out how to get home."

"Hey, what about the elevator?" Anxious, I jogged ahead but found furniture stacked high on the elevator rail. The door slid on its track, hit a chunky chair and bounced open.

Y'sindra snorted. "We took care of it."

"So I see. That should hold them for a while, but we should get home." I made a U-turn for the back door.

"Aren't we worried more moon fae will be waiting?" Y'sindra asked and tottered through the door I held open for everyone.

"Excuse me. I might have helpful information." Lonwie followed my sister but stopped in front of me. "To my knowledge, that portal is the only way in and out of Outerlands. If the barricade we built prevents it from returning, we should remain safe."

"Outerlands. Is that the old space between Ta'Vale and Shadwe before the portal was sealed?"

"Sure is." He gave me a thousand-watt smile and skipped to Y'sindra. Dude was entirely too chipper, but he seemed to know quite a bit. Lonwie might prove useful after all.

"Moon fae have to be familiar with an area to open a portal," Mae said. "I get the impression Etta'wy opened a portal and that's how Nyle first found his way to our property."

"Who?" Y'sindra asked.

"Nyle is the guy Mae shoved through a portal," I told her and stopped on the edge of the deck to appreciate the view. Stars danced over the waves. Foamy white crests, glowing beneath the moon, rose and fell. I'd love to linger, but we didn't have the luxury of time. I took all three stairs to the beach path in a single hop. "I'm with Mae. I suspect Nyle's the only one who could teleport to Interlands."

"Why?" Y'sindra fell into step at my side, flitting into the air every few steps to test her wings.

She didn't sway or stumble from magic exhaustion. Good. One less thing to worry about.

"Because he's like us—specialized. Etta'wy's contact, her handler of sorts."

"And her murderer," Y'sindra said as she rose to my shoulder height and then dropped back down.

True, but not a reminder I appreciated. "He'll pay for that soon enough."

"The RFG won't be gentle," Mae said.

"I'd be disappointed if they were."

Y'sindra's feet scuffed the wood planks, sending her off balance, but Lonwie was there and caught her. Damn fairy gripped his arm instead of pushing him away.

My brows snapped together in disbelief. "Anyhow," I drawled. "It's possible more corrupted moon fae can get to Interlands but not probable.

The only other moon fae I saw were those guards, and they aren't going to leave those three—whoever they are—unattended to chase us down."

"Makes sense." Y'sindra hovered outside the druid circle. "So, we gonna give this thing another go?"

Mae stepped off the wooden path and grimaced as sand flowed into her stupid strappy sandals. Conceding defeat, she waded into the circle. "I don't think we have a choice."

My stomach soured at the thought, and I pressed a fist to my belly. When was the last time we ate? Or slept?

Holding back to ensure the circle didn't accidently trigger short one sister, I let Y'sindra and Lonwie join Mae and then followed. As soon as I broke the perimeter, the same static charge vibrated through my veins. My breath crackled in my lungs.

"This circle, it does something to me." Arms crossed, I scraped my hands up and down the sleeves of my jacket. Whatever was happening, I didn't like it. "You guys seriously don't feel that?"

"It is very warm," Lonwie said.

"Sure is, but that's not what I meant." I clenched and unclenched my hands. "It's electric. My insides are...fizzy."

"Nope, don't feel a thing," Y'sindra said. "You gonna get us home or what?"

I tossed my hands in the air. "As if I know how this thing works. Mae's the one who spends her free time in Eodrom's library."

"No one knows how these circles work." Mae peered from stone to stone and shrugged.

"Well, that's great. How are we supposed to go—"

The world dropped out from beneath my feet.

24

I WANTED TO SCREAM

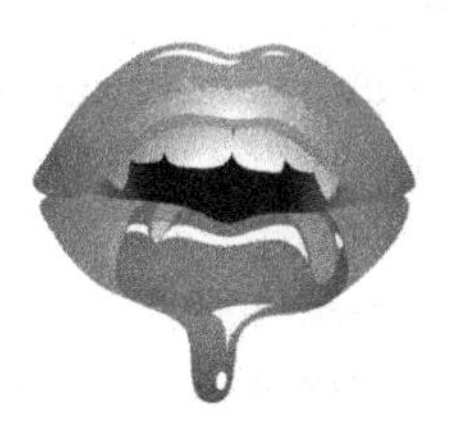

The mid-afternoon Las Vegas sun glared down at us. I lay on the ground groaning. The desert grass—oxymoron—warmed my jacket while its heated blades pushed against my neck. At least my stomach wasn't trying to turn itself inside out, but why was the sky spinning?

I lifted my head enough to see my sisters. Mae sat on her toes, draping her torso over her thighs to press her forehead to the ground. Y'sindra and Lonwie leaned against a tree. Everyone made it through and got out of the circle. Good.

My head still swam, and I lay back down, breathing deep through my mouth. I guess my sisters were half right. We did travel when I said "go," but I didn't believe it had anything to do with me specifically. I sure as hell didn't plan to test that theory anytime soon, or ever.

Above the trees, the cloudless sky rippled. That second trip through the stones must have scrambled my brain. I pushed onto my elbows and waited. For what, I wasn't sure.

A cluster of black birds flew toward the building, while a single wispy cloud drifted away. A sight-seeing helicopter scraped over the high-rises at the other end of the Strip.

I kept an eye on the birds as they flew closer. Getting pooped on would be the icing on the crap cake.

Everything we'd been through was a blur. I still wasn't sure what happened, but as far as I was concerned, our work was done. We found where the moon fae were hiding, the RFG could collect their own stones. Nyle was in custody, Duskmere could interrogate him all he wanted. I was certain he had means of extracting the information they needed. They found out about Etta'wy after all.

Maybe I could convince Duskmere to confiscate Nyle's middle fingers for me. A trophy payment. I chuckled at the thought. Mae and Y'sindra already hated my macabre choice of sundial decor. They'd love a pair of middle fingers mounted over the mantle.

The dark dots of the birds grew larger. They crossed above the building's perimeter. Their forms wavered, subtle and brief.

My chest froze on a gasp, breath locked in my throat. The grass tickled my palm, but my fingers didn't twitch.

Above, the birds appeared normal. The breath I'd held puffed past my lips as I tracked their flight. They passed overhead, moving behind me, and I flipped to kneel in the grass, keeping my gaze glued to the blackbirds as they neared the far side of the building.

"Distorted!"

"Did you hit your head?" Y'sindra wobbled away from the tree.

"No, the birds. There's something above us." I stood and raced to the closest tree, pulling myself up through the limbs. "Didn't you wonder why we've never seen pictures of a druid circle on the Blackthorne rooftop?"

"No, but now that you mention it..." Mae's voice came through the branches.

"I didn't think about it either." I pulled myself up another branch. The earthy, subtle minty scent of fig leaves brushed against me. "But it's weird right? We should have."

The trees were pruned to a manageable ten feet—and no wonder—they were on a high-rise rooftop. I passed the final limb and broke through to the surface and the clear blue sky. The black birds smudged the horizon. Hot metal and a clean scent, like chlorine, wound past the sweet, green odor of rooftop fruit trees.

"What's up?" Y'sindra rose to my level. Her body seemed heavy, but it was a good sign she could fly. She nestled into the treetop next to me, wings tucked tight to her back.

"This." Green figs, unripe and hard, dotted the branches. I plucked one and tossed it upward. The fruit flew about fifteen feet before bouncing against an invisible barrier. A wafer-thin crease against the blue sky rippled outward from the impact of the fig to the edge of the building. It folded at the corner and ran down to the rail.

"What in Odin's hairy beard?" Y'sindra squinted at the empty space above. She gripped a branch on either side and balanced on her toes. The ripple had dissipated and left nothing but clear sky behind. "The same stuff as the elevator walls?"

"I think so."

"What's going on up there?" Mae called.

"Hang on." I slid through the branches and dropped onto the grass. With a wave, I gestured for her to follow me to the edge of the building.

We wound through the assorted fruit trees and shrubs. Once we reached the railing, I took her hand and pressed it toward the empty air above the rail. As anticipated, her palm hit resistance at the far side of the railing.

Mae yanked her hand back and cupped it against her chest. "What is that?"

"I don't know, but I've seen this magic before." I tapped at the weird elastic, invisible wall for emphasis. "First in the sun fae dungeon and again in the elevator. Same feel, same smell. Whatever it is, it surrounds this rooftop. I suspect there's something extra shielding the rooftop from view, maybe hides whatever the creator was interested in keeping secret."

"The druid circle," Mae said.

"Yep. Which leads to the question, is this a form of druidic magic? Do you realize the implications if it is?"

"That the druid built it. Big whoop." Y'sindra twirled a finger in the air and yawned. Lonwie, who I'd once again forgotten about, smothered a laugh.

"Built all of it." I tilted my head waiting for it to sink in.

Y'sindra rolled her eyes so hard, she probably gave herself a migraine. "That's what I said, genius."

"Oh, stars." Mae caught on first. She regarded me above the fingertips pressed to her lips. "The druids built the dungeon."

"Bingo." I made a finger gun. In the greater scheme of everything going on, I wasn't sure where this new bit of information stood on the shit-scale, but we definitely needed to evaluate it further. Or maybe never. It wasn't our problem anymore. "Let's get out of here. Duskmere is going to be pacing a hole in our porch if we don't get home soon."

"Well, you did shove some rando at him and throw a phone at his head," Y'sindra said.

I bared my fangs at her. Lonwie scooted closer to the fairy, to protect her or hide, I wasn't sure. Shaking my head, I crossed to the spiral staircase and started climbing down.

Mae followed on my heels. "She's not wrong."

"You too?" I hopped to the balcony and waited as she descended the last few steps.

"Oh, I think it was the right choice, but I agree he's going to be angry we went without him or any Royal Fae Guard."

"Fair point." Hands on hips, I watched the stairs, waiting for Y'sindra to come down.

"Boo," she whispered in my ear.

Talons raking air, I leaped back, and my hip collided with the knotted wood end of the stair's railing. "Why the shit would you do that?" I massaged the latest addition to my collection of bruises and glared until I realized what —or rather who—hovered in the air with her.

Y'sindra, knowing my knee-jerk reaction to surprise had easily dodged my swipe and dropped to the ground along with Lonwie, where she stood grinning. "Didn't know he could fly, did you?"

"Pfft. Of course I did. It was obvious." It wasn't obvious at all. Where did he hide those wings? All fairies, male and female, wore loose, light clothes for a reason. The backs were easily tailored to accommodate wings. I'd been trying to convert Y'sindra to tunic and leggings for years, but still hadn't broke her of her baby doll dress habit. In contrast, Lonwie wore something that could pass for a potato sack.

"Mmm hmm, sure." Y'sindra slow winked and skipped toward the far side of the balcony with her new friend in tow, followed by Mae.

I trailed behind my sisters, cutting beneath a shaded overhang and skirting a long planter backed by a trellis covered with of all things, grapes. This guy loved his fruit. Was it magic or money that kept everything growing in the dry Nevada climate? Mae had the green thumb, and she hadn't yet marveled at the assortment, so it must be money.

Leaning over the railing, my stomach quivered at the seven hundred-something-foot drop. All the conditioning I endured, climbing the trees on our property day after day to push past my crippling terror, hadn't prepared me for this height. This was so much higher than those trees.

My lungs weren't large enough for all the air they needed. A buzz hummed between my ears. My knuckles bleached white on the railing, but I wouldn't pull my gaze away.

I could have polished off a bucket of cheesy poofs in the time it took for my pulse to slow from a gallop to a trot. To be fair, I was a slow eater.

I'd conditioned myself to overcome this very reasonable fear, but the recent fall triggered memories best left buried. Battling back the panic, my grip relaxed and eyes slid shut. I let my head fall forward, enjoying the stretch in my neck as my muscles relaxed. A swath of hair, loose from Y'sindra's elaborate braiding, fell across my face. I smiled against the strands tickling my lips. I'd done it.

"We might have a problem." Mae's voice was tight. She swatted at my shoulder. "Lane..."

I turned to Mae and found her staring not at the cityscape, but behind us, at the penthouse. Following her gaze, waves of needles rolled from my scalp to my toes.

Mr. Black carried paper bags from his entry to the kitchen.

With nowhere to go, none of us moved. Y'sindra's wings didn't so much as shiver.

I breathed through my mouth. Maybe he wouldn't see us. Maybe he wouldn't look up. And maybe I could shoot rainbows out of my ass. How could I have forgot the druid returned to Vegas before we did? Stupid, simple mistakes would get us killed. I wanted to scream, but that meant moving.

Pulling something from the bag, he placed it on the counter, looking up as he did. He reached back into the bag, looking down, but his arm stilled. His head snapped up.

He saw us.

25

TOO SLOW. TOO LATE.

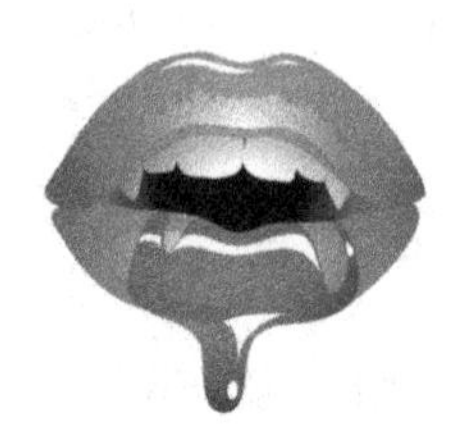

Mr. Black shouted, but the closed glass door effectively blocked his words. I didn't have to hear him to know he was pissed.

"Go, go, go!" I waved my arms to herd Y'sindra and Lonwie over the edge of the balcony. They shot over the rail. One worry down.

I spun to collect Mae, but infrasound pounded my eardrums and the world tilted. My knees cracked onto concrete. My vision grew fuzzy around the edges, pulsed. I couldn't hear it, but the wave of familiar dizziness pulled me dangerously close to unconsciousness. I melted to the floor, and my head thunked the cement. Involuntary tears pooled at my temples, ran into my hairline. This couldn't happen. Mae would be trapped here without me, helpless.

"Lane!" She knelt and tried to pull me up.

Beyond Mae, the druid leaned on his staff as he came toward us, holding a wooden horn to his mouth.

Had Etta'wy told him about me? About me being a blood fae? Infrasound: the one sure way to stop a blood fae. Suddenly, being able to weather a banshee's wail didn't seem like such a good trade.

I tried to push to my feet, but my limbs refused to cooperate. Mae was tough, but her magic wasn't offensive. She couldn't maintain her protection forever. Damn it, I couldn't lay here and let this happen.

My consciousness rolled in and out, never quite pulling me under, but leaving me unable to do more than watch the druid's relentless walk toward us.

At least Y'sindra got away. She could tell Duskmere what happened. He could bring the RFG down on this asshole.

The glass door slid on its track. Mr. Black, in loose beige lounge pants and fuzzy navy slippers, stepped onto the balcony. At least they weren't bunny slippers. I couldn't live with being killed by someone in bunny slippers.

With his dark gaze glued to me, he lowered the horn, waist-length, silvery brown braid swaying behind him. "I was wondering when you'd show up. Etta'wy might not have believed you'd figure it out, but she was a fool. I knew it was only a matter of time."

What was with these guys thinking my tainted blood made me some sort of mastermind? First Nyle and now Mr. Black.

My equilibrium tried to find its buoyancy. It sloshed side to side in my skull. I licked my lips and pushed onto an elbow, but my arm shook, threatening to refuse the weight.

"How?" Did I actually speak? I wasn't sure, but if I could keep him talking, keep his mouth away from that horn, I could get enough strength to do...something. My arm already shook less, but I didn't want to show it. I let myself collapse to the ground.

Mae crouched over me. The heat of her magic turned my jacket toasty as she prepared to throw a shield over us. Sweat beaded on my forehead, my neck.

"This is all a misunderstanding." Sweet, pacifist Mae tried to reason with Mr. Black. He didn't look like a monster. Therefore he couldn't be one in her eyes. Ha! "It sounds like you did your research on us. If that's the case, you know we hold no allegiance to Ta'Vale. We were doing a job, that's all."

The druid's gaze slid to my sister. Good girl, smart. Keep him distracted. While his attention was diverted, I let my body relax, gain strength.

"We both know that isn't true. For your sister, that's probably the case. You? I'm afraid not."

That was a lot of specific information to know about us. Maybe Etta'wy wasn't the only one with contacts in Eodrom. Although Mr. Black was obscure enough, ordinary enough, he could have come and gone from Interlands and Ta'Vale—even Eodrom. No one would have suspected a thing.

My brain had stopped sloshing around my skull. The shakes were gone. If he stayed focused on Mae long enough, I could rush him, smash that stupid horn.

I had one shot. It needed to count.

Keeping my moves tight, I crawled my hand toward Mae who knelt by my hip. A squeeze to her ankle let her know I was awake. Hopefully, she'd interpret the intention. *I'm okay. Be ready.*

Her magic shuddered but quickly coalesced, heated, readying.

Relief coated me. Mae understood. She'd stay out of the way. One less thing for me to worry about.

I closed my eyes and pulled deep breaths through my nose and pushing the breath out and over my lips. Oxygen rich blood flooded my limbs. I tensed, readying for attack.

"Bonzai!" a squeaky voice shrieked.

She wouldn't.

My eyes popped open and dropping all pretense of being incapacitated, I leaped to my feet.

She did.

A tiny cyclone, otherwise known as Y'sindra, zoomed over the balcony.

Loyal to her wintery marrow, the stubborn troublemaker didn't listen to me. She hadn't fled. Damn her.

Stars, I loved her. I would also throttle her if we made it out alive.

Mr. Black spun toward Y'sindra and lifted the staff, holding it parallel in front of him. Understanding iced the blood in my veins. He didn't need it to stand or walk. The staff was his focus. Shit. He would nuke my sister. My feet propelled me toward the druid before my brain registered the action.

"Y'sindra, no!" I wouldn't get there in time. I might be fast, but not faster than magic.

Little more than a shifting of shadows, Lonwie rose above the rail behind Mr. Black. He barreled into his back, sending him staggering.

The druid swung around, arms wide, swiping the empty air with his staff.

Y'sindra blitzed from behind and snagged the horn from his other hand. She kept flying and dove over the railing.

Lonwie flew for the opposite side of the deck, his quad dragonfly-like wings a furious hum. Mr. Black had a bead on him. Lonwie wasn't going to make it. My stomach took flight. I couldn't let him get hurt.

"Hey!" I rushed the druid, balcony floor vibrating beneath my heavy boots.

Too late, the druid began to turn. I bulldozed into his side.

The beach window had been made of stronger stuff.

The world fractured, cracked against my eardrums. I pressed my face into the druid's shoulder as I rode him through the glass door, down to his living room floor.

"Oof." Beneath me, the druid grunted.

Mae's magic coated me. Through the shimmering shield, pressure pinged against me. Glass shards bounced against my shielded back.

I rolled off the druid and forward into the room. Behind me, Mr. Black screamed. I spun and raced for the shattered door, a spike of glass sticking out of his arm caught my attention. Served him right. "Hope that's your horn arm."

The druid spat curses at me as I flew past him, toward the balcony. Glass splintered beneath him as he rolled to his feet, crying out as new shards drove into his body.

I leaped over the jagged ring of glass and without pause, grabbed Mae and swung her behind me. She knew exactly what to do. Her arms circled my neck and legs clung to my waist. I vaulted a teak lawn chair and swerved around a potted palm.

"Lane, no!" Mae shouted, realizing I wasn't taking us into the penthouse and out the front door.

Mr. Black had already gained his feet. He owned the entire building. Even if we got past him, one call would bring security. We'd never make it out alive.

I didn't give myself time to panic, time to think about how high up we were—shit, *now* I was thinking about it.

My fingers gripped the railing. I pushed up and over into the nothingness of open air. Nothing above. Nothing below.

My nerve endings ignited. My stomach climbed into my mouth.

And then I let go.

26

IN THE GRAY

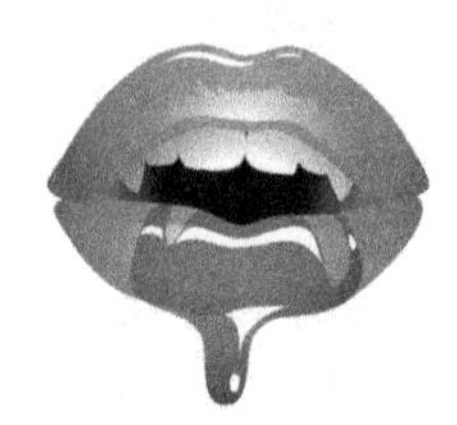

MAE SHOUTED MY NAME. THE WIND TORE IT AWAY AND CARRIED IT OUT of earshot, even as her magic sizzled over my skin. The shield would save my face if I brushed against the exterior, but it wouldn't do a damn thing for us if I didn't stop our fall. Floor after floor screamed past at dizzying velocity.

A balcony flew by. I slammed my hands against the steel frame beam, but my talons didn't punch through. Sparks rained over us. A high-pitched whine stabbed my eardrums.

No, no, no! I scrambled against the side of the building but couldn't catch hold.

I'd miscalculated horribly. We were going to die.

We plummeted past another balcony.

My stomach left my body. I was hollow.

Another floor.

Too fast. We were going too fast. Even if I caught hold now, the force would rip my claws from my hands.

Steel transitioned to concrete. Relief itched along my spine.

My hearts hammered my chest, threatening to break me open.

I pulled back my arms and flung them forward, driving my talons into the reinforced concrete. We jerked, didn't stop, but slowed. *Come on stop, damn you*! Hellfire roared in my shoulder sockets. Pain tore down my arms, up my neck. The wind stole away tears of pain before they could wet my cheeks.

Traces of concrete pummeled our protective bubble, stinging like a thousand bee stings, even through the shield. My retractable claws extended further than they were meant to, tearing at the quicks. Waves of darkness chased across my vision. I screamed.

My talons would snap. I'd have no way to stop us. We'd fall.

The shield pressed into the building beneath my claws, leaving slivers of fingertips exposed. Flesh and blood smeared down the side of the building. Pain reached into my gut and tried to pull it inside out.

Our descent stopped. I sucked oxygen and blinked wind-dry eyes at the pool next to me extending from the face of the building. The pool deck. We'd only dropped eight floors. Not as far as it felt, but probably why my shoulders were still in their sockets, and Mae and I weren't fae soup on the sidewalk.

I panted in agony, in relief. If not for the extra layer of protection from Mae's magic, I'd be short ten claws.

Mae pressed flat against my back, her face buried against my neck, legs pretzeled around my waist. The pressure of her knees on my ribs was nothing compared to the torture in my arms, in my fingers. Easy to ignore.

Wind chased across the building's face and broke against an eight-inch-thick acrylic glass box containing one of the hotel's prize features—a suspended pool. Gusts pulled at my clothes, tugged my hair, but otherwise left us relatively undisturbed in the box's shadow.

Mae's shield dropped, and a chill from its sudden absence chewed into my bones. Blood rolled onto my fingers, down my hands to dry before it reached my wrists. The wind swooped over and under and tore loose what hair remained in my braids.

Butterflies filled my chest, clogged my throat.

"We're alive." My voice came out raw. I reached out with one leg and propped it against the Plexiglass barrier to hold steady, but made the mistake of looking down.

My stomach executed a triple axel. Panic grabbed hold, squeezed.

"It's okay," Mae shouted to be heard. "You're okay."

I nodded and closed my eyes. I had to calm the fuck down and get us to the ground, or we were dead.

Mae's face ruffled in my hair. "Um, Lane."

My eyes cracked opened. "What..." The words dried on my tongue. To our left, on the other side of the plexiglass, a cluster of people gathered in the waist-high water. The pool extended about ten feet past the hotel front, and these crazy tourists were clustered at the edge of the overhang, gawking, some still inside but most on the floor hanging over empty air. They were insane.

"Get inside." They couldn't hear me. I bared my fangs to scare them away. A camera phone flashed. Idiots.

"If you can get closer," Mae shouted. "I can reach the barrier and climb over."

Poor, naive Mae. She still thought we were going through the hotel. Security had to be swarming the place by now. Even if I could get through them all, could my sister? Either of them? Not worth the risk. I could do this. Probably. Maybe. I wasn't a deep well of confidence, more like a puddle.

Beyond the gawkers, men in sleek black suits and reflective Ray Bans gathered at the edge of the pool—security. They were the kick in the ass I needed to get moving.

The building's face below us was concrete broken by regular bands of steel-framed windows. I'd have to time this perfectly.

Inside the box, vampire Vaughn had joined the security guards. He looked both shocked and pissed to see us out here. Mostly pissed. It was now or never. "Hold on!"

"Wait. What? No!" The wind ran away with Mae's protest. Her octopus grip on me tightened, and her magic burned over us, hot and bright.

I ripped my hands free and dropped.

Seconds passed fast in free fall, and it wouldn't even take ten to hit the ground. I needed distance from the druid. Twenty or so more floors were enough. After that, I'd Spider-Man crawl us to the ground.

Steel flashed below my toes. I drilled my talons into the building. Too soon. They ticked against the base of the steel-framed window. My vision went wobbly with fear, but the tips of my claws punched into the wall inches below the frame.

My arms jerked, and we slid in a cloud of concrete dust. It coated my lungs, stuffed my nostrils. The further we dragged down the wall, the deeper my claws dug. My damaged fingertips grazed concrete. A wave of dizziness rolled beneath my eyelids, bright white flashes of agony.

We came to a halt. Fire licked over my shoulder muscles, down my arms. Pain pulled tears from beneath my lashes. I opened my eyes and blinked away the moisture. Sunlight filtered through concrete dust. The soles of my boots found traction on the wall and helped hold us steady against the buffeting wind.

There were no sounds above the hammering of my pulse. No shouts from the balconies above or street noises from below. I swallowed and looked down. My neck pinched, but I didn't lose myself to panic.

We'd dropped at most fifty feet. Not as far as I'd wanted, but this was too risky. I'd crawl from here. It wouldn't be as fast, but it would still get us to the ground before the druid. Hopefully before security could assemble.

I yanked my right hand free. Pieces of the building came away with my talons and rained bits of plaster over us. I reached down with my right arm until elbow met knee and extended my left leg at the same time. Embedding my talons into the wall wasn't as easy without the force of the fall behind them. At least I'd keep my fingertips, what was left of them.

"You can do it," Mae said against my ear. I nodded and repeated the process.

Left, right, left. Calm chased the remnants of panic from my shaky limbs. I climbed at a slight diagonal and then down between the steel framed windows. Once there was nothing but concrete between us and the ground, I lost myself to the repetitive action.

We did it. We found the moon fae. Y'sindra got pictures of their hideout —Outerlands—no doubt where they'd tucked away the stones. We captured the finger flipper and faced down a druid. I'd say all in a day's work I hoped never to do again.

Daydreams of trashy reality tv marathons, long naps, and never-ending bowls of cheesy poofs occupied my thoughts as I continued the slow crawl to freedom.

"Lane." My nerves twanged, and I froze at Lonwie's voice so close. If Y'sindra insisted we bring him home, I'd put a bell on him. "You must move."

I turned my head enough to see him. "Y'sindra?"

"Safe." His voice grew and fell as he flew side to side above me. "Please hurry. The druid."

I looked up. Beyond the near-invisible infinity pool and its crowd of tourists who still hadn't retreated inside, Mr. Black hung over the side of his balcony. We'd made it halfway down and he was little more than a stick figure —waving a stick. His staff. Shit.

"Hold on," I shouted to Mae and ripped both hands free. We dropped.

Mae's magic warmed but no shield followed. She must have overtaxed her sun shard. Good thing we had a big bag of them at the house.

I caught hold but immediately let go. Short bursts. Two floors at a time. Cut out recovery. Who needed fingertips?

Green magic smashed into the wall at my hip, showering us with more concrete. A ball of writhing vines unfurled. Thorny arms stretched outward, toward us, seeking.

What the ever-fucking fuck?

I tore my claws free and fell. The wait for two windows—two floors—took ages. We cleared the second window, and I drove my talons home without the wrenching pull on my shoulders. We dropped again. Again.

Faint car horns, a siren, and the rush of traffic penetrated my haze.

We were so close. Exhaustion stuffed itself into every pore. I pressed my forehead to the building. A few more falls and we'd be in the parking lot—safe.

"Watch out!" Lonwie yelled.

My muscles tangled together. I pulled flush with the wall and tilted my face to the sky.

Above, Mr. Black was a smudge against the sun peeking over the balcony's edge.

Lonwie put himself between us and the druid, shouting for me to move. My brain ran sluggish, couldn't process the events fast enough, and I clung there, frozen.

A sphere of thrashing vines encased in green magic grew larger and larger behind Lonwie.

"Lo. Behind you!"

"No!" Mae screamed.

The ball collided with Lo, engulfed him in a cocoon of vines and thorns. He hurtled toward the ground.

Instinct pushed me from the wall, and I reached out to intercept his fall.

Razor-sharp thorns pierced my body, went deep. I shrieked.

Oh, stars, don't let them stab Lo. He's so small. Please let him be alive.

We hurtled toward the asphalt. Mae let go. I sent a desperate prayer to the universe that she had enough magic left to dampen her landing.

I curled my body around Lo, tucking and rolling. The impact shoved thorns into my belly. I screamed. The druid's magic burned where it pierced flesh.

As soon as we stopped rolling, I unfurled and twisted to kneel by my precious cargo. "Lo." My voice shook, and I ignored the painful cramps twisting my stomach. "Lo!

No response came. My sisters sprinted toward us.

"Lo!" Y'sindra's bare knees hit the asphalt. She turned her liquid gaze on me.

"He saved us," I said. "We'll take care of him."

She nodded and swiped a shaky hand over her damp cheeks. Mae put her arm around Y'sindra's shoulders.

Inside the nest of vines, Lo groaned. We all three jumped.

"Lo?" Y'sindra leaned toward him.

I grabbed her hand before she could touch the thorns. "Don't. There's magic on them."

A cough came from within the nest of vines.

Y'sindra sobbed her relief and dropped to eye level with Lo. "You fool. Don't do that again."

Fool? Wow, that was an incredibly nice insult coming from her.

"Lo, we're here. Are you hurt?" I asked and crawled around the vine ball. There had to be a way through.

"No. I...I think the thorns are on the outside." His voice emerged muffled by the magic and vines encasing him. He shifted, and the ball stretched with his movements. "You called me Lo."

I sat back and pressed my throbbing fingertips to my mouth. Despite my obvious distrust and reluctance to help him, Lo had still risked his life to save my sisters and me. Salt in my guilt wound. Here he was happy I'd called him by the name he reserved for friends.

Shame gripped me. "I'm sorry, I should have—"

Asphalt sprayed in every direction, and a crater opened next to us. I slung a protective arm across my face. A cloud of dust floated from the impact. Thorn-laden vines whipped from the fading debris.

"What is that?" Y'sindra backpedaled.

"Car. Now." I scooped Lo up, barely registering the thorns that sank into my palms, and sprinted for the valet desk. My toe caught on the curb, and I stumbled. My legs were heavy. I shook my head to clear the cobwebs. Something was wrong.

Mae stiff-armed the valet away from the stand and dug through the cabinet of keys. "Got them!" She came away with the wolf's head key chain.

I struggled to lift my legs, and with each step, my feet grew heavier. Teddy's orange Trans Am was a beacon. Thank the stars I'd had that hundred to get us parked so close. My steps grew sloppy. I stumbled, cracking my hip against the trunk. Everywhere the thorns had touched burned.

Mae opened the passenger door, took one look at me and ran around the car to throw herself into the driver's side. Great, her driving sucked.

"What's wrong with you?" Y'sindra hovered next to me, her anxious gaze bouncing between me and Lo.

"Thorns poisoned." My tongue was thick in my mouth. I could barely speak. Couldn't stand straight, my feet anchored to the ground.

Using the car as support, I slid along the side. Y'sindra scrambled ahead and flipped the front seat forward.

The engine let out a throaty roar.

I flirted with consciousness. My feet tangled—twisted. I teetered in the gray, body tilting toward the ground.

"Lane," Y'sindra shouted, frantic.

Her voice broke through. Faint. I sank a fang into my tongue, the sharp pain cut through the lurking darkness.

"M'okay." I pushed upright. Heat circled my neck. I wouldn't last long.

One foot in front of the other, slow and plodding, I finally reached the passenger door. Though I wanted to lift my arms, they weighed a thousand pounds. I had to get Lo inside the car. My chest pulsed with a sob. We'd made it, I couldn't fail now. If I didn't get him inside, Y'sindra would try herself. I wouldn't let her be poisoned, too. Not if I could do something about it.

"Stop!" Shouts came from the casino's entrance. Security finally caught up.

Damn it, I could do something. I would.

I swiveled my body away from the car and back toward the open door. My dead weight arms swung inside the car, and I let go of Lo.

"Ah!" The colossal effort pulled a shout from my lungs. The vine ball rolled across the cramped back seat. I tried to follow but my vision wavered. I couldn't focus, couldn't hold my balance.

My chin hit the door frame, and I fell backward.

For a split second the bright blue sky filled my vision before my head cracked against the asphalt. Darkness swallowed me whole.

27

BORED, BROKE, AND OUT OF BUSINESS

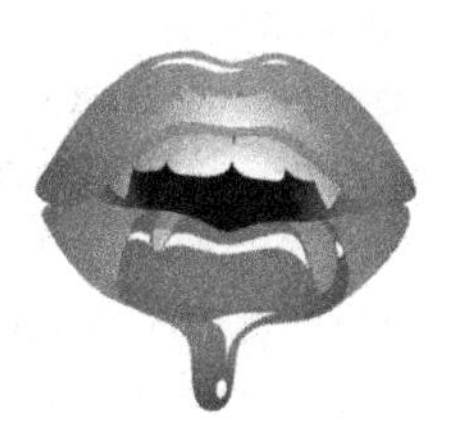

I CAME TO WITH A TWITCH, A SNORT, AND HORRIBLE CRIMP IN MY NECK. A lump throbbed on the back of my skull. The car rocked through a pothole, bouncing my head against the door frame. A string of curses flew from my mouth. I loved my sister, but Mae's driving sucked.

Groaning, I pushed upright in the backseat and wedged myself into the corner for stability. Pieces of torn seat scraped beneath my palms. I followed the line of punctures to Lo's prone form and winced. He lay on the bench seat, one leg dangling off the edge. The thorny vines were gone, but they'd left a trail of destruction in their wake. Couldn't wait to explain this to Teddy.

At the litany of curses and groans, Mae twisted to look over her shoulder at me. Y'sindra's bright white head leaned into the center console space.

I squinted against the sun glaring through the windshield and flicked my hand at Mae. "I'm okay. Watch the road." My voice came out rough and raw, as if someone had stuffed cotton and razors down my throat. I forced a swallow.

Defying all logic, despite the multiple near-death escapes we had executed, my first coherent thoughts were of Teddy. The sun was out. I'd missed my dinner date.

"We shoulda done the quokka maneuver," Y'sindra said.

I rubbed a hand over my face. It felt puffy. "That will never be a thing."

Her obsession with small furry creatures was ridiculous. My gaze slid toward Lo fast asleep on the seat next to me. Small furry creatures.

"But quokkas throw their young for a diversion. I'm a helluva diversion."

"Urban legend, Y'sindra." I swallowed the desert in my throat. "They don't actually do that, and why throw you? You can fly."

"Dream killer."

Next to me, Lo snuffled. I rolled my head on the seat in his direction. A scratch on his right cheek flamed crimson beneath the nearly imperceptible fur on his face, and thin traces of green surrounded the wound. Related to the druid magic? He shivered and pulled his knees toward his middle. My general lack of empathy, of which I had none, did a full reverse. Careful of my as of yet unhealed injuries, I slipped free of my jacket and laid it over Lo's still form.

"Did you check to see if the thorns got him anywhere else?" I asked, tucking the edges of my jacket beneath his sides to prevent it from sliding.

"Of course, duh." Y'sindra's tone was gentler than her words. She had that doe-eyed look about her again.

"Why so protective? You didn't even know the guy yesterday."

She plucked at the frayed edges of her seat. "He wanted to help. No strings attached. How many folks can you say that about?"

"Point taken, but this level of nice from you is unheard of."

"You know my history." She pressed her forehead into the back of her seat, leaving only a puff of snow-white hair visible. "I know what it means to be abandoned."

Despite the stabbing pain in my abdomen, I reached around the front seat to squeeze her shoulder. "And to be saved."

Y'sindra lifted her head and nodded.

"Fair enough. I promise to give him a chance." And I would. He deserved that and more.

"Damn straight..." Y'sindra began but shook her head. "Thank you."

Sincerity hurt my sister. She didn't show her heart often, but it was in there, and it was huge. Awake, but still groggy, I smiled and eased back.

"How do you know he was abandoned?" Mae asked.

"He found me while I was taking pictures, came out of nowhere. I blasted him from the air and was about to turn him into an ice cube, but instead of defending himself he warned me about a patrol headed my way." She gave a one-shoulder shrug. "After the patrol passed, I asked Lo what he was doing there. He said his master left, and he was waiting for him to return."

"Master?" Disgust snapped my spine straight, and I bumped my head against the roof.

"Yeah, but it gets worse," Y'sindra said, and damn if her icy blue eyes didn't mist up. "Whoever this master is, he left shortly before the sun fae sealed the veil between Ta'Vale and Shadwe, or rather, Outerlands."

Mae gasped.

"What?" My talons dug into the already mutilated seat. "That was over a hundred years ago. This master better hope I never find him."

"He better hope *we* never find him," Y'sindra amended. "I plan to put the deep freeze on his nards."

"You're a scary little thing." She made me proud.

"Scary things come in small packages."

Wasn't that the truth.

In the rearview, I caught the wink Mae gave Y'sindra. "Glad you're on our side."

"Yeah, yeah. I buy your love with fear."

My sisters' banter wrapped around me like a fuzzy blanket. I rested my forehead against the warm glass of the tinted passenger window and took in our surroundings. We cruised down an unfamiliar street in some nondescript suburb. Xeriscape yards with rocks for lawns and drought-resistant greenery rolled past. "Where are we?"

"We had to take a detour." Mae started to turn in her seat but caught herself. "Some cars pursued us from Blackthorne, but I think we lost them. I'm headed home now. Hopefully no one's staking out Root."

"Doubt it. They have a multi-million-dollar hotel to maintain." Sure, we broke into the elusive owner's penthouse and effectively hotwired his druid circle, but we didn't steal anything. Mr. Black had a hotel to run, sun stones to hide, and a corrupt race of fae to assist. "How long was I out?"

"About thirty minutes." Y'sindra rested her elbows on the console and chin on her fists.

I pushed higher in the seat. Tacky and heavy from blood, my shirt resisted any attempt at movement. I tried to pluck the saturated cotton from my belly, but threads pressed into half-healed puncture wounds pulled. My vision tilted, and I dropped the shirt. Sooner or later I'd have to yank it free.

Preferably sooner, before the punctures healed completely, but who knew when that would happen.

"If you don't break out the medicine when we get home, I'm telling Mom." Y'sindra stared at my blood-soaked shirt.

That was no small threat. Mom was a force of nature. I stuck out my tongue. "I will. I have to."

If the throbbing knot on my skull was any indication, my healing had slowed to a crawl. Bumps and bruises were the first to heal, and they hadn't. Time to rip off the bandage. I took a deep breath and tore my shirt from my raw flesh.

"Shit." I pounded a hand against the doorframe. My head dropped back against the seat, and I breathed through the pain.

Mae whipped toward me in time to plow through another yawning pothole. My teeth clacked together but thankfully missed my tongue. The Trans Am's frame heaved and shuddered in defeat.

"The idea." I swallowed and licked my chapped lips. "Is to avoid the holes."

"I'm trying."

"Not hard enough," Y'sindra said, climbing back into her seat after falling into the footwell. If she would only wear a seatbelt.

Fresh, warm blood seeped beneath my shirt. Between Mae's driving, the druid thorns, and me bleeding all over the place, Teddy's car was ruined. Hopefully, this wasn't the thing to chase him away.

After everything my sisters and I just went through, that was the last thing I should be concerned about, but I was. Then again, I had suffered a head wound.

I folded up the hem of my shirt—which at this point felt more like damp cardboard than fabric—for a better look at my stomach. Violent pink ridges surrounded the thorns' entry points, but the holes themselves were congealed globs of glistening blood. Not even scabs had formed. The deeper punctures still leaked. Paper-thin green lines circled the edges of the wounds. This was definitely related to the druid magic. I'd wait until I started sprouting leaves or developed a sudden fondness for trees to be concerned.

The partially healed wounds didn't gush blood, but they oozed anew. Careful not to tear anything else, I used the fingertip of my ring finger—my least damaged digit—to massage the tender flesh surrounding the wounds. The skin wasn't hot to the touch, and the muscles beneath didn't hurt.

Overall, the damage from our brush with Mr. Black wasn't as bad as I'd feared. I let the heavy shirt fall and leaned back on a sigh.

More ruined clothes, and damn it, I liked this shirt.

I found Y'sindra smirking at me. "Keep this up and soon you'll have to go naked."

"Or you can finally wear those dragon skin leathers."

Of course fashion obsessed Mae couldn't resist pointing out the incredibly rare, nearly priceless, and almost indestructible leathers I came by pretty dishonestly. I neither slayed the dragon nor stole the skin.

Mae hung a right at the end of the street. Still no cars followed. We turned left onto another twisting side street, passing through another nondescript neighborhood on our winding way back to Root. I had no idea where we were, but Mae drove with purpose. Between her uncanny memory and Y'sindra's navigational ability to always locate true north, we'd find our way home.

Fate, that fickle bitch, had put those two in my father's path and granted me better sisters than I deserved.

Brief exchanges between my sisters and Lo's quiet snores had become the soundtrack to our road trip home. The druid magic still tugged at my lids, and I dozed on and off until I spotted a familiar landmark.

"We're close." I pointed through the center console to the fast-food joint ahead. The permanent message on the marquee read *Last burger before Interlands*. Y'sindra and I were regulars.

"Food at last." Y'sindra stood in her seat and pressed her palms to the dash. I shook my head at her continued lack of a seat belt. "We're stopping, right?"

"We'll be home soon," Mae said. "I'll cook."

Kale and quinoa? No thank you.

"I'm with Y'sindra. Feels like I haven't eaten in days." My stomach took that as a cue to let out a mighty rumble. I pressed a fist into my belly. "See? I'm starving."

"Fine, we'll stop." Mae squinted at me in the mirror as if I'd orchestrated the stomach growl. "If we get spotted by Blackthorne security, it's on you two.

"I'll take my chances." I propped my crossed ankles on the console. "Get me three animal-style burgers. Four, no, five orders of fries, and a strawberry milkshake."

The car went quiet, and I looked up to find Mae gawking at me in the rear view and Y'sindra grinning.

"What? I'm hungry. Should probably order something for Lo, too."

"We don't know what he eats." Y'sindra came away from the dash and leaned on my ankles.

I rolled my head on the seat toward our sleeping passenger. "Order a plain burger. If he doesn't eat vegetables, we've got him covered. If he doesn't eat meat, he'll have the bun and fries."

"And an extra shake," Y'sindra added.

Mae flipped on the blinker and steered us into the fast-food parking lot. "That has nothing to do with you wanting one of every flavor, right?"

"Absolutely not."

Next to me, Lo finally sat up with a stretch and a yawn. He caught me watching and froze, then his fine furry face transformed into pure joy. "Hello. I must have fallen asleep."

"You could say that." Mae's laugh came out on a breathy rush of relief.

"It's okay. Whatever magic hit you, also knocked out Lane." Y'sindra hooked a thumb in my direction. "She just woke up too."

That wasn't entirely true, but I got the feeling she wanted to put Lo at ease, so I didn't contradict her.

We pulled up next to the digital menu and a voice floated out. "Welcome to In-N-Out Burger, how can I help you today?"

"Gosh, hello! Do you know—"

I pulled Lo from the window and shook my head.

Mae recited our order into the speaker.

Leaning close to Lo, I lowered my voice. "We are ordering food. Have you been to Earth before?"

"No. Is that where we are?" Lo stood on the seat and pressed against the window.

"Yes, that's where we've been since we came through the elevator." I bit the edge of my lip. Why hadn't Lo left Outerlands before we got there? An elevator wasn't exactly a two-person job. "You never went through the elevator—the portal?"

"I had to stay so I could report to my master when he returned. Once the druid parted the veil, I just knew he'd be back soon." Lo shook a fall of curls from his brow and sat down. "My master promised to come back for me, and he is true to his word. Only I couldn't wait any longer. It's getting too dangerous, and he must know. I will find him."

I doubted that. Not only was it a great big universe out there, whatever piece of garbage abandoned this guy, they had no plans to come back for him. "Your...master ordered you to stay?" The word left a foul taste in my mouth. One I wanted to rinse away with a strawberry shake.

Y'sindra scooted onto the center console facing Lo and me. I pushed up from the seat to peer over her head at the line of cars. Three vehicles separated us from lunch.

"Golly, no. I stayed because as Shadwe's crown prince, he would need to know what was happening so close to his realm."

Shell-shocked, I fell into the seat. Y'sindra's jaw dropped open. At least a hundred questions sat on my tongue, but I settled for one. "Your *maste*r is the prince of Shadwe?"

"Yes...well, no. Not *the* prince. There are two. The eldest was in that room you escaped from."

That meant we escaped two princes: the moon fae who could be none other than the despicable Prince Miro and this Shadwe prince. Fan-fucking-tastic. May I never see any of them again.

"My master is the crown prince of the Barbout bloodline. Well, he was. I wish to the shadows he hadn't, but my master renounced his name and any claims on ruling. That is why we left Shadwe. We had a home in Outerlands, but Prince Aventheo—that's my master." Lo paused his tide of words to swell with obvious pride. "My master left to find a new home for us."

Lo's fondness for this so-called master shined through in his every action, every word. I wrinkled my nose in distaste, but aside from the illusion of ownership, nothing about Lo said he'd been mistreated.

Fine, instead of making this Aventheo bleed, I'd turn him over to Teddy. We'd done damage aplenty to his car, and Teddy could take it out of this prince's hide. I settled into my seat with a smile. Sometimes, I had strokes of brilliance.

We inched a car-length closer to the drive-thru window. Despite the oniony, earthy scent of fried potatoes and hamburgers wafting through Mae's open window, my eyelids drifted shut. The druid magic still pushed that sluggish feeling through my veins. My breath deepened, the purr of the idling Trans Am lulled me deeper.

I woke to a hot paper bag hitting my lap. I blinked stupidly at the large cup Y'sindra waved in my face.

"How did you fall asleep that fast? Take the shake, I need to help Mae with the rest of the food."

Mae balanced a drink holder that contained four more shakes in one hand and a full-to-the-top paper bag in the other, waiting to hand them to Y'sindra. The bubblegum chewing cashier leaned against the window, three more paper bags waiting on the pass through.

We might have ordered too much.

"Yeah, sorry." I took the cup from Y'sindra, who in turn relieved Mae of the drink holder and paper bag.

Lo gripped his shake with his knees and opened the greasy paper bag on the seat next to him to peer inside. His nose twitched, taking in the aromas, and his eyes went wide. "What is this?"

"Food of the gods." I pulled a hot fry from my own bag. "Go ahead, give it a try." We rolled away from the window, and Mae pulled across Root, steering us toward home. Salty goodness exploded on my tongue. I took ten seconds to savor the deliciousness before hunger took hold. I pulled my first burger from the bag and settled into the ride.

Halfway through my second burger, we turned off Root onto the no-name stretch of dirt that ran past our house. Things were about to get bumpy. I folded the wrapper over the half-eaten sandwich, put it back into the bag, and slurped down the rest of my shake.

Lo burped and licked his fingers. Fair to say he liked his food. Y'sindra leaned through the console to give him a fist bump. Confused, Lo cringed away from her raised fist. I laughed and displayed my sister's intentions, which he quickly mimicked when Y'sindra tried again.

If life were always this simple...well we'd be bored, broke, and out of business. But damn if this wasn't exactly what we needed after the past few days.

A void in the trees appeared ahead—our driveway. We were so close now. I needed a week-long nap, time to heal. Time to digest everything we'd been through. My bones grew heavier with anticipation. I pressed a light hand to my stomach. Blood still seeped beneath the fabric. I'd hoped food might help, but I needed the damn blood medicine. A special blend—Mom's recipe—frozen and revolting. She'd changed her recipe about three years ago, and while it tasted so much worse, it worked almost as well as blood straight from the vein.

"Uh oh. You're in trouble, Lane." Y'sindra stood on her seat and peered at me over the headrest.

I leaned to the side for a view through the windshield, and there in all his flannel and denim glory stood Teddy propped against a column on our front porch. My hearts double-tapped my breastbone. A warm flush scoured my body. How long had he been waiting, and why were my palms sweaty? I ran a hand over the fly-away halo of hair surrounding my head.

Unable to sit still, I rocked against my seat. I shouldn't give a damn about Teddy and his opinion of me, but I did.

You are so much more than this.

His words burned joy into the fiber of my being, and I pressed a fist to the ache of emotion swelling dead center to my chest.

The car slowed, and the motor died.

Teddy looked through the window, spotted me, and stalked to the passenger side. Y'sindra snickered beneath her breath.

Panic pulled my gaze to the oily bottom of the fast-food bag sagging on the floor, to the thorn punctures and gaping holes scarring the backseat, and the blood. So much blood. I slumped. We might as well have set off a bomb back here. Teddy would never trust me again.

The door wrenched open, and I ducked my face.

"Where have you been? I've been going out of my mind with worry."

He hadn't seen the damage yet. Anytime now.

"Sup Tedster." Still laughing, Y'sindra hopped from the car. Traitor. She shot me two thumbs up from behind Teddy's legs.

The front seat flipped forward, and Teddy crouched in the open space. "Shit, what happened to you? Are you okay? Talk to me, Lane."

"Oh. Oh my!" Lo leaped to his feet. He bumped his head on the roof and fell back on his rump.

I reached to steady Lo, who vibrated, on the verge of doing the same thing again. What was wrong with him? Delayed reaction to the poison? He was fine minutes ago. There weren't any healers in Interlands I trusted. I could call Mom. She could heal anything, almost anything.

Tears wet Lo's fuzzy cheeks. He scrambled to all fours and crawled across my lap. Oh, sweet Ho Hos that hurt. "Prince Aventheo!"

Pain swept aside the flutter in my belly that twisted and turned sour. No, this had to be a mistake.

"Lo! Buddy!"

I recoiled from the door, from the crown prince of Shadwe. Teddy. We'd found Lo's master.

28

FERAL AND DANGEROUS

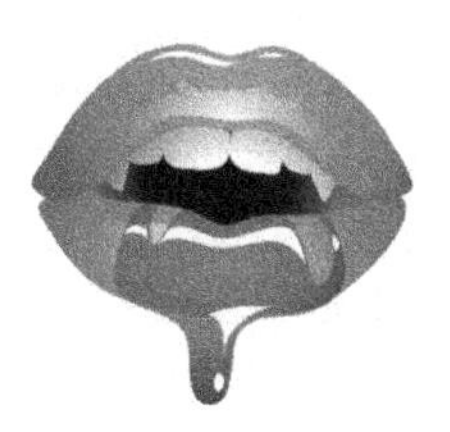

A VACUUM OF WHITE NOISE BUZZED IN MY EARS. TEDDY'S LYING LIPS moved in rapid conversation with Lo, but their voices didn't penetrate the buzz.

Prince Aventheo.

Crown Prince of Shadwe.

A realm that agreed to take a corrupt race with a penchant for genocide off the sun fae's hands. They might be regretting their decision. Teddy could have come to Interlands seeking revenge. Was he playing some twisted long game that included cozying up to someone—me—distantly related to the sun fae court? The bitter taste of regret and loathing filled my mouth, and I wanted to spit out all traces of Teddy.

I wanted to rage, to rip him apart, piece by bloody piece. I could only breathe through this terrible new pain wracking my body. Drinking blood wouldn't heal this wound.

Unless it came straight from Teddy's veins.

My gaze narrowed on the source of my hurt, my blinding fury. How could I not have seen this coming—any of this? I was a detective, and I hadn't detected a fucking thing. Even loud-mouthed Y'sindra stood to the side, stunned speechless.

Mae moved first. From the corner of my eye, her head swiveled in my direction, and she reached through the console to place her hand on my knee. I sucked in a breath at the contact. That was all it took.

The white noise dropped, and voices filled the space. Everyone's words tripped over one another—Teddy, Lo, my sisters.

"I haven't stopped trying..."

"Lane?"

"Master, there is so much to tell you..."

"Not master...missed..."

"Come inside..."

Time snapped into hyperdrive. I exploded from the car, fist first, and punched Teddy square in the jaw. His head snapped to the side.

I panted, the sudden silence roaring against my eardrums.

Teddy's head slowly came back around. Something feral and dangerous flared in his bottomless black eyes. His muscles tensed, bulged, strained as he fought to hold in check whatever beast warred inside him. Under normal circumstances, I would acknowledge the predator beneath the skin and proceed with caution.

But nothing happening here was normal.

Anger and hurt threatened to tear me apart. I barged into Teddy's personal space and shoved him, a furious scream ripping from my lungs. His arms flew wide and he backpedaled, feet twisting, and Teddy hit the ground.

He rose to his elbows but stopped short when I stepped over him, my feet straddling his hips. I flashed fang and bent forward at the waist. A pea-sized portion of my brain recognized he'd leashed whatever caged beast he had inside him. He let me shove him. Even now, he let me dominate him. That pissed me off even more.

"Who the hell are you? You lied to me," I snarled. "Did you think getting close to me would get you into Eodrom? Boy, did you pick the wrong girl. If you knew why I left Ta'Vale..." Words twisting on my tongue, I shook my head.

Teddy fell back on the grass and folded his hands across his chest. My mouth dropped open. *Are you kidding me?* This wasn't a picnic, but there he was, in full repose. Acting like he hadn't been exposed for all his filthy deeds. I was going to rip out his throat and then go cry in the shower, damn him.

Eyes closed, Teddy's chest expanded on a deep breath. "Can we talk now?"

"What the..? I *am* talking. Haven't you been listening?"

His lids cracked. "I've been listening, but I don't think you have."

A needle of doubt wedged beneath my anger. They'd all been talking—all four of them—happy and laughing, and I hadn't heard a word.

I'd punched Teddy.

No! I wasn't in the wrong here. Tracing my tongue along the seam of my lips, I forged ahead. "Well, what about Lo? You abandoned him." I glanced to my right where Lo bounced nervously, hands wringing over one another in front of his heart.

I wanted to do the same thing to Teddy's throat. My fingers twitched.

"No, no, he didn't—" Lo said, but Y'sindra silenced him with a hand on his elbow. His chin wobbled, but Lo's liquid gaze said what his words hadn't. He didn't believe Teddy—*his master*—had abandoned him.

Behind the pair, Mae silently watched the scene unfold. When our eyes met, her mouth twitched to the side, and she shook her head. What did that mean? Was she upset with Teddy? *No, not him*. I knew the expression. That look spoke of disappointment. Disappointment in me. What the hell had I done?

A fresh scream built in my throat, pressed against my clenched teeth. I shoved my hands into my snarled hair. My vision swam behind a watery veil of frustration, and I stalked away from all of them.

My body sagged on a defeated sigh. I tilted my face toward the sky and banged my clenched fists against my outer thighs. What right did I have to be this angry? We'd kissed, big deal.

Yet until this moment I hadn't realized how Teddy had slowly but surely burrowed into my hearts, made me believe I was more than a monster, that I was *worthy* of being more. The worst part—the part grinding its heel into my soul—he made me begin to believe in myself.

The building scream tore free. I clenched the hem of my jacket and stomped my foot. Once, twice, I couldn't stop.

"Malaney Callaghan." Mom's voice froze my foot mid-stomp.

I twisted toward the house, throwing myself off balance, and fell. The punctures on my stomach pulled and ripped. Tiny explosions rolled over my eyes. I groaned and curled in on myself.

"Hrmph. That's exactly where a temper tantrum gets you. Now stop acting the fool and help that boy up." She tsked. "Come drink your medicine when you're done."

When the pain turned from razor wire to sandpaper against my abdomen, I eased into a seated position. Mom, mouth set in a disapproving line, wiped her hands on her *Will Cook For Blood* apron. She was small, but mighty. Though I didn't have the black-on-black blood fae hair and eyes, I took after my mom. My features, my curvy figure, my stature, they were all Mom. She was the Betty Crocker blood fae version of me.

Mom hmphed again, lifted her nose into the air, and followed it into the house.

All the bluster ballooning inside me evaporated. I fell back onto the ground and stared at the sky. "Shit."

How did she get here? We hadn't been gone long enough for her to make the trip, unless she set out before we even left.

Mom called Teddy—the former crown prince of Shadwe—"that boy." A laugh bubbled in my chest. I smiled and shook my head, the grass crunching beneath my head with the movement. If she only knew. She would know soon. I'd have to tell her. "Shit."

"You know there are other words in the vocabulary, right? A lot more curse words. I can give you a comprehensive list." Y'sindra bent over me. "See you inside, sucker."

Teddy's low voice brought my head up. He knelt next to Lo, whose fuzzy cheeks were damp from tears—happy tears. Smiles wreathed both their faces. When Teddy reached out and pulled Lo into a tight embrace, my hearts cracked.

Just a little.

The crest of emotions I'd been riding crashed, leaving me a shell for confusion and regret. Even if everything wasn't what it seemed with Lo, Teddy still lied.

Or at least omitted the truth.

Though, I'd never asked where he came from, never asked anything about him.

Irritated, confused, and just damn tired, I bounced my head against the soft ground. *Huge mistake!* Pain grabbed my skull and said hello. Right, on top of everything else, I'd passed out in the Blackthorne parking lot and given myself one helluva lump. I turned my cheek to the grass and squeezed my eyes shut. Shame simmered beneath my skin. The painful clarity that maybe I had no right to be angry bullied its way into my scrambled brain.

Fatigue seeped into my marrow. More than every other emotion I'd experienced on this roller coaster, I felt loss. Loss for something that didn't yet have a name. One question ran on loop in my head. Now that I knew Teddy's true identity, could I ever look at him the same?

A shadow fell over me. My lids cracked and there he stood. I reached for anger to stem the ache swelling beneath my breastbone, burning behind my eyes, but it wasn't there.

Teddy raked a hand through his hair and then reached down to me. "I'd appreciate the opportunity to talk."

My loose fists pressed against my sides, fingers scratching my palms. I should get up and walk away, avoid his bar forever. Or move away from Interlands. Moving would probably be best.

I looked at his still-outstretched hand. "Don't take this as me forgiving you, I can use the help. I'm bleeding all over the damn place." I put my hand in his.

Teddy took care easing me to my feet. I stumbled forward and our chests brushed. My traitorous pulse beat in the base of my throat.

Gods damn this male.

29

THE FINAL EMBER

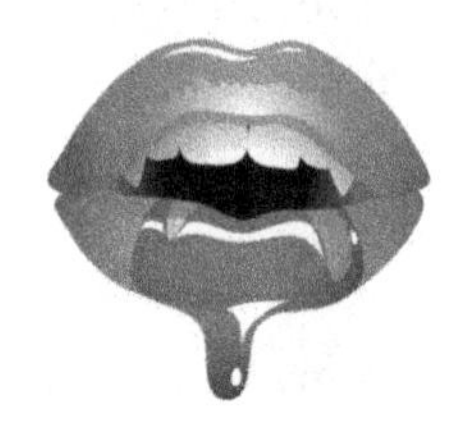

THE PORCH SWING CREAKED. TEDDY ROCKED HEEL TO TOE WITH THE motion while my feet dangled above the wood slats. He reached across the distance between us and tugged the corner of my heavy, blood-soaked shirt. "Yours?"

I nodded.

"You're okay, though?"

I shrugged. Physically, I'd be all right. Emotionally? Not so sure.

Teddy puffed a breath and let his head drop onto the back of the bubblegum pink bench seat. I'd wanted to keep the swing its natural wood tones, but Y'sindra had campaigned hard for pink. Mae was the deciding vote. Traitor.

After several beats of silence, "I like Meghan."

I finally looked at Teddy, really looked. Pale purple half-moons hung below his eyes. His jeans were dirt stained and his flannel buttoned crooked. While Teddy dressed for comfort, he was never messy, unclean, tired. I scowled. I would not feel bad for this male. "How exactly are you on a first name basis with my mother?"

"Duskmere." Teddy spat the moon fae's name with the same disgust I reserved for brussels sprouts. Those two really did have some sort of history. "He showed up at the bar yesterday with your phone and your mom."

"Yesterday? I gave him the phone a couple hours ago." Or was it yesterday? Doubt crouched in my brain. I hadn't questioned the night-to-day cycles or my crushing fatigue, what with fae and druids intent on killing me every which way I turned. But now that I had time to breathe, the time cycles from Vegas to Treasure Island seemed...off.

"Lane, you've been gone three days."

I jerked upright. *Not that off!* The swing's chains jingled from the sudden motion. "Impossible. We borrowed your car yesterday."

Teddy shook his head. "Today's Saturday. You borrowed the car Thursday morning. Three days, Lane. Three days, I've been losing my mind."

"No." I shook my head. "You're lying."

"Why would I lie? Lane, I've never—not once—been untruthful with you. Not since that first day you barged into my bar asking for directions and a bottle of human red." His voice crackled with frustration. I cringed at the memory. I'd proved as allergic to human blood as fae. The worst kind of allergic. The type that made be black out and kill things. Thank the stars I'd both waited to get home to open the bottle and that my sisters hadn't yet arrived in Interlands.

"I'll be right back. Wait here." Teddy pegged me with that super intent look, and I sighed. Whatever he asked, I would fold like origami. Misunderstanding my sigh, he added, "Please."

"Well, since you said please."

He shoved away from the bench, setting the swing swaying like a cheap carnival ride. The erratic motion forced my head to swivel back and forth to keep my half-hearted glare bull's-eyed on Teddy as he headed for his truck.

The swing had slowed to a nearly imperceptible swish when Teddy jogged up the porch steps and rejoined me on the bench, a small black rectangle in his hand.

"Why do you have my phone?" I tried to grab for it, but he held the phone up and out of my reach. His thumb continued to scroll through the photo album.

"Dumbass Duskmere couldn't figure out how to use it. Left it at the bar along with your mother. Here." Teddy handed over the phone.

I snatched it from his grip and turned it on. A picture of Y'sindra rubbing mud on Mae's head popped up. I opened the home screen. "How'd you get into my phone?"

"The moon fae remembered what you told him, though he didn't know what it meant."

Yep, Dumbass Duskmere.

Unable to wait, Teddy risked losing a digit by tapping open the photo gallery. At first, I wasn't sure what I was looking at. Images taken from above the treetops aimed straight down. Not a single one looked important, only trees, and beneath the canopy a river and some rocks. Great. Y'sindra wasted time on nature shots while Mae and I were being ambushed and nearly turned to dust.

I flipped from one image to the next—tree, bird, big bear by a river, building, moon fae under a tree, more moon fae, rocks, tree. My brain spasmed, and I flipped back. No, it couldn't be. Pulse thumping in my throat, I pinched my fingers on the screen and dragged them to the edges, zooming in.

"That sneaky fairy." My shocked gaze flew to Teddy's. "Those rocks, they're the sun stones."

He nodded. "Now go back to the album and see what day the picture was taken."

The stones were buried—planted—just as Iola said they would need to be. The grounders. That had to be the job they were hired for. What did that Smurf fart say—not just a hole? But they didn't say holes, plural. Was there another job? And did I care? Nope.

I continued to gape at the image. Y'sindra did it, she found the stones. We had photographic proof of where they were. I wouldn't presume to call us heroes, but if the cape fit... I should get a cape. I'd make the announcement from the top of the sun bridge, on the spot where those bastards tried to end me. Images of a giant banner unfurled over the side of the bridge, with me standing above, arms raised—

"The date, check the date."

"Let me savor this, will you?" But the moment was ruined. I clicked back to the photo album and checked the time. "Day after we left, but we got there at night. So what?"

"Check today's date."

Muttering about wasting my time and needing a nap, I returned to the home screen, and stared.

Six-seventeen p.m., Saturday. Impossible. Yet there was no disputing the digital evidence. We left early Thursday. The unanswered calls, voice mail, and new text message icons glared from the top left. I didn't have to look to know they were from Teddy. I clicked anyhow.

The texts began about five hours after we'd borrowed the Trans Am, when he told me to meet him at the bar after we returned. I scrolled through text after text. His tone began light, joking, but gave in to concern by hour twelve. Concern escalated into anger, but circled back to worry. Some foreign emotion made a mess of my insides at the final text that came in yesterday afternoon, probably right before Duskmere showed up.

"I'm angry in some. I know, and I'm sorry. I was...concerned." Teddy scraped his hands down his face, and a tiny piece of me softened. He'd worried about me, and this wasn't the first time. He'd done so many small things to show me he cared. Of course, there was the one big ass thing when he rolled full throttle into Eodrom to rescue me, even if I hadn't needed saving. He deserved for me to listen.

Teddy's panicked words screamed at me from his final text. All caps. *I'LL BACK OFF. JUST TELL ME UR OK!!! PLS COME HOME!!!* It was hard to swallow, what with the giant wad of emotion camped out in my throat.

"It's not like you to disappear, but after our last encounter, I thought you got spooked and ran. Stupid, I know. But you'd told me you planned for a quick trip to Vegas and back, so once it hit the twenty-four-hour mark I wasn't thinking rationally."

The compulsion to apologize for his pain sat heavy on my tongue, but it wasn't my fault. And I wasn't ready to play nice. We had too much to talk about first.

"I went to Eodrom," Teddy said.

"You what?"

He shrugged and gestured to his dirty denim and rumpled flannel. "Still in the same clothes. I'd just got back when Duskmere showed up."

"Okay." I paused to lick my lips and angle toward Teddy on the bench. "Time for some answers. How the hell are you so fast?"

His nostrils flared. "It's who I am. I've never tried to hide that from you. I told you that before."

"No, you didn't. I mean, yes, you used those words." Those exact words, I'd been paying attention. "But you didn't tell me you were a prince of Shadwe."

"Because I'm not."

I leveled a flat look on Teddy. "You said you never lied to me."

His hand slid along the pink slat seat, and his pinkie traced the back of my hand. I didn't pull away. "Yes, I was born a Barbout—the ruling family of

Shadwe. I'm the youngest of three, but when my shape manifested as the black wolf, I became heir apparent. I was nine at the time, and still too young to rule."

My brows pinched together. "Your shape."

"Yes." He shook his head, fatigue drawing brackets around his mouth, at the edges of his eyes. "It's a lot to explain, but my family is a line of shape shifters going back as far, if not further, than your keepers."

"So you're some sort of werewolf?" Hot damn, I'd been right.

Teddy chuckled his warm, velvety laugh. "Shifters and weres are different in every way possible. Weres are born one thing—human—and changed due to a magic-born disease. Shifters *are* magic."

"Makes sense." No, it didn't. The whole thing made no sense to me, but I knew someone who would get it. I'd corner Mae later.

"So you're a black non-werewolf wolf, and that's how you can cover distances so quickly?" I dragged my talons along the wooden bench slats, picking at the ugly pink paint. "You must have crazy stamina to make Eodrom and back in a single day. Twice."

His brows climbed, and he flashed a row of straight, white teeth. "Oh, I do."

Walked right into that one. A blush sizzled across my cheeks. I fanned my thick hair on my unbearably hot neck and pulled the length over my shoulder.

Teddy reached forward to play with the ends trailing to my waist. I swallowed and shifted.

"What about Lo?" I blurted the question, trying to rekindle my anger and failing. My righteous fury had neared the bottom of a downward slope, and I couldn't seem to push it back up that hill. Wasn't sure I wanted to. I'd be a hypocrite to judge Teddy for what he'd been born.

Teddy angled toward me and laid one arm along the back of the bench. His fingers toyed with the hair at my nape, fingertips brushing the sensitive flesh beneath, and I fought not to bend into his touch. "I assume you didn't hear any of our conversation?"

"What conversation?"

He chuckled and tugged my earlobe. "The one I had with Lo when he tackled me. Thank you for saving him. I've been trying to find a way back since the sun fae sealed the veil."

"The weeks you disappear from the bar?" I pressed my hand to my forehead. Of course.

"Yes." His fingers grazed my throat. "I've been looking for a lead on a druid but haven't been able to find any. In the absence of that, I run the border between Ta'Vale and Outerlands a couple times a year. The sun fae were hasty with their work. If you are sensitive to magic, you can still feel the scar on the veil."

"I wonder if that's something Mae can see."

"Auras are visible to your sister?"

I nodded.

"She might. Magic lives on every wavelength. It's a vibration for me. I feel it, but your sister might be able to see where it's weak." His fingertips stroked my neck, the increased touching not lost on me. I fought the war inside myself not to leap on Teddy here and now, or limp onto him. I was pretty banged up. "I should've talked to you about this sooner. Might have saved me some effort."

"If you'd talked to me sooner, I wouldn't have punched you."

He gripped his jaw and worked it side to side. "You've got a mean uppercut."

"I know."

Teddy barked a laugh. "That's my girl."

Though his words were meant as a joke, we both sobered.

"I'd like you to be," he amended. "When you're ready."

I licked my lips but held my thoughts to myself and met Teddy's earnest gaze. There was still something he needed to answer for. "Lo called you his master?" The accusation slipped into a question.

Teddy's chest rose and fell on a heavy sigh, and he pulled his hand from my hair to rest behind my head. Staying close but not intruding. "That's Lo. His family serves mine. He helped raise me even though he wasn't much older. When I left home and moved to Outerlands, I invited Lo to join me. Never could break him of that word."

With that, the final ember of my anger extinguished. The parallel of our lives across realms, across years was astounding. He left home to escape who he was, same as me. I should apologize, I wanted to, but the words wouldn't leave my mouth. I hated myself for judging him, but then again, Teddy didn't know what I was, either.

"I'm not a blood fae. Not really. I'm... I'm a monster. A hybrid fae." I stared at my hands knotted together on my lap and waited for the disgust.

"I know."

"It's okay, I under... Wait, what? How?" I surged to the edge of my seat and twisted toward him. Pain exploded in my abdomen. I yelped and folded over.

Teddy jumped from the bench and braced his hands on my knees, halting the swing's erratic motion. "None of this is important."

"It is," I argued through my clenched teeth.

"You need to get inside and let your mother help you." Teddy tipped my chin, forcing me to look at him. He smiled. "You aren't getting rid of me. I'll come back tomorrow, and we'll talk. Nothing else matters until you're healed."

Damn him, he was right. I could barely cobble together a coherent thought. "Fine."

I tried to stand, but the pull in my stomach sent starbursts wheeling across my vision.

"Stop trying to do it all yourself and let me help."

My jaw worked, chewing on my frustration. Being helpless wasn't my thing, but I also didn't think I'd make it very far on my own.

I released my grip on the seat and Teddy crouched to ease a shoulder beneath my right armpit, sliding his opposite arm beneath my knees.

A groan escaped me, and he froze.

"It's just my pride, I'm fine."

He chuckled and rose. "You look terrible. Let's get you inside."

"That kind of flattery will get you nowhere."

"I promised I'd never lie." Teddy winked, and while still cradling me like a helpless baby, crouched to twist the doorknob.

"Yeah, well, if you think I look bad, you should see your car." My petty comeback echoed through the foyer.

"About time." My mom popped out of the kitchen, shaking the dreaded thermos of stale blood and whatever the hell else she put into the foul mixture.

I cringed and grabbed the edge of the door. "On second thought, I could use a little more fresh air."

"Sorry sweet fangs, time for your medicine." Teddy kicked the door from my grip, and it closed behind us. He whistled all the way to the kitchen.

30

I GOT GREEDY

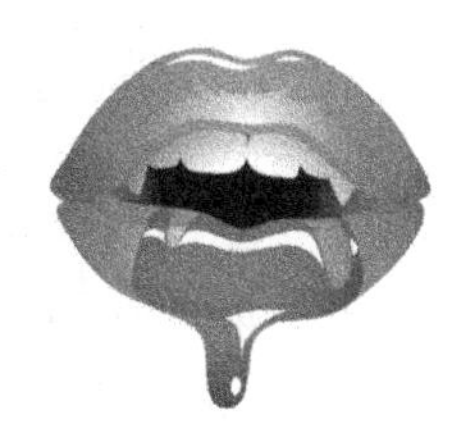

THUNDER SHOOK ME AWAKE. I CRACKED A LID AND WINCED AT THE morning sun's lemonade light leaking through the shutters. No rain. Not thunder. Groaning, I tugged a pillow over my face and let sleep settle in my veins.

The heavy boom came again. I flung the pillow from my face and shot up on the bed. Son of a bitch. "Answer the damn door!"

"Wash off your stink and get down here." Y'sindra's muffled voice floated up the stairwell and through my closed bedroom door.

Fresh brewed coffee and bacon dug into my nostrils. That, I'd get out of bed for. I flopped my legs over the edge of the mattress, and a sharp cramp corkscrewed my guts. I doubled over on a groan.

Probably a reaction to the "medicine" Mom forced down my throat last night. The stuff looked like something she scraped out of the garbage disposal. Tasted worse. Precisely why I resisted drinking it until I couldn't. To this day, I didn't know what she added to make it tolerable to my system, and I probably never wanted to.

Flakes of blood and dirt formed a ring on the floor around the boots still on my feet. After several deep breaths to settle my stomach, I looked over my shoulder at the disaster zone I'd made of my favorite robot unicorn blanket and ironically pink sheets. Mae would have a hissy fit when she saw I'd bypassed the shower for bed last night.

My jaw cracked on a yawn, and I heaved into a vertical position. The butter-soft texture of my leather jeans didn't feel very buttery. Dried sweat and blood had turned them stiff. The pants saved my knees some damage, but as I popped the fastener and attempted to peel the material from my hip, I put serious consideration into the merit of sweatpants.

A short hallway led to the bathroom, flanked on one side by a square walk-in closet and a seated vanity on the other. The bones of the house had been standing longer than electricity existed on Earth. Passed down through generations on Mom's side of the family, the ancient place had been expanded and updated over time. My sisters and I did our fair share when Mom gifted us the keys.

Turning to face the vanity, a zing of surprise chased away the last vestiges of sleep. "What a fucking mess." I leaned into the mirror, angling side to side. No wonder my body insisted I'd been run over by a herd of elephants.

Chalky concrete dust smeared in blood and coated with grass stains and dirt painted me in a macabre camouflage pattern from my hair to my toes. This is how Teddy saw me, and he hadn't run away.

I shrugged out of my jacket and carefully peeled off the inflexible shirt to drop it on the growing pile of clothes to be burned.

Goosebumps tickled my cool flesh. I stepped closer to the vanity and winced, studying my torso in its reflection. Punctures ran from the bottom of my rib cage to my waistline and side to side, with the worst concentrated center right, where I'd tucked Lo during the fall. A few had sealed while I slept, leaving angry purple-pink ridges surrounding thick scabs, but most still wept blood. Great, more medicine.

I flexed my fingers and made a fist. The soft new flesh across my fingertips pulled but otherwise healed, thank the stars. Mae's shield saved my hands from the worst. Palm and sole injuries hurt the most. I couldn't stop touching things, and I certainly couldn't stop walking.

I'd almost pushed things too far this time. One day I might if I didn't respect my limitations. But if the choice was saving myself or saving my sisters, that was no choice at all.

My boots and socks were next, but the pants wouldn't come off. Between the blood and sweat, I couldn't push them down my legs. Instead, I had to lie down and wiggle out of them backwards. I wiggled fast. No way would I let anyone get an eyeful of this humiliation.

The pants lay like a sculpture where I'd crawled out of them. Damn, I'd spent a fortune I didn't possess to have this special blend of materials made. Durable like leather, lighter like jeans, they were perfect. They also made my butt look great. Two pair left, but at the rate this week was chewing through my wardrobe, who knew for how long.

The shag floor runner in the hall gave way to the dove gray and white bathroom tile. On reflex, my toes curled away from the chill. Inside the shower, I rotated the faucets to high and danced out of the way of the frigid stream, waiting for the water to heat.

The mirrors fogged at warp speed. We'd pulled a job in the infancy of YML for the co-owner of a Las Vegas plumbing company on contract with more than one high end casino. Our client got her prenup-protected divorce, which included the business, and we got excellent plumbing. Right now, this was exactly what I needed and where I planned to spend the next hour.

Not thinking about near deaths.

Not thinking about Teddy.

Not thinking at all.

Near-scalding water pounded my shoulders and slid down my body. Gods this felt good. The steam opened my lungs. With each breath, twisted muscles loosened, knots released. A sludge of brown swirled down the drain. I turned and tilted my face toward the downpour.

Banging began on my bedroom door. Someone had a death wish. "Go away!"

All I wanted was a minute of peace and a shower. *Several showers*. A full day to sleep would be nice. Not too much to ask, considering my week.

Banging resumed. I grabbed a bar of rosemary soap and began to methodically cleanse inch after inch of grimy flesh. If I ignored them, they would go away.

Yeah, right. Because that's ever worked for me.

The shower head shook and drops of water splintered as a loud thud on the opposite side of the wall announced someone slamming open my door. My aggressive grip on the soap sent it shooting from my hand.

"Malaney Callaghan."

Son of a Fomorian. My molars ground together. This asshole had some balls barging in here, and if he didn't get out, I might remove them.

"We must speak. Immediately."

"Get out." The intruder did no such thing and instead moved from the hall into my bathroom. His features blurred behind the steamy glass, but even if I hadn't recognized his voice, the stick-up-his-ass posture was unmistakably Duskmere. "Are either of my sisters dying?"

"What? No. The—"

"My mom? My father?" This guy wasn't just rude, he was dense. I mean, read the room, the one I was currently wet and naked in.

He hesitated. "Your family is hale and whole. That is not—"

"Whatever you need to talk about can wait until I'm done. Now get the hell out of here."

"It is critical we speak."

"What part of 'get out' did you not understand?" Being naked wasn't what bothered me. The interruption of my *me* time, that pissed me off.

Another form loomed behind Duskmere. Even in shadow I recognized the shaggy outline of his hair, the broad shoulders, and despite the tightly wound tension humming through the misty air, his easy stance.

Not sure Teddy felt the same indifference to the moon fae's presence and my unclothed state.

"She said, get out." Teddy's menacing growl cut through the tap dance of water on tile.

Oh, I wanted to see this. Glass squeaking, I swiped away the condensation in time to see Teddy grab Duskmere by the collar and yank him from the bathroom.

Even though I'd already experienced Teddy's surprising strength during his close encounter with Duskmere, this was another reminder that there was a lot more power in that lean form than I'd ever realized. I wasn't mad about it.

The two collided with my bed, rocking the mattress on its frame. Comforter and sheets tangled around their legs, stripping the bed as they wrestled from view. I hummed and resumed spreading suds. Someone would break this up before things got out of hand.

In the other room, the pair banged into something solid. The glass surrounding me rattled in its frame.

Or maybe no one would come. If their nonsense required me leaving this shower stall, I was going on the warpath.

"That's enough!" At Meghan Callaghan's scare-the-pants-off-you angry voice, the ruckus in the other room ceased. It was a tone I was familiar with. They made the right choice.

I threw water on the glass for a quick clean and watched my not even five-foot mother push the two big males toward the door. My mattress was off its frame, the bedding scattered across the floor, and the nightstand closest to the bathroom lay face down. All evidence of the mess I'd left behind last night, destroyed.

At least one good thing came from Duskmere's visit.

Though I tried to lose myself in the lull of rosemary suds and hot water, the urgency in Duskmere's usually monotone voice needled me. Damn him. All this because I got greedy on a job and grabbed a sack full of sun shards. I couldn't help but wonder if the RFG would have found the missing stones without our help. Doubtful. Sure, my sisters and I were good, but in this case, I wasn't exaggerating. Without the ability to enter the garden, they would have never known. Without my maybe ability to get through a druid portal, they definitely wouldn't know where the stones had been moved.

The shards falling into my lap might not have been a bad thing if it meant ensuring my father's and Mae's power, and therefore their minds, remained safe. Even if that also meant saving the rest of the homicidal-toward-hybrids sun fae in the process. We found the stones, all they had to do was bring them home. Case closed.

So why Duskmere's urgency? I had to assume someone had contacted him after I went to bed and let him know about the images Y'sindra captured. Mom probably did before we even returned from our unplanned trip to Outerlands if she'd seen the pictures after Teddy unlocked the phone.

That did it, I'd lost the serenity of my shower, and I wasn't getting it back. With an angry crank, I cut off the water and grabbed a towel from the rack.

I'd go see what this was all about, but first Duskmere would know how much I didn't appreciate him showing up whenever the mood struck. This was the third time, and I was starting to hate his face.

I slid into clean sweats, and after fishing my favorite fuzzy slippers from beneath the askew mattress, stomped toward the stairs. As soon as I hit the landing the heavy scent of warm butter and sugar pulled me into its embrace, and my mouth pooled with saliva. Mom's cookies. She knew how to deflate a situation.

At the bottom of the stairs, I rounded the corner into the kitchen and found the room bathed in sunlight and chock full of family plus three. Duskmere and Teddy sat at opposite ends of the island, making a point of not glaring at one another, while Lo sat with Y'sindra along the side.

My eyes tracked to the ridiculous battery-powered sundial clock I bought as a housewarming gift to myself, and my sisters hated. No sense of humor. Were we even related? Technically, no.

It wasn't quite eleven, yet my nose told me the coffee was fresh. Mae would be responsible for that small favor.

I found my saint of a sister reaching into one of the two ovens mounted on the far wall to pull out a tray of golden cookies. Mom was busy pulling plates from the cabinets. Y'sindra huddled at the island with Lo. I liked Lo, and me liking anyone happened almost as infrequently as Y'sindra liking anyone, which made this entire experience worth every bloody bump.

Y'sindra giggled—*giggled*—at something Lo said and fed him a piece of bacon. Bacon! This was serious. Who was this fairy and what happened to my sister?

Teddy saw me first. At the far end of the kitchen island, he came to his feet but didn't move in my direction. A bruise colored his left cheek, and he'd haphazardly finger-combed his hair into place.

Duskmere sat at the opposite end of the long island, back facing me. Elbows on the counter, head slumped onto his fist, he pushed the food in front of him around his plate. He did not deserve those cheesy eggs and bacon.

When our eyes met, Teddy didn't smile. Unease teased my nerve endings. What changed between last night and today? Hell, what changed between him dragging the moon fae from my bathroom to now?

As if sensing the energy shift in the room, Duskmere straightened and turned to face me. A wiggle of worry squirmed between his pinched brows. The sight of his bloodied nose and oncoming black eye hit me with a swift jolt of petty satisfaction.

"Malaney Callaghan." His words set my teeth on edge, but his tone tossed acid into my stomach. Something was wrong. Solemn-faced, my mom approached the counter. Mae followed behind to set a tray of still-steaming cookies on a cooling rack in the center of the island. Even Y'sindra stopped yammering. Shit.

I ignored them on my way to the coffee pot but didn't miss my phone lying in front of Duskmere. The screen was open to the blurry, zoomed-in shot of the stolen sun stones. Great, drama incoming. This required a double dose of caffeine. The average-sized mug I'd grabbed went back on the shelf, and I took down the super-sized mug—all the better to inject caffeine directly to the brain. I took a big slurp and aimed the bottom of the mug at Duskmere. It featured a prominent middle finger.

"How'd my phone get down here?" Keep the questions neutral, get out of here without any more insanity.

Crossing the kitchen, I hip-checked the island counter halfway between a melodramatic moon fae and a moody Teddy. Y'sindra pushed the cookie plate across the counter toward me. I took three and dunked one into my coffee. The soggy half kerplunked into my mug. I swirled the dark elixir, shrugged, and took a sip of my chunky coffee.

"Malaney Callaghan, you must take me to this location immediately." He tapped my screen with all the subtly of a woodpecker.

I smiled at Duskmere and tipped my mug back in his face. This guy had some nerve coming at me with demands after he woke me up, interrupted my shower, brawled with my—with Teddy—and wrecked my already wrecked bedroom. I shoved half a cookie into my mouth.

"Firf uf all, lay off muh phone."

"Don't talk with your mouth full, dear." Mom shook her head at me.

I slurped more coffee to wash down the cookie and ended up with more cookie, only soggy. Damn, forgot about that. I held up a finger and swallowed. "Second of all, I don't need to take you anywhere. The druid circle is on the roof of the Blackthorne. Call an Uber. They charge an arm and a leg for Interlands pick-ups, but with your RFG bucks, you can afford it."

Duskmere stilled. Mom yelped in surprise and pressed a trembling hand at her throat.

My gaze tracked to Mae, and I raised my brows in question. She shrugged.

"Uh, something you two care to share?"

"Blackthorne?" Duskmere pressed his palms flat to the counter, tendons standing along their backs from the pressure.

"Yeah, used to be called The Solstice." I eyed the lumpy layer of coffee at the bottom of my mug. To fill or not to refill. "Same owner, minor facelift, new name."

"We go for the Beltane brunch every year. It'll blow your wings back." Y'sindra bumped her shoulder into Lo's. "You just missed it, but you're coming next year."

"This is the location of the druid circle?" Duskmere asked.

"He's the owner, original owner if our contact there is right. Owner's name is Mr. Black." I shoved the last cookie into my mouth, pushed my stool back, and took my mug to the sink.

Duskmere and my mom's hushed voices stirred my suspicions. This couldn't be good. Mom huddled at the moon fae's side, her dark head bent to his silver one.

"What now?" Arms and ankles crossed, I leaned against the cabinets.

My mom looked up. Her lips set in a tight crease, hands busy wringing the life from one of our dishtowels.

"Lane, sweetheart, we need to talk."

31

IT SURE WAS CATHARTIC

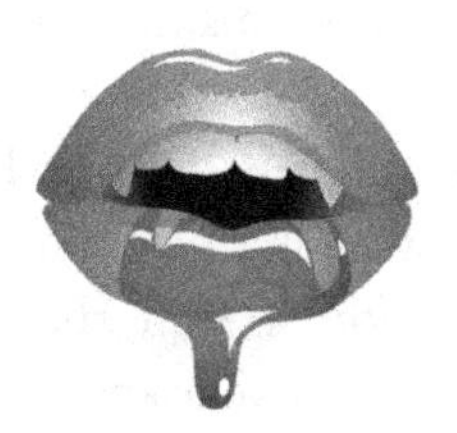

We rocked to a stop at the pileup of cars waiting to turn onto Las Vegas Boulevard, my clenched jaw flexing with the Bronco's motion. Here we were, exactly where I didn't want to be. Every time I thought things would return to normal, life rang the doorbell and yelled "surprise."

Turned out I was related to a druid. When I'd tried to punch Duskmere in his big, fat, lying mouth, Mom confirmed. She had conveniently left that leaf off the family tree until now.

Pissed at the world, I glared at nothing out the window. I'd learned to cope with my blood fae–sun fae self, but now there was a new player in the genetic game. I knew squat about druids, for a reason. They were realm roamers, nomads, a fae race so adept with nature magic they were able to alter the very fabric of it and had long ago wandered into the annals of history.

Except the lone druid who took sides during the Great Divide, who created the spell that turned moon fae to blood fae. He disappeared before the war ended, and according to Duskmere he was Angus Blackthorne, his name taken for the type of wood he used for a focus.

And according to Mom, he was my great, great, great—too many greats to count—grandfather.

This sucked. All of it. I wanted normal the way I wanted a long, steamy, uninterrupted shower.

Until a couple days ago, normal meant chasing down sleazeballs who owed money to bigger sleazeballs. Tracking down missing persons predictably led to one of two places—a bed not their own or a ditch. Or my personal favorite—introducing an abusive spouse's teeth to their windpipe.

My sisters and I were private investigators. We dealt in small-scale local business—Interlands and Vegas. As far as I was concerned, this intra-realm bullshit wasn't in our service area. I projected another death glare at Duskmere in the rearview. "This seems like something you could do without me."

My sisters were along for the ride because Duskmere insisted he needed me. They in turn insisted I wouldn't be doing anything alone. Surprisingly, the moon fae requested Teddy join as well, though Teddy had already made it clear he'd be coming before Duskmere asked.

"I must mark new locations in order to create a portal without a summoning stone."

"You gotta pee on something?" Y'sindra asked.

"I send a piece of my energy into the earth and am then linked to that location. Moon fae have a limit on links, I must release one."

"Feel free to forget our address." I flashed him a smile sweeter than Mom's cookies in the mirror. "Let's get back to why you need me."

"You are a hybrid."

My jaw flexed again. Here I thought my social skills were poor, what with all my fang flashing and impressive array of nasty looks, but Duskmere's blunt, robotic demeanor had me beat. Much more time spent in this guy's company, and I'd snap a fang.

"She knows that. What's your point, pretty boy?" Y'sindra plucked a raisin from a handful of trail mix and flicked it at Duskmere.

Pretty boy? I glanced between Y'sindra and Duskmere. Prominent cheekbones, winged eyebrows, long lashes, perfectly cropped silver hair. Okay, I could see it.

"Your sister's manifestations of each race's DNA in her bloodline is unpredictable."

"Understatement." I dug a flake of dried blood from my nail bed. Retractable claws were a bitch to clean.

"You should not have been able to pass through the druid portal, not without a druid." Duskmere had a dramatic pause moment, and I tensed.

Dramatic pauses were never a good sign. "You, Malaney Callaghan, are a druid."

"What? No. I barely have a handle on the DNA I've dealt with for twenty-three years, and you expect me to just waltz through druid portals? Bullshit." I slapped my hands on the steering wheel.

Teddy reached across the space between us to rub the knot of tension lodged between my shoulder blades.

"There was no predicting the fallout of evolution from moon fae to blood fae. Something that should have taken hundreds to thousands of years was forced on a handful of my kin in less than a year." Duskmere's voice turned rough. The horror of his words scooped me hollow. "So many did not survive. Meghan Callaghan did. I am not surprised she has such an extraordinarily singular daughter."

The line of cars rolled forward, and I lifted my foot off the gas to move a whole car length.

Duskmere meant to compliment me, but his words reinforced the hateful monikers still hanging heavy around my neck. The number of first-generation blood fae was under fifty. Six second-generation children from those, and the dishonor of being born hybrid went to me. Lucky, fucking me.

"Different and special are worlds apart, and apparently you didn't get the memo. I'm different." My attempt to shoot laser beams through the rearview failed. One day it would work.

We idled at the lightning-quick stoplight. It turned green, but tourists taking their sweet-ass time still clogged the crosswalk. I cursed under my breath and laid on the horn. Didn't help, but it sure was cathartic.

Clearly sick of waiting, the stretch limo in front of us shoved its nose into the pedestrian traffic, forcing the tide of humans to momentarily part. I followed the car's lead before the crosswalk could fill again and gunned it down the Boulevard. Hot, dry air swept in through the open windows, chasing away the remnants of our conversation.

"What if the druid is home? He nearly killed us last time. How do you plan to get past him?" Ever the planner, it was a wonder Mae waited until now to press Duskmere for details. I'd been pondering that same question.

"I do." Duskmere failed to elaborate.

We rolled to a stop at another light, and the car to the right honked. I leaned forward to look around Teddy and laughed. The limo from the stop light idled next to us. The bachelorette party inside flashed their boobs at the two males seated on that side of the Bronco. One woman climbed out and threw a cocktail napkin into Duskmere's lap. "You're *hot*. Call me."

"Nice necklace. Where'd you get it?" I asked the woman. Teddy's expression was incredulous. I kept an ironclad hold on a straight face and shrugged. "What? Who doesn't like a penis necklace?"

The eye roll he gave me was so aggressive, I wondered if he got a glimpse of gray matter.

"Not the time sweetheart." Y'sindra tossed a handful of trail mix at the woman leaning into the window. "Shoo."

Plucking peanuts and raisins from the front of her frilly white crop top, the woman stumbled back to the limo. Mae, true to form, leaned across Y'sindra and Lo to pocket the phone number still lying in Duskmere's lap.

"Hey, lover boy." Y'sindra threw another raisin at Duskmere. "About this plan, you gonna share, or are we supposed to guess?"

The light turned green, and we rolled ahead with traffic.

Teddy shifted in his seat and growled. He actually growled. "If we run into trouble, the moon fae will open a portal into the dungeons and send your druid there."

"How did..." Oh. Oh! It was clear from his expression Teddy spoke from experience. Holy forsaken gods, this was the beef between them. I glanced from Teddy to Duskmere and back. Wow. "So that's what happened."

"What happened?" my sisters chimed in simultaneously.

Duskmere shifted uncomfortably in his seat and spoke to the back of Teddy's head. "My queen tasked me with investigating the Shadwe prince recently residing in Interlands."

It made sense now why, if Iola knew who Teddy was, she'd vanished when he showed up looking for me, metaphorically beating his chest. Maybe a little literal chest beating, too. She wouldn't want to risk bad blood with Shadwe when they housed Ta'Vale's worst enemies.

"Odin's shriveled balls, you pushed Teddy into the dungeon." Y'sindra cackled. "And you're still breathing. Guess you aren't a complete creampuff."

Duskmere's eyes tightened, the right one twitched. Sore subject apparently.

Of course the RFG captain would assume the worst, act first, and ask questions later. The bitter taste of hypocrisy coated my tongue. Exactly what I'd done—minus the dungeon.

If I didn't stop with all the introspection, I might start caring about feelings. I had a good track record of not giving a shit.

The light turned green, and I rolled across the intersection. Ahead, the sky-high garden peeked from above the other casinos. I steered into the outside lane. Duskmere had gone suspiciously quiet. I glanced in the mirror and found him staring out the window. While I knew he'd been earthside before, I didn't know how recently or how often.

A twinge of sympathy pinched my chest.

Great, I was going soft. The problem was, Duskmere wasn't a bad guy. In fact, he was a hero. I wouldn't exist without him. My parents would have died in those dungeons. For that reason, I tried to appreciate him, but he was kind of a dick.

"How are we going to get into the crazy druid's place without being spotted?" Y'sindra squeezed onto the console between Teddy and me, jostling my arm. "Even if we do make it to the elevator, they've got cameras."

"Not to mention it's the middle of the day," Mae said. "You'd be spotted scaling the wall in an instant."

"You're right. I've been thinking about that." I hit my blinker and turned off the Strip, pulling through an elaborate casino drive that by-passed the front entrance and headed for parking. "Y'sindra and Lo can fly to the roof and use Duskmere's portal stones to bring the rest of us up."

Excited to be included, Lo bounced in his seat.

"I'm not eager to get my wings fried off." Y'sindra, clearly not sharing the sentiment, flopped into the back seat. My talons ticked against the steering wheel. I wasn't eager for that either, but considering our previous exit from the casino, we'd drained our already shallow well of options.

Mae leaned toward Duskmere's open window and twisted her neck to look up at the casino we passed. "This isn't the Blackthorne."

"Sure isn't, but they share a parking garage." A shadow passed over the Bronco as we left daylight and eased into the artificially lit space. Door-to-door cars lined the entire level. A car pulled out of a spot at the end of the row. Prime real estate, but this wasn't our stop. "Y'sindra and Lo can fly out from the roof and go up the side of the Blackthorne. So long as they follow those fancy wood beams to the penthouse level, they won't pass over any windows and won't be seen."

The stench of garbage bins that needed changing, stale cigarettes, and old oil infiltrated the SUV. I fumbled with the window button while navigating the crowded pavement. The six-story parking garage situated behind the hottest shopping promenade on the Strip was a sprawling obstacle course of people and poorly parked cars. Though the higher we climbed, less of both filled each level.

Sunshine splashed through the windshield as we exited the covered parking and drove onto the roof.

As predicted, only a handful of vehicles parked on this level—for good reason. It wasn't surface-of-the-sun level yet, but very soon cars up here would be pressure cookers on wheels. Rookie tourists were easy to spot by the welts on the backs of their thighs.

Not even noon, and the heat already radiated through the soles of my Adidas. I filled my lungs to bursting and turned toward the Blackthorne. My confidence shriveled. I wasn't ready for this.

Anxiety plowed across my body. My hands shook, and I pressed them to the front of my thighs, gathering the light cotton material of my joggers into my palm. The pant legs rose with each nervous twist, a dry breeze brushing my ankles.

I wasn't frightened often, but I'd spent most of this past week on the upper end of the fear scale. This entire misadventure had been a real kick in the ego.

The druid's balcony wasn't visible from here, but the building still elicited an emotional reaction to my involuntary free fall. To the fact that I'd almost killed myself. That I'd almost killed my sisters.

Through the SUV windows, I spotted Mae, sitting alone. She clenched the new sun shard hanging center to her chest. The chain rubbed against the still unhealed cut Nyle had inflicted on her neck. Watching her, my pulse grew thick in my throat. Guilt was a hard pill to swallow.

I released the grip on my pants and shook out my hands. *Suck it up, Lane.*

Mae didn't ask me to help. She didn't pressure me. My sister faced the uncertainty of losing her power without a word of judgment. She bowed her head and then left the truck to join the others.

My gaze went to Teddy at the back of the Bronco. I should probably shut the hell up about how much I couldn't do and try to do what everyone seemed to believe I could. Even if they were wrong, I could still try.

Shoulders back, chin up, I joined the group gathered behind the truck. Duskmere was in the process of explaining to Y'sindra precisely how to use the portal stones. She rolled the shiny stones in her palm, paying zero attention to his words.

Fantastic. The plan relied on a fairy who got distracted by her own reflection.

"Hey." Mae snapped her fingers in front of the fairy's face. "Focus."

Y'sindra stuck out her tongue, but she secured the stones in a fanny pack slung bandoleer-style across her chest. Thank goodness Lo hung on Duskmere's every word. It gave me a sliver of confidence we'd make it to the roof.

"Squeeze the stone, throw the stone. We're not inventing the wheel. I got it." Y'sindra dusted the front of her dove-gray leggings, the same color as her dress. It was convenient and obnoxiously adorable how she matched Lo's monochrome attire. At least her knickers were covered.

The barest hint of green colored the top of the Blackthorne. "Don't forget about the barrier surrounding the garden. Hug the roofline from the side of the building where you fly up to the front to the balcony. From there, you can take the staircase and avoid being seen from inside the penthouse."

"Through the window you broke? Yeah, got it." She popped her wings wide and fluffed the skirt of her dress.

"You sure you're okay with this?" Apprehension grabbed hold. This was a terrible idea. It should be me, not Y'sindra. Her magic level was still so low, it couldn't fill a snow cone. I pressed my talons into the sides of my thighs. "We can figure another way up. If we wait a few hours for dark, there's a better chance I can scale to the top."

"And miss my chance at being the hero? You're not stealing my blizzard."

"Thunder."

"Whatever." Y'sindra hovered to eye level and hugged my neck.

Warmth flooded my aching chest, and I swallowed twice to choke down all the dumb emotion. "Get out of here." My voice wobbled. "Don't do anything stupid."

"Your definition of stupid or mine?" She cackled and gestured to Lo. "Time to go save some butts."

My raw nerves twitched watching Y'sindra's fragile form shrink into the distance.

We'd sent the smallest of our team to potentially confront the most dangerous of unknowns all alone, armed with snowflakes.

32

IN THE NAME OF EVERY FORSAKEN GOD

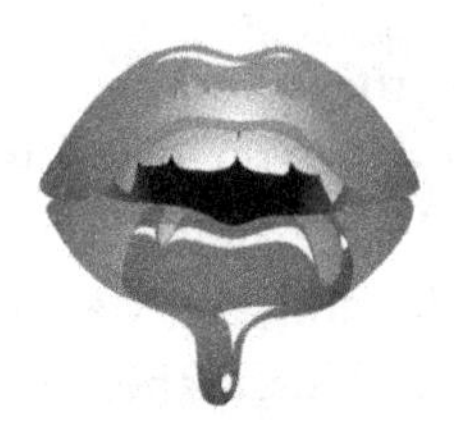

WAVES OF HEAT RADIATED FROM THE CONCRETE. PERSPIRATION BEADED, pasting loose hairs onto my forehead. I dragged the back of my hand across my slick brow and squinted in the direction Y'sindra and Lo had flown.

"It's a good plan. She'll be okay." Mae squeezed my hand.

"She will." She had to.

Mae continued past me to the front of the Bronco and cocked a hip against the hood. She threaded her arms over her chest and watched our sister ascend more than fifty floors.

Teddy's shadow replaced Mae as he approached.

I glanced at him and rounded on Duskmere. "Why didn't you tell us Etta'wy had a contact inside Eodrom?"

"It did not seem relevant."

Every time I wanted to give this guy the benefit of the doubt, he said stupid crap like that. I squeezed the bridge of my nose. "You approached me for help based off information from this captured contact. Still doesn't seem relevant?"

Duskmere traced his tongue along the ridge of his teeth. Oh yeah, he realized his mistake. "Your help was sought because of your skill set."

"Right, and the fact that I could get into the sun garden when you couldn't." I snorted and shook my head. "Any other information you don't think is relevant? For instance, who the contact is?"

His nostrils flared. Oh, he did not like me questioning his competence. Tough shit. "Look, if my sisters and I are going to put our asses on the line—"

"And an exceptional ass it is." Teddy winked, and I flashed him an appreciative grin. Cheeky male.

"Right, so if we are putting our exceptional asses on the line for you, I expect transparency."

We dueled with our glares for a heartbeat. He nodded once. "The fae in question was a lower kelpie from Palough's court."

"Was?" Duskmere needed to learn to shape his tenses better if he wanted to be sneaky. He'd never make it in my line of work.

A muscle feathered in his jaw. "She's missing."

I blinked. That dungeon wasn't exactly a vacation destination to come and go as one pleased. She sure as shit didn't tunnel her way out. Wait, grounders? Nah. "Come again?"

Sunbeams spiked off his steel gaze, which slid away from mine to fix somewhere over my shoulder. "The kelpie believed herself to be currying favor with her swamp prince, Palough. When she learned otherwise, she was quickly convinced to give us a name in exchange for being returned to her home to face punishment. She named Etta'wy."

I glanced over my shoulders to see what Duskmere was looking at. Nothing. The not-so-tricky moon fae couldn't meet my gaze while trying to skirt details. "And?"

Mae moved to my side, arms crossed, fingernails tapping an irritated rhythm on her biceps.

"For her cooperation, the prisoner was being held in rooms rather than the dungeon while awaiting an envoy from the Marrowghan Swamp. Shortly before Cirron and I arrived at your home, her guards were found unconscious with no memory of the events." He paused. "The kelpie traitor is gone."

"Son of a bitch." I covered my mouth and pushed angry breaths through my nose. Gone? He thought this wasn't relevant?

To my left, Teddy uttered curses beneath his breath, while on my right, Mae sucked in a sharp breath—shock in surround sound.

This went so much deeper than I thought. "What in the name of every forsaken god is going on inside Eodrom?"

"That, Malaney Callaghan," my name sounded less a sign of respect and more a curse, "is what I seek to discover."

"What is your partner doing to find out?" If Duskmere had a stick up his ass, Cirron had a two-by-four. I wasn't complaining about the continued absence of his company, but all things considered, the missing sun fae was pretty damn glaring.

Duskmere drew his gaze to mine. "Cirron has been questioning Rathmore."

"Who?"

"The corrupted you captured. His name is Nyle Rathmore and was the known spy master for the moon fae ranks before and during the war." A muscle ticked at the edge of Duskmere's jaw. "He is not one we would have wished to survive the exile, but we are glad to have him in our dungeons. Rathmore is an extremely dangerous fae."

"Yeah, well, you're welcome." I rubbed a hand across my sweaty neck. "He's the moon fae I smelled on the stones in the garden. Make sure your partner asks about that."

"Cirron is currently accompanying Finnlay to Interlands. They will be at your home by our return and should have news."

Mae and I looked at each other, silently communicating our mutual surprise. Finnlay Callaghan enjoyed leaving his precious lab less than I loved asparagus.

"I am concealing nothing from you. I informed you of Etta'wy's involvement during our first meeting at his bar." Duskmere thrust his chin toward Teddy, who stood next to me, absorbing the exchange.

"But not about the contact. Especially if they escaped and can fucking shape shift." My voice echoed across the roof lot. I ground a finger into the vein twitching at my temple.

Teddy's arm snaked across my shoulders. His warm breath tickled the shell of my ear. "A horse in the palace would probably draw attention."

I barked a laugh. "Clop, clop, clop."

His lids sprang wide, and he howled.

Mae chortled and bumped my shoulder with hers as she retreated behind the Bronco.

The laughter was infectious. I giggled, and the giggles rolled into full on belly laughs. Tears squeezed from the corners of my eyes. "Whew." I dragged a knuckle beneath my damp lashes. I'd needed that. I slid a glance at a still-chuckling Teddy and smiled. Yep, runaway prince or no, he was one of the good ones.

Our eyes locked, and his humor faded. He took my hands and pulled me to face him. "Promise me if we see Dacian, you do not engage."

"Who—"

"My brother. Lo said you saw him. Promise me." His intense gaze sparked like obsidian chips.

"Oh, right. Him." Two princes. My nose wrinkled at the memory.

"When we return, when there's time, I will tell you anything you want to know. There is nothing about me I would hide from you."

Intriguing. "No secrets?"

"None."

I tilted my face to study the bright blue sky. Everything in me screamed to trust him. Neither the energy nor the desire remained to hate this male. "All right."

The tight line of his shoulders loosened. Pleasure purred inside of me. My response mattered to him. I mattered.

His hands flowed up my arms, around my neck, and threaded into the loosely bound hair at the base of my skull. The pressure of his palms pulled me toward him, and my hearts hopped behind my ribs. It was happening, right here, in a parking lot with my sister and Duskmere for an audience, and I didn't give a damn. I melted against Teddy's hard chest.

An electrical clap ripped through the stale desert air, and I jumped away from Teddy, jittery limbs shaking with shock. Oh shit, the portal. Time to get serious.

From the dark oval rising above the scalding tarmac, Y'sindra appeared in the garden, waving. Relief unspooled inside of me. Thick green grass hugged her ankles, the druid stones in the background. At least she didn't open the portal inside the circle. I wouldn't put it past her.

"Two at a time." Duskmere's pale gaze flicked between Teddy and me. He strode forward and pressed three more portal stones into my hand. "In case Y'sindra Callaghan has none left. The both of you go first. Use these. Maerwen Callaghan and I will follow."

Steps away, but hundreds of feet between us, Y'sindra gestured for us to hurry.

Squeezing my fingers tight around the cold lumps in my palm, I jogged through the portal, Teddy on my heels.

The moment my feet sank into the grass, pain ballooned in my ear canals from the instant altitude change. I staggered a few feet away, pinched my nose, and blew. Y'sindra's muffled voice was gibberish beneath the pressure. I squeezed my eyes and blew again. *Pop!* Sound rushed back and the discomfort vanished.

"...not home." Y'sindra's voice caught up to her moving lips.

The simmering worry that we might be forced into another showdown settled. Even if the druid was home, he didn't hear Y'sindra, and that fairy does not know how to be stealthy. My eyes went to Lo blending into his surroundings behind her. Now he was sneaky.

Note to self: Watch what you say when Lo's nearby. Or better yet when he's not. Basically, always watch out.

"Lane, we should hurry." Teddy touched my hand still curled in a death grip around its precious cargo. "The portal."

I winced and nodded. Here I'd accused Y'sindra of getting easily distracted. I plucked a stone from my palm and squeezed.

"They won't take in the grass." Y'sindra hovered at my shoulder and gestured to a nearby fig tree. "I bounced it off that."

"Good idea." I wrenched my arm back.

"Don't miss."

My arm fell to my side. "Are you trying to make me miss?"

"Just saying." Y'sindra hitched a shoulder. "Took me three tries, last one hit. Found out the hard way once you activate 'em, you only get one shot."

Great. Sure, I could bury a blade in a bullseye, but now she'd jinxed me.

"Today?" Y'sindra prodded.

I deadpanned my sister. "Go. Away."

Her indignant buzz drifted toward the edge of the garden overlooking the patio below. One could hope she did something useful, like double check on the druid.

Before she could turn to watch and make me nervous, I let the stone fly. It hit the trunk with a hollow thud, froze on the rebound, and expanded into a view of Mae and Duskmere on the parking garage below. I moved away to give them room, shoving the extra two portal stones into my pocket—for future just-in-case moments. Mae jogged through, followed by Duskmere.

"According to Y'sindra, the druid is gone," I said. "If we're lucky, he's on vacation. If we're not, we might cross paths in Outerlands."

"Wait for us!" Y'sindra and Lo zoomed toward us across the garden.

"Any change?" I asked.

"Nope. Lights off, no one's home."

"She knocked on the glass," Lo supplied helpfully.

"You did what?" What was wrong with her? That fairy would be the death of me. "You know what, never mind. Teddy, Lo, are you sure you want to come? This isn't what you signed up for."

"I signed up for you." Teddy brushed a calloused fingers whisper soft across my cheek. "If you go, I go."

"And me. I'm going," Lo chirped with a puffed chest.

"I suggest Duskmere binds to Treasure Island." Mae preemptively cut off the moon fae's objection. "It's safer for us now and you in the future. Outerlands is an unknown. Wouldn't it be better to find somewhere hidden that isn't in the middle of enemy territory?"

That's my clever sister.

Duskmere hesitated. At least he didn't outright object.

"You should listen to Mae," Teddy said. "It's a sound suggestion."

"I agree. Even if you don't want to, the rest of us are staying on the beach." I started walking toward the stone circle. Something about it seemed off, but I couldn't put my finger on what. "Everyone inside the circle before me. I still have my doubts, but we're here, so let's try."

They broke the circle perimeter, but I took my time following, tracing the stones one-by-one. Something was wrong, like the darkest corners only visible in my peripheral. I was seeing something, but I couldn't focus on what.

I shook away the unease and stopped at the outer edge of the circle. "Everyone ready?"

"The faster we get there, the faster we get home. Let's go." Y'sindra snapped her fingers at me. On principle, I frowned at her, but didn't disagree.

"You okay?" Mae asked.

"Yes. I don't know. Just my imagination. Let's get this show on the road. The DVR is going to start deleting shows to make room soon, and if I miss the final rose on *Forever After*, I'm gonna be pissed."

Teddy grinned. "I knew you were a romantic."

"Pah-lease." Y'sindra cackled and hovered next to Teddy. "It's all about the drama."

Shaking my head, I completed my path around the circle. Something still seemed off, but I couldn't figure it out.

"Hey, we should submit the security vamp at the Blackthorne for next season." Y'sindra's wings hummed, shedding snow from her excitement. "He's hunky enough."

"I'd watch that," Mae said.

I stepped inside the circle. No spark. No fizz. No electricity. I took another step. Two. Three. I passed the center point of the circle and still no sensation.

A strangled breath pushed past my lips. Wrong, wrong, wrong.

"We need to go." I headed for the edge of the circle. "Now. We need to get off this roof."

Spaghetti thin vines and thorns erupted from the ground outside the circle and folded over the stones, forming a dome. I stumbled backward. My hearts shriveled and stomach shook. *Trap!*

A form separated from the closest tree. As the shadow slipped free of the bark, the grainy wood textures faded away and were replaced by Mr. Black. "I wondered when you'd return."

How did he know we were here? How did we not know he was? He'd been right gods damned there, listening to everything.

"Keep him talking, lure him closer." Teddy's voice was barely a breath in my ear.

"No one touch the thorns." My sisters knew, but my words were for Teddy.

Duskmere moved to stand behind me. He looked to Teddy and gave a subtle nod toward the druid. Were he and Teddy actually working together?

All right, I'd play. "You got us, Mr. Black—or is it Blackthorne? Sorry, I didn't recognize the name. I guess no one does. Must suck to barely be a footnote in history."

The druid's low laugh twisted in the dry air. He moved closer.

"Footnotes are subtle but vital inserts. You, for instance, are my insert."

"I'm not your anything." My throat scratched out the last word as my gaze landed on a broken stone. Like the druid's description of his mark in history, the change in the circle was subtle. It was a small piece broken off the top and wedged beneath the rose bushes beyond.

The druid broke his own circle. Short of a road trip or airplane—not happening—we had no way to reach Outerlands. Of course, neither did Mr. Black.

"Ah, I see you've spotted the change. Smart girl." The druid sounded pleased.

From inside the vine dome, Teddy inched closer to the thorn wall.

"I hope you didn't have plans to hop a ride with Nyle." I studied my talons and shrugged. "He's the most recent addition to the sun fae dungeons."

"You got us, so now what?" Y'sindra buzzed in tight, agitated circles, stopping briefly at my side to mean mug the druid. "Planning on cooking us up here? Turning us into lifeless husks? We heard that's your specialty."

This guy was the source of the druid bogeyman, the legend. Changing the genetic course of an entire race wasn't his only crime. He'd drained the lifeforce of other druids who left Ta'Vale with him and left their dry husks to petrify under the desert sun.

Through the mosaic of vines, I looked from his navy blue slippers, up his waist-length braid, to the crown of his salt-and-pepper head. He couldn't possibly be capable.

"That was not me, but I'd be happy to try on you. Payment for the horn."

"I smashed it in the parking lot." Y'sindra bobbed in the air like a yo-yo. "Did they bring you the splinters?"

The druid took another step. I felt Teddy coil before I saw him move. A dark slice of dungeon opened behind Blackthorne. Guards waited at the ready.

Teddy surged. His body met the vine wall, and the dome shrank, folded around him. He bucked and twisted, encased in a net of vines and thorns. Dots of bright red burst beneath the green veil as the thorns sank deeper into his flesh.

I had to get that off him. I reached for Teddy, clawed at the vines. Thorns ripped my palms. I didn't care. It could kill him.

My hearts slowed. I spun on Blackthorne, a growl building in my chest. He twisted to look behind him.

If he hurt Teddy, by gods he would fix him.

I catapulted into motion, slamming into the druid, shoulder to chest. He staggered, arms sweeping wide to catch himself. His momentum tilted him forward, away from the open portal.

"No you fucking don't." I stepped in and pushed, sending him stumbling across the threshold where the guards waiting in the dungeon cell converged and pulled him to the ground.

33

SOUL BRUISED

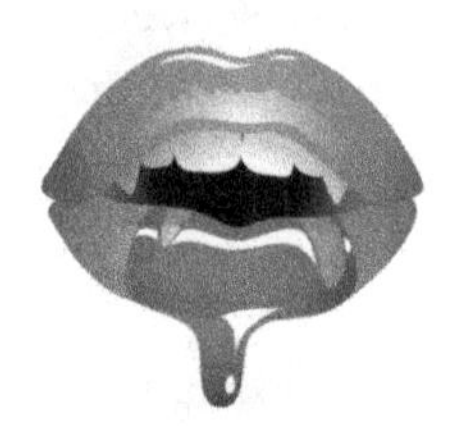

I SHOULD HAVE FELT TRIUMPH, BUT INSTEAD A SUCKING VORTEX OF nothing settled in my core. A wavy haze pulled at my vision as I stared into the dark depths of the cell and shrieked a bottomless pit of rage at the druid. All this—everything—because this asshole opened a doorway to Outerlands.

But first he manufactured my genetic cesspool.

"Lane." Mae's fingertips brushed my elbow.

Laser focused on my singular thought to follow the druid and rain a lifetime of caged fury down on him, I shook my arm and stepped toward the pulsating portal. A polished length of wood lying on the ground stopped me. Blackthorne's staff. It warmed my palm as I wrapped it in a tight grip. A tingling sensation sizzled from my fingers to my shoulder. I wrenched my arm back and took aim at the kneeling druid's skull.

Another scream exploded from me and followed the staff through the portal. Blackthorne's face came up and caught the end of the staff on his forehead. His head rocked back. The portal snapped shut, burning the image of the druid sagging between the guards behind my eyelids.

I'd missed my chance. The brief satisfaction humming through my veins at felling the druid turned sharp. My panting grated against my eardrums. Utter silence behind me hit harder than an ogre's uppercut.

Teddy. The memory of him collapsing into a net of thorns and vines plowed to the forefront of my brain. A yelp of panic burst from me, and I dropped next to where he lay motionless inside the druid-spell cocoon. This wasn't Lo's small scratch on the cheek or even the few punctures I took. Unlike the spell that Lo was caught in, these thorns pointed inward, into Teddy. Too many thorns pierced his body, too much magic in his system. Would he wake up? Would he die?

Lo hunched opposite me, shaking with desperation. Y'sindra wound her arms around his trembling shoulders. I suspected it was as much to comfort as to keep him from trying to pull the thorns from Teddy's body.

"He's breathing," Mae said, her light touch returning.

I squeezed my eyes shut. This was why she'd been trying to get my attention. I'd shaken her off, too caught up in my own selfish emotions, my self-pity. I could be a heartless bitch.

"Stop it. His aura is strong." Mae rubbed my shoulder. "He's out, but his breathing is even. Let's take him to Mom."

Mom. If anyone could help Teddy, she could. A natural healer with druidic knowledge. I gasped a breath. "Yes. You're right."

"Malaney Callaghan, I must reach Outerlands."

Incredulous, I rose and rounded on Duskmere, my hands clenching and unclenching at my sides. He couldn't possibly believe I'd take him there now, even if I could. "What you must do is open a portal so I can get Teddy home. It was your lunatic plan that put him in this position."

"I must—"

"You must open a portal. Now!" I descended on the moon fae like a thundercloud. Unease flickered in his pale eyes, but to his credit—and his stupidity—he held his ground.

Not for long. I slammed my palms against his chest and sent him staggering for balance. "The druid broke the circle, jackass. Don't you see it? Blackthorne knew we were coming. Someone warned him."

Mae's hands flew to her mouth. Guess it hadn't occurred to her either.

"Impossible." The thick doubt in Duskmere's voice belied his denial.

The druid knew we were coming. He knew we were coming at the time we did. The reality of that sank in. My bones grew heavy with the knowledge. After pouring a lifetime of anger onto the druid, I was drained, exhausted, my soul bruised.

"How many knew you were making this trip, Duskmere?" I asked, and Mae edged closer to me, waiting for his answer.

He licked his lips, silver orbs skipping from me to Teddy and around the group. "There will be an explanation."

I'm sure there would. Like, someone close to him was leaking worse than a sinking ship. At the gaping crack in his usual self-assurance, a small part of me felt sorry for him. A very small part, but enough to force me to soften my tone.

"Listen, I understand your urgency, but the druid circle is broken. We can't use it to go anywhere, but we can use your portal to go home." My nostrils flared against my frustration, thrashing to be set loose. *Stay calm, Lane. Stay calm*. "Teddy needs help—right now. Get us back, and I promise I will help you figure something out."

I hated making that promise, but for some revolting reason I hated the kicked puppy look on his face more. Besides, I promised to help find a solution, not be his escort into hostile territory. I didn't know exactly where the place was located, but the Internet worked magic. I'd find it, put a big red dot on a map, and send Duskmere on his way.

"I swiped a pamphlet," Y'sindra said. "We've got the address."

It'd be nice if she'd grabbed it out of forethought and preparation, but no. Her magpie tendencies drove her to grab every new shiny she came across. We had a basement full of useless junk as proof.

"See, we know where it is. We can figure out a way for you to get there." I gave my sis a nod of thanks, even if her intentions hadn't been deliberate, they helped. "Open the portal."

Duskmere bent at the waist, getting a close-up of the broken druid stone, as if mentally calculating the truth of my words. I swore, if he told me to take him through the busted-ass circle one more time, I'd escort him off this roof via the balcony.

"All right," he said after a too-long pause. "Remember, two at a time. You must move the black wolf on your own and move him quickly."

Even as I watched, the smallest of the vines melted from Teddy's limp form. I knelt at his side, calculating the best way to move him. His legs were clear to the knees, as was his head and shoulders. The thorns were close to his armpits, and while I might prick my hands gripping him there, it seemed a better option than pulling by his feet with more risk of injury to Teddy. Besides, I already cut my hands on the thorns once and wasn't asleep yet. Fast tolerance buildup, or small dose.

"All right." I moved behind Teddy's head and slid my hands beneath his shoulders. "Open it behind me. I'm ready."

"I have your word you will get me to Outerlands?"

Oh, for fuck's sake. "We'll run a search on the damn hotel the minute we're all back and Teddy is in Mom's capable hands."

He looked at me like he wanted to argue, and I looked at him like I'd remove his tongue from his skull if he dared. He pressed his lips together so tightly, his charcoal flesh turned chalky white. Duskmere's eyes tightened, but he kept his trap closed and prepared to work his magic. Wise move.

Pulling up the portal happened fast and without ceremony. A quick clenching and unclenching of his fist, a nano-second flare of the moon crystal at his throat, and the oval wavered to life. Much different from when my father worked his hybrid hocus pocus, and much more accurate.

Scooping my fingers beneath Teddy's shoulders and around his armpits, I began dragging him backward. My hair lifted and scalp itched as I slowly backed through the portal. For the second time in a single week, I made an undignified ass-first entrance. At least this time it was voluntary.

I pulled a very heavy, very unconscious Teddy straight back until his feet cleared the portal, and veered to my left, making room for whoever came through next.

In my peripheral, I caught a glimpse of a tall figure with a shining copper cap of hair. My lip curled—Cirron. Fantastic. Not what I needed to deal with right now. On the other hand, I could shove the hotel's address and a map at him and Duskmere, and be done with them both. *May I never see another RFG member this century.*

I eased Teddy down on the warm, afternoon grass and knelt at his side, rubbing my sweaty palms on my thighs. His chest still moved. The steady rise and fall of deep sleep loosened a knot gathered between my shoulder blades.

The clap of the portal closing ricocheted across the landscape. I jumped, but Teddy didn't flinch. He needed Mom's ministrations immediately, but I'd be damned if I left him vulnerable with Cirron so close. I flicked a glance in his direction, and he quickly looked away. *Right.* As if he hadn't noticed me or the portal. What a prick. It would make my day if he turned out to be the traitor. He might be Duskmere's partner in every sense of the word, but I didn't like him and didn't trust him.

I dismissed the sun fae with a sneer and turned my attention to Teddy. A few vines still tangled at his waist. They had withered to the size of shoestrings. Soon, they would be nothing.

"Teddy?" I whispered and moved to lay my ear to his heart. It beat strong and steady. My head swam from relief as my body eased its grip on panic.

Catching my lip beneath a fang, I trailed my fingers down his face, memorizing his features by touch. He needed to wake up. By the gods, he better wake up. If it came down to it, I would storm the dungeon and beat the antidote from the druid.

My fingers splayed on Teddy's chest. This male was vital to me. Not because of a good kiss and a great ass, but because he believed in me in a way that forced me to believe in myself. A spasm of panic shook me to my marrow and then melted away.

I didn't care who or what Teddy was born to be, all that mattered was who he'd become. What he'd become knocked his unnecessarily chivalrous self unconscious trying to save my sisters and me, but it showed what he was made of—pure gold.

I'd still kick his ass when he woke up. I didn't need any male saving me, even if the gesture did put a flutter in my stomach.

Across the lawn, Cirron dropped all pretense of not noticing me and headed in my direction with the expression of someone who had stepped in a still-steaming pile of shit. Apparently, the dislike was mutual. He stopped several feet away.

"Teddy is hurt," I said. "Go get my mother."

Cirron didn't move. If he expected a please, I'd throttle him. I laid my ultimate death stare on the sun fae.

Unaware his throat was on a collision course with my fangs—blood allergy be damned—he completely missed the effort I put into my murdery look in favor of studying Teddy. Cirron inched closer.

"If you value breathing, you'll back away while you still can."

"This is the black wolf." Scrubbing a hand up and down his forearm, Cirron leaned closer to Teddy but then took that step back. He gestured toward the empty space I'd just walked through moments before. "Where is Duskmere? Are the others with him?"

"I know who the fuck he is." This arrogant prick ignored me. Wrote Teddy off. In fact, I got the distinct impression he would finish Teddy if I turned my back. My hands curled into loose fists, pressing my talons to my palms, curbing the urge to plunge them into his eyeballs. "Cirron. Go get my mother. Now."

At last, he shifted his focus to me. His weird amber orbs took in my tense posture, the slip of fangs, my hooked hands. *That's right. Give me a reason, asshole.*

Proving he had at least a single shred of sense in his otherwise empty head, he strode for the front porch. I glared at his back, ensuring he did in fact go into the house.

Like a sleepy dragon's eye, an oblong circle, vertical to the ground and resembling an oil slick, opened in the yard. The glistening black oval dissipated and revealed the druid's rooftop garden.

As predicted, Y'sindra and Lo sped through hand in hand. What I didn't expect was for them to take a hard right, clearing space in front of the portal. From there, Lo flew straight for Teddy to kneel on his opposite side, but Y'sindra turned to face Mae's image growing larger by the second. Shit, she was going to come through. Duskmere said two living beings at a time.

"What are you doing?" My hearts triple tapped, and I surged to my feet. I didn't know what would happen, but that thing snapped shut with the speed and force of an atomic guillotine. So help me, if my sister got herself chopped in half, I would strangle her.

Lungs frozen, I watched Mae sprint through the portal.

She cleared the threshold, jogged to me, and gripped my tingling arms hanging limp at my sides. "Breathe, Lane. It's fine, I'm okay." She glanced around the yard. "Where's Mom?"

"Gods! Are you trying to kill me?" I scrubbed my face with trembling hands, feeling angry, terrified, but mostly relieved. "What were you thinking?"

"I'm a big girl, Laney. There were risks, but Duskmere was pretty sure Y'sindra and Lo were small enough he and I could also pass through."

"Pretty sure? You risked your life on a maybe? Why doesn't he know how his own portals work?" My furious glare jerked over Mae's shoulder to Duskmere, who came through the cosmic doorway.

"Just like sun fae, moon fae magic varies with each individual's ability to manipulate it." Out of what I assumed was respect for Duskmere, Mae leaned close, her voice hushed. "Very few can open portals. Most that could are banished."

"Because." Duskmere stepped onto our weed-dotted lawn. The portal sliced shut close enough to trim the ends of his already close-cropped hair. "Knowing you have two hearts informed me the portal is not reacting to living creatures. I will need to do more research, but I believe it is mass based."

"A preventative against an invading army," Mae mused.

I snorted. "Unless it's a fairy army, apparently." Thank the stars fairy tribes were unsociable creatures who barely tolerated their own kind. The thought of an invading fairy army turned my insides to jelly.

"Cirron is here." I gave Duskmere my judgiest head-to-toe look. I had a lot of looks. "That guy sucks. You should think really hard about that relationship."

Instead of the argument I'd expected, Duskmere dipped his head in acknowledgement. Maybe he deserved more credit.

The front door thumped open, and we all turned to face my apron-clad mom, who hustled down the steps and raced toward Teddy. Loose pants and tunic flowing, my father appeared and made his way toward my sisters and me. It had been at least three years since I'd seen my father in the flesh, and a heavy anchor of guilt landed in my chest. I didn't miss home, but I missed my parents. When this was all over, I would visit more.

Cirron's shadow filled the open front door, and he followed at a slower pace. Duskmere needed to dump that guy.

"What happened and how long has he been unresponsive?" All business, Meghan Callaghan, the healer, knelt and placed her fingers to Teddy's throat. "His pulse is strong."

"He took a big dose of druid magic. The same stuff knocked me out, but way more than I got hit with." I wrung my hands and inched closer. "He's going to wake up, right?"

Mom peeled the edge of Teddy's flannel from his flesh. A gasp exploded past my lips. I locked my knees as the ground roiled beneath me. The gray and red flannel had masked Teddy's blood. So much blood. I'd been so distracted, I missed the growing stains on his denim, the crimson pool collecting in the hollow of his throat. *Oh, Teddy.*

Y'sindra slipped her hand into my clammy one. "He'll be all right. You looked bad too, but you woke up."

"She's right," Mae said. "He'll be okay."

"The black wolf would not be this easy to kill." Duskmere arched a silver brow.

"If that's supposed to help..." I bit back the sharp retort digging into my tongue. His words had been meant to comfort. *Don't be an asshole, Lane.* "I hope you're right."

"Shall we speak?" My father didn't greet my sisters and me with a hug, but he'd never been the type. Probably where I got it from.

"Let's give Mom room to work." Mae moved away and they all followed, gathering in a loose circle.

I hesitated, loathe to leave Teddy.

"Go," my mom said without looking up. Her nimble fingers worked over his wounds. "I will tend to him. You can do nothing more."

"Duskmere." My father addressed the moon fae as I approached. "Torneh contacted me on the journey here. He is concerned the RFG has been compromised and needs you and Cirron to report back immediately."

While my direct interaction with the imposing sun fae ruler was on the order of nonexistent, unlike Iola, Torneh had been a regular fixture in my early life. He and my father were close, sharing the same passion for developing a hybrid magic of sun and moon. I didn't know much more about the male, but my estimation rose considerably hearing he wasn't oblivious to the machinations inside his court.

Next to me, Duskmere dipped his head toward my father. "Your daughters and I share these concerns. I will return once our business here is complete. Thank you, Finnlay Callaghan."

"Meghan will see to Prince Aventheo's wellbeing," my father told Duskmere. His regard for my mom knew no bounds. It was one of his better attributes. "You needn't worry about any issues with Shadwe."

"What?" I gawked at my father. "Why would they care? Teddy walked away from them."

"That is not the business to which I refer." Duskmere spoke over my objection. "Blackthorne broke his circle, severing our connection to the newly sundered veil to Outerlands."

Cirron had approached the group, but rather than push his way into our loose circle and join the conversation, he paced the perimeter.

"Mmm, yes that is troubling." My father assumed his thoughtful stance, face tilted forward, steepled index fingers pressed to his lips. "I do not expect it to be easy, but perhaps you will get the information you need from Blackthorne."

"That won't be necessary, not immediately. Your daughters can provide us with the location."

"Yep, that's me. I got the address." Y'sindra fluttered her wings with pride.

I pulled my suspicious gaze from Cirron to my crowing sister and resisted reminding her we could have searched the Web for the information.

"So you will be able to set a portal to the location. Excellent."

"Thanks to your daughters, yes." Duskmere giving us credit forced me to rethink his status as a giant asshole. He could be a small asshole. "The sun stones will soon reside in the garden once again."

The hushed voices of my father and Duskmere were drowned out by the distinct sound of a moon fae portal ripping open. My gaze whipped toward Mae and the open oval behind her.

"I'm sorry." Cirron's eyes were glued to Duskmere even as he grabbed my sister by the waist and yanked her through the portal.

"No!" I screamed and tripped toward the window into Outerlands. Beyond Cirron, my nemesis, Nyle, grinned and wagged his fingers at me. *How the fuck... Cirron.* He'd freed Nyle.

Mae clawed toward us. Bloody welts rose on Cirron's arms. She rocked her head back toward his face, but he avoided the blow.

The furthest from the portal, I wasn't going to make it. My lead-filled feet couldn't move fast enough.

"Cirron!" Duskmere leaped for the opening.

Whump. Whump.

The hollow thud of a blade meeting flesh sounded. Duskmere staggered, and I registered the two daggers embedded to their hilts in his chest.

Acid turned in my gut. I reached for fighting clarity, but my feet rooted and chest pumped with my out-of-control breaths. Everything happened too fast.

Duskmere staggered forward another step, wavered, dropped to his knees. Nyle turned his back, dismissing the fallen RFG. He pulled my flailing sister from Cirron's grip and dragged her away.

A long-winded groan wheezed from Duskmere's stilling lungs, and he toppled to his side.

Cirron bellowed. He struggled for the opening, for Duskmere, but a guard landed a hammer punch to his temple, knocking him to the ground. Another guard kicked Cirron to keep him there.

A flash of ice blistered past me. The interior ring of the portal frosted over. The smooth edges of the shrinking oval immediately began to crack but held long enough for Y'sindra to barrel through. The portal blurred and snapped shut.

"Oh gods, no!" They were gone.

Both of them.

My sisters were gone.

34

GONE

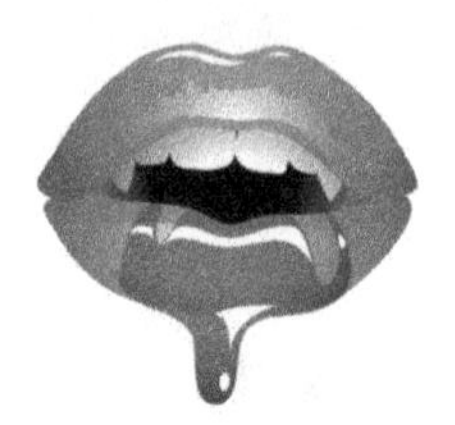

I LOST EVERYONE.

A desperate hollowness threatened to swallow me. My sisters were gone, and I didn't know how to get them back—my guiding lights in the murky sludge of my questionable existence. Without them, who was I?

My breath came in sharp, short gasps. I stared unblinking at the spot where my sisters had vanished. My eyes burned, but if I looked away it would make it real.

This was a nightmare. It had to be.

Mom rushed by, breaking through my direct line of sight. My eyelids fluttered. This was happening. This was still real. I choked on a sob and ground the heel of my palm against my breastbone, massaging the near incapacitating ache. I couldn't survive this.

"Lane, get over here and get pressure on this." Hunched over Duskmere, Mom had slipped on the mantle of healer—serious, no nonsense, dispassionate. Meghan Callaghan. She'd removed one dagger and pressed a ball of cloth ripped from her apron against the wound. "Fin, contact Torneh. We need to get Duskmere to the Eodrom healers immediately. I don't have enough supplies."

I looked from the chalky gray moon fae to Teddy, who still hadn't moved. My hearts spasmed.

"But Teddy—"

"Is not about to return to stardust." Mom's retort boiled with impatience. The brittle sound of fabric shredding echoed against my eardrums as she ripped Duskmere's shirt wide and tore another strip from her apron. "Best I can tell, he's asleep. Either he'll wake or he won't. Only time and Blackthorne know. Now get over here and keep pressure on this. If you can't do that, go get my bag."

The soil beneath Duskmere couldn't absorb any more of his blood, and it pooled beneath him. Crimson ribbons pushed over Mom's knuckles and down the sides of her hands, the first strip of apron saturated. He'd already lost so much blood, and it wasn't slowing down.

Dread's clammy hand brushed across my nape. The small nick on Mae's throat from Nyle's blade still hadn't scabbed. Shit, I'd noticed but hadn't unpacked what that meant.

Hot air pushed from my nostrils as I stared unblinking at Duskmere's free-flowing blood. If Nyle was a known spymaster and apparent assassin, his blades were probably poisoned. Anti-coagulant. Duskmere would never survive the two-day ride to Eodrom.

Acid churned in my belly, burned my chest, up my throat. The boy-hero of the Great Fae Divide was going to die on my front lawn. That bothered me—a lot—and it pissed me off. I shouldn't give a hairy ogre's ass if the arrogant prick met the stars, but damn it, I did.

I dropped at his side and took the freshly torn strip from my mom's hands and pressed it to the open slit in Duskmere's chest.

"Finnlay," Mom shouted, peeling the torn fabric from Duskmere's wounds. "My bag."

My father stood some distance from us, speaking to a projection of Torneh, Iola, and a cluster of RFG behind them through his communication crystal.

"Lo can..." The words dried on my tongue, and I blinked at the spot Lo had just been. Teddy lay all alone, his companion gone. Where the hell did he go?

"I'll get it. More pressure, Lane." Mom sprinted for the house. Distantly, it occurred to me that while I didn't make it to the portal, neither did Mom—a full blood fae who was faster and stronger.

Through the furious haze of tears pooling in my eyes, I ignored the thoughts gorging on my guilt and turned my focus to those gathered in the hologram. Everyone was tense. Torneh looked ready to explode. Iola glowed with anger, literally, glowed. Even with my contacts in, the brilliance of her form forced me to squint.

The blood fae from the dungeon stood to one side of the pair. This time she wasn't glaring knives at me but instead stared helplessly at Duskmere, who continued to bleed out beneath my hands. Our eyes met, hers and mine, and the stark terror there shook me. To care that much, even when your love is not returned. The air grew heavy in my lungs, and I looked over my shoulder to another still form laid out on my lawn. "Come on Teddy, wake up."

Duskmere's body twitched beneath my fingers. I tensed, pressed harder, but blood ruptured from the oversaturated rags. Duskmere shook with an involuntary spasm. He was dying, but his body fought to hold on.

My mom dropped to her knees next to me and yanked open her medicine bag. A wave of sharp, sweet, and bitter herbs punched my nostrils. Blood fae couldn't perform magic, but Mom was a healer before she evolved. She continued to keep a vast garden curated for healing plants.

"We need more than your medicine bag." I pulled off my shirt and tore two quick strips from the hem. "You need to get the other blade out. I'm certain it's coated in at least one poison. Definitely an anti-coagulant but don't know what else."

Her hands stilled in the bag. She grabbed the discarded dagger she'd already removed and dragged it beneath her nostrils. Duskmere's scent was heavy on the blade, too heavy for me to detect anything below the surface.

"You're right. Oleander." Her lids fluttered, and she pulled in a deeper breath. Her brow dipped. "Blood Nettle, Sweet Greville, Starbane. Be ready to put pressure on the second wound. We need to remove this from his system."

That was all the warning I had before she leaned over Duskmere and yanked the blade from his chest. The dry sound of metal scraping bone was followed by the wet slurp of his flesh trying to keep its grip on the dagger.

I pressed a fresh strip of my torn shirt to the weeping slit. My shaky breath was hot in my nostrils. Within seconds, bright red rivulets wept from beneath both sides of my palm. "This isn't stopping. Do you have anything to slow the blood?"

"Working on it." A mortar and pestle at her knee, Mom dug through the bunches of fresh-cut herbs in her seemingly bottomless bag.

First, a spade-shaped green plant smelling faintly of garlic appeared, and then a red, round-leafed plant, its spicy scent scratching my throat. Bunching them together, she pressed the herbs into the mortar and dove back into the bag with her free hand to retrieve a rich purple, plum-sized berry. She mashed the berry between her palms, scraped it into the mortar, and began grinding the concoction.

I recognized each ingredient, knew how each would smell, taste, what properties they held. There was a time in my life I'd trained with the great Meghan Callaghan. I'd aspired to be like her—respected, loved, necessary. Someone who healed.

My eyes followed the motion of Mom's blood- and berry-stained fists working the mortar and pestle.

I'd been stupid, naive. For a minute I thought finding the sun stones would get me those things. Childish dreams. Now, I might have lost Teddy just when I found him. I didn't have my touchstones, my sisters. I'd had everything I needed and had been too blind to see. I hadn't appreciated it. Now I had nothing.

A sob caught in my throat, and my mom's glittering obsidian gaze whipped to me. A salt and pepper swatch of hair escaped her bun and fell forward to bounce against her cheek as she continued to grind the plants into a paste. "Focus. Remember your lessons. Duskmere Blademoon's life depends on you being present."

My brow bunched. I didn't know enough about the dying male beneath my hands. Despite always being somewhere in the periphery of my life, I hadn't even known his formal name—Blademoon. My gaze roved over his long, sharp face—like a slice of new moon. Fitting.

The sticky wet of his lifeblood cooled over the tops of my hands, still warm beneath my palms.

Lo missing.

Mae taken.

Y'sindra gone.

Teddy somewhere in between.

Duskmere dying, and there wasn't a damn thing I could do about any of it.

The sharp edges of my vision faded, turned dark. I squeezed my eyes shut. It was too much. I couldn't come back from this.

"Lane."

Pushed from the sun bridge, breaking my body, that was nothing to this. Blackthorne shattered me. Cirron stole my soul.

"Lane."

I struggled to breathe past this pain. Teddy might sleep forever. He might meet the stars. Try as Mom might, there was no hope for Duskmere. I was up to my elbows with the evidence. Even with a map, I didn't know how to get to my sisters. The druid might have closed the veil along with the circle.

"Malaney Callaghan." Mom's frigid tone shocked me from my misery. Her furious gaze shamed me. "Now is not the time. I need you here. Now. Your sisters need you focused. One thing at a time."

The blade of guilt twisted in my chest. My sisters needed me. They were alone.

"One thing at a time," she said again and eased my hands from Duskmere's wound. Numb, I watched her scrape the black paste from the mortar and push it into the hole I'd been pressing against. She repeated the motion until the herb mixture was a mound, before flattening it against his flesh, sealing the puncture.

She'd already covered the first dagger hole while I'd been lost to self-pity and regret. The herbal paste bubbled as blood pressed into it, but the bleeding had slowed. Thin trails of watery red wept from the edges. The freshly packed wound still flowed from beneath the medicinal mixture, and Mom used a clean cloth to continually brush away the blood.

My father's lanky shadow fell across Duskmere. "When the bleeding has slowed enough that you deem it safe to move him, we will take him through the portal."

He'd ended his call. How much had Torneh, Iola, and the RFG my father had been speaking with seen?

"Soon," Mom answered.

"What portal?" He couldn't mean...

"Mine. They will be waiting to take Duskmere." His gaze flitted a few feet away. "And your Prince Aventheo."

I surged to my feet and took a wide-legged stance. "Are you crazy? What happens when we end up somewhere no one can reach us?"

"Mind your tone, Malaney Callaghan." My mom's stern voice cracked like thunder. "That is your father, and he is the chief royal wizard for a reason."

"But—"

"It's been years since the incident." My father's lips thinned. He was a proud man, but he had reason to be. No sun fae matched Finnlay Callaghan for magic. "I was granted special permission to have the wards lifted in our yard because hybrid travel is of the utmost importance to Torneh."

"Trust your father, Lane."

I clutched my hands to my chest, turning my head to take in Teddy's still form. "Do I have a choice? Let me take Teddy first."

"Duskmere must be brought through. He is vital." My father gripped his hands behind his back.

"Teddy is vital to me. He goes first."

"Do it, Fin. These herbs need to dry before we move Duskmere. Lane can take Prince Aventheo now and return for Duskmere." Mom raised her dark brows at me. "I'll need your help. We'll have to be careful not to put any stress on the wounds."

"Very well. Ready yourself, Malaney." My father's voice took on the sharp edge of irritation. "The portal lasts longer than that of a moon fae's, but not so long as you can linger. Deliver the prince and return immediately."

The fight went out of me. This situation couldn't get worse. I needed Teddy to wake up. I wanted my sisters, and I saw no clear path—or path at all—to achieving either of those things.

Damn it, all I'd wanted to do was prove myself, and I'd done that all right. I'd proven to be the complete genetic fuck up all those sun fae bigots believed me to be. Now they'd eventually lose their power and wither to the stars, but there was no triumph in that.

"Lane—"

"Hurry, I know." I pressed a hand to my sternum. "I do know, Mom. Just...this hurts."

Her features softened. "We will get them back. *You* will get them back, but not yet."

"Not yet." Or not at all. I resumed my position at Teddy's shoulders and began to lift his torso but hesitated and looked at my father. "Can you guarantee me no harm will come to Teddy, that they'll do everything in their power to help him?"

My father's face contorted, and he lifted his knobby nose into the air as if trying to avoid something rotten. "Of course they will. He is the crown prince of Shadwe. No one will risk making those housing our enemy into our enemy as well."

Except Teddy wasn't a prince, but if that made them work to bring him back to me, I'd take it. I heaved his shoulders from the ground. "Let's get this over with."

"Meghan, you take the prince's legs." Pulling a stone disk embedded with several sun shards from his pocket, my father moved behind me and pressed the disk into the ground. Roughly the size of his open hand, half the disk protruded from the dirt. He stood, brushing his hands, and burrowed his bright blue gaze into mine. "If you overturn the projector, you will sever the connection."

I glanced at the lumpy, half buried disk, gauging its placement. This object was something new. My father told the truth He had been refining his portals. There was a thread of hope. Teddy's weight shifted, and I turned to find Mom at his feet.

"Open the portal, Fin." Mom kept her gaze steady on me. I ignored the trickle of sweat slick on my spine. They were counting on me, and I didn't like the feeling.

A soft click sounded behind me and a cool breeze stroked my half-bared neck, lifting loose hairs.

"Go." My father's voice boomed with urgency, and I started backward, watching my feet for the disk.

I should probably ask what would happen if I kicked it over.

"Easy, Lane. You're almost there."

Then again, who needed that kind of pressure? Best I didn't know.

We shuffled across the portal into my parent's garden and were immediately surrounded by robed medics and royal fae guard who relieved us of Teddy's still limp body. Watching him be carried away matched the helpless ache of watching the portal close on Mae's receding form.

"He better be alive when I get back," I warned.

Iola stepped forward from behind the group. Her sunset eyes flared, and I stilled. "Our healers will do everything in their power to bring Prince Aventheo back to you."

To me. She would do this for me.

"Let's go, Lane." Meghan Callaghan's stern, no nonsense command pulled me from the bottomless depths of Iola's gaze.

Mom and I stepped from their yard to mine. We took care lifting Duskmere while my father collapsed the portal, placed a second disk, and reopened it, ensuring we would have the time we needed to make our way slowly from one realm to the next.

At the sight of their esteemed captain, a hush fell over those gathered. Several RFG members moved in and took exquisite care receiving the burden. Strangely, I still felt the weight of Duskmere's waning life, even after his body left my hands.

A lump of bloody fabric lay at my feet. The healers had relieved him of the shirt Mom had sliced, and his jacket. Obscenely, a single boot lay on its side in the grass. Crouching down, I retrieved the jacket and tied it around my waist. Duskmere will want this if he woke. When he woke.

Mom made her way to the healers and began explaining what she'd done to slow the blood flow, about the suspected poisons. A gentle click sounded as my father stepped through the portal. He retrieved the two projector halves buried between our yard and theirs, most of their sun shards dark, depleted of their power. The group headed into my parent's back door, and my father brushed past me to follow.

While Teddy had been taken to the healing grounds of Eodrom, Duskmere was deemed too critical to travel that far and had been taken into my parent's home. The yard, chaotic and full moments ago, was empty. Absence gnawed in my hollowed chest, and it hurt. For a moment I'd had purpose, and now I was back to nothing. No one.

I gripped the dangling arms of Duskmere's bloodied jacket, still knotted at my waist. Blackthorne, the source of all this chaos, all this destruction, and all the answers that could help me save everyone, everything, was so close.

Yet he might as well be at the top of the Drifta mountains. At least there I could reach him. Here, he was locked away in a magic-warded dungeon.

There wasn't a soul in Eodrom I could beg for an audience. Even if I could find a sympathetic ear, no one was going to give me access. Not with the rate they'd been losing prisoners. Not with the traitors. Not with Cirron's recent betrayal.

Pain twisted my ribs. Mae. Y'sindra.

My thumb brushed over the ragged edge of a tear in Duskmere's jacket. He would have brought me to Blackthorne.

I stilled.

Duskmere would help.

Fingers bumping over the raised edge of the RFG emblem, my breath quickened.

Only RFG had access to the dungeons, and I had the captain's emblem. Pulse thumping in my throat, I took in the empty yard.

Not giving myself time to second guess, I unwound the jacket from my waist and pulled it on as I strode for the garden gate and the druid.

35

FUCK THIS GUY

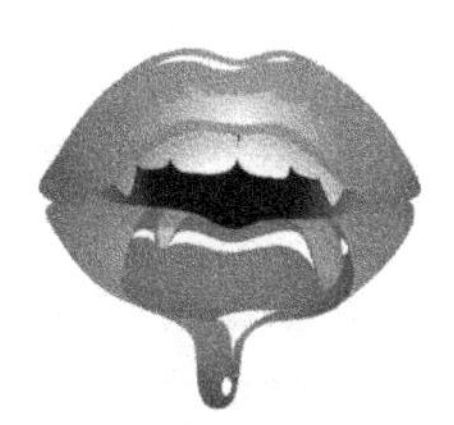

THE DOWNWARD SPIRAL FROM HELL WAS AS LONG AND MONOTONOUS AS I remembered, but this time there were voices, happy voices, laughter, the carefree shouts of children. My eyelids warmed, and I blinked quickly.

How did I miss this on my last pass? The buzz of rage and fantasies of murdering Duskmere must have drowned out everything else.

I paused in the shadowy crease between the stairwell and the interior wall, and stared into the dark depths of the arched corridor opposite me. The moon fae who remained in the Grian Valley. Rather than reside beneath the Lann Ridge mountains, they'd made a new home here, beneath Eodrom. And for the first fifteen years of my life I'd been too self-absorbed with the fallout of my own genetic mess to notice.

No. I wasn't the asshole here. These fae weren't genetic mutts like me. They'd escaped into the accepting embrace of their forgiving enemy, integrated into a new living structure, had a place in this world.

I was and always would be *other*—and I didn't give a damn. It took losing everyone who mattered to me to understand. My sisters, and by some miracle, Teddy, didn't just accept my differences, they embraced them.

Something I should have done long ago.

My chest vibrated with a growl.

Movement at the bend above me cut the sound short. My sharp vision caught them before they spotted my still form tucked in the shadows. Two young female fae, one moon, one sun, hand in hand, all giggles and smiles, the picture of childhood innocence. My throat swelled. Fucking *feelings*.

Twin gold braids bouncing on her shoulders, the adolescent sun fae saw me and stopped two steps above.

"What..." The moon fae stumbled into the other girl and steadied herself with a hand on the girl's shoulder.

"Hi," the sun fae said. The shock of finding me skulking along in the dark having passed, she smiled, innocent, wide, and genuine. "I've never seen you. Do you need help finding someone? Uru can be confusing if you've never been before."

Uru? That must be the new moon fae home—Strong heart. How...appropriate.

"Don't be silly, she's Royal Fae Guard." The young moon fae pointed over her friend's shoulder toward Duskmere's jacket. Of course the moon fae's eyes would be better in the gloom. Hopefully not sharp enough to see the copious blood stains.

"You girls be careful." I loped away from the pair and past the stone arch into the moon fae's new world. Short I might be, but I let my strides carry me three steps at a time. The acceptance I saw between the girls cleaved my hearts.

Seeing two diametrically opposed races clinging to one another in joy and laughter seared through me with hope and sorrow. That's all I'd ever wanted. As a girl. As a grown woman. I'd lied to myself. I'd called it respect. I'd wanted acceptance.

No more. Now, I wanted my sisters back. I also wanted the stones, but not so I could be raised up by those who looked down on me. Not for the savior notoriety but to keep Mae whole.

Heedless of the noise coming from the next three arches, I pushed myself faster and faster. Glittery chips embedded in the rough-cut stone walls streaked past like flights of shooting stars.

The solid clomp of my heels crashed into the walls and bounced back to my ears, louder, faster.

I didn't know my way around the dungeons, but I knew how to reach the only cell with portal capability. The cell we sent Blackthorne to no more than two hours ago, and even less time since Cirron betrayed the sun fae in the worst possible way imaginable. My money was on the fact that the last thing the RFG was concerned with was relocating the druid.

I curled my fingers, bunching the excess length of Duskmere's jacket sleeves in my palms.

Mom was a brilliant healer. The sun fae medics had healing magic. They might save him.

But all that blood.

Because of my nature, I knew how much blood a body could lose. Duskmere lost that and more. There were powerful beings but no true gods. There were no miracles, only stars and the infinite universe beyond. Duskmere would be joining them.

May his stardust have a peaceful rebirth.

At the base of the stairwell a line of crystals climbed the arch and met at its apex. My feet hit the dungeon floor with a hiss of gravel.

As I passed beneath the arch, the embedded crystals flared gray, then dusky blue, turquoise, and finally a vivid emerald green. The shoulder of Duskmere's jacket heated my collarbone. I shrugged out of the leather and turned it inside out. The RFG insignia magically stamped into the material was already fading. I'd been right, the insignia was the key to entry. Not terribly secure, which worked for me.

Pale blue fairy lights dotted the high dungeon ceiling. The walls and ground, so deeply dark, seemed to gobble the smallest particles of light that dared reach them. They sure went for the creepy factor in this place.

I licked my lips and squinted into the inky darkness.

No time to be tentative, I threw back my shoulders and pulled up every inch of my five-foot stature. Fangs bared, I plowed forward. Blackthorne would see death when he saw me. I needed him to know his life meant nothing next to the answers I planned to pull from him. Sure, I couldn't actually kill the bastard if I wanted him to talk, but I could get damn close. Inevitably, even the hardest shells crack in that liminal space. It's not seeing their end that does it. It's the fear of not reaching that release.

It should worry me how okay I was with torturing this male, but honestly, fuck this guy. He was the reason my life was a shit show and the little that mattered to me had been ripped away.

I crossed the threshold from hallway to dungeon proper. Empty cells behind black stone bars hummed with what I now recognized as druidic magic marched alongside me and faded into the distance. This place was enormous. It could take hours to find the right cell. Maybe days.

Doubt scratched inside my brain. What if they moved him? Maybe they had an even deeper and darker place for the druid's level of evil.

Continuing past empty cell after empty cell, my pace increased with each. Desperation drove me. This was my only opportunity to confront Blackthorne. If I got caught down here, it was over. At best I'd be escorted out and lose my shot at ever finding a way to wake Teddy and rescue my sisters; at worst I'd be the dungeon's newest resident.

Not gonna happen. I clenched my fists, the scrape of talon against palm spurring me faster.

"Blackthorne!" My shout rolled into the dark distance. "Come out, come out, wherever you are."

Silence answered me. But then laughter. My steps stuttered. Low laughter that grew deeper and louder.

Anticipation coursed down my spine. My arms tingled with relief. He was here.

"I expected you sooner." The disembodied voice snaked down the corridor. Not sure who he expected, but I doubted it was me. I'd never heard of druids being omniscient. Then again, I'd never heard much about them at all.

Mae would know.

"Is the black wolf still alive? I wasn't expecting him to join you in my garden. Wasn't expecting anyone to do anything so stupid, either." He chuckled again. "You looked rather upset. I hope he wakes up."

Blackthorne knew it was me. And he knew Teddy was this black wolf. Mildly surprising, but anyone old enough to have lived through the Great Fae Divide seemed to know, and gramps here was older than most dirt.

"You better pray he wakes up." Forehead leading the way, I charged toward the voice. It had come from ahead and to the right, in the cell with two bent bars. Teddy's handiwork. The same cell Duskmere had thrown us both into.

Memories of my anger toward the moon fae punched me in the gut. Why did I have to be such a jerk? Sure, Duskmere was a prick, but he'd been doing his job. Doing what he believed in. If he pulled through, I'd be nicer.

I scowled and stomped toward the cell, spraying gravel. Duskmere's current condition was this guy's fault, too. Cirron wouldn't have had a chance to turn if the druid hadn't created the opportunity.

Blackthorne waited at the front of the cell, looking no worse than when we tossed him through the portal. No beating, no torture, no sign of any damage—if one didn't count the lump on his forehead. The skin had split where I'd hit him, but there was no blood on his face. It stained the hem of his shirt, probably from wiping his face clean.

I stepped close to the bars, inches from Blackthorne. He smiled—fucking smiled—unsurprised and unafraid seeing me here like this. I bet it was the baby fangs. Whatever the reason, it was rude. I put a lot of effort into looking scary.

"You're alone." The druid's gaze slid past me and then to Duskmere's jacket. "That's a lot of blood."

"You're still breathing. I didn't hit you hard enough with your stick." He'd expected Cirron. He'd expected to be set free. "And I'm happy to inform you, Cirron is gone. Hope you like your new digs."

Blackthorne blew out an exaggerated breath and smiled, leaning a shoulder against the bars, no concerns in the world. "It'll do. I'd appreciate it if you would inform the chef of my dietary restrictions on your way out. I'm vegan." His carefree attitude plucked at a nerve between my shoulders. "I suppose you're here to ask me why I did it?"

"I don't care why, I want to know how. Your buddies have something that matters to me, and I want it back." He didn't need to know they took Mae. That Y'sindra was gone. I casually studied my talons. "Tell me how to fix your circle."

He pressed his palms against the invisible barrier threaded between the bars while he did a full head-to-toe look-see. I tapped my fingers against my thighs. The idea of getting the once over by an ancient baddie was uncomfortable.

"You're one of my creations."

"No, I'm not." I laughed, raw and angry. This guy had a serious god complex. The truth burned in my chest. "I'm a mistake."

Blackthorne's eyes went wide. "No, my dear. Blood fae are the mistake. You are perfection."

36

WHY NOT HEAR HIM OUT

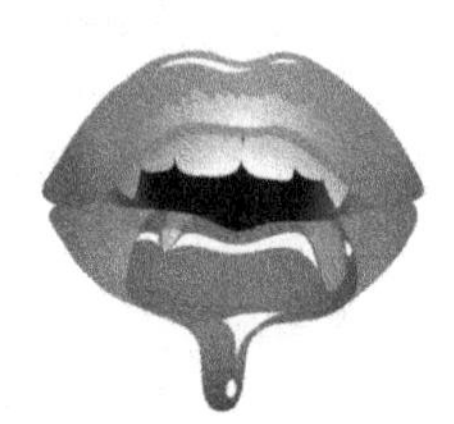

THIS GUY WASN'T A DRUID, HE WAS A SHITTY COMEDIAN.

"Listen, I don't have time for underhanded insults. I need information, and you're going to give it to me."

"You take admiration as insult?" He clucked his tongue and looked me over once again the same way my father studied one of his spell theories or Mom with her plants. "I didn't add a drop of druid blood to the creation spell, yet you stumbled your way through my circle. It took my genetic material to trigger the correct spell reaction. I guess this means you can call me grandpa."

"A little vain?" I snapped. "What makes you think you're the druid I'm related to?"

"Because there are no druids outside of my bloodline left alive." His gaze drilled into mine. "She saw to that."

"Oh, yeah. Your desert massacre. Boy am I lucky to be related to a mass murderer." Must be where I got my violent tendencies. "Listen Blackthorne, I need to get to Outerlands. If I got through the circle, I can fix the circle. Now are you going to volunteer the information, or do I need to beat it out of you? I'm cool with option two, but I'm on a time crunch and need to get a move on it if that's the direction we're headed."

He chuckled again, a sound I was coming to loathe. "I don't particularly care for the moon fae princeling nor his corrupted sun fae. No reason not to help you."

His lack of loyalty was good news, but damn, I'd been rooting for option two. All at once, the pent-up aggression I'd been holding onto to slipped out of me. I bowed my head and stuffed my hands into the ridiculously shallow pockets of my joggers. This new wardrobe experiment was a mistake. "So how do I fix the circle? I'm guessing it's gonna take more than super glue."

Laughter ripped out of him, full and deep. I'd been wrong, this was way worse than the chuckle.

Blackthorne drew his fingertips beneath his eyes. "I like you. We're more similar than you know."

My lip peeled up, and I put my fangs in his face. "You and I, we're nothing alike. I'm far from a saint, but I would never do the things you've done. Gods, man, you altered an entire race. You didn't even do it because you had some zealot's belief in the moon fae cause. Here I thought I was the monster."

His animated face went still as stone. "I did it for love."

"Then you're a damn fool."

"Am I? What would you do to save the black wolf?"

A boulder hit the bottom of my stomach, and I reeled back from the bars. "What game are you playing old man? Are you telling me he won't wake up? You expect me to do something for you to save Teddy."

Head tilted, the druid held his hands to the side, palms up in the universal gesture of I don't know. "No game. No expectations. Simply a question."

My shoulders curled inward from the pain lancing my hearts. I'd tear this universe from end to end and onto the next to bring him back, but love?

I'd known Teddy for years and we'd been friends, but things had changed between us. They'd been changing for a while, if I was honest with myself (which I frequently was not). Sure, he had an award-winning ass, and I'd learned he could knock my boots off with his kisses, but, again, love?

"What of the sun fae and the snow fairy?" He tapped a finger to his bottom lip. "What would you do for them?"

His question dumped ice into my veins. *Anything*. I would do anything for them, all of them. I'd even set this bastard free if that's what he asked.

"I think you might understand what drove my actions after all."

"No one I care about would ask me to commit genocide." This guy knew exactly what buttons to push. I'd have to be careful. "That you loved someone who did makes you an idiot."

"You might be right, but what's done cannot be undone." Blackthorne gripped his hands at his lower back and paced along the front of the cell, from one side to the other. I recognized the posture. It was the same as my father's lecture stance. "I did not agree to aid the moon fae, despite what history will write."

"Wrote—happened a long time ago, gramps. And I don't care, just tell me how to fix your circle."

His steady pacing didn't skip a beat. "I agreed because my love asked, and because I saw a problem that needed to be corrected. Two birds, one spell." Blackthorne glanced at me as he passed on the other side of the bars. "She is like you, you know?"

"A monster?"

"An outcast." The word crashed into me and rattled through my brain. "An unintentional product of moon fae mother and sun fae father, she came into this world sun."

"She wasn't a hybrid." I didn't know where this was going, but it wasn't there.

"No, but she was unwanted. Her moon fae mother abandoned her to her noble father at the sun fae court."

I snorted. Whoever this female had been, it wasn't her parent's race that ostracized her, rather their abandonment. Same reason I had an adopted sun fae sister. When Mae was brought to the court as an orphan by the young snow fairy that found her, Y'sindra, they were both shunned and turned away. Good thing my parents were different, collecting and nurturing broken things.

"So you understand she was his in name only, held in disdain. Later, becoming a mere shadow to her exalted half-sister. Living at court was cruel for her, torture."

But was she thrown from the sun bridge? I snorted. "Poor thing."

"Indeed. She mourned not being born moon fae, believing that was the source of her mother's abandonment and father's rejection. It ate at her, rotted her from inside with every taunt and blow she took for her lineage and disgrace until her blinding hatred of what she was turned her to the moon fae's side when the war began in earnest." He stopped and faced me. "We had performed the binding, and I had no choice but to follow."

I whistled low. "You bound yourself to this unstable female? I was right. You are an idiot."

"Mark my words, granddaughter, love controls us, not the other way around. You'll see. You have no idea what the black wolf is, do you? If you did, you would thank me for knocking him out and drop him into a deep dark lake before he woke."

"I'm more than capable of handling an overgrown puppy." This guy wouldn't shut up. Unfortunately, he kept going on about the wrong shit. I reached over my shoulder to tuck the length of my braid beneath Duskmere's jacket in preparation for going into that cell and getting answers. "Listen, old man, this isn't *Love Connection*. Tell me how to fix your stupid circle, or things are about to get ugly."

"If you're in such a hurry, why waste time with the circle when you can walk through the veil?"

"I..." I could do that? What was I thinking? Of course I couldn't. "Shut up. Just shut up and tell me what I want to know."

"Which is it?"

"What? What the fuck are you talking about?" The urge to choke the life from Blackthorne, answers be damned, was powerful. His penchant for slipping from archaic being to modern human with his speech was maddening.

"I cannot both shut up and tell you what you want to know, so which is it?"

My lids slid shut in a slow blink, and I screamed, primal and furious. I surged for the bars, snaking my arms through, going for his throat.

He chuckled and danced out of reach, spryer than he had any right to be at his age. As I considered opening the door and going in after him, it dawned on me that whatever magical barrier was smeared over the bars was a one-way thing. I poked the four-foot-tall, one-foot-wide rectangle of open space, and my finger passed straight through. Yep, one way. I could easily squeeze through. Why even bother with the bars? Unless the magic only stretched so far.

I stepped back and shook my arm. "Why does this place reek of druid magic?" Felt like it, too. I chose to keep that to myself. Gramps here already felt too much camaraderie for my liking.

Blackthorne's obnoxiously white teeth flashed in the murky cell. He approached the bars, leaning a shoulder to the wall and crossing one ankle in front of the other.

The bastard was too comfortable. I made another grab at him. My shoulder slammed into the bar as my fingers grazed his shirt, and he scooted out of reach.

"How long are we going to do this?"

"You're older than dirt—and I'm being literal." I rolled my freshly bruised shoulder. "How are you so quick?"

"I take vitamins."

An aggrieved sigh puffed past my lips. "Come on, old man. Tell me what I need to do to wake Teddy up and fix the circle so we can end this."

"Teddy?" Brows rising with his question, Blackthorne returned to his upright lounging position.

"The black wolf."

"Ah, Aventheo. Teddy. Not a terribly clever name change. I suppose he chose it for conformity with the humans. I've spent lifetimes conforming."

"And I suppose I don't care." I pinched the bridge of my nose. I had one nerve left, and he was stepping all over it. "Tell me what I need to know, or I'm coming in there."

"You're welcome to join me." He leaned close enough for the glossy eggplant shade of his eyes to show. Here I'd always assumed my violet eye came from my sun fae DNA, but it could be the druid in me. "The circle would be an easy fix for you, but I think you want to reach Outerlands quickly. Days would be wasted on repair and travel. Instead, I'm going to teach you to part the veil."

I opened my mouth to argue, but why not hear him out? Feet splayed wide, I crossed my arms over my chest. "And Teddy?"

"He won't die. The thorns were magicked with a sleep spell, but the fool took a massive dose. Enough that it would kill some, but not the black wolf, and not you." Blackthorne lifted a shoulder and let it drop. "He will wake when he wakes."

My molars ground together, fangs clacked, setting fire to every ache and pain in my skull. "And he'll wake when?"

"When the spell runs its course. He could already be awake, or it might be days, even years."

Years? I gasped and wheezed. Teddy would wake up. He *would* wake up. But years? Damn.

"So, granddaughter."

I squeezed my lids shut, letting go of my panic about Teddy, and opened them to slice a lethal look at Blackthorne. He needed to stop with this familial shit.

"Many, many times removed granddaughter. So removed, we're barely related."

"Two leaves, same family tree." He waved a hand through the air like the leaf he'd compared me with.

My jaw flexed, and I stared at him. The silence was alive and loud against my eardrums. Fine. We were related. He was a monster, but so was I. Time for me to take advantage of that fact. "All right. Tell me how to fast-track a trip to Outerlands."

"You did both of us a favor when you gave me this." Blackthorne peeled away from the wall, tapped the lump on his forehead, and pointed past me. "Grab my staff."

I turned to find the knobby length of wood I'd drilled Blackthorne's skull with leaning against the opposite cell. Well, damn. I rubbed my oddly sweaty palms on my pants and crossed to the stick.

If this worked, I'd try for the sun stones, but my sisters came first. If I couldn't get Mae and Y'sindra, I'd be cliché and die trying.

Hefting the staff from its resting spot, I approached Blackthorne and knocked it against the bars, sending a couple of attached seed pods flying.

He watched the gesture with a satisfied grin. "Very good. Let's get started."

37

NOT ONE LIKE ME

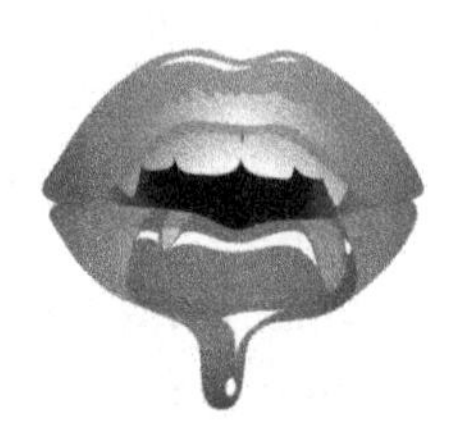

I'D DISCOVERED THE SECRET TO THE DEEP, DEEP, TOO FUCKING DEEP, dungeon. Forget shards beneath the talons or fang pulling, this was the torture.

Sunlight blasted into the corridor above me, and my knees went Jell-O-like with gratitude. Leaning against the rough stone wall, I paused to punch some life into my thighs and think through the challenges ahead.

Challenges. *Ha!* If the speed lesson with my ancient and evil relative was any indication, this climb was the easy part.

"Just find the old door to Shadwe, grab hold, and jiggle a little magic into the veil." I rolled my fist down one thigh, and then the other. All I needed to do was hotwire the universe. Sure, no problem.

Thoughts swirling, I pushed away from the wall and put my thousand-pound legs into motion. Even if that crackpot Blackthorne's minimal instructions paid off, and I reopened the door to Outerlands, sundering the veil didn't come with an instruction book.

As if I read instructions.

Flat ground greeted me as I rounded the final curve. With no more stairs to climb, my legs shed those pounds, and I wobbled across the landing like a newborn giraffe.

I watched my feet and focused on my situation. Somewhere between

Blackthorne's outrageous suggestion, accompanied by his shitty instructions and my clumsy reentry into the courtyard, I'd shaped my scattershot thoughts into some semblance of a plan. Once I rescued my sisters—because I *would* rescue them—I needed more than a way into Outerlands. I needed a helluva lot of rope and an army.

The idea of being surrounded by armed fae who wanted me dead wasn't my idea of a good time. They were coming for one thing and one thing only. It was a safe bet the moon fae roped the stones and hauled them through Nyle's portals in the sun garden, straight into Outerlands. Based on the size of the stones, it stood to reason a lot of moon fae pulled, thus my need for an army.

A mostly empty courtyard greeted me, but I still had a ways to go. It was a genuine possibility I would die from exhaustion before I made it out of Eodrom and gave the moon fae a shot at me.

Grumbling a litany of complaints beneath my breath, I steered toward a path that would take me the long way around the murdery grove and sank into the task of putting one foot in front of the other. Five minutes or five hours might have passed by the time I crossed the stream running through the heart of Grian Valley and marking the center of the castle.

I left the courtyard behind and navigated the halls with speed and purpose. More fae populated the interior of Eodrom than I'd crossed paths within the courtyard. I ignored the blatant stares and whispered gossip these assholes didn't even have the decency to do behind my back.

Until a few days ago, when Duskmere dragged, or rather shoved me back, I hadn't been to the palace since leaving Ta'Vale. I had no idea where the original door into Outerlands was, but the man who knew all—aka Finnlay Callaghan—did, and he could get me there. Assuming the successful portal from my Interlands front yard wasn't a fluke. I traced my tongue over my teeth. I'd bet my fangs I'd find Iola, Torneh, and my father together.

A one-stop shop—army, rope, portal.

Despite the urgency pulsing through me, my steps slowed as I neared the wing leading to the healing gardens. I had spent more days here than I cared to remember. Fortunately, I didn't remember much, what with the whole cracked skull and punctured heart situation. I rolled my shoulders back and expanded my rib cage. Memories couldn't hurt me. No one here could ever hurt me again.

I approached an exterior archway. Like the floors, it was carved from creamy alabaster stone. Unlike the floors, it was thick with embedded sun shards. Would the power-hungry sun fae resort to chipping away at the décor if the stones weren't recovered?

Could be I didn't need to bring all of them back. The moon fae who remained in Ta'Vale survived on three stones. Still, I wondered how much stronger Duskmere would be with all five?

Or would have been. I pressed a hand to the cool stone of the archway and bowed my head. I had to stop thinking that way. If anyone could take two well-placed daggers to the chest and survive, it was that stubborn bastard.

As I passed beneath the arch and into the meadow beyond, I dragged my fingers over the amalgam of rough shards and smooth stone. Soft emerald grass and pastel flowers exploded around me, their sweet floral and verdant scent heavy in the air. Ten large wood and stone cottages dotted the modestly sized field. Trees with long ropey limbs swished in the breeze. Manicured serenity designed to promote quiet minds for optimal healing.

The largest cottage set opposite me across the wide lawns was my destination. I hugged my arms over the ache in my stomach. Memories bulldozed into me. A pale pink cobbled path led to the building where I'd spent months teetering on the edge of death. This was not a place I'd ever planned to revisit.

A modest crowd spilled from the porch onto a wide waiting area laid before the main healing house. The right side of the patio opened to a sprawling pavilion covered with an ornate lattice roof interwoven with climbing vines and colorful trumpet flowers. Stone benches, tables, and potted plants filled the covered space.

Voices rode the breeze, bringing pieces of conversation to me. Duskmere and Teddy were alive, but that was all I could gather. No details on their conditions, but alive was enough.

Among the many heads bent together, I spotted my father, a hair taller than most of the gathered, but also thinner. An academic to the core, he couldn't be bothered with exercising anything but his brain.

At the center of the group stood a male and female sun fae leaking so much power only my father breached within five feet of them, giving me a clear path to Iola and Torneh. Good, I could get everything I needed and be on my way, but first, Teddy. I searched for my mom's dark head, which should stand out in this sea of blondes, but couldn't find her. The weight of disappointment settled heavy in my chest, and I ground my palm against the suspicious ache behind my breastbone. I'd hoped to find her with news of Teddy.

Sucking in a shaky breath, I sent my gaze skating across the rest of those gathered. Almost all RFG, and here I was behaving like the scared little girl I used to be. That wouldn't do. I dropped my arms and skirted wide, hoping to pull Iola and my father aside without drawing attention.

"Hey!" A roughened voice boomed over the organized chaos.

Not wanting any part of the drama, I put my head down and steered clear of the group. Someone jostled their way free of the cluster and drew a long shadow over the cobbles in my path.

Oh, good, I was the drama.

With an exaggerate sigh, I faced the solidly built fae stalking in my direction. He had unusually pale hair for a wood fae, like birch bark, and one green eye. A thick scar slashed from his hairline, across a milky left eye, and over his cheekbone. That sort of scar meant battle-tried, seasoned. I could probably take him, but I'd prefer not to get into a brawl with both Duskmere and Teddy clinging to life only feet away. Teddy would be amused. Duskmere, not so much. What I wouldn't give right now for Y'sindra and one of her cutting remarks.

The corners of my mouth pinched. Damn that snow fairy. Why'd she go through the portal?

Hands on my waist, I drummed my fingers on my hipbones and stabbed the wood fae rudely invading my personal space with an epic death stare. I knew the type, trying and failing to intimidate me with the disproportionate difference in our heights. I got it, he was tall, I wasn't. "I'm in a hurry, so let's pretend I let you have your say and move on. M'kay?"

His nostrils flared, and a vein throbbed on each side of his throat. "How dare you show your face. You are responsible for my captain's condition."

This old song? It got boring always being the one to blame. "So, we're doing this?" I shook out my hands and bounced on my toes.

"You wear his jacket."

"Oh, that. I, uh..." A flush scoured my body, burning all the way to the pointy tips of my ears. What the hell was I supposed to say? I took it and busted into your dungeon to question Ta'Vale's most wanted? "He loaned it to me?"

Yeah, that simply oozed confidence. Dungeon cell, here I come.

"A lie. My captain would not part with his insignia for anyone." Spit flew with Scar's words and landed on my foot. Unintentional, still nasty. "Let alone to a mutt."

This guy had some big ol' balls coming at me like that, and in front of this crowd. I looked around the angry fae to my father and raised my brows, the signal for 'a little help here'? He shrugged his bushy brows right back.

My attempt to project daggers from my eyeballs predictably failed. Finnlay Callaghan's word carried weight, which I suppose justified his reluctance on not speaking up when he believed I could handle myself. I could, but sometimes it'd be nice for him to be Dad, not the royal wizard.

My glare snapped from my father back to Scar and all his indignant fury. "Get the fuck out of my way." I smiled. "Please."

"First, I will have my captain's jacket back, and then I will escort you to the dungeons." He tapped an eight-inch dagger against the scarred cheekbone beneath his cloudy eye. Good blade. Maybe I should take it. "I have dealt with monsters."

If he'd asked nicely, I would have given him the jacket, but he'd gone and involved my pride. "Not one like me. I'm a monster for monsters."

"Malaney Callaghan." Iola's melodic voice instantly pulled me from my battle-ready stance.

I narrowed my eyes on Scar's angular face. Lucky bastard was saved the embarrassment of an ass kicking in front of his fellow RFG. Forcing my lips into a smile, I turned to the exquisite female gliding to us. "Iola."

As one, the gathered RFG hissed an astounded breath. My smile widened. *That's right, I called your queen by her given name. Suck on it.*

Iola's fingers trailed over the heavy leather jacket.

"This belongs to Duskmere?" she asked.

"Mmm." I hummed an affirmation, my confidence shriveling, and I prepared to be smote.

"The druid." She nodded to the knob of wood peeking over my shoulder from beneath the jacket. "Clever of you to interrogate him. Duskmere woke long enough to report on the broken circle."

Hope fluttered, and that terrified me. Fingers knotted, I studied Duskmere's crusted blood on my hands. "Will he be all right?"

"Unfortunately, only Mother Sun knows if he will wake again."

Code for fat fucking chance. I nodded and picked at the blood caked beneath my talons.

"Considering your relation to Blackthorne, I presume you wish to repair the damaged circle and retrieve our sun stones?"

My head came up. No judgement colored her sunset gaze, only questions. Her words had been loud enough to carry over everyone gathered. Scar was horrified. I wasn't sure if that resulted from his precious queen asking for my assistance, my relationship to the druid, or the realization that his fate was in my monstrous hands. Probably all of the above.

"I...yes. I spoke with Blackthorne." I slid a gaze over the group and was met with a mixture of shock, horror, and for the first time in my life, curiosity. Iola's public show of confidence was everything I'd ever wanted, but nothing changed. No seismic shift occurred in the universe. Ogres wouldn't start farting rainbows. Vampires wouldn't survive on apple juice. Y'sindra wouldn't stop cursing. Acceptance might have been what I wanted, but it was never what would make me whole.

"Let us discuss what you will need." Iola gestured to a bench beneath the pavilion.

Unable to resist, I blew a kiss to Scar and sought my father. His lips were settled in a deep scowl. What was his problem? A girl had the right to a little fun before saving the universe. Okay, maybe not the universe, but at least a very large piece of this world.

With a stiff jerk of my chin, I indicated he follow and set off after Iola.

I pulled the length of wood tucked against my back from beneath Duskmere's jacket and sank onto the bench next to Iola. Relieved of that knobby pressure, I twisted side to side, and my spine let loose a symphony of loud cracks. Iola's brows jumped. I knew how to make an impression.

My father joined us, as did Torneh, and my stomach wobbled. If Iola emitted an aura of power, Torneh pulsed with a supernova of it.

My knees locked around the staff, and I hugged it to my shoulder. Why should I be uncomfortable? Their problem got my sisters snatched. I was here doing them a favor while Mae and Y'sindra suffered who knew what at the hands of the sun fae's enemies. Sure, Duskmere might yet die, but I didn't throw the daggers.

I lifted my eyes from my lap and laid a weighted look first on Iola, then to Torneh, and finally my father. "I'm going to try to get the stones."

"You must retrieve the sun stones," Torneh said. Of course the first words he'd ever spoken directly to me, and they were a command.

"The only thing I must do is get my sisters, and when I've rescued them, I will try to get your stones." Try, not will. I wouldn't make a promise I wasn't certain I could keep.

"The stones are more important." Torneh's expression might be softer if it were carved in stone. For all of Iola's gentle warmth, her other half was an ass.

The fear his caged power had inspired vanished. Boy did I have bad news for him. This guy might rule a realm, but he had no say in my life. More importantly, he needed me.

"They're your stones and they're the reason my sisters are gone." I clicked my talons against the staff. "The stones come second."

"The existence of every race in Ta'Vale depends on the return of those stones, even the moon fae. Even your family."

Why not pull the daggers out of Duskmere and plunge them into my heart? I bowed my head and stared at the junction of Blackthorne's staff and my knees. "Listen, I'll do everything I can to get them back but, and I cannot stress this enough, my sisters come first."

Torneh shifted, but Iola put a hand over his. Their gazes met, seeming to speak in silence. After a long stretch, his broad chest expanded on a deep breath, but he said nothing. In a snit, he tossed his ridiculously luxurious gold mane and turned away. To be able to convince with a look rather than fist and fang—I needed that skill.

But I did enjoy punching things.

Iola turned her Torneh-taming smile on me. "We know you will do everything in your power. Now you are here seeking an audience, so please, what do you need from us?"

I leveled a look on each of them, even Torneh, putting some weight into the silence. This was a big ask. "I need an army, rope, and portals."

For the first time since I met her, Iola appeared stunned. Her mouth worked. "An army?"

"I can do no such thing." My father put a hand to his chest, as if personally insulted.

"Impossible. We have no standing army," Torneh barked over them both.

"Okay, and one more thing." I picked at a loose thread on my pants. This next bit was probably going to land worse than the first. "So, I'm going to need the rope and the army delivered to the old door to Outerlands."

Iola surged to her feet. Gold light boiled beneath her skin.

"Yeah, forgot to mention I have to reopen that door." Eyes watering, I squinted and waved my hands in the air, jazz-hands style. "Surprise."

38

NOT DESIGNED FOR AMOROUS AEROBICS

THE BANDOLIER OF DAGGERS ACROSS MY CHEST WAS MORE LIABILITY THAN protection. The most dangerous and most vital situation I've ever been presented with lay before me, and I had secondhand weapons.

Everything from throwing knives to a claymore taller than me hung on my walls at home. I'd spent years mastering them. I knew their weights, their balance, their lethality. I could cleave the wings from a fly at twenty paces with my carbon blades or crush them with my torpedo daggers.

I straightened the crisscrossed harness that kept pulling to one side back onto my shoulders. The best I could say about these borrowed blades were that they weren't dull and mostly well kept—no rust and no blood. Beggars couldn't be choosers, but what I'd been begging for was a ride home to get my own stuff.

One portal was all Finnlay Callaghan would commit his magic to. Too many portals meant too many shards, which would end in magic burnout. In his own aloof manner, my father loved us, I knew that, but I'd long ago accepted that his job and the sun fae would always come first. With a potential war on the horizon, it wasn't something he could risk. Not if I couldn't guarantee the return of the stones. Not even for my sisters. I worked my jaw and gave the harness an especially hard tug.

That meant no quick trip home to collect my stuff. I was left to borrow all the gear I needed. Fun. No portal for my backup plan, either. I had to make this fly-by-the-seat-of-my-pants shit work. Wouldn't be the first time.

The solid treads of my new boots struck the stone floors as I marched toward the balcony at the end of this hall. They were taller than my typical work boots, and clung all the way to the knees. Honestly, I wasn't sure if they were designed for fighting or S&M. I glanced down to the rounded, steel-plated toes. Most likely fighting, but considering the previous owner, I wasn't ruling anything out. I had no doubt Teddy would be a fan. He had better wake up so I could put that theory to the test.

After loading up with weapons, I'd been forced to raid a closet—a closet belonging to the blood fae I'd met in the dungeon. Of every fae in this gods forsaken place, we were the most similar in size, all the way down to my too small, too narrow feet. While the boots were questionable, at least what's-her-name-that-I-refused-to-learn had good taste in work clothes. The leathers I'd confiscated and had zero intention of returning poured over my every curve like liquid armor. Not as good as dragon skin, but close.

"Hey, I didn't say you could take my sword!" She-who-could-not-be-named shouted after me. Two weapons lay crossed over my back—Blackthorne's staff and the blood fae's sword. I never had a flair for the dramatic before, but with the cherry red fighting leathers I'd helped myself to and the armory strapped to my body, I was really leaning into this warrior-sex-goddess vibe.

The sword was good quality, and now it was mine. I stalked through the open doorway at the end of the hall, into daylight, and across the balcony. After leaping onto the balustrade, I turned to face the fanged tornado flying toward me. The fastest way from point A to point B was not through the palace.

"Tootles." I gave a finger wave and stepped backward into the open air.

The ground screamed toward me. Flexing my core, I wrangled control of the fall.

Deep breath.

Loose limbs.

My knees were soft and legs already folding the moment my feet touched ground, body tucking, and I rolled away from the impact. Half-rolled.

"Oof. Ow. Shit." The pommel of the sword buried in the ground, bringing my roll to an abrupt stop. The hard leather holsters covering my chest dug into the side of my throat, my ribs. Gods that hurt, but I wouldn't show it to my one blood fae audience. Joints weeping, I jumped to my feet and swaggered away with a little wobble and a lot of hip swing.

Peace greeted me between the palace and my childhood home, still situated within the sprawling Eodrom compound, but away from the royal cesspool. The fields between were sparsely paved with crushed stone paths and dotted with the occasional cottage. Wind whispered, and the playful swish of wild grass soothed some of the tension of the coming unknown.

The final nail in my plan coffin hit after Torneh finished choking on my surprise announcement of reopening the old door to Outerlands. I couldn't be certain if his reaction came from the mention of reopening the door or specifically *me* reopening the door.

Torneh stated it would take two moonrises to march to the border. Annoying, but I could work with three days. What I couldn't work with were the twenty-seven Royal Fae Guard Torneh committed to the cause, which he claimed, and Iola agreed, were the most they could spare without leaving the Grian Valley defenseless.

Twenty-seven fae did not an army make.

I was so screwed. Shame Teddy was still comatose and wouldn't be delivering said screw. When one sees the end coming, one can pinpoint the things in their life they wished they'd had the opportunity to experience.

"Going somewhere without me, sweet fangs?"

Shock scorched my nerve endings raw. I executed a whiplash turn to find Teddy, in the delicious flesh, leaning against the gray stone fence surrounding my parent's property. Awake. Alive. He'd never looked so good in thorn-shredded denim and a flannel hanging on by one stubborn button that revealed most of his glorious chest.

Fate totally deserved an edible arrangement for this one. Who said she didn't know how to deliver a gift? Not me. Never again.

Screw keeping my cool. I broke into a sprint, and Teddy caught me as I leaped at him. My man, my exceptionally strong man, grunted and fell against the stone rail to brace himself. Still in his arms, I leaned back to absorb every line of his familiar face.

A frown pinched my brows together. His toasty tan complexion had a definite green undertone. Not the swarthy olive type, more like his brush with death was still TBD.

I framed his face with my hands. "You're awake."

"I'm awake." He smiled and his lips brushed my brow. "Where are we going?"

"You're going to bed before you fall down." Pleasure and gratitude for finding Teddy on his feet flooded me. Damn druid might not have been all wrong.

"Only if you plan to join me."

Warmth bled into my bones. I bunched his parted flannel in my fists and rested my forehead against his nearly naked chest. Teddy's shirt smelled of sweat, pine, and vanilla—a little sweet, a lot woodsy, and all delicious. My fangs tingled as I pressed my nose to the fabric, filling my lungs with his scent.

"Lane."

"Mmm," I replied, burying my face in the soft flannel.

His rough laugh vibrated his shirt, tickled my nose. "Let me look at you, sweet fangs." He tucked a finger under my chin.

Our gazes tangled. His dark gaze sharpened, glittered with sudden hunger—for me. Instant, intense molten desire pooled in my belly. My lungs tightened, and a breath skipped over my lips.

Sensing my reaction, Teddy's lazy smile snapped taut. His arms twitched, tensed. The heat from his hand splayed over my spine branded me, pulled me closer. So close. My hearts beat against his.

"Lane," he whispered, voice strangled, tortured.

Any restraint I'd been holding onto tore free at his broken voice. I'd put him out of his misery. Reaching up, I tunneled my fingers in his thick hair and pulled his face toward mine.

He growled and our mouths met without hesitation, greedy and insistent. Oh gods, I almost lost this. Why did I wait so long?

More, I needed more.

I pushed against him, hard. His hot breath rushed over my lips before his mouth again claimed mine.

Teddy's big hands stroked a path of fire down my back and followed the curves of my ass until he cupped a cheek in each palm and squeezed, pushing my belly against the thick evidence of his desire. His needy growl sent spears of pleasure to my core while his hands readjusted, roaming, pressed into the sensitive flesh at the apex of my inner thighs. Oh gods. I groaned as his fingers dipped dangerously close to exactly where I needed them to go.

The leather was too thick, too restrictive. I writhed against him, and his grip tightened. Still not close enough. Bracing my hands against his shoulders, I leaped up and wrapped my legs tight around his hips, squeezing until I could no longer discern my heat from his.

His head fell back, exposing the passion-tense cords of his throat. "What are you doing to me?"

"Not nearly enough." Sealing every inch of my body to his, I leaned forward, applying delicious friction to the hard ridge cradled at the sensitive juncture of my thighs. My legs trembled from want, and I scraped my fangs over his bared column. He bucked and whirled, wedging me against the stone. The weapons crossed over my back ground against bone. I barely noticed. Who was I to look a gift wolf in the mouth? I'd much rather kiss it.

I drew his bottom lip between my teeth and pressed my fangs lightly into the tender flesh. His muscles clenched in response. Oh, I was a bad girl. I smiled against his lips and dropped to the ground for better access, letting my hand drift south over the hard ridges of his stomach. My seeking finger dipped into his jeans and brushed against the satin and steel length of him. I almost collapsed when his cock twitched and hardened even more from the brief touch.

"Fuck, Lane."

My sentiments exactly.

His reaction was heady. It made me weak, and I wanted to do that again. To take all of him in my hand and milk him until he didn't just moan my name but shouted it. How had I waited so long for this?

Teddy's hooded gaze set my blood on fire, and it scorched a path to my throbbing core. I gave him a slow smile as I popped a talon beneath the button on his jeans and it hit the gravel drive with a double plink.

My gaze dropped and mouth flooded with saliva. I swallowed before I drooled all over myself. Silly male never wore a belt. Lucky me. The waist sagged open, caught only by the zipper. No problem. Taking the tab between my forefinger and thumb, I dragged the zipper tab down. My fingers once again brushed against the thickening length of his erection as he sprang free and—

"Malaney." My father's voice, as effective as a bucket of ice water, doused my lust.

Are you fucking kidding me? I dropped my forehead against Teddy's shoulder. He imitated the fence post behind me and froze. By the feel of the not insignificant ridge beneath my naughty fingers, he'd need a minute.

"Little busy here," I said through clenched teeth.

"Yes, I have eyes. However, I believe you were in a hurry."

"A little bit."

"In a hurry to depart for the border." My father stood on the top step of his front porch, hands folded in front of him. "If you had *things* to attend to before departing, you could have saved my power source and agreed to march with the troops Torneh and Iola are providing. However, you were quite insistent speed was of the essence to reach your sisters."

Cheap shot, but not wrong. Guilt wrestled the final vestiges of my libido into submission. Mae would approve of my extracurricular activities, still... "The faster the better."

Teddy's fingers dug into my hips and pulled me to him once again, but my father had done an excellent job of extinguishing my desire.

"I like this outfit," Teddy whispered into my ear, giving it a nibble before a final ass grab. My lips twitched, but plunged into a deep scowl when I spotted the scarred fae. He leaned irreverently against the door frame of my parent's home, eating a sandwich.

"You," I shouted and jabbed a finger in his direction. "You fuck right off."

"Malaney," my father scolded. "Odollam is Duskmere's second, and Torneh has tasked him with escorting you, which is a great honor."

"Right, well, Duskmere was tasked with, I'm going to say, annoying me, and it was no honor."

These leathers were not designed for amorous aerobics. I wiggled and twisted on my way to the front porch, pulling my pants from my crotch and zipped jacket from beneath my boobs.

Teddy slung an arm across my back. Considering the amount of weight he settled over my shoulders, I wasn't sure if he was trying to get me or his body to behave. He might be awake and feeling horny, but Teddy wasn't entirely recovered. I'd make sure my father settled him into one of the extra rooms before I left.

He leaned down as we walked, lips brushing the shell of my ear. Goosebumps tingled across the back of my neck. "To be continued."

A warm shiver raced from my scalp to my core and got comfortable. To be continued, indeed. I slid him a sideways smile, admiring the denim clinging precariously to his hip bones. While I appreciated the view, I needed to find something to belt his pants.

At the top of the two-step stairs, I pushed past my father until I stood nose to neck with Scar—otherwise known as Odollam. I'd give the fae some credit; he didn't give an inch.

"I am to escort you into Outerlands if you are able to open the door." Scar took another bite of his sandwich.

The emphasis on his use of the word *if* wasn't lost on me. Had I been sure of my abilities I might be offended, but I wasn't.

"I'm a big, strong girl, I don't need an escort." I gave him space, but only so he could properly appreciate my sneer. "Certainly not you."

Scar studied my face. "The file I have on you says you have two obsidian eyes. Are your bi-colored eyes a mark of your affliction?"

I sputtered, words racing through my mind, insults, threats. My talons extended and dug into the palms of my clenched fists. "A mark of my—"

"Lane has already agreed to allow me to join her." Teddy's arm, still coiled over my shoulders, pressed me to his side.

The fae's green eye snapped away from my discolored orbs and took Teddy's measure. He didn't quake, but he didn't puff his chest, either. "The black wolf or no, you do not appear to be in any condition to protect her."

Her. Not Malaney Callaghan. No sign of respect. At least he didn't call me hybrid, or worse. Lucky him. The tether on my temper was wafer thin.

Teddy laughed. "You misunderstand, we'll be going to a world I abandoned. She'll protect me."

The angry adrenaline shooting through my body came to a standstill. In a convoluted way, Teddy defended my honor.

So not the time to dwell on how this male made me feel, but after the seed the old druid planted in my head, I could barely think of anything else. Damn, Blackthorne. Damn him to the deepest darkest hell. If it could get deeper than that dungeon.

Odo seemed at a loss for words. He studied Teddy, and I studied him. My eyes drifted from his scar to... "Take off your belt."

39

BRAVO ON THE EXIT

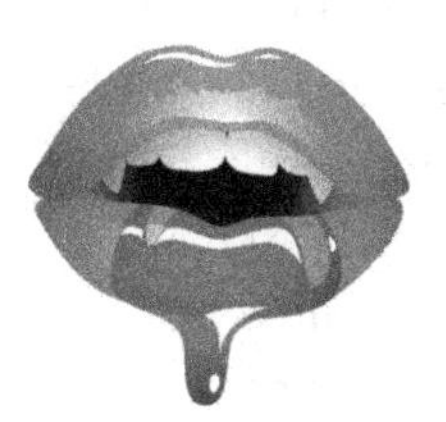

Odo had the build of a stout tree trunk. Teddy had an athletic build but securing the belt, if you could call the rope that, required a wrap and a half around his waist. So long as the knots didn't slip, his pants would remain above his ass. Helpful for him, since he didn't wear a stitch beneath the denim. Disappointing for me.

On the other side of the portal, my father had already left, he'd said to attend to Duskmere.

Scar, with his now sagging pants, and seven other RFG took my father's place. They huffed and puffed and muscled the last spool of rope through the portal, transferring the burden to Teddy and me. While blister bark weighed less than any other material, the size of the spools and amount we required was significant.

Between Teddy and I, we could move them to the door, but first we had to find it. By taking the load off the troops marching to join us, it would speed up their travel. Scar claimed he'd see us in half the time, maybe faster. I had my doubts. If all went well on the rescue, I expected to need the rope before the fae reached us.

The blood fae female was one of seven with my buddy, Odo. I gave her another finger wave. She opened her mouth, but the portal closed, not with the violent ripping sound of a moon fae portal, but a melodic chime. I wondered what she was about to say. Probably something about how good I looked in her leathers and I should keep everything. Sweet. *Don't mind if I do.*

A small stone shining with chips of sun shards remained. Half of the portal projector my father designed. If sun shards were in such short supply, and my father needed more and more, the least I could do was save these scraps.

The slice of stone had wedged into the soil. I loosened it with a talon and tucked it into a utility pocket on the bandolier, all the while keeping an eye on Teddy. The big dope had no business being out of bed. My sensitive parts still hummed from our encounter, and while I'd like to be in the same place —bed, with him—things were about to get serious, and I didn't need the added responsibility of ensuring he remained vertical.

My desire was a barely contained thing. With the condition he was in, I might kill him if I decided to continue our raunchy rendezvous. Still, my fingers curled as if holding onto the satiny feel of his erection.

Teddy leaned against a tree, trying for casual but missing the mark. The dots of sweat on his forehead gave him away.

"You look like crap." I dusted the dirt from my hands and headed in the direction my father said the border lay. The portal's coordinates didn't put me at the border to Outerlands but at Mom's favorite herb monger, which my father assured me was a short walk to the old door. Teddy pushed away from the tree and fell into step at my side. "You should've stayed behind and rested."

"I'm fine, beautiful. Do your thing, and I'll be right there with you."

"Don't piss in my glass and call it a margarita. You aren't fine." I veered left around a small tree sprouted in the center of the old path. "I'd put money on you passing out before we even get there."

"What is it with you and this new obsession with gambling?"

"Seems lucrative."

"Sure, if you don't lose."

"Haven't so far." If one didn't count the Etta'wy wager.

"Listen, consider me your guide." He rolled his hand forward and bent at the waist. "I did live in Outerlands."

"Hrmph." Smart ass, but he had a point.

Guilt overcame my petulance, and though he didn't ask, I stopped walking to give Teddy a break, busying myself adjusting the bandolier of punch daggers strapped across my chest. Mine were better, shorter, but their serrated edges made ragged cuts did more damage. The spiral tri-blade daggers on my hips were another story. I ran a finger over the long, thin leather holsters. Nice. These babies might find their way onto my wall.

"If I didn't know better, I'd think you were trying to make me jealous the way you're fondling those weapons," Teddy drawled, but a rumble of laughter rode beneath his words.

"Hrmph," I grunted again and pulled a square of hide from one of the bandolier pockets. "Take this. I'm not really the map type, and this thing is ancient. You're old, should be right up your alley."

Teddy had no choice but to take the map I thrust at him. "I'm not that old."

With a saucy one-shoulder shrug, I swaggered in the direction of the border, granting Teddy a view to admire.

Leather flapped behind me as Teddy shook out the map and laughed. "Bravo on the exit, but sweet fangs, you're going the wrong way."

"I knew that." No, I didn't. "Just evaluating our surroundings. Looks good." I spun on my heel and marched in the direction Teddy pointed.

"According to this we're exactly three wind songs from the border. What the hell's a wind song?" Spirits higher—and I couldn't imagine why—he jogged to catch up and matched my pace.

"Roughly a mile. The fae—well most of the fae—don't measure distance that way anymore." I snapped a branch from a tree and tapped it against the map. "That map *is* old."

Teddy took care folding the scrap of ancient leather and wedged into his back pocket. "We follow this path, and it'll take us right to the old door."

"That's easy."

The path ran straight if not smooth. Weeds and grass choked the edges of the crushed stone walkway, reclaiming it for the wild. Tree limbs, some low enough to limbo with, spanned the distance, forcing me to push, break, or saw our way through. If nothing else, the mess in our wake would serve as an obvious indicator to the troops marching this way.

"Almost there." Teddy's first words in the past hour startled me. "How are you supposed to know where the door is if it's closed?"

"Good question."

He walked close enough for our hands to brush, and his curiosity itched across my skin.

"And?"

"And I don't know." Slowing my pace, I opened my arms wide with frustration. "That loopy druid said I'll know it when I see it. Whatever that means."

"Hang on." Teddy grabbed my extended arms and turned me toward him. "We're doing this on the druid's recommendation? The one who tried to kill us?"

"Pfft." I puffed air between my lips but couldn't quite meet his eyes. "No, *I'm* doing this, you're just the guide, remember?"

Teddy shoved a hand through his hair, leaving a fly-away mess. It should be a crime he could still manage to look that good. "Lane..."

"Okay, listen." I put one hand on my cocked hip and held up a finger with the other hand. "First, he didn't try to kill us."

"Could have fooled me." Taking a wide stance, Teddy crossed his muscular arms over his chest.

"That's because you're the fool who ran headfirst into a massive dose of sleep spell." I took him in from toes to kissable lips. My posture went soft, and I puffed a breath. "I'm glad you're okay."

Those kissable lips melted into a cocky grin. "I could tell, and I liked it. Wanna show me how glad you are again?"

"Absolutely, but we can't. Not right now." But I wanted to. Badly. And I would when this was over. "Save Mae. Save Y'sindra. Find out where the hell Lo went, and then I'll show you until you can't see straight."

Teddy's brow dipped into a frown. "I gathered both your sisters were missing, but Lo too? What did I miss?"

"Long story, come on." As we navigated the path, I filled Teddy in on the chaos that went down after he knocked himself out. When I got to Lo's disappearance, Teddy's dark eyes crinkled with humor. "The guy's good. Best spy my family ever employed. They weren't happy when he left with me."

The pride in Teddy's voice warmed me somewhere in the upper region of my torso. He loved Lo, no denying it. Yep, I'd had it all wrong, and Blackthorne might have had it all right. I was a goner.

While the cicadas sang and grass whispered, I memorized Teddy's profile. I'd resigned myself to the fact I might not walk away from this rescue mission, but Teddy forced his way along. I couldn't lose my sisters and him. Well damn, I guess I had to survive.

"We should be close." Teddy's words broke into my no-death

introspection. "It's been a while, but this area is familiar. There should be markers over there."

I cut through the knee-high grass and found the markers—stumpy rocks dotted with lichen and strangled by vines. Following the direction carved into the rocks indicating where the barrier should be, I looked right. Nothing. I scanned slowly to the left. "I don't suppose you know where the old door is? How am I supposed to find... Oh."

"Oh?"

"Yeah, oh." I gestured to the jagged, kaleidoscope slice of light stretching from dirt to sky. "I think we found the spot."

40

LEAVE ME TO DIE IN SHAME

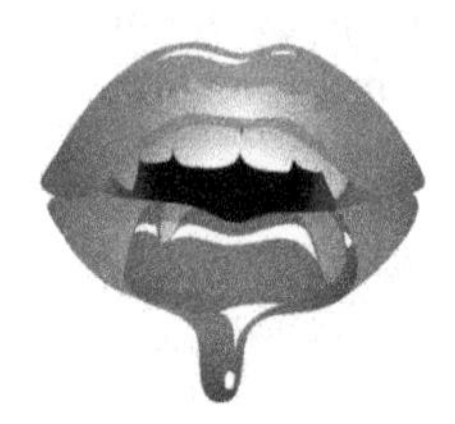

THE THIN SCAR ON THE VEIL STRETCHED FROM SOIL TO STARS. COLORS swirled and lights collided inside the narrow glimpse into galaxies drifting inches and millions of miles away.

Teddy saw the same thing he'd seen since we left the herb monger's—weeds, grass, and trees—no veil, no scar.

Not counting the accidental jump through the druid circle, finding the scarred veil was my first real druid ability. And my last. The old entry to Outerlands had yet to give an inch. I glared at the strip of magical space.

This was ridiculous. It was like looking through the keyhole of a locked door missing its handle. With my legs crossed and staff laid across my lap, the thigh-high grass almost swallowed me whole. A stalk twisted in the low-key breeze and scratched my cheek. I ripped a handful of blades loose and tore them into tiny pieces.

Stupid sun fae. Stupid veil. Stupid grass.

In the distance, Teddy snored not so quietly. He'd left me alone hours ago, he'd said, so I'd have space to work. I was no closer to cracking the code than before he fell asleep. All I'd managed was to shake a few more seed pods loose from this stick, which got me exactly nowhere.

Stupid veil. Stupid grass. Stupid stick.

Trust your gut, Blackthorne said. Feel the magic within you and pull it free. Shape it. Guide it. Bend it to your will.

Right. The only thing in my gut was indigestion.

"Well, if you can't fix it, hit it." I jumped to my feet, rolled my shoulders, and held the staff Louisville Slugger style, the dark wood warming unnaturally beneath my palms. Choking up on my grip, I wrung my hands on the smooth length once, twice, and swung for the fences—or the veil—but the staff passed straight through. Its momentum whipped me around until I faced the path behind me.

My balance bailed, and I lost the fight with gravity. "Oof." I hit the ground, and my lungs deflated faster than burst balloons. I gasped and stared at the darkening sky. Gold streaks from the setting sun arrowed up from below the treetops, but the deep dark of the plum sky gobbled them bit by bit. Soon it would be night, and I might still be right here.

Odo claimed he'd arrive tomorrow. Fuck. If that guy got here before I even scratched the veil... A growl rumbled my chest, and I coughed. That hurt. I flung an arm over my eyes and forced deep breaths into my too-tight lungs.

"So, I guess you won't be joining the bar's softball team next year."

From beneath my forearm, I punched him with a look that promised murder. One of my best looks. "Not funny."

"It is." He was steadier on his feet now with some sleep under his—Odo's—belt, and he didn't appear intimidated by my murdery look. Not even a little bit. Thumbs hooked beneath his waistband, he stood over me. "Need help up, or should I join you?"

"Leave me to die in shame before those fae fluffs from the palace get here."

Teddy took my arms and tugged my dead weight into a vertical position. Rude. He let go, and I melted boneless toward the ground. "No you don't." He caught me and kept me upright.

"Let me lie here and wallow in my failure."

"Stop being such a baby."

"Wah."

He rolled his eyes but didn't release me. I let my head flop back.

"Never knew you to be a quitter." Teddy tried to poke my pride, but the joke was on him. I had none left. "Can I help? What did the druid say you need to do?"

"No, and not a whole lot. Use my focus." I shook the staff in my limp arm. “He said the magic is in my blood despite me reminding him blood fae do not have magic. Dumb ass. Frankenstein should know his monster.”

“Isn’t that the druid’s focus?”

“Yes, but...” My teeth clacked together, and I stared at his brilliant face. Blood fae might not perform magic, but they were magic, and they didn’t rely on a stick, or a shard, or anything else to funnel their power—except blood. Well, damn. I knew what had to be done. “Do you trust me?”

Teddy let me go and stepped back. This time I didn’t go limp. “With my life,” he said.

“You might regret that.” Would this idea work? Mae always told me to trust my instincts, but this instinct was crazy. I rose to my feet. “Give me your arm and maybe don’t watch. This is gonna hurt.”

His brow furrowed, but he held his arm out to me. “What are you planni—son of a—ow. What the hell, Lane?”

A thin red line stretched from the inside of his elbow to his wrist. Small bubbles of blood beaded along the cut I’d made.

“Now who’s being the baby. It’s barely a scratch, and I *did* warn you.” I licked the thin sheen of blood from my talon. My stomach quivered with ecstasy. Jaw aching, I tamped down the impulse to attach myself to his throat. The tiny taste wasn’t going to incite a blood drunk rage, but it sure fanned a desire for more. *For him.* Gods, I’d never tasted anything so good.

“Barely,” Teddy muttered. Completely unaware of me eyeing him like a hamburger with special sauce, held his arm to his chest.

There wasn’t enough blood for what I needed to do. I hadn’t cut deep enough. He would hate this next part.

“Sorry about this.” A little sorry.

“It’s okay, you did say it’d hurt. Small cut, it’ll heal.”

I smiled, gently pulling his arm to me, and cradled it in my hands. “I’m not sorry about that.”

“What?”

“I’m sorry about this.” Before he could ask what I meant, I bore down on the split flesh of his forearm, forcing blood to pool against my palms.

“Ow!” Teddy curled his forearm to his bicep as soon as I let go. “Is this payback for tagging along? Be honest.”

Running my hands from end to end of the staff, I painted it with Teddy’s blood. My magic came from blood. That’s what Blackthorne said—not my blood, *the* blood. This had to work.

Breath in. Breath out. Grip the staff.

In a heartbeat, my nerve endings sizzled. My blood went carbonated, fizzed, hummed against my eardrums.

"Lane? Lane!" Teddy's voice was faint against the magic maelstrom building inside me.

Holy shit, holy shit, holy shit. Something was happening. This might be the moment. "Stay back!" I flipped the tip of the staff forward. *Follow my gut*.

My gut said to rip this sucker open.

I thrust the bloody, super-heated staff into the scar. A scream tore from me and my legs went weak, threatened to fold. Not today, bitches. I locked my knees and held firm.

A concussion of air shook my bones. It threw Teddy backward, out of my field of vision. My arms vibrated, but I pushed forward, drove the staff deeper.

The staff tried to shake free of my grasp. "Open up, gods damn it!" I screamed again. A continuous wail scraped my lungs. Frigid air blasted against me. My knuckles burned from the freezing air. I forced my eyes open and stared into the rippling abyss. Ice crystals blurred the air.

"I knew you could do it!" Teddy shouted.

I wanted to roar and beat my chest, but I wasn't done yet.

Beyond the edge of the scar, ice crusted the staff but melted in a blink. I panted. Exhaustion sucked the marrow from my bones, turning my movements brittle. I should take a break. Try again in five.

Shit, no. I had to keep going. All or nothing, and I wanted all.

In the widening gap, I stood stationary inside a hyperdrive. The stars created contrails in their wake, seeming to shoot into the distance, growing fainter. The scar grew twice my size, triple, stopped.

My hearts slammed against my rib cage. I knew what just happened. Blackthorne didn't tell me, I didn't read it in a book. Deep down, I knew. I bound two realms. Instinct guided me, told me to combine the two foci—staff and blood.

Fucking hell, I was a druid.

41

I NEEDED A TIC TAC

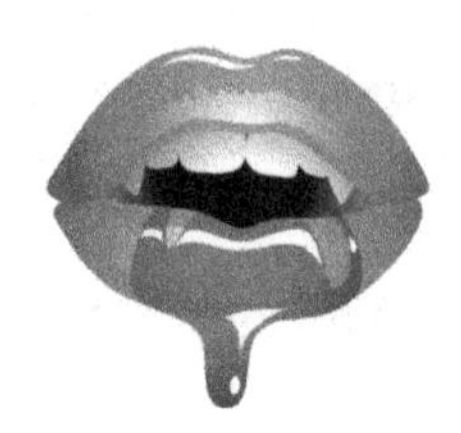

"Fucking hell, you're a druid."

"And blood fae." Sure, I just told myself the same thing, but hearing it out loud made it real. Real was a bummer. I shot Teddy a narrow-eyed challenge. "Don't forget the blood fae part."

"Never." His delicious lips slid into a grin every shade of wicked. "It's the best part. Gave you that spectacular ass."

He wasn't wrong. I turned to give him a good look at said spectacular ass but froze mid-shake.

Haze hanging beyond the infinitely tall, but literally door-wide, gap began to swirl and clear. Similar trees to those this side of the border, but smaller, their leaves darker, loomed from behind the milky haze. The same path beneath my feet ran through the parted veil and into the distance.

It worked. Outerlands. The blip of protective space between Ta'Vale, Shadwe, and now Earth. Just a narrow slice open between the two realms, but it was enough. My sisters were in there. Excitement rattled my breath. "We've gotta move." I bolted for the barrier.

"Lane, wait!" Teddy called.

Nope.

"Damn it, Lane, wait. We don't know what we're walking into." Teddy's voice grew deeper, rougher, with every word.

A sudden gale roared past me. Loose hairs flew, and the thick end of my braid whipped around to slap me in the face. I threw an arm across my eyes to protect them from a dust devil of dirt and shredded grass.

The garbled voice of wind died down, and I lowered my arm. Teddy stood in my path. Dust still floated around his legs, coated his boots. He'd done this. He said he moved fast, but damn.

My gaze rose to his, and I froze. A crimson ring pulsed around the small pupil at the center of Teddy's black orb, completely black. Spikes of red shot from the ring and traced to the edges of his eye. The thin red lines retreated, seeming to pull the blown-out darkness back with them until his irises were their velvety brown-black, and the pupil a small round orb.

What the fuck?

Seriously, what the fuck?

Teddy opened his mouth to speak, but his oxygen-deprived lungs objected. He swayed and dropped to a crouch, bending his head forward. "Please..." He gulped air. "Don't make me do that."

"Because you're out of shape?" His granite abs said otherwise.

"Because eventually I won't be able to pull back from the change."

Oh. What did I say to that? Indecision burned in my brain, and I clutched my hands on my head, torn between Teddy and the parted veil. The chance to save my sisters was right in front of me, but Teddy, so big, so strong, right now was so vulnerable. We should have a plan, I knew that, but I was so close to my sisters.

I buried my face in my hands and let loose my frustration until my lungs were raw.

Every atom in my body screamed to get through the door this instant and find my sisters, but I couldn't leave Teddy like this. Not because he'd laid a brain-scrambling kiss on me, but because he asked. And because damn it, I cared.

Grass crunched, swished, and Teddy's strong fingers circled my upper arms. He was okay. I huffed into my palms. Wow, I needed a Tic Tac.

"You waited." Teddy squeezed my arms.

"Don't get a big head about it. I didn't want to drag your carcass to Interlands." I hooked my hands over his forearms and met his deliciously dark gaze, no trace of crimson to be found. "We are going to talk about whatever that was, but not yet. My sisters are in there. I already waited too long. We have to go. Now."

Teddy's fingers relaxed and he ran his hands slowly up and down my arms.

"Hang on, let's think about this. We don't know what we're walking into, but more than that, what if the veil doesn't stay open?"

"Looks steady to me."

"But if it's not, we're trapped there with an unknown number of enemies." He ducked his head forward, staring through his lashes, directly into my eyes. "Your sisters won't be any better off if we get locked up with them."

The elation of my accidental triumph burned away, leaving an ache in my chest from the truth in his words. How dare he assault me with logic. I pulled away, my movements jerky. "You don't have to come with me. I didn't ask you to and don't expect it. But Teddy, I have to go. They're all I've got."

He closed the distance I'd created and crushed me to his chest. I tensed, but his earthy vanilla scent seduced me, melted me, and I buried my nose in his flannel. I just found this thing between us, and I'd miss it with my entire soul if I lost him.

"You've got me." Teddy's baritone voice rumbled the pillow I'd made of his chest. His large hand cupped the back of my head, fingers threading beneath my braid, massaging my scalp. I'd never get enough of this. "I promise, you've got me, but I understand. You need your sisters. All I ask is that we're careful. Recon first instead of rushing blind into the center of town."

I hated when someone was right and it wasn't me. Brushing my cheek against his shirt, I studied the thin slice in the veil. Nothing moved on the other side, but who knew for how long? "Okay, I won't rush, but we need to go." I stepped away but couldn't force myself to drop the fistfuls of flannel I clung to. "I need to go."

He touched his forehead to mine. "You had it right the first time. For now, can you do something to secure the veil?"

Secure the veil. Sure, no problem. I rolled my eyes, and my rolling gaze landed on the staff, the parted veil, and finally Teddy. I smiled. "Trust me?"

"You're going to cut me again, aren't you?"

"A little." I held my index finger and thumb close to indicate how much.

He groaned but extended the same arm I'd already sliced. For such a strong, scary guy, Teddy was a real pushover.

"Feel free to use a fang. In fact, I intend for you to do exactly that when this is all over. Right here." He pressed a finger to his carotid. His voice dropped into husky territory as he drew a line to his chest and tapped above his heart. "And here."

Saliva pooled in my mouth and my traitorous fangs tingled. Oh yeah, Teddy didn't know about my condition. Damn blood allergy.

"I bet you do." Poor guy was going to have his dreams dashed when we had this conversation. The feeling would be mutual. I gave a tight-lipped smile and took Teddy's arm. "Sorry."

"You'll make it up to me later." Teddy's smile turned my insides molten.

I scraped a talon down the cut I'd already made, and blood welled immediately.

"Didn't need to dig so deep," Teddy complained.

"And you don't need to keep...frustrating me."

"How am I frustrating?" Teddy paused. A twinkle—an actual fucking twinkle—lit his eyes, and he chuckled. Smug bastard.

"Shut up." I glared into his twinkling eyes as I dragged my hands down his forearm, painting my palms with his blood.

This relationship was officially in the weird zone. *Hey, Lane, what'd you and that hot hunk of man-meat do today? Not much. Cracked open the universe. Practiced paint-by-numbers with Teddy's blood. Tried to bind two realms together so I could rescue my kidnapped sisters. Technically, one kidnapped sister, one run away. You know, a Tuesday*.

Was it Tuesday? With all this new chaos in my life, I had no idea what day it was.

I stomped toward the veil. Without breaking stride, I snatched the staff from the ground and approached the torn scar, stopping directly center of the line between one realm and the next. I stared into the hazy distance.

A chill skated down my spine. I could do this, I had to do this. The door to thoughts of Teddy and Tuesdays slammed closed.

I let my eyes slide shut and focused on the blood beneath my palm, the whorl of the wood. *Instinct*. I called the power. A vibration buzzed beneath my skin. It worked. Not from contact with the bloody staff, I willed it up from my core. This magic shit came so naturally. Too natural, too fast. Elation fist-bumped terror in my chest. Power didn't come without a price, so what had I sacrificed to make space inside of me for this magic?

Gramps left that part out of his crash course.

"The staff is glowing. You're getting good at this." Teddy's voice pulled me back to the moment.

I cracked a lid, eyeing the pale green light emanating from the ancient wood. "I won't be casting any spells, but raw power? Apparently, I have that in spades."

"Who says?" Teddy tucked his hands in his pocket and approached to peer through the gap.

"Blackthorne."

"He doesn't make the rules."

"You never know." With one end of the staff pressed to the dirt, I bobbled the staff from one hand to the other. "He's old with a capital O."

Teddy turned and gave me a crooked smile. "Like dragons. All creatures of the universe are."

My mouth opened and closed. Creatures of the universe? The staff fell over, and I scrambled to pick it up. "Druids are fae."

"Yes. Probably among the first, and that's why they're different. They are fae and more. My family is the same." Teddy's eyes tightened. His voice got low and gritty. "Same as every other sentient inhabitant of Shadwe, and then we are more."

I pressed a hand to my belly, the staff warm against my body. So what did that make me? My eyes squeezed shut, and I filled my lungs to capacity. After a slow count to ten, I expelled the excess air and gripped the staff with both hands. We were here to do something, my mutated DNA sundae with a giant turd on top wasn't a concern. Not right now.

"Back up. I need room to do this." Stars bless him, he didn't argue, didn't ask what I was doing. He backed up.

Clamping down on the staff, I focused on the power simmering in my core. Picturing a loose thread sticking out from the ball of energy, I pulled. The electric spike in my veins came instantly. The scent of lightning and pine filled my nostrils but faded. Well, that was new.

I stepped wide and braced my legs. *Follow your instinct.* Hopefully my instincts didn't get Teddy and me killed.

Pressure built in my skull. Something—magic—raced from my core to the staff, taking the pressure with it. Tiny sparks of power bit my fingers. Sucking in a breath, I lifted the charged staff above my head, and with all my considerable strength, drove it into the soil.

Chartreuse flames fired away from the staff, along the ground, and up the sides of the veil to disappear in the sky. I flushed hot and cold. Awe stole my breath. The streak of flames burned out but left behind a faint glow, not so bright it would draw immediate attention, but there was no hiding the entry to Ta'Vale.

Teddy approached again and touched the still-vibrating staff with a tentative finger. "Impressive."

I licked my lips, not yet trusting my voice, and nodded.

The staff had driven a foot into the ground. Not nearly far enough. I frowned at the stupid stick. I'd put everything I had into staking the border with the staff, but it still stood hip high. "This isn't Excalibur. Anyone can come by and take it."

"You want me to help?"

"I can do it myself." I shouldered Teddy out of the way. The nerve, to think I needed his help with anything strength related. If he wasn't so scrumptious in denim, I might hold the suggestion against him.

Leaning onto the staff, I pushed. And pushed. Shadows scribbled across the edge of my vision. The staff still didn't move, not an inch. This was embarrassing. I eased back on the pressure before I passed out and shot a look at Teddy. He wisely made it a point to study a tree. This was bullshit. I pressed both palms to the top of the staff and pushed. My arms shook and shoulders screamed. This time it moved, but barely. Great.

I put my hands on my knees and panted.

"We aren't here for the view," I snapped. "Get over here and help me. Must be hitting rock or something."

"Hmm." He said no more as he bent and took hold of the staff. Smart guy.

My arms were wet noodles, but we had to give this one more try. "Ready?"

"Yes." Teddy wrung his hands on the shaft, testing his grip.

"Now!" I shoved down with everything I had, and it didn't move. Teddy's biceps bulged, and all at once the staff slid into the earth. We followed it down to the ground, leaving the knobby crown nestled in the tall grass.

"That should do it." Teddy scuffed a toe at the soil around the staff. He came toward me and tucked a strand of hair that had come free from my braid behind my ear. I bent into his touch. "I think you were right. Must be a layer of rock down there."

I pressed a fang into the corner of my lip. Except it didn't feel like rock. "Must be. Hope we didn't break the staff. It didn't—"

A javelin rocketed inches from my nose. I leaped backward, slamming into the edge of the veil, rattling the sword crossed over my spine in its sheath. I never wondered if the veil turned solid anywhere, and this wasn't when I wanted to find out.

Intent on returning the weapon pointy side first, I snatched it from the grass, but yelped at the burn of ice and dropped the melting spike. Ice! Could it be? My heartrate skyrocketed, and I bolted across the veil into Outerlands.

42

CHAOS AND CONFUSION

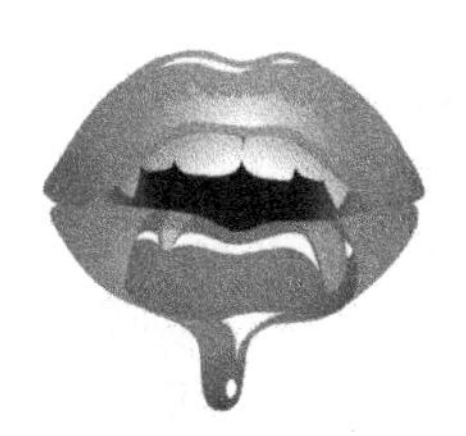

"Y'SINDRA? Y'SINDRA!"

Across the border, a bush trembled, and a small figure emerged. "Lane?" Y'sindra barked a sob, tripping forward when her dress caught on a branch. "Son of a rock troll's bald ass."

The open veil gave no resistance as I raced for my sister and her escalating litany of ear-blistering swears. She ripped free of the bush and launched into the air, barreling into my chest with the gentle touch of a bowling ball.

"I couldn't stop them. I tried." Her voice broke, along with my hearts. She cried into my shoulder, and it wasn't a cute, dainty sniffle. The cries came with huge gulps of air and no doubt tons of snot all over my shoulder.

Y'sindra's silky wings shivered beneath my hands, coating my fingers with fluffy dollops of snow. My frosty sister was an iron maiden when it came to her emotions, keeping them locked behind a cage of snark and profanity. I ignored the cold burning into my joints and continued to stroke her back.

At least some measure of her winter magic had returned. We were going to need every weapon in our arsenal to get Mae and get out of here alive. The more time that passed, the less keen I was for that cliché "die trying" ending.

A hiccup echoed into my ear, and Y'sindra rubbed her snotty nose on my jacket. Another piece of wardrobe destined for the trash.

I glanced beyond my sister's shoulder and did a double take. Lo waited next to Teddy. That guy's camo game was strong. Lo twisted his hands round and round one another, watching Y'sindra's meltdown. *Same buddy, same.* I worried too, but Y'sindra was the strongest of us all. Mentally, anyhow.

"The stones are gone." She stepped back, brushing wrinkles and twigs from her ruined dress. "Thank Freyja's fruitcakes we can check that off our to-do list."

I straightened and wedged my hands into my hip pockets. They were tight, like my throat. Clearly we were going to pretend her emotional break didn't happen.

"There's one stone left." Lo eased from Teddy to Y'sindra.

Who cared about the stones? Whatever was happening here was way more important. I fought a grin watching Lo sidle up to my sister and my sister allowing her shoulder to lean into his.

"Not for long. You heard them." Y'sindra looked to Lo, mouth twitching to one side.

"He heard them?" I gave Lo the critical once over. Small, weird natural camo, adorable. He was sneaky, but the idea that he got close enough to eavesdrop boggled the mind.

"Yep." She bounced, torn dress hem waving. "Lo is a good spy. Really good. We should put him on payroll."

Their hands came together like magnets.

For my own safety, I bit my lip before I said the C word. If cute came out of my mouth, Y'sindra would ice me. "You aren't the most inconspicuous fairy. How did you get away?"

"That's just mean."

My brows inched up.

Her brows slashed down.

Teddy coughed.

"Fine." She punctuated the word with a sassy hair toss. Lo blew away the strands that caught on his mouth. "When I followed Mae through the portal you were too slow to catch, I didn't have enough magic to cause frostbite, so I flew away. The end. Speaking of slow, we should get moving."

Y'sindra's twisty maze of remarks came with extra salt. Whatever helped her cope. She'd definitely glossed over the facts, but she got away, alive. How didn't particularly matter.

The moon chose that moment to come out from hiding and glinted off the polished surface of the knobby top of the staff protruding from the ground. I doubted anyone would wander this way, but I didn't want to take the chance.

"Hang on, I need to take care of something." Picking handfuls of leaves, I made my way to the staff and scattered them over the top, and more in the general vicinity. Brushing my hands, I stood and looked down the direction Teddy and I had just come through Ta'Vale, and then turned to follow the same path winding into the woods here in Outerlands, a reminder of the days when the two realms were previously connected. Already the warm, dry air of Ta'Vale intermingled with the cool, moist air of Outerlands, creating a new environment along the border.

I jogged to catch up to Y'sindra and Lo, who were already heading in the opposite direction of the veil. "How'd you know to come to the veil? And why'd you try to skewer me?"

"Lo and I were in the sky when we saw the green lights and thought it was the moon fae getting freaky with the veil." She tossed the answer over her shoulder without slowing. "How'd you two do that? Your black wolf have unknown powers?"

"Something like that." I wasn't ready to confess my new abilities.

"Slow down," Teddy said. "If you were in the sky, does that mean they have no fliers?"

"Nope." Lo skipped twice down the path with his one-word answer. Such a chipper fellow, no matter how dire the situation.

"Where's my brother?" Teddy stopped walking. "Hold up, we need a plan."

Grumbling some very unflattering insults, Y'sindra faced Teddy with crossed arms and a mighty glare. "Got a plan. Break my sister out of the cage they have her locked inside."

A jolt of horror stabbed me. "Cage? They put Mae in a cage?"

"She didn't give them much choice." Y'sindra mimicked a one-two punch. "Our girl knocked a couple teeth out of that sun fae's skull, and then some crazy light exploded out of her. Blinded your finger flipper—he still can't see by the way. It was either kill her or lock her up. They picked the cage."

Blinding light? That was Iola's ability. I'd never heard of anyone else with that type of power.

"I couldn't stop them. Without my magic, the only safe place was the sky." Y'sindra looked away. "I should have tried harder."

"And then what would I have done?" I squeezed her shoulder. "I need you. Together, we'll get Mae out of there."

"I'm going to freeze the nads off the guy that took her."

I barked a laugh. "I want to see that."

"Y'sindra, you said the only safe place is the sky?" Teddy asked, I assumed steering the conversation back to the topic of a plan.

"You don't have to tell me what I said."

"If they don't have fliers," Teddy ignored her snark, "where is my brother? Dacian eats, breathes, and shits chaos."

"I saw your brother leaving with a sun stone as we arrived. I'm sorry Ted-D." Lo's slow, deliberate pronunciation turned Teddy into a first name and surname. It was better than master. They must have had the talk. "I wanted to follow, but they were trying to capture Y'sindra. I had to intervene."

Teddy nodded. "Of course. I would expect nothing less."

"The situation was under control," Y'sindra snapped.

Ah, so that's why she omitted how she escaped. It would gut my fiercely protective sister that she had help getting away while Mae was thrown in a cage. It wouldn't do much for her pride, either.

"Oh! I'm so sorry. Did I misunderstand the situation? They had you pinned—"

"So, your brother can fly." Y'sindra spoke over Lo's response, and I snorted a laugh. "You got wings, too?"

"No."

"Geez, fine, don't tell me."

Teddy stared at Y'sindra, a confused expression bending his brow. I knew the feeling. Confusion was Y'sindra's best skill, right behind chaos. Or maybe it was chaos before confusion. Too close to tell.

"If Dacian isn't here," Teddy said, giving my sister a dubious look, "and there are no other fliers, I presume there are also no patrols."

"Nope," Y'sindra answered, popping the P.

Teddy peered into the trees and then both ways down the path. "If I remember, we have about an hour walk to town."

"Yep." Y'sindra popped another P. "Too bad you don't have wings. We'd be there in five."

"Let's get moving." Teddy swept an arm forward, gesturing for the pair of them to take the lead, and then rested a light touch on my lower back. "You two can fill us in on what to expect once we reach town."

Y'sindra trotted to me and held out her arms.

I stared down at her. She made grabby hands.

"Seriously?"

"Come on, I'm tired. I've had a rough two days. Lost one sister. Almost got killed myself before the other finally showed up."

My mouth opened, closed. *I take back everything I said about missing my sister. This sister in particular.* "Argh. Sometimes, I really don't like you." I crouched so the miniature manipulator could hop on my back.

"Yeah, yeah, I know." Y'sindra trotted behind me and climbed aboard. "But you love me. Now giddy up."

Teddy and Lo pointedly ignored the situation, walking ahead.

Y'sindra gave my neck a fierce hug and whispered, "Love ya, sis."

Pressure punched my eyes. Damn that fairy. I tilted my head to the side and rested it against hers. "Let's go save our sister."

43

WEIGHT TO MY BONES

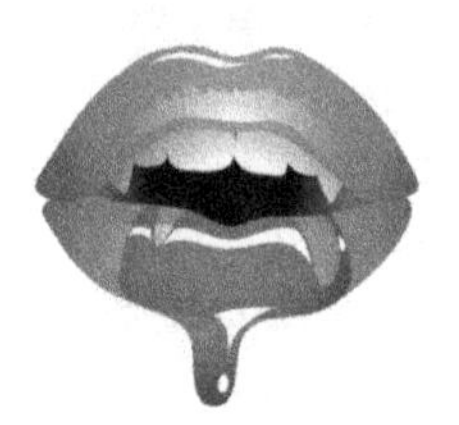

OVERLAPPING SHADOWS CROWDED TEDDY AND ME. WE HID INSIDE AN old, abandoned bar across the street from the building where my sister was in a cage. The same building we narrowly escaped from less than a week ago. Every piece of me argued that had been months ago. I held the exhaustion at bay by sheer stubbornness and absolute determination to get Mae and Y'sindra out of this shithole safely.

In truth, the only thing shitty about Outerlands was its name. What the fae lacked in creativity, they made up for in less creativity.

Except for the complete absence of population, it was the clean version of Interlands. The building fronts weren't decrepit, the landscaping along the main street was overgrown, but not out of control. There was no desert dust, no duct tape patches on buildings, no overgrown hamsters with rotten attitudes.

"This bar is almost as nice as yours." It was better, fancy.

Despite the lack of booze, it was clearly a bar. A weirdly well-kept one at that, not a speck of dust on anything. The center of the large room featured a square bar with a spiral staircase for a centerpiece. Glass orbs intended for fae lights hung suspended by copper rods over the bar ringed by wood-back stools. Round tables filled the space between the bar and cushy booths lining the outer wall.

"This is my bar. Was my bar, before I walked away. Looks like Lo's kept the place up." Teddy hitched a thumb toward the spiral stairs. "That's his room."

I leaned onto the cherrywood bar, straining to see the mystery room above. "What happened to everyone else who lived here?"

"They probably left when I did, after the moon fae moved in."

Well, that was a surprise. "I thought the moon fae were exiled to Shadwe."

"They were. The king and queen honored their agreement with the keepers—Iola and Torneh."

"The king and queen—your parents?"

"Misfortune of birth." Teddy's mouth twisted into a sneer. "In exchange for two moon stones, my parents accepted the corrupted moon fae, but settled them here after I left Shadwe. I think in hopes it would drive me to return. They didn't expect me to pack my shit and move across realms."

I bit my lip and studied his tense profile. Teddy had devolved into a rebellious teen instead of acting like the hundred-plus-year-old that he was. Wisdom did not come with age, or at least maturity didn't.

We had so much to discuss when this was over. I wound my fingers with Teddy's and fell into his gaze.

Y'sindra glided through an open window on the side of the bar and landed in a spray of snow that spattered my face. I let go of Teddy's hand to scrape the wet cold off my face.

"Get ready." Tension wound through Y'sindra's voice. "Lo says they've packed up and will move soon."

"How many?" Still no movement behind the smoked glass windows across the street. Mae was so close. I scanned left and right down the grassy road, checking for any more guards—all clear. We took out two guards an hour ago, but no one had come looking for them yet.

"Ayo, that sun fae, your finger flipper, and three guards."

"That's it?" Wow, this place really was deserted. "Cirron is mine. I want the pleasure of removing his head."

"Not *that* sun fae, the sun fae chick. The one with the corruption. They put Cirron in a cage. Well, a cell, not a cage. According to Lo, the building they're squatting in used to be the town hall. There are two floors of cells beneath, all of it unused until now."

A muscle feathered in Teddy's jaw. *Interesting.*

"True?" I asked.

"Yes." His reply was more of a growl. "My parents had it constructed and tried to order me to keep the law here after the moon fae arrived. That's when I moved."

Wow. Okay first, Teddy as sheriff—hilarious. Second, well, that was the only thing.

I shook my head. "So, Mae is in the dungeon?"

"Nope, Mae's in a literal cage." Y'sindra's iridescent wings shivered with anger, dusting more snow. "It has a blanket over it, too."

"What the hell?" I faced the building across the street and attempted to blow a hole in the wall with the force of my glare.

"Aren't you proud?"

"A little."

"Our pacifist is all grown up." Y'sindra climbed onto the window's wide sill. "Cirron and his sister are in the cells."

My stomach cramped. Shit. Cirron had a sister, and these fae had her. Nyle probably kidnapped the sister to force Cirron to play puppet. Bummer, that meant I couldn't kill him. I really wanted to kill him.

Nyle on the other hand? He was dead.

Moonlight and shadows danced in the alley across from us. The shadows stretched. I sucked in a breath and went rigid, my talons driving into the windowsill. "Where did they come from?"

A group of ten or more moon fae clad in sturdy leather armor emerged from a wedge of darkness running between the building we were watching and the one next to it. Flashes of moonlight splintered off swords hanging at their hips. They waited in the road while one guard, not a fae and not in armor, broke from the group and went inside.

"Oh no." Y'sindra pressed against the window, her winter magic blooming frost across the glass. "Lo and I saw two large groups camped near the sun stone, but when we checked later, they were gone. We assumed they left for Shadwe."

"Why would you assume that?" Teddy leaned onto the windowsill, craning his neck to search the street.

"Lo overheard Prince Pestilence and his sun fae hussy making plans for the last of their troops to escort their people to their new home."

"Dacian. He's the reason they dare returning to Shadwe." Teddy ground his knuckles on the sill and leaned toward the window. "He always wanted to be heir apparent, and me leaving clearly didn't change his status."

Fear curled in my belly and twisted my guts. This was bad. None of us were at our peak, and the odds were stacking up against us. Prince Miro, Nyle, and the sun fae female plus their guards would be a challenge. Now there were more armored bodies to go through to get to Mae. What if Teddy's brother came back?

If Rip were taking bets, I wouldn't put money on us.

"It's happening," someone said behind us.

I spun toward the voice, whipping two push daggers from their holsters. "Damn, Lo." My ears buzzed from the adrenaline coursing through my system with no outlet. "Stop doing that." I paused. "How do you do that? No, never mind. Later."

If we had a later.

"Oh, I'm so sorry." Lo's small, clawed hands fluttered.

Y'sindra and her side-eye joined us. "Want to put the pointy things away?"

"Oops." I tucked the daggers into the bandolier. "What's happening, Lo?"

I willed the doors across the street to stay closed. For all my rushing before, I felt woefully underprepared. This wasn't my first time staring down the barrel of failure, but it was the first time my sister's life hinged on evading that barrel.

"They are preparing to leave." Lo's small round ears twitched. "A group of escorts arrived, soldiers. I spotted a second, larger contingent heading this way."

Dread added weight to my bones. Our dire situation got worse. I licked my lips. "We need to do this, before the others arrive."

"The plan is solid." Teddy rolled his shoulders. "But you're right, we should do this before more come. Lo, you ready?"

"Yes, sir!" Lo's tiny chest puffed. His hand went to his forehead and whipped away in a sharp salute.

Teddy shook his head. "Better than master."

A smile threatened but couldn't break through my creeping dread. Mae might say to trust my instincts, but right now my instincts screamed our chances of making it out of here alive were abysmal. But I had no choice. I couldn't let them slip the border with Mae. I might never see her again.

Y'sindra pulled Lo into a crushing hug. "Don't get caught."

Emotion clogged my throat, and I turned away. *No room for emotion. Shut it out. Shut it down.* I rolled my head side to side and bounced on my toes, loosening up. "Stick with the plan, Lo. Get their attention, pull as many as you can away from the building."

Teddy brushed my hand, and I flexed my fingers. *No emotion. Death*. I would bring death. Eyes forward. Focused.

"Get into position." I tugged down the hem of my jacket and made for the back door Teddy pointed out earlier. We'd each go our own direction, but we needed to exit the building with stealth.

This could be the last time I saw any of them, or the last time they saw me. I slammed the door on that train of thought and focused on what needed to get done.

Get Mae. Kill Nyle. Get out.

"No one deviate. Stick to the plan." I speared each of them with a look. "Survive."

The shiny doorknob was cold beneath my palm. I twisted it and pulled open the door. Fire arced through my veins, and then I froze.

"Hello again." Nyle stood across the threshold, dark magic dripping from his fingers, and armored troops at his back.

44

I RODE HIS CORPSE TO THE GROUND

I SLAMMED THE DOOR.

Y'sindra snapped her wings. "Why'd you do that? We can take him."

A knock rapped on the door.

"We can't take all of them, plus the magic he has prepped." I paced in front of the door.

Nyle knocked again. "Open up, or I'll huff, and I'll puff."

"And I'll blow your head right off your shoulders," Y'sindra shouted.

I grabbed the back of her tunic and yanked her away as the door shuddered from a kick. No way Nyle could hold his spell long. It took too much power, sapped too much magic strength. He'd let loose as soon as he was inside, and we needed to be gone.

"You and Lo up the stairs." With my hand still wound in Y'sindra's shirt, I slung her toward the bar. My sister knew my game face. She kept her trap shut and took wing, aiming for Lo's room.

"With me." I grabbed Teddy's hand and pulled him toward the still-open window to our left. I raced for the moonlit square.

Weapons bristled across my body. They forced me to navigate my exit carefully. *Slow. Too fucking slow*. My breath pulsed against my eardrums as my heartrate ramped up. *Don't look back, Lane. Keep moving.*

I dangled both legs over the window ledge. We were higher than I thought. No time to waste, I pushed off. My knees bent to absorb the impact until I crouched and put my hands on the ground to steady myself. More noise than I wanted to make, but Nyle and crew were busy knocking down the door. Above me, Teddy slung a leg over the windowsill.

Breathing through my mouth, I hugged the wall and hurried toward the back corner of the building.

The banging on the door intensified. "Open the door you stupid bitch."

Nyle was no longer amused. My fingers tingled, itching to rip that corrupted fae's throat out. I clenched my fists until talons pricked my palms. With pain came clarity. My surroundings were hyper focused—sharp, high contrast.

A loud bang reverberated through the still air and the wall next to me shuddered. Shit, they were inside. Please don't let Y'sindra do anything stupid.

I dropped all pretense of stealth and sprinted for the corner. The thud of Teddy's footsteps followed. At least, I hoped it was Teddy.

The corner came up on me too fast. I gripped a drainpipe affixed to end of the wood slat wall, and shoulders straining, slung myself around the corner, toward the open back door. No, not open, missing. Jagged splinters surrounded the door frame.

Laser focused on the leather-clad back beyond the threshold, I pulled two push daggers from the bandolier. My fingers wrapped around the crossbar handles. Cool metal sang against my palm. This would feel good.

Fighting calm settled over me. Time slipped sluggish, went silent. I drove my left fist into the meaty back of the soldier blocking my path to Nyle. The hard leather armor resisted, but the scent of fresh blood filled my nostrils, sour and sharp.

The male twisted wide, side to side, swatting over his shoulder at the sting in his back. I'd gone for the kidney, but between the leather and short length of the blade, I'd missed my mark.

I danced out of reach, waiting. The soldier spun on me. I stepped forward and punched up with both fists. The blades drove into the underside of his jaw. No protection there. His hot blood sprayed across my face.

Even as I pushed, I torqued my wrists and angled the blades toward his brain stem. His eyes rolled until I saw the bloodshot whites. I ripped the weapons from beneath his jaw, scraping bone as gravity pulled him down.

The thud finally alerted the next guard, who came at me. His armor was different, softer. Two punches to the gut, twist, rip up until my daggers lodged in leather and sternum. He exhaled and watched his guts spill onto my boots. I pushed him off my blades. He hit the hall wall.

A long shadow fell across me from behind. I tensed to stab backward.

"I've got these. Get the leader." Teddy's voice stopped me from skewering him even as he reached past me to grab the fae coming at us by the skull and twisted.

Buoyed by Teddy's faith in me, I pressed to the wall and side-stepped past the surprised soldiers crowding the hall. They didn't have time to come at me with Teddy tearing into them from behind.

The scattered group inside was busy searching for us. Anticipation pounded through my veins. Fangs lengthening, I smiled. *Surprise, mother fuckers.*

I leaped onto my first target's back and shoved both blades into his neck. Sweet- and bitter-scented blood misted my face. The fae's death came swift, and I rode his corpse to the ground. As soon as my feet touched the floor, momentum carried me blades first into my next target. Not a fae this time. They were built different, bigger, wider, probably from Shadwe. Died like a fae.

In the confusion, the next three went down with the same ease. I sliced my way to my sixth victim.

Play time ended. The short-lived shouts and thuds finally clued the rest of the thugs in the room that they had company.

From fighting stances, they evaluated me and the bodies in my wake. Fine then, not thugs, soldiers, seasoned fighters. Beyond them stood Nyle. He pointed at me and crooked a hand, beckoning.

My fingers squeezed the dagger handles, grinding the metal bars against the bones in my palms. Nyle was already dead, he just didn't know it. I pointed a dagger at him and slid the blunt side of the blade across my throat, painting it with a line of his cohort's smelly blood.

Motion blurred to my right. I ripped my gaze from Nyle and kicked the chair next to me into the path of a female rushing my way. Nimble and ready for me, she leaped over the chair. Two can play this game. I angled my hips, blading my body, and planted my feet.

A soft scrape behind me was all the warning I had a millisecond before a sword slashed down through the air. A burst of adrenaline stood the hair on my neck on end. I kept my feet rooted in place but twisted my body left, my right arm flowing with the movement into my mystery attacker's sternum.

He grunted, but that damn leather armor kept the short push-dagger from driving deep enough to do any real damage.

Bad idea leaving the female at my back. I released the blade embedded in my other attacker's chest and moved to his side, putting the female in my peripherals. An obvious righty, the fae I'd already stabbed gripped his sword in both hands and swung, following me to the left.

I ducked and punched into the vulnerable armpit his wild swing left exposed. The fae grunted through his teeth and reached for the dagger I pushed to the hilt in his armpit. He might be trained, but not well enough to stay focused on his opponent when wounded. Idiot.

The tri-blade daggers at my hips slid from their holsters with a slick sigh. Spinning them in my grip, pointy side forward, I slammed them into the injured fae's chest and immediately ripped them free. Blood gushed, pouring from his sternum and pooling at his toes. Mouth locked in a shocked O, he stumbled away from me, tripping over the chair behind him, and slammed into a table, tilting it onto its side.

His death would come slow, but certain.

The female wisely bided her time, waiting for me to be distracted by the killing blow. I'd missed her closing in until her booted foot met the right side of my rib cage. I flew into table the dying male had flipped. My breath abandoned me. Falling to my hands and knees, my vision flashed vivid, faded. It pulsed in and out as I rode a wave of pain. Holy mother of troll fuckers, did she have a lead leg?

"You don't look so tough from down there," the fae female taunted.

Stupid. Fighting 101: Don't waste time with taunts. It never ends well.

Her foot came at me again, but I dropped to my belly and rolled—or tried. The pommel of the sword strapped to my back stopped me mid-roll. Did I not learn my lesson the first time? She caught me on the backswing of her kick. Her heel drove into the other side of my ribs.

Blood fae bones weren't easy to break, but I still tasted blood from my tender insides those bones were grinding against. She followed the stomp with a jab to the temple.

In my star-studded vision, a bearded fae skidded across the floor. Teddy appeared and gripped beard guy's skull between his hands. The fae's eyes rounded, grew wider, wider. Blood vessels burst, drowning his gray eyes in red. Veins bulged on the column of Teddy's throat. A high-pitched shriek whined from the fae's open mouth.

Whoa. Was Teddy doing what I thought?

Bearded guy's bloodshot eyes bulged in their sockets. Blood bubbles bloomed in his nostrils. The bubbles popped, and a crimson river poured from his nose and over his still wide-open mouth. Still screaming.

Yep, that's what I thought he was doing. Impressive but gross.

Bearded fae's heels scraped the floor with desperation.

A sloppy, wet crunch brought an abrupt end to the ear-piercing shriek. It didn't happen like in the movies. The moon fae's head didn't explode, it went squishy, malformed. Blood didn't paint the room. I wasn't sure if I was disgusted or turned on, and what did that say about me? Probably that I should consider therapy.

Fortunately, the bitch who kicked me couldn't seem to turn from the brutal death tableau, either. I popped to my feet, right in her face and grinned. "Hi."

She blinked, focusing on me. I shoved one tri-blade dagger into her gut. The leather stopped it before I could drive it to its hilt. I twisted and pulled back. She screamed.

"That's for kicking me." Shit talk was dangerous, but it was fun if you won the fight, and she was dead on her feet.

Still slick with her blood, I drove the same blade into the side of her throat. The fae's shriek turned into a choking gurgle.

Behind her, a bear hitting a table pulled my attention from the female moon fae's dull eyes. A bear? The table let loose a loud crack and split down the center beneath the creature's considerable mass, collapsing inward.

It shook its massive head and roared. I stared, unblinking. "Yep, that's a bear."

Teddy stomped into view, his broad shoulders blocking whatever he did to the animal who had no business in a bar. Teddy moved on, leaving not a bear, but a soldier slumping on his own sword, pinned inside the broken table's crevice.

Now that was weird.

The dead female dropped from my dagger. I had a clear view of Y'sindra buzzing around a heavily corrupted moon fae. Panic strummed my bruised ribs. What was she thinking? No way did that damn fairy have enough winter magic to be in this fight.

Frost jumped from her hands, and she formed a snowball, smearing it over the corrupted fae's face. He waved his arms wildly, but Y'sindra hovered out of his reach.

"Now," she shouted.

Lo zoomed in from above and drove his clawed hand into the blinded fae's throat. Well, didn't the tiny terrors make an adorably bloodthirsty pair?

But they also made great targets for Nyle. His turn to die. I took a step toward the bar, but he was gone. I choked on my panic. No, he couldn't be gone. I twisted side to side. Bodies, lots of bodies, but his wasn't one of them.

I spun for the next soldier, but none were left standing. At least twenty lay dead, or close enough. All except Nyle, who rose from behind the far side of the bar. The coward. I sheathed the daggers and pulled the sword from the harness across my back. I'd make a kabob out of him.

He spotted me and waved, his fingers wreathed in a glove of sparkling black magic. I went cold. Nyle never released the magic. That shouldn't be possible, unless he extinguished the spell and then prepped it again. The amount of control that would take was terrifying.

I scoured the pile of bodies with my gaze. We'd fought through a lot of soldiers. Maybe he had held it but couldn't get a clean shot. He could now. We'd done him a favor and made ourselves easy targets.

Instinctively I backed up. Y'sindra stood facing me on the bar between us. On the side of the room, back to Nyle, Teddy had a chokehold on a barely conscious soldier. None of them saw the threat.

Nyle's cold gaze met mine but slid to Y'sindra. My oblivious sister laughed and flexed at Lo, who watched her from the ground.

"No," I screamed. My legs went weak, but I forced them to obey my brain. Foreboding pressed painfully against the backs of my eyes. Arms outstretched, I surged for my sister.

Nyle let loose his lethal magic. I screamed again, a primal sound. Words failed me as horror hollowed me out.

Y'sindra looked at me, laughed, and went up on her tip toes to perform a pirouette.

The magic could miss. *Please miss. Please miss.*

A writhing black ball of magic hit Y'sindra. We screamed in tandem. The impact threw her small body from the bar. She slammed face first into the floor.

Images of Etta'wy's gruesome death filled my brain. *No. Not Y'sindra.* It couldn't happen to my sister.

Behind Y'sindra's convulsing form, Teddy vaulted the bar toward Nyle. Lo rose to follow Teddy but quickly turned and dropped to the floor by my sister.

I fell to my knees next to Y'sindra. Her wings slapped the floor, and I saw it—the magic. Half her left wing was already gone, dusted. My fingers flexed on the pommel of the sword. No, I couldn't do that. I couldn't cut off her wing. Oh gods, I couldn't.

If I didn't, she was dead.

The magic ate away another inch of her wing. It was almost to her shoulder. If it touched her flesh, it would consume her body.

I raised the sword. My arms shook. "I'm sorry."

Her glacial eyes pinched with pain. Tears streamed from their corners. "Do it," she sobbed.

The blade came down neatly across her wing, severing it a millimeter from the dust. *Oh gods.* I took her wing. Y'sindra's sobs were the most pain I'd ever felt. Worse than my broken body after the fall. Worse than a pierced heart. Worse than anything.

"You saved her." Lo tugged my hands from my face. "You saved your sister."

I swallowed and looked at Y'sindra. She lay curled on her side. Ice crusted the wing stump. She'd been aware enough to freeze the wound, stop the blood. Her chest pumped with rapid breaths.

"Lane." Her voice was low, rough. She gritted her teeth and pushed to a sitting position.

My hands trembled, and I forced them into my lap. Her wing was gone. I did that.

"Lane," she said again, and I met her brilliant blue gaze. "Thank you."

I shook my head. *No. No. I won't accept gratitude for this.*

Teddy dragged a subdued Nyle around the corner of the bar and dropped him next to us. Bruises covered the moon fae's face. One arm hung limp at his side, and he wiggled to sit up.

Teddy put a toe to Nyle's chest and kicked him over. "Want to do the honors?"

"You're too late." Blood ran from Nyle's mouth with his garbled words.

He laughed, a terrible grating sound. "They're gone. Sister's gone." He choked and nodded at Teddy. "Came for him."

That's why there were so many bodies. Odds were his brother sent them after Teddy. And I thought my family had issues.

I looked from Teddy to Y'sindra.

"Do it," she growled.

No more encouragement needed. My fingers tightened around the sword still stained with my sister's blood. Gripping the hilt with both hands, I rose to my feet, walked to Nyle, and swung. The cut was clean and the sword sharp, but the angle didn't make for good decapitation.

The blade hit his spinal column, stuck. I put a boot to his chest and pushed Nyle's dead weight from the sword. Bone scraped metal, and he hit the floor.

All eyes were on me. I crouched down and wiped the corrupted blood on the dead moon fae's leg.

"Lane," Y'sindra said, and I looked up. An icicle shivered on the end of her wing stump. "Lo will get me to the border. You bring our sister home."

45

TIME TO LET THE MONSTER OUT OF THE CAGE

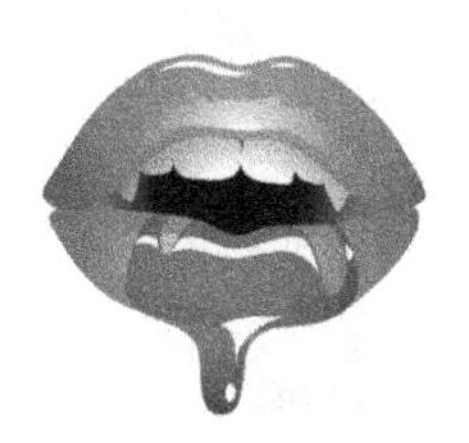

THE GRASS WAS NOT ALWAYS GREENER ON THE OTHER SIDE. SOMETIMES IT was painted red and slippery as fuck. My right foot skidded backward, propelling me face first toward the ground. I tried to catch myself but instead took it on the chin. Vanilla, honeysuckle, and ginger assaulted my senses—sweet and spicy.

Panic pulled my vision askew.

Not just any blood on the grass—Mae's blood. Other scents hid there as well, musky, earthy, sharp, sour. Pride ballooned in my chest. Mae did some damage.

Don't stop. Keep moving.

Though I was on all fours, I drove forward, pushing with my feet, pulling with my hands until the momentum carried me upright and across the road to the building where Mae was held.

Is, damn it. Is being held. Y'sindra said Mae put up a fight when they brought her in. The blood could be from that. And Nyle was a filthy liar. They had to be there.

I rushed up the stairs to the white-wood porch and didn't stop until my booted foot met the door. It cracked but didn't break. From sole to hip, pain vibrated along my bones. *Shit, ow.* What happened? I've kicked many a door, and they all went down. I gritted my teeth and rammed my heel into the splintered wood. A hole broke open, trapping my foot half in, half out of the building. I slammed my palms into the door and blasted the compromised slab of wood from its frame, but the door didn't release my leg and yanked me forward as it fell into the building.

This was ridiculous. First the staff, now the door.

Splinters gripped my calf. This felt like a bad slapstick scene. I frantically scanned the room as I struggled to tug my leg free. The pressure of the splintered wood dug deeper with every profanity-laced wiggle, but they didn't pierce the leather.

Teddy pounded onto the porch. He crossed the threshold and stomped on the door next to my leg, releasing me from its grip.

"I escorted them to the trees. They've got it from there."

Despite Y'sindra and Lo getting over the border being the right thing, I couldn't put a lid on my worry.

"Maybe letting them go was a bad idea." I bit the edge of my lip.

"No. They're safe, Lane." Teddy bent his face toward mine, took my hands, pulling me chest to chest. "Lo is carrying your sister. It'll just take time. They need to navigate the trees to avoid my brother." He squeezed my hands and retreated through the door to search the sky.

"You saw him? Your brother?" I followed Teddy outside, across the broken door. Only clouds and moon hung in the sky.

"No, but he'll come for that final stone."

Okay, I could do what I needed to do. Y'sindra would make it. Two wings, one wing, she was fierce. I nodded and went back inside the building, finding it silent, hollow. But the echoes of shouts rubbed against my skin. My sister's screams. Chairs were backed away from tables, some tipped on their sides, as if their former occupants had rushed to evacuate the building. The door to a fae-sized cage hung open. Fat pillows lined the floor. Plates of uneaten food were stacked inside..

All at once I felt light-headed. The blood outside wasn't old. I let them escape with my sister. I let them hurt my sister. I clutched my stomach and dropped into a crouch. Impotent fury clawed my throat. I shoved my face into my palms. The cold, killing mantle I wore evaporated beneath the scorching reality of my failure.

"Get up, Lane." Teddy's unyielding voice rattled me. His heavy steps crossed the floor to my side. My hands slid away, and I glared up at him. "This isn't you. You're Malaney Fucking Callaghan—ass kicker extraordinaire. They couldn't have gone far. Now let's go."

His words burrowed into my sluggish brain. Teddy made a good point. I was a lot of things, but quitter wasn't on the list. Time to let the monster out of the cage.

I grinned, vicious, humorless, and rose to my feet. The dried blood coating my lips cracked. I pressed a hard kiss to Teddy's mouth, leaving behind flakes of our enemies. "Thank you."

"Anytime, sweet fangs." He winked and kissed me back—quick, hard, savage.

Holy mother of Twinkies. The things this male did to me, even amidst a crisis. He ran his tongue along the seam of his lips as if savoring the taste of our kiss. My hearts accelerated and lady bits tingled. I shook my head. *Down girl.*

I returned to Mae's blood and scanned both ways down the street. This wasn't a lot, but enough that there had to be more. I smelled it behind us. At the mouth of the alleyway, another spatter of blood.

"This way." I ran between the buildings, Teddy close behind. He was right, they couldn't have gotten far. The familiar detachment slid into me. I became cold, methodical. No emotion.

Though at least a dozen feet separated the buildings, this felt cramped, dangerous. I pushed steady breaths through my mouth, searching shadow to shadow.

I burst from between the buildings and stopped short on another street, more overgrown but also empty. A dense forest encroached on the other side of the grassy lane. Younger trees grew in the road. I studied the ground. *Which way to go?*

No more blood. Damn. Good news, Mae wasn't hurt badly enough to keep bleeding. Bad news, I couldn't track her—not easily. Shit. I spun and paced right, then turned back, heading left, stopping next to the tree line.

"We shouldn't split up," Teddy said, picking up on my dilemma.

"Hadn't considered that." I had, but not now. It wasn't worth time spent on a losing argument. I crouched close to the grass. Good night vision or not, the darkness didn't help. A pale blue haze bled from behind the jumble of clouds covering the moon. It was still not enough to see by, not reliably.

Tilting my head until my left cheek touched grass, I sought the shine of blood. Something glistened to the right. Pure willpower held my excitement in check. It could be dew. I hustled to the damp grass and Mae's spicy-sweet blood wafted to me before I reached the spot. My hand trembled above the stained grass.

It was only a few feet to the right, but it gave me something. I jumped to my feet and pointed in the direction the fading trail led. "This way."

Keeping close to the buildings as we moved, I fanned a continuous look side to side. The moon had emerged bright and strong, giving me as good a look as I needed to track.

Hopefully they stuck to the street. If they went into the trees, we'd lose the light, and I might lose Mae. If Y'sindra were here, she could track from above.

Guilt barreled into me, and I almost doubled over. My steps faltered, and Teddy was there to help. I shook my head, wouldn't meet his eyes. Y'sindra would never be the same. She might never forgive me.

Stop that. She's alive. You still have another sister who needs you. I fought for the clarity I needed to save Mae, scraped the guilt from my hearts and buried it deep.

Another sprinkle of blood glistened ahead. Even as I moved toward it, I searched from building to tree line to avoid an ambush, but I kept returning to the stain. The moonlight faded, grew darker.

Turning a scowl to the sky, I sucked in a shocked breath and leaped to the side, pressing tight to the building. My chest pumped with an overdose of adrenaline. That wasn't cloud cover.

"Watch out!" I reached for the sword sheathed on my back, but the shadow was already gone. Did I imagine it? I hoped so, because if not, we were fucked. I edged tentatively away from the wall and searched the star-studded sky. "Where'd it go?"

"Where did what go?" Teddy must not have seen the same thing. He followed my gaze upward.

Legs planted, I had my elbows out, hands loose and ready. "A dragon. Smaller, though. I didn't get a good look." Not that I knew a lot of them, but in silhouette, it hadn't looked much different from the only dragon I'd ever met.

Teddy growled and charged to the center of the street. What was that brave idiot doing? Had he never watched a movie? Overconfidence gets you eaten.

"My brother."

My arms dropped. The tip of my sword thumped in the dirt. "Come again?"

"He's a shifter," Teddy said by way of crappy explanation.

"Your brother's a weredragon?" Information I could have used before now. And what the holy hot sauce did that make Teddy?

"We went over this. Shifters are magic. Weres are a magic-born human disease." His nose wrinkled while his upper lip lifted in a sneer. Oh, the disdain. Guess he didn't like being compared to weres. Fair enough. I didn't like being called a vampire. "As Ta'Vale's population are fae, Shadwe's are shifters."

Shifters. That explained the bear in the bar. "So there's a bunch of dragons flying around Shadwe? You didn't think that might be important in case, you know, we ran into a few?" I waved the sword to the sky.

"My family, and my family alone, are wyverns." Teddy tilted a look in my direction. "Every Barbout is a wyvern."

"Even you?"

"Except me."

"So not *every* Barbout. Unless you're adopted." On a scale of one to ten, my curiosity pinged at ninety-nine. I narrowed my eyes at Teddy. If I squinted hard enough, maybe I could see...

"I am not." Teddy was done with the subject of family. "Which way did he go?

I nodded toward the tree line. "That way."

Concern didn't nip at my heels, it sank its fangs deep. Anything could hide in that forest. No, not anything. The canopy would hide us from enemies above, but it would also provide deep cover for anything within.

Yet that's the direction Teddy's brother flew. This screamed ambush, but he could also be escorting the others through the forest. Lo did say there was a single stone left. He could have come back for that.

A cloud drifted toward the horizon. Cloud, not wyvern. Teddy's brother had momentarily moved on, just as we should. I licked my dry lips and inched further from the protection of the building.

Beneath the pale blue moonlight, another spray of blood glistened ahead, along the other side of the road, close to the trees. Too damn close.

It was more blood than the last few spots. Dissociating my thoughts from Teddy's scaled relation somewhere in the sky, I hurried to the wet grass and knelt for a sniff. Satisfaction crested and swelled over my dread. I picked up more sharp notes, rotten notes, less clean cutting scent of Mae. Most of this wasn't hers. My sister was still alive and still literally kicking.

From the bloody patch of grass, I slowly expanded my search, sweeping my gaze in a wide arc farther and farther from the source. They couldn't be far. Mae's fight had to slow her captors' escape, which didn't bode well for my sister.

Teddy stepped in front of me, his delicious lips pressed into an uncompromising line. He gave the forest a hard look. "These fae had your sister locked up. Why didn't they leave her behind?"

I stood and brushed my hands on my thighs, partly to disguise the nervous tremor. "Funny, I was wondering the same thing."

Doubt danced over the back of my neck, pulling goosebumps up along the naked flesh. I reached behind to adjust my braid beneath my jacket. It would have been easier for them to leave Mae behind. If she caused too much trouble, they could change their mind. I might not find my sister. I might find her body.

Shouts crashed into the silent night. Electric surprise jolted me. I heard Mae's voice. I went dizzy with proof of life until her shouts were answered by angry bellows. Not far. I cried out and ran toward my sister's voice. She appeared, a furious wraith tearing down the street with a handful of soldiers in pursuit.

"Lane!" Mae shouted and angled in my direction.

I fought the urge to run to her and tensed my muscles for a sudden stop. Let Mae get behind me. I couldn't let her get caught in the crossfire. My hearts pounded hard enough to rattle my ribs. I strained to keep my trembling muscles steady and planted my feet shoulder width apart, left foot facing the coming assault, the back foot turned perpendicular. Balancing my weight between both feet, I dropped my bladed body into a slight crouch. Elbows up, arms steady, I kept my sword locked in a two-handed grip over my right shoulder.

A long breath pushed past my lips. *Calm*, I thought. *No emotion.*

Behind Mae, Teddy erupted from the woods and barreled into the first soldier. They went down in a spray of torn grass and flying dirt. Well, I didn't see that coming.

I rolled my shoulders and flexed my grip on the sword. The unmistakable sound of flesh on flesh had its hooks in me, tried to pull my gaze to Teddy.

Focus. Eyes on Mae.

She drew close. I gave her a quick once over. Mae limped, but despite the blood I'd found, no injuries were evident. Good enough for now. She flew past me, her ragged breaths heaving.

"Watch out," she panted.

A halo of white light blurred her pursuer. I squinted against the brilliance. The light faded, leaving a cat the size of a pony pounding toward me. I blinked. Did I hit my head harder than I thought? No bones crunched, no howls of pain. She didn't even slow her steps. She...she shifted.

Teddy's words jangled in my brain. Weres and shifters were nothing alike. *Understatement.*

"Used all my magic," Mae wheezed from behind me, but not too close. "Can't..."

A thud pulled my head around. Mae lay crumpled in the grass. Fear whistled in my ears. Was she breathing?

The heavy beat of rushing paws yanked my attention to the imminent feline threat. I deepened my crouch and dropped my arms to hold the sword at my side, tip tilting toward the ground. Big cats were deadly, but also predictable. She'd jump.

Sure enough, ten feet out the shifter's muscular shoulder's bunched, her chest dipped toward the ground and her powerful hind legs launched her into the air.

I held steady.

Massive paws splayed wide. Claws much longer and thicker than mine extended. Jaws open, ready to eat my face.

My sword swept out and up, its sharp edge catching the big cat in the ribs. The feline's scream morphed as she shifted. The weight behind my strike drove the blade deeper, pushed her. I turned with the swing, avoiding the path of her out-of-control descent.

She lay silent on the ground, eyes open but sightless. In the same fluid motion of my turn, I dragged the blade from her sternum and spun, ready for the next attacker.

He was already there, dual swords arcing toward me. I ducked under his singing blades, and putting all my weight behind a forward thrust, drove my sword through his chest.

The frenzied attacker was slow to register his own death. He kept pushing forward on the blade, each push slower, weaker, until his breastbone met the hilt. Hot blood ran over my fingers, turning them slick. I squeezed my hand to maintain my grip.

Slate-colored eyes met mine, widened, and dislocated from my gaze, fogged over. His arms fell to his sides. The razored edge of one blade bit into my left shoulder. Adrenaline did funny things to a body. No pain yet, but soon.

His death rattle fanned my face. Dead weight torqued my wrists forward and dragged the sword tip to the ground.

Three more soldiers pounded toward me. The big body on my blade tilted to the ground and pulled the slick hilt from my grip.

This had to end quick. I needed to get to Mae. And where was Teddy?

Head down, shoulders squared, I pulled both tri-blade daggers free and rushed to meet the attackers. My gaze narrowed on the unlucky bastard in the lead. Ducking and punching, I worked my way through all three with less effort than it took me to kick down the city hall door.

The third soldier's features were locked in a dumbstruck expression, not quite comprehending she was supposed to die. I shoved her over and ran for my sister, sheathing my daggers before I stabbed someone I shouldn't.

Mae hadn't moved. Her head twisted one way, legs the other, while her arms lay akimbo. *No, no, no.* This couldn't be happening. I crouched to check her pulse, the damp grass cool beneath my knees. My own thundering heartbeat overrode any sensation.

I leaned back on my heels and shook my hands. Fear choked me. Vertigo tried to tip me over.

Mae issued a soft moan. Her lashes fluttered, eyes rolling side to side beneath their lids. Alive. She was alive. Fear fled me in a great gush, leaving me shaky, weak. I had to get her home.

I lifted my sister, curling her tight to my chest. The cut in my shoulder flared to life, sudden, sharp. I groaned, almost losing my grip. With the battle adrenaline gone, pain bulldozed past every other sensation. Shit, that hurt. I was no wimp, but dropping Mae was a real possibility here.

Jostling my sister in my arms, I flipped her over my right shoulder. The impact forced a wheeze from her unconscious body.

"Sorry." I winced but couldn't stop for pity. She'd wheezed. She was alive. More soldiers would come to retrieve her soon and find their cohorts dead. I planned to be across the border before that happened.

My shoulder throbbed. The cut must have gone deeper than I'd thought.

This would be an inconvenient time to pass out. Blood ran thick and free beneath the jacket sleeve. My left arm hung on the edge of tingling and numb.

Had to keep moving. Had to get Mae home.

My leg throbbed where I'd trapped it in the door. I clenched my jaw and limped in the direction of the city hall. It wasn't too far. If I limped faster...

An explosive bang assaulted my eardrums. My hearts lodged in my throat. Teddy. Where was Teddy?

I ducked my head between my shoulders and spun, retreating to the protection of the buildings, and desperately sought Teddy. He stood less than ten feet behind, but he didn't move toward me. Our gazes caught. His mouth worked while he pressed a hand to his chest.

"What was that?" My brows collided. Why was he just standing there? "You okay?" I took a step in his direction, but then I saw it. A stain bloomed from beneath his hand, slowly unfurling crimson wings across his chest.

The sight was a sledgehammer to my soul. Grip on Mae forgotten, she slid from my shoulder.

"Run..." Teddy groaned, and his legs folded, bringing him to the ground.

46

WHY COULDN'T I DIE LIKE A NORMAL FAE

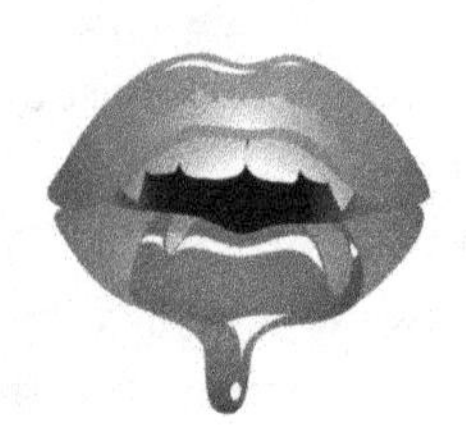

SHOCK ROOTED MY FEET IN PLACE. "GET UP," I WHISPERED, BUT TEDDY lay still.

"You fae are such pussies about guns." My head snapped up. Dacian stood on the far side of Teddy, still holding a gun—aimed at me.

My focus zeroed in on the weapon. The air left my lungs. Time turned to molasses. His finger tightened, tensed. The trigger compressed. The muzzle flashed. A dark smudge burst through the orange flare. Heat blistered my cheek. Splinters exploded from the building next to me. Chips of wood pinged my cheek and pelted my jacket.

The bullet had veered wide.

Fangs tingling with anticipation, I grinned. No humor, just the promise of death. "Fae aren't pussies. We know guns don't play nice with our magic. Dumbass."

Dacian dropped the gun and roared, the sound morphing as he lit up like a roman candle. My eyes watered at the sudden burst of brilliant light, and I turned to the side. When the lightshow ended, the wyvern screeched a challenge.

"Let's do this." I ripped two push daggers from their sheathes and tore down the street toward Dacian's beast. My left grip felt weak. Good thing I was right-handed.

The wyvern reared, stretched, and flared his wings. He whipped a dagger-tipped tail side-to-side. Long neck pulled high, mouth gaping, he prepared to turn me into a snack.

Not today. Not ever.

I dropped to my back and slid for his belly in a move that would have Teddy begging me to join his stupid softball team next season.

Seashell-sized scales the color of a sunrise—all pink, orange, and cobalt blue, covered the wyvern's gullet. I punched the daggers up, but they bounced and slid off the too-pretty scales.

The short blades were useless against that armor.

A grating laugh shook the beast's belly gyrating in my face.

My eyes narrowed. I'd show him funny. I dropped the push daggers and focused on a spot where two scales met, dug my talons beneath their seam, and tugged. The laughing morphed into a roar.

"Something wrong?" My turn to laugh. A deranged response considering the situation, but man was I pissed.

The bi-pedal beast backpedaled. With my talons hooked beneath his scale, the motion pulled me upright. I planted my feet and pulled in the opposite direction. I couldn't stop myself from being dragged along with him, but the harder I tugged, the more desperate he grew to escape.

I wiggled the scale. One side tore free, and I let loose a triumphant shout. "This is coming with me."

Dacian bellowed. His wyvern head whipped forward, and he snapped the two-inch teeth lining his jaws at my face.

I twisted left, putting everything I had behind my good arm. Sounding like a massive piece of Velcro, the scale tore free. My arms windmilled. I staggered, stumbled, and ate dirt, but by the gods I held onto that fucking scale.

The ground shook. I flipped to my back and scuttled backward, but Dacian's clawed foot locked on me hip to chest. My bones ground together. *Son of a mountain troll, that hurt.* Involuntary tears wet my cheeks.

I'd managed to keep my arms free and clawed at his toes, but the scales were smaller and harder. That trick wouldn't work twice

Dacian surged straight up to hover. I focused on the naked spot on the wyvern's chest, reached for it. My talons scraped through the air, but I was close.

"My brother's stink is all over you." Dacian's voice came out weirdly normal.

The mention of Teddy constricted my hearts more than the wyvern's claws, and I turned my head, desperately seeking his form. He lay curled on his side, so small now. Still hadn't moved. What was that down the street? It was bright and orange. Oh, great, the sun stone. A laugh fizzled in my chest. Figured.

The bloody spot on Dacian's chest was so close. It taunted me.

His head arched toward me, and the slit nostrils on his narrow snout flared. "I smell what he sees in you."

I punched him in the nose.

His head whipped away, and his grip momentarily tightened. Pin pricks of white light wheeled across my vision. His hold eased, and I shook some sense back into my brain.

With each flap of his wings, his legs lifted, drawing me close to the chink I'd ripped in his armor.

Dacian's clawed foot left a gap in his toes over my left hip, leaving a tri-blade dagger free for the grabbing. I pulled the weapon from its sheath and slowed my breath—not easy with my ribs constricted—timing it with the rise and fall of his legs.

Up. Down. Up. Down. Up. My arm arced toward the bare spot. I missed. I shook my head and exhaled. Up. Down. Up. I swung again. The blade bit into soft flesh, sank deep. A scream tore past my lips as I threw my shoulder into a twist.

Dacian screeched and bucked. He twirled in a frenzy. The world rushed by on fast-forward, tilted. Oh gods, I was going to hurl.

His foot spasmed, opened. I cartwheeled away, head spinning, limbs flailing. The icy air froze the scream in my chest, and then I was falling.

Above, light flared. The wyvern vanished, and Dacian went into free fall. Hot satisfaction burned away the chill of rushing air. I went down swinging and he was going down with me.

Tree tops scraped the edge of my vision, roof tops. I hit the ground with a gut-churning crunch. My legs snapped easier than toothpicks. I might have blacked out. Probably did. Suddenly, I was screaming, fighting the wave of darkness trying to drag me under. Pain wrung through my body but not my legs.

I lifted my head to look down my body at the twist of bones sticking from my shins and the right thigh bone pushed down over my kneecap. Couldn't feel it, so I must have broken my back. A small mercy.

Down the street a new cluster of sword brandishing soldiers closed in. *Fuck*. Why couldn't I die in the fall like a normal fae? *Oh, I know, because Fate's a bitch.* Now I had to lie here helpless and suffer. I didn't even know if Teddy and Mae were still alive.

I dug my talons into the ground. Hot tears burned paths from the corners of my eyes. Unfair. So fucking unfair.

A hallucination of Y'sindra appeared in my erratic vision.

"Hold on, Lane. For the love of Freyja, don't you dare die."

I gulped air and swallowed. Weird. My hallucination sounded exactly like my sister, but she wore a blanket tied over her shoulders. Y'sindra would never cover her wings.

Feet rushed past Y'sindra in this bizarre vision. Shouts, followed by the clang of metal meeting metal. Maybe I was already dead. Why couldn't I be on a tropical beach having hot sex with Teddy?

Teddy. Oh gods, what happened to Teddy?

A pair of feet behind my imaginary sister stopped, and the last face I should see in a death vision appeared. The thick scar crossing Odo's face pulled one side of his mouth higher, giving him an unbeatable sneer.

"No surprise finding you like this." He took in my twisted body, and something that looked remarkably like pity clouded his mossy gaze. Yep, I was definitely imagining this. "We'll clean up your mess."

Hallucination Odo was an ass, just like the real one.

Darkness smudged the edge of my vision, and my lids grew heavy. I couldn't even feel the pain. Shock? Nope, dead, remember?

I let my eyes slide shut.

"Lane? Lane! I swear I'll pee in your cheesy poofs if you die."

Yep. Exactly like Y'sindra. I chuckled, coughed, and the darkness captured me.

47

HAIR OF THE BLACK WOLF

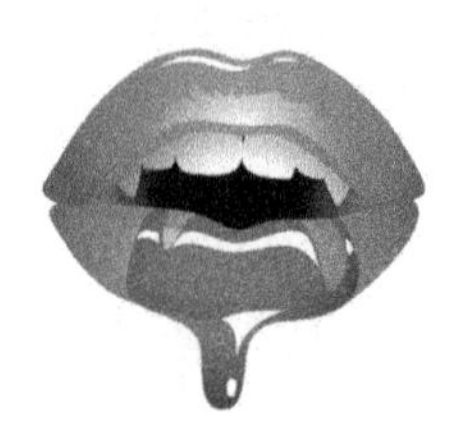

I CAME TO, FANGS DEEP IN A THROAT. DIVINITY FLOODED MY MOUTH, sweet as liquid sugar with a hint of smoke and salt. *Mmm, delicious. Familiar.*

My eyes flashed open, and I scrambled back in a bed. A headboard rattled against the wall and the pink sheets—*my* ironically pink sheets—slid to my hips. I grappled for the covers and tried to focus. The room played tilt-a-wheel with my vision.

Three things filtered into my swampy brain: I drank blood, I was naked, and I was alive. Also, I was naked.

My stomach wrung like a wet towel, and I bent over the side of the bed to return the blood I didn't ask for.

"Don't do that, Lane."

Teddy. He wasn't dead. And I drank from him.

His warm hand stroked my back, and he gently pulled me away from my retching position. "Your mom removed the infusion line today. You need to keep that down."

I swallowed, tasting Teddy's blood anew. His throat had my full attention. A thin line of blood oozed from beneath the palm covering the punctures on his neck.

My hands flew to my mouth. I should have warned him when I had the chance. He had to get out of here before the blood drunk phase kicked in. There was no telling what I would do to him.

"Teddy, no. You don't understand what'll happen." I leaned for the side of the bed once again, but he caught my shoulders and sat me up. That tricky blanket fell back to my waist.

The gentleman he was, Teddy ogled my boobs. Scowling, I snagged my trusty robot unicorn blanket and yanked it to my throat. Or not so trusty. It wouldn't stop flashing Teddy.

I savored his warm-syrup chuckle, rich and deep. "I do understand, but it won't happen. I promise."

"My mom mixes medicine for me." I used the term medicine loosely.

Oh, how the mighty had fallen. I ran my hands over the blanket, its familiar velvety threads tickling my palms. This entire conversation was mortifying. I was less worried about flashing my boobs than letting my vulnerabilities, my deficiencies, hang out.

Absently it registered I fell from the sky. Beneath the blanket I moved my legs, twisted side to side. Everything worked, but everything also hurt.

"Did you ever wonder where she got the blood from?" One brow rose along with the mischievous curl of his lip.

My hands stilled and mouth fell open, closed. He couldn't be implying... "No."

"Yes."

"Impossible."

"It's not."

"That blood *medicine* is disgusting."

Teddy's laugh shook the mattress. He reached out, engulfed me in his arms, and curled me to his chest. "That's the deathwart root sap she mixes in." He shuddered. "Swears it keeps the blood fresh."

The deathwart explained a lot. Smelliest tree in existence. It would have been easier on both me and my tastebuds if she'd told me who's blood I'd been drinking. I could have tapped that years ago. Tapped that vein, but also that ass.

"You could have told me." I picked at the loose thread on the tip of the unicorn's horn. Uh, hold on. My brows smashed together, and I glared. "You let me order all those disgusting Bloody Marys knowing I couldn't drink them?"

"Shhh. Don't waste your strength." He pulled me back to his chest, a laugh rumbling beneath my ear.

Sneaky bastard, but since I was alive, I had plenty of time to tease out all his secrets. Speaking of teasing...I inched toward the bead of red nectar rolling down the corded column of his throat. If it was safe, why not? If it wasn't, too late now.

My tongue traced circles on Teddy's warm, melted butterscotch flesh. He groaned and tipped his head back, settling into the pillows. The motion pulled me tight to his side. His big body blasted delicious heat, and I crooked a leg across his hips. His hands fisted against the blanket on my backside, pulling me closer.

"The reason my blood works is because shifters are blood magic." Teddy nipped my lower lip. "Sorry to say, sugar fangs, but I'm your only choice in town."

Sugar fangs? I liked it.

Despite my rusty joints, I managed to climb onboard and straddle Teddy's hips. Amazing, I definitely broke—at a minimum—both my legs in the fall. His diluted blood worked wonders. Lingering pain aside, this felt like I'd earned invincibility. I grinned and held his arms to the side as I leaned close to that luscious throat of his.

"You know, I screwed up my last job." I lapped away the last of his leaking blood, swirled my tongue over the nearly sealed puncture. My legs tightened and knees locked against his hipbones. Holy mother of stars. I was going to have an orgasm before I even saw his cock. But I felt it, hard and growing harder with only a blanket between us, stopping him from being inside me. "I might not be able to afford this."

Teddy's strong fingers gripped my hips. "I think we can work something out," he growled. "Besides, you found the sun fae's precious stone. They owe you."

Ugh. Talk about an ice bath for the libido. At this rate, I'd never get laid. I growled and rolled off Teddy. "I don't want anything from the sun fae."

"You sure?" Teddy tilted onto his side, propping his head in his hand, and watched the path his fingers took as they trailed over my bare hip. "You went through hell to get that thing."

"I went through hell for my sisters. I don't care about the rest of them, and besides, there's still two stones missing."

Teddy squeezed my ass—he really liked doing that. He pressed his lips to my forehead and then fell onto his back, tucking his hands behind his head. "Thanks to you, we've got Dacian, and we also have a way to follow the stones into Shadwe. We'll get them back."

Thanks to me. Surreal. Nobody ever thanked me for a damn thing. "Your brother didn't die? Too bad."

"Probably wishes he did. The shame alone might kill him." Teddy chuckled, and my heart went gooey at the rich tones of pure evil. "Brought down by a female smaller than his big toe. In wyvern form, of course."

I returned his grin, pride settling warm in my belly. A monster for monsters, indeed. This hybrid thing wasn't so bad. I did need new business cards.

Teddy's words—all of them—hadn't escaped me. He said *we'd* get the stones back, and there wasn't a bit of me willing to fight him on that. He'd snuck up on me, broke through my barriers, fit himself into my life like the final corner piece of that stupid jigsaw puzzle sitting unfinished on our dining room table for the last six months. I'd bet all my Ho Hos that Y'sindra burned that piece for fun.

Oh gods, Y'sindra. I sat up. "Where are my sisters? Are they okay? Is Y'sindra..." I couldn't say it. I couldn't ask about her wing.

"I'm fine, you slut." The eavesdropping fairy's voice came from the hall.

I squealed and leaped from the bed, my bare feet slapping across the remarkably clean floor. Oh, shit. Clothes. They weren't where they were supposed to be—on the floor.

I ran to the bed and yanked the blanket. Teddy's bare chest stared at me. His nearly flawless chest. A light dusting of dark hair didn't hide the light pink scar puckering the skin above his heart. Thank the gods his brother had shitty aim. My gaze dropped to the sheets bunched at Teddy's waist.

The devious male chuckled and swung his legs out from beneath the covers. My mouth twisted into a scowl. It was just rude to wear sweatpants in bed.

"Tease." I laid the most disgruntled look I had in my arsenal on Teddy. He had the audacity to wink. Hopeless male. I shook my head and ran toward the door.

"Hate to see you go, but drop the blanket and I'll love watching you walk away."

"Yeah, yeah. Never heard that one before." I rolled my eyes. My traitorous unicorn blanket, as if listening to Teddy, twisted between my legs and dragged to the floor, leaving me bare assed.

"We can come back later," Mae hollered through the door.

"Ugh, no. Don't you dare."

"You two decent?" Mae questioned

I pushed to my feet and yanked the blanket up. "Yeah, I just—"

"Who cares." Y'sindra burst through the door.

She looked at me. I avoided looking at her missing wing and focused on her deceptively cherubic face.

"Lane..." Y'sindra rushed toward me. I fell to my knees and engulfed her in a desperate hug. Her cloud of snow-white hair cushioned my face.

My hand brushed her wing stump, and my voice broke on a sob. "I'm so sorry." I sniffled into her curls.

"You shut your mouth. Unless you're sorry you saved my life." Her small hands fisted my blanket. "Besides, now you have no excuse not to do the quokka maneuver."

Leave it to Y'sindra. I pressed my forehead against her neck, fighting the urge to ugly cry.

Footsteps approached, and an arm curled across my shoulders. I knew that scent. With a smile, I melted into Mae's three-way hug. The tears leaked.

"Thank the stars you're okay," she said. "We've been so worried."

"Pfft, what? You know me, I always bounce back." I rolled my stiff shoulders and turned away, catching my tears with my fingertips, not quite able to meet their eyes. I couldn't shake the uneasy feeling that things were different. What those things were, I wasn't yet sure.

Mae pulled my hand from my lap and squeezed. "Lane, it's been over two months."

"Two months since..." My eyes rounded with the realization of what she said.

"Not as long as your sun bridge siesta." The nervous twist of Y'sindra's hands betrayed her snarky words.

"You were in a bad way. We didn't know when—if—" Mae's voice caught, and she swallowed. "Mom said if anything could help, it would be Teddy's blood."

My gaze traveled between my sisters and then to Teddy. "You've been here the whole time?"

He shrugged and pulled on his usual flannel, this one green and blue. My eyes fell to his throat—no excessive bite marks.

Teddy crooked a smile, apparently able to read my thoughts. "Today was the first time for that."

A blush scorched my cheeks.

"You bit him?" Y'sindra cackled.

The blush turned to wildfire, racing from my cheeks, to throat, and over my chest. "No."

"You've got blood on your mouth."

"Shut up." I dragged the back of my hand across my damp lips. Well, shit. The fairy wasn't lying.

Teddy's bare feet padded into my line of sight. The male had some sexy toes. Ugh, what? Toes? Where did that thought come from? Probably lack of food. *Solid* food.

"Nothing to be ashamed of. Meghan could tell you were waking up. That's why she unhooked the infusion line today. Your body craved what it needed." Teddy sifted his fingers through my tangled hair. "I'll leave you with your sisters."

I grabbed his hand, unwilling to let him leave, irrationally desperate for him to stay.

He came back and dusted a kiss on my lips. "I'll see you downstairs."

"Yeah he will. Dude's basically moved in," Y'sindra said loudly to Teddy's retreating back.

"And he brought Lo with him." Mae elbowed her.

Y'sindra huffed, trying to act indignant, but couldn't hide her love-struck smile.

I pulled Y'sindra into another hug. She put up a half-hearted struggle, and I laughed. "Thank the gods some things never change. Love you two."

"Yeah, yeah." Y'sindra wiggled from my hold, and I let her go. For all her bluster, she didn't go far, and leaned against my side. "Spill the tea. Your guy have wings or what?"

We were back to that? My eyes did a tour of their sockets. "Nope."

The rich, smoky smell of bacon twisted into my nostrils. Accepting the aromatic invitation, I pushed to my feet and followed Y'sindra toward the door.

My stomach clenched at the sight of the bedazzled wrap covering her wing stump. She seemed okay, but I also knew she'd be buzzing around me like an annoying gnat if she still had her wing.

"No, he doesn't? Or, no, you failed to find out?" she asked.

"No." I wasn't going to indulge her, mostly because I still had no idea what Teddy was—an issue I would rectify as soon as I got some food in my empty belly.

She looked at me over her shoulder and waved her sparkly stump. "You going down like that?"

"Like what?"

"Clothes," Mae said.

"Pfft, I knew that. Uh, where are all my clothes?"

"Where they should be."

"And that is?"

Mae nodded toward the hallway leading to my bathroom. "Closet."

"Just testing you." I padded into the closet to toss on a pair of sweats and a tee.

Mae grinned when I emerged and slipped her hand into mine, steering us out into the hallway. "The guards Torneh and Iola sent after us got the sun stone."

I grunted. "Guess that means Scar wasn't a hallucination."

"Scar?" Mae pursed her lips.

"Odo. Real asshole."

"You think they're all assholes." Mae shook her head, swishing my shoulder with her honey-gold ponytail.

"Because they are."

We reached the stairs, and my legs balked at the idea of going down. I gripped the banister to prevent gravity from doing its job.

Mae went down first, moving at the speed of a snail, stopping on each step to check on me. "True, except these assholes went against Torneh's orders not to enter Outerlands."

"Why the hell would Odo do that?" My temper brought my foot down hard, sending wicked bolts of pain up my leg.

"He found Y'sindra and Lo at the border and told them to bring the RFG to you."

Leaning against the wall, I massaged the offended muscle and eased down a step. "Hrmph. Probably wanted all the credit."

"Probably, but they also paid us." Mae gestured to the bright, overhead light.

"Good." I limped down another step. While I truly didn't want a thing from the sun fae, I also wasn't an idiot. Most of the time. Electricity was good, and that shit was expensive. Humans ran the stuff from the Earth side of the border, and they tacked on what they called hazard pay. "I guess we can keep the lights on for the next month."

"Much longer than that. Rip sent over more money than we can spend in a year." Her breezy laugh warmed me to my toes. Mae was home. Y'sindra was okay. Teddy... I had all the time I wanted to explore that mystery. Bonus, I drank his blood and so far, I hadn't blacked out and murdered anyone.

"Rip?"

"Mmm, yes. Something about a wager you made about Etta'wy." She tilted her head in question.

Well, I'll be damned. I didn't exactly bring her in, but I did take her down. Rip saw it with his two creepy eyes, and the ogre kept his word.

"Duskmere's awake."

My foot froze on the next step. I looked to my sister. She nodded.

"Thank... I mean." I blew out a breath. A brush with death didn't mean I had to go soft. "Hope they healed that stick out of his ass."

The pop and sizzle of bacon in the kitchen wound up the stairs. *Screw this. What's a little pain?* I limped faster and cleared the last few steps to the landing, scooting past Mae.

"They brought Cirron and his daughter back."

Pity. "It'll be a good day if I never see that guy again."

"Lane..."

I gritted my teeth and hobbled double time across the living room. Fried onions underscored the bacon. Maybe I died after all, because this was too deliciously good to be true. The drone of voices mixed with popping grease.

The oven door's old springs groaned.

"Hot stuff, coming through." The smell of Mom's butter biscuits ballooned into the fragrant breakfast air.

My stomach jumped up and shouted hallelujah. I put my hand on the wall outside the room, taking a moment to absorb all this joy.

"Still nothing on where he took the stones?" my father asked, with an obviously full mouth. The gang was all here.

"There's something you need to know." I turned at Mae's urgent whisper in my ear.

From the other room, someone answered my father. "No, Barbout refuses to speak, and they rightfully do not want me in the interrogation."

That. Voice.

My wide eyes locked on Mae. I forgot how to breathe. *This better be another hallucination.*

Someone slapped the countertop.

"Watch it," Y'sindra said. "Laney will shoot you again if you break her coffee pot."

"If they don't get anything from that son of a bitch soon, then I will," Teddy promised.

I shook the shock from my system, rounded the corner into the kitchen, strode to the knives, and pulled the biggest one from the block.

Mae hurried across the kitchen and flung her arms around Cirron. "Lane, no."

I stopped mid-step. What the actual fuck was this?

Cirron's jaw worked, and while he held himself erect in his seat, embarrassment clouded his gaze.

"Told you someone needed to warn her." Y'sindra snorted and gave me the thumbs up with the hand Lo, seated next to her, wasn't holding.

"I tried," Mae complained, still holding onto Cirron. The traitor looked resigned, but also, enamored?

Mae and Cirron? I should have stayed in the coma.

"No. I forbid it." I waved the extra-large knife at Cirron. "That lump of ogre dung should be dead."

Teddy slid one arm over my shoulders and with his other, guided my weapon wielding hand to the counter. "Simmer down, my fierce little monster."

I glowered at my sister snuggled up to the traitor.

"They had his sister, Lane. Used her to manipulate him." Mae eased onto a stool at Cirron's side. "He didn't have a choice."

"Depends. You have a backup sister?"

"Lane!" A thunderstorm brewed in Mae's blue eyes. "You would have done the same thing for either of us."

I shrugged a single shoulder. "Maybe." Okay, I would, but that didn't mean I had to like him.

Teddy popped me on the butt. "Let's eat."

"You should listen to that boy more often." Mom set two plates at the end of the counter and spooned a steaming pile of scrambled eggs on each. "Everyone's been worried about you. Eat, eat."

"She already did." Teddy laughed, following me to the island counter.

A fresh blush burned over my tattletale cheeks, and I shoved half a slice of bacon in my mouth.

Laughter filled the room. Happy laughter. So much joy. Voices that soothed my soul. I fought the burn in my eyes, the pressure thumping in my chest as I watched this group.

Y'sindra's spirit was mightier than a missing wing, and now she had Lo. Mae was bruised but not broken. Cirron...fuck that guy. Mom, she was always looking out for me, no matter how far apart we were. My father showed up. For me. And Teddy...I shivered. I'd never woken up so good.

The male in question put a folded napkin at my elbow and a Bloody Mary on top of that. Ew, gross.

"A good bartender would know I hate those things."

"I'm a phenomenal bartender, and you'll love this one." Teddy inched the stool next to me closer until our thighs brushed.

I couldn't keep the ridiculous smile from my lips. "What makes it so special?"

He leaned in and gave the drink a stir with a nauseating stalk of celery. "A little hair of the black wolf."

***

Thank you for reading! Did you enjoy? Please add your review because nothing helps an author more and encourages readers to take a chance on a book than a review.

And don't miss more in the Blood Fae Druid series, by S.L. Choi coming soon!

Until then read more great books like WICKED MISERY, by City Owl Author, Tracey Martin. Turn the page for a sneak peek!

Also be sure to sign up for the City Owl Press newsletter to receive notice of all book releases!

SNEAK PEEK OF WICKED MISERY

BY TRACEY MARTIN

The perfect scumbag entered the bar around ten. I straightened, my bottle of cream stout pressed to my lips, and focused my gift on him as he crossed the crowded room. He blended in well. The leather jacket, tight T-shirt, and faded jeans were the standard fare for a Saturday evening at Kilpatrick's. But the malice oozing from his pores—definitely not. It tasted foul, like burnt oil. Yeah, this guy was a class-A asshole. Just the sort I was looking for to be my next soul donor.

I swigged my beer, but even old Sam Adams was helpless to defeat the nasty coating the guy left on my tongue. Luckily, the bleached blonde two tables over did a better job. I didn't know why she was so morose, but that banana-cream sadness of hers washed away some of the guy's foulness. Tasty and energizing, and—most importantly—guilt free.

Steph, my best friend and occasional partner in quasi-crime, returned from the bathroom and sat across from me. "Jess, you almost done with the beer? I need a smoke break."

"I thought you were trying to quit the nic-sticks." Much as I wished she would quit for her health, I hated when she tried. Diffuse anxiety like that was the one negative emotion—well, besides evil—that bugged me. Not only did the taste remind me of spearmint, which I couldn't stand, it made me jittery.

"I can't quit until Jim does. How am I supposed to give it up when he's smoking in the apartment?"

"Fair point." As he was the first decent guy Steph had ever dated, I couldn't be too annoyed with Jim for the smoking thing. Everyone has their goods and their bads—something my twisted-to-hell-and-back gift had been reminding me of since I turned eighteen.

With the bottle, I motioned to my scumbag. "I'm going hunting. You in?"

Steph assessed my target, her long purple nails tapping against her lip as if there should be a cigarette between her fingers. "What's he going to do?"

It was a good question, yet not one I could answer with certainty since my goal was to prevent the crime. Even when someone's intent was so overwhelming I gagged on its foulness, I couldn't always get a read on the specifics. Sometimes, though, emotions were tied to plans, and plans to images that I could tap into.

Granted, most of the time I'd be happier not knowing those details. To me, evil was evil. I'd been cursed to taste it for ten years now, and it was unmistakable. Still, if it eased Steph's mind...

I closed my eyes and stretched out my gift toward the scumbag. My nervous system danced as a giddy energy swept through me. This guy's cruelty could power me to run a marathon.

And that was bad. Damn it. I bit my tongue, and the pain grounded me. Furious at myself for lurking in his heart so long, I dragged my attention back to my beer. I'd need to scrub out my head with a Disney movie later.

"Once and would-be future rapist," I told Steph. "Keep an eye on him? I have to go check for work. And don't be so obvious that you're staring."

Steph's sneer faded as she picked at the last of the French fries.

I worked my way through the chaos near the restrooms, wishing the bar was less cramped. There simply wasn't enough room for the pool tables and the dartboard. And whose brilliant idea had it first been to give drunk people darts to throw anyway? As if using a bar's bathroom wasn't already an unpleasant proposition. But Steph's cousin owned Kilpatrick's, and he lived for the arguments and brawls. If I didn't know better, I'd swear he was a rage addict. Really, though, he was a Boston-Irish dude with a perverse sense of humor. Almost as dangerous.

Both bathrooms were unisex, but it was the one on the right that I needed. I knocked.

"Use the other one."

"Other one's occupied."

I leaned against the wall and watched my scumbag sidle up to a vanity addict at the bar. Peachy. Had my would-be rapist found his victim? If they left together, how was I going to ditch her? Targeting rapists could be such a pain, and yet it was also incredibly satisfying. Must be something in my female DNA.

Oblivious to the guy's intentions, the vanity addict smiled at him. Shuddering, I wondered how far gone she was.

As a kid, it had been my dream to join the Angelic Order of the Gryphon and become one of those humans who cured addicts and fought the preds who enslaved them. Then somewhere along the way a pred had cursed me, twisted my magic into a lousy imitation of its own power. Because of that, I'd been denied my dream. But also because of that, I'd grown up more determined than ever to save humanity. I just got to be picky about who I helped.

The person on the right finally finished, and I prayed the bathroom wouldn't stink worse than usual.

After locking the door, I climbed on the toilet seat. Seph made fun of me, but I liked my low-tech means of contacting clients. She called me paranoid. I preferred cautious. It's not like I was a Luddite, but I knew enough about tech to know that nothing online was ever truly safe, especially in my unskilled hands. Tech, on the other hand, was how Steph made her living, so she's appointed herself my social media manager. She monitored discussions about Boston's mysterious Soul Swapper, kept me updated on anything I needed to know, and occasionally stepped in using one of her many aliases when necessary. Which was kind of her. That's what best friends were for—protecting your ass.

As far as I was concerned, however, if a potential client thought it was beneath them to communicate with me via a plastic container hidden behind a tile in the ceiling of the right-hand bathroom in Kilpatrick's Bar on Boylston Street, well it's not like I was desperate to read their pleas for assistance. Enough people reached out to me for help as it was. I didn't need to maintain a website advertising my services on the dark web, and I definitely didn't need a fucking Instagram account for it.

On my tiptoes, I pushed the tile aside and grasped the edge of the Rubbermaid container. Already I could see strange handwriting on the notepad inside. Sweet. Potential client, here I come.

I skimmed the note, which was signed with only initials. Good for J.G. Some morons signed their whole names. Not that any of this business was technically illegal, but it sure skirted the line so close that I'd need a better lawyer than I could afford if I got busted.

Okay, so maybe it was a slight, eensy, teeny, nano-bit illegal. Or would be if someone had the foresight to make a law about it. But people didn't devote time to making laws about things deemed impossible.

Things like me.

I wrote back to J.G. *Monday, midnight, the Hatch Shell.* Then I tucked the whole thing back in the ceiling over the toilet.

That's the other thing online communication couldn't give you—the personal touch. I needed to meet clients face-to-face so I could assess them.

Escaping from the restroom gave my nose a new appreciation for the odor of sweat and stale liquor. My scumbag was putting the moves on the addict, and Steph was twirling her lighter around. Magical addicts and typical addicts—in some ways they weren't so different.

Whereas nicotine was Steph's metaphorical demon, the vanity addict's demon was literal. Sort of. We shared the planet with five races that preyed on human weakness—anger for the furies, greed for the goblins, jealousy for the harpies, lust for the satyrs, and pride or vanity for the sylphs. Once, humanity had referred to them as monsters or demigods. Back in the Middle Ages, the Christian Church had collectively given them the name demon. These days, however, most humans just called them predators, or preds, for short.

Not that the name mattered.

In the end, all it meant was that in the vanity addict's case, somewhere in Boston was a sylph who'd broken the addict's soul, binding the vanity addict to itself and using that connection to drink in the addict's negative emotions. Like me, the sylph got a magical hit from humanity's negativity. And while Steph got miserable if she went too long without nicotine, the vanity addict had lost all ability to feel happy or good about herself without the sylph's approval.

Sadly, in the end, both types of afflictions could be deadly.

I finished my beer and tried not to let pity bog me down. Steph would—rightfully—kick my ass if she could hear me comparing her to a vanity addict, and if I let my heart break over every magical addict I met, I'd be as wretched as they were. The problem with having magical blood was that I could identify addicts, and addicts were everywhere. Most people would freak if they realized how many prominent politicians or celebrities had a pred on their back, but there was truth to the whole cliché about selling your soul for success.

Thirty minutes later Scumbag finally made his move. *Idiot*, I wanted to yell at the addict. Although she couldn't read the guy's intentions, she had to have heard the news about a serial killer targeting twenty-something-year-old women in the area. I despised victim-blaming, but really—a little paranoia was not a bad thing to have.

Lips pursed, I watched the would-be rapist help her down from her barstool. Some people were simply too trusting. Fortunately for her, I was on the case.

Steph knew the drill. Ten seconds after Scumbag and his lady headed out the door, we followed them into the night.

***

The subway's yellow lights turned everyone a ghastly hue. As much as I loathed the thought, I extended my gift toward Scumbag. The odds of losing him were too good. My mind latched on to his anticipation, and the feeling made my skin crawl, yet at the same time adrenaline flooded my veins.

I cursed the blissful rush, which was why I'd started hunting people like him in the first place. It was that or let my own shame overwhelm me. What I'd become wasn't my fault, but the words "not my fault" were overused and hollow, however truthful they were.

Scumbag and his addict got off the train at one of the last T stops. That was going to make concealing ourselves a lot more difficult.

"How are you going to get rid of his date?" Steph asked as we hightailed it out of the station.

The night was darker along the city's edge, and we had to hang back to stay unseen. The couple cut across the small parking lot and headed into residential streets. A few drab trees had been hacked to make way for power lines, and their unnatural branch formations seemed to flip off the neighborhood.

"Got me. Maybe I can swipe his blood while you distract her."

"How?"

"I don't know. Throw your wig at her?"

Steph nudged me in the ribs. Unfortunately for her, she'd begun losing her hair in college before she'd transitioned, so she'd amassed an impressive wig collection over the last decade..

I grabbed Steph's arm and pulled her into the shadows with me as the addict led the way toward a house up the hill. A swarm of imps danced around the nearest streetlight. The largest of them was no longer than my longest finger, but their wings beat in an effervescent haze. Not quite glowing and not completely transparent, they caused funky shadows to flit about the houses, making it difficult to see.

I kept a wary eye on the imps as the addict unlocked her front door. Imps were attracted to magical blood, and a single sting could leave me powerless for several minutes. Neither me, nor the addict who didn't realize she was depending on me, could afford that.

"Looks like he's making a call. Let's go."

I charged across the street, Steph struggling to keep up in her three-inch heels. We weren't going to make it. Scumbag was already putting away the cellphone.

The porch's screen door slammed, and the light turned on. He hadn't gone in yet. I ducked behind a scraggly rhododendron. A couple of imps swooped down from the streetlamp, and I swatted them away, cursing under my breath.

What was this guy up to? He paced between the clutter and sorry furniture on the porch, playing with a knife and looking up and down the street as though he expected company. Creepy. Lights were on upstairs, and I could make out the addict moving around.

I checked my watch. Scumbag's impatience tasted like bitter tea. The last thing I wanted was for someone to arrive as I did the magical equivalent of bashing him over the head. On the other hand, waiting around all night wasn't going to do me or the addict any good. Not to mention I had to get up for work tomorrow morning.

"Hide if you don't want him seeing your face," I told Steph, then I pulled my hood around my head.

I crept to the front of the porch, gathering magic into a ball in my stomach, then cracked the door. Scumbag looked over in surprise.

"Hi." Simple, to the point and the perfect word for exhaling a gush of power. A smoky cloud blew from my lips and coiled around Scumbag's head. He couldn't see it, but he felt it. His face slackened.

The smoke vanished, but my gut registered the familiar tightening that told me the magic connected us like a rope. If I were a pred, that rope would make my victim an addict. Preds had a harder time creating that bond, but when they did, they could extend their ropes for miles or give the magic a tug and send an addict's emotions spiraling toward them. Since I wasn't a pred, I had to rely on words to manipulate people, every bit as effective but only so long as my victims heard me.

"Come with me."

I didn't wait for him to follow. He couldn't help but obey. Until I broke the tie, he was incapable of anything but lusting and yearning for me, and was thus highly malleable. Though I had to admit, the thought of this bastard yearning for me made me want to hurl.

It was bad enough that I'd been cursed with a pred's ability to get a magical high from human misery. Talk about living with guilt. But also being cursed, specifically, with a satyr's ability to drive people mad with lust? Definitely not something I'd have asked for. And not something I understood. If I had a deadly weakness, it would have to be rage or jealousy. I mean, I had a temper and I knew how to use it. And as for jealousy, much as I hated to admit it, the fact that I didn't wear a Gryphon uniform constantly ate away at my insides.

So why, for the love of dragons, did I not tempt with one of those emotions? Why lust instead?

I could only assume it was some quirk in the universe, not that different from how I ended up with a mop of dark brown curls when my parents both had straight hair. In other words, shit happened. Usually to me, it seemed.

Scumbag followed me into the rhododendron's shadow, oozing evil like an infection oozed pus. Steph was on the ball tonight and had already pulled out the blood-collection kit from my backpack. All I needed—or rather the preds I traded with needed—was a couple drops. Steph worked for a local hospital's IT department, and she'd swiped me one of those thumb-pricking devices diabetics used to monitor their blood sugar and Gryphons used to monitor an addict's magic levels.

Scumbag stumbled over the rhododendron's roots and landed against me. I shoved him off, but he didn't want to let go.

"Can I do you here, beautiful?" He had some sort of Eastern European accent, and his hands fumbled with his belt buckle.

It had to be the nature of my magic, but unrequited lust tasted like the best thing on earth to me. If I was longing for a steak, it melted on my tongue like filet mignon. If I desired ice cream, it tantalized my taste buds like a chocolate peanut butter sundae. Tonight, it filled my mouth with the flavor of a hot brownie straight out of the oven.

I gave the would-be rapist a more forceful shove, and he hit the side of the house. Scumbag was disturbed by my refusal yet undaunted. I had to be quick. I knew where those hands of his would be next, and I had no desire to see him whip out that particular weapon.

"Not tonight, thanks. What I want is a little blood." I held out the lancet.

"What do I do with this?"

Maybe because I was a mere human wielding a pred's power, my magic didn't simply drive people lusty. It made them stupid to boot. "You put it like this, and press down." I positioned it for him.

"Will you do it for me?"

Steph snorted.

I shot her a dirty look. "What's your name?"

"Pete Donovich."

I swallowed down my disgust and grabbed his hand. "Pete Donovich, do you offer your blood freely? Say it."

"I give, offer, my blood freely." His words were starting to slur.

I clicked the device and gathered a couple drops of blood in a vial. Mission almost accomplished—the quasi-legal part anyway. After all, it was perfectly legal for a pred to bargain for someone's soul so long as the person gave it freely. The blood symbolized the contract and gave the pred a means for calling the person when the agreement kicked in.

Using my magic to convince Pete, or anyone else, to donate blood was technically legal in the sense that preds did it all the time and it was damn hard to prove coercion in any court. Ethically, I'd be the first to admit it was wrong. But since Pete intended to tie up the vanity addict in this house, rape her, and do about twenty other things to her that would require serious drinking on my part to forget, I wasn't going to lose sleep over stealing his soul.

No, if I lost sleep, it would be from the nightmares Pete gave me. And because of that, I couldn't let him waltz into the addict's apartment now that I was done.

"Turn around and kneel."

If I had the power, this guy would be locked up for life. But, alas, the Gryphons considered me a failure, my gift a dud. Granted, if they knew the truth about me, they'd probably hunt me down like a pred, so life could have been worse. Yet there were times when all this secrecy got in the way of doing good deeds.

I gathered the magic once more. "Forget me." Then I sent it shooting out through my hands and into Scumbag Pete's head. He moaned.

With a decisive chop, I snapped the rope of magic that connected us. The pressure in my gut vanished. Pete shook himself. Before he could figure out what was going on, my steel-toed boot met his skull. He grunted and collapsed. One scumbag off the streets, if only for the night.

I fished through Pete's wallet and pocketed his ID. I'd never remember his name without it, and the pred I traded with would need it. Besides, in the ten years I'd been passing myself off as a vigilante for the hopeless, I'd nicked quite a few souls. I had to have some way to remember the faces of those who I'd taken blood from because I could only do it once per person. After I'd handed a soul over to one pred, another pred couldn't have it at the same time.

"Did you see that?" Steph asked.

"See what?"

"Thought I saw a shadow move."

I scanned the vicinity, closing my eyes and stretching out with my gift. Theoretically, it was possible that if anyone was watching, they wouldn't be miserable or frightened or nervous or angry or feeling any other negative emotion. And if that was the case, I'd miss them completely. It was damned unlikely though. Everyone was unhappy about something.

But all I picked up on was some marital discord across the street. "I've got nothing."

Steph frowned. "A van pulled up a couple minutes ago. I don't like this."

"Well, we're done. Let's get out of here."

We started down the street, and Steph grabbed my wrist. This time I'd caught it too. A flicker of black to my left. The shuffle of feet cutting through un-mowed grass. Steph's breath rattled in my ear as I reached under my jacket for my knife.

"Stay here."

With a dry mouth, I took a couple steps in the shadow's direction. Yet still my gift registered no signs of life. Disturbing. Maybe whoever we saw wasn't human? Even more disturbing. My knife would be useless, and I didn't have a protective charm on me.

"Jess!" Steph's harsh whisper made me jump. She beckoned me back.

I squinted into the hazy darkness and decided she had a point.

Steph relaxed once the subway's glow encompassed us again, but I kept checking over my shoulder. That van had parked close to the addict's house, so why hadn't I sensed the driver? Why hadn't I sensed anything in the bushes? I swore I felt that absence of emotion standing behind me the whole way home, but all I saw were humans.

Paranoia. If this business of mine didn't kill me, it would drive me insane. One of these days, I'd take up a normal hobby. Something just as useful. Maybe knitting.

Don't miss the next Blood Fae Druid book coming soon, and find more from S.L. Choi at www.slchoi.com

Until then, discover WICKED MISERY, by City Owl Author, Tracey Martin!

Jessica Moore only has five days to catch a killer.

Thanks to a goblin's curse, Jessica gets a magical high from humanity's suffering. While the guilt of thriving on misery could bury a girl, she atones by using her power to hunt the bad guys—until one of them frames her for his crimes.

In desperation, Jessica seeks refuge with the one person she trusts—a satyr named Lucen. Like every member of his paranormal race, Lucen uses his lusty magic to control Boston's human population, and Jessica isn't immune to his power.

But the murder victims belong to a rival race, and when they discover Lucen is harboring Jessica, dodging the cops becomes the least of her problems.

With time running out, Jessica faces a danger every bit as serious as the brewing magical war—succumbing to Lucen's seductive power. Will their tenuous relationship survive, or will more misery prevail?

ACKNOWLEDGMENTS

Cat on lap aside, these words would never have made it to print without my amazing husband, Bryan. Your endless encouragement and (sweet but misguided) belief that I can do anything, means everything. *KSH*

A heartfelt thank you to my editor, Heather McCorkle. Your passion for BAD GIRLS DRINK BLOOD really made this story shine.

Thank you to the awesome City Owl Press team, Tina, Yelena, Marianne, and Charissa, for your hard work behind the scenes and incredible patience for my constant questions and suggestions. All of your inboxes (and DMs) have my deepest condolences.

To Julie Gwinn, my agent, who stepped in to hold my hand (I need a lot of hand holding) at the start of this journey. Your enthusiastic words and keen eye for edits remind me everyday I'm in the best hands.

Gabi, what can I say? You've been my rock. Serendipity that we met. BGDB wouldn't be the story that it is without you. I can't wait for all the books we work on together!

Lauri, my emotional support human, whose feedback I value, and whose place in my life is invaluable.

Kelly, the jelly to my peanut butter, and my biggest, cheeriest cheerleader.

Markella, I'm so grateful Julie placed my manuscript in your hands.

To Susan, for being an ever-encouraging friend.

To the Quokkas, who are the definition of support.

To Elaine and Jana, for being my early, guinea pig readers.

To the urban fantasy authors who opened my eyes to the captivating world of vampires, shifters, angels, demons, and every delicious, paranormal thing in between.

Writing is a solitary journey built on a wide network of support. There are so many people who have said or done something small to keep me going, without even realizing it. I've heard you. I've seen you. Thank you.

Finally, to my mom. I miss you.

ABOUT THE AUTHOR

S.L. CHOI is an urban fantasy author with a deep love for humor, fast-paced action, and hit-you-in-the-heart feels. She grew up imagining goblins living in the rocks outside her bedroom window, while fairies flew through the flowers. When not writing, she is either photographing the beautiful New England area, hiking, gaming with her equally nerdy husband, or attending to the small furry overlord who rules them both.

www.slchoi.com

instagram.com/@SLChoi_author
facebook.com/@AuthorSLChoi
twitter.com/@SL_Choi
tiktok.com/@SLChoi_author

ABOUT THE PUBLISHER

City Owl Press is a cutting edge indie publishing company, bringing the world of romance and speculative fiction to discerning readers.

Escape Your World. Get Lost in Ours!

www.cityowlpress.com

facebook.com/CityOwlPress
twitter.com/cityowlpress
instagram.com/cityowlbooks
pinterest.com/cityowlpress
tiktok.com/@cityowlpress